ECHOES OF TIME

A Jaipur Murder Mystery

Dr Ramesh Pattni

PARTRIDGE

ISBN: Hardcover   978-1-5437-1053-3
               Softcover   978-1-5437-1054-0
               eBook   978-1-5437-1055-7

To order additional copies of this book, contact
Partridge India
000 800 919 0634 (Call Free)
+91 000 80091 90634 (Outside India)
orders.india@partridgepublishing.com

www.partridgepublishing.com/india

CONTENTS

CHAPTER 1

The ancient stones of Amber Fort loomed over the magnificent city of Jaipur, their sandstone facets bathed in the faint moonlight. In the shadows, whispers of a centuries-old curse seemed to stir in the night breeze, unheard by the sleeping city below. The air was still, tinged with the faint scent of the nearby Maota Lake and the distant sighs from the slumbering city below. Once a symbol of Rajasthan's royal might, the fort now stood as a silent guardian, its secrets etched into the very stones.

Kuldip and Ranjeet, the night guards, patrolled the ramparts, their footsteps reverberating in the quiet of the night. They were an odd pair—Kuldip, tall and lean with a neat beard, and Ranjeet, a shorter, stockier fellow with a cheerful face. Despite their differences, they had formed a close bond over their years of service together.

As they patrolled, Kuldip couldn't help but feel a sense of unease. He had patrolled these walls countless times, but tonight something felt different; the air seemed heavier, the shadows a bit deeper, and the silence more oppressive than ever.

Ranjeet, noticing his partner's discomfort, broke the silence. 'It's quite a night, isn't it?' he remarked, his voice sounding oddly loud in the surrounding stillness.

'Hmm . . .' Kuldip nodded, his eyes scanning the moonlit landscape sprawled before them. 'It's too quiet,' he murmured, his hand instinctively resting on the hilt of his sword. 'I don't like it.'

Ranjeet chuckled softly, trying to lighten the mood. 'You worry too much, Kuldeep. It's just another peaceful night.'

But Kuldip wasn't convinced. His instincts were on edge. His gaze drifted to the Ganesh Pol, the ornate gateway leading to the fort's inner chambers. 'Do you remember the stories told about this place?'

Ranjeet raised an eyebrow. 'The tales of the old kings and their dark deeds?' Ranjeet hesitated, his grin faltering. 'Sure. But they're just stories.'

'Stories don't leave scars on walls,' Kuldip muttered, his eyes never leaving the gateway. 'They say these walls have seen things . . . *terrible* things.' His voice was low. 'These walls hide many secrets,' Kuldeep said as a sudden gust of wind swept past, carrying with it a metallic tang.

Ranjeet's smile faded. 'Do you smell that?'

Kuldip inhaled sharply, the scent unmistakable. 'Blood.'

The two exchanged a look before drawing their batons, moving swiftly toward the Ganesh Pol. As they stepped through the gateway, the scent grew stronger, mingling with the musty odour of ancient stone. Kuldip's torch cast a flickering light on the courtyard, revealing the source.

A man lay sprawled in a pool of blood, his limbs twisted unnaturally. A jewelled dagger, its hilt bearing the royal insignia of Jaipur, was buried deep in his chest. His eyes had been gouged out, leaving gaping sockets, and his lips were frozen in a grotesque grimace. Around his neck, a gold chain had been wound so tightly that it had cut into the flesh.

Ranjeet staggered back; his face had gone pale, and his eyes were wide with shock and disbelief. 'What . . . what is this?'

'We need to call Supervisor Mohan,' Kuldeep said in a shaking voice, barely able to control the panic rising in his chest. 'Now.'

Twenty minutes later, the stillness of the early morning was shattered by the wail of sirens. Police vehicles swarmed in the narrow streets leading to Amber Fort, their lights casting red and blue hues against the ancient walls.

Within minutes, the once-peaceful courtyard became a hive of activity as dozens of police officers and forensic experts swarmed on the scene. The air hummed with the crackle of radios and the low murmur of voices as the authorities set about the grim task of investigating the horrific crime.

Inspector Rajesh Singh stood at the centre of the chaos, his sharp eyes scanning the chaos. He was the kind of man who drew attention without trying. At well over six feet, with broad shoulders and an imposing solid frame, he carried himself with a quiet authority that made it clear he wasn't to be trifled with. His neatly trimmed beard, streaked with the faintest hints of grey, framed a face that was both rugged and thoughtful, the lines around his eyes suggesting years of experience rather than age.

His eyes, dark and piercing, had an uncanny way of seeing beyond the surface—a trait that served him well in his 20 years on the force. They held a balance of sharp intellect and weariness as if they had witnessed both the worst and the best humanity had to offer. Yet behind that sharp gaze was a subtle warmth, a hint of empathy that softened his otherwise formidable demeanour. This duality—steadfast in seeking justice yet profoundly compassionate behind the badge—earned him respect from his colleagues and the individuals he aimed to protect.

Though his expression was calm, his jaw tightened as he took in the gruesome details before him. Two decades on the force hadn't prepared him for this. The staging of the body, the carefully arranged artefacts around it, and the symbols carved into the stone near it pointed to something calculated, something sinister.

His eyes lingered on the strange etching into the stone near the victim's body, an intricate fusion of royal emblems he didn't recognise. He crouched down, studying it closer. A chill ran down his spine as the stories of Amber Fort's bloody past whispered in his mind—tales of betrayal, greed, and revenge. Singh shook his head, pushing aside the unease growing in the pit of his stomach.

He again looked at the body and the historical objects arranged around it. This was not an ordinary murder. He thoughtfully looked at his team of forensic experts clad in stark white suits and armed with an array of high-tech equipment, moving with clinical precision and carefully documenting every detail of the crime scene, and noticed how clueless they all appeared.

As some of his officers worked to clear the growing crowd of onlookers that had begun to gather at the scene's periphery, Inspector Singh knew he'd need help in solving this murder.

High above the chaos of the crime scene, a solitary figure stood upon the ramparts of the Amber Fort, obscured by the shadows cast by the ancient walls. He watched the scene below with a keen, unwavering gaze, his eyes following the movements of the police and forensic experts as they went about their work.

He was dressed in nondescript dark clothing, his face hidden beneath a headcloth. He blended seamlessly into the shadows as if he were a part of the stones themselves—a silent, watchful presence that seemed to exist outside the bounds of time and space.

And then, as silently as he had appeared, he was gone, disappearing into the shadows like a ghost.

࿗

As the sun climbed higher, casting long shadows over the courtyard, Inspector Singh scanned the sea of faces surrounding the crime scene. His sharp eyes moved methodically, lingering on a bystander whose nervous shifting stood out amid the muted whispers of the crowd, and then on the constables attempting to contain the growing throng. Every detail was catalogued, every movement weighed for meaning. Singh was a man who thrived on patterns, on finding the thread that connected chaos into something coherent.

Still, this case defied the familiar logic he relied on. The symbols etched into the stone and the ritualistic precision of the murder—they were unlike anything he had encountered before. Calling in an expert wasn't a decision he made lightly. He knew it would ruffle feathers in the department, especially among those who preferred tradition over innovation. But Singh had always prioritised results over appearances, and this time, he needed someone who could see the story buried in the symbols.

In the face of such deliberate evil, the only thing more terrifying than confronting it head-on was the thought of letting it run unchecked, consuming everything and everyone in its path. And if he was going to stop it, Singh knew he would have to act not just with his instincts but with precision—and an ally who could decode the killer's twisted message.

As the victim's body was taken away for autopsy, he got into his jeep. As his driver started the engine, Singh looked back at the towering fort. He could feel the weight of centuries of history and the looming spectre of the present like a physical weight. He couldn't help but feel a sense of foreboding. It was as if the very stones of the fort were warning him of the darkness ahead.

࿗

Back at the police station, Inspector Rajesh Singh sat at his desk, brow furrowed as he pored over the crime scene photos spread before him. The strange symbols and the meticulous staging—they all pointed to a killer who knew exactly what they were doing. His mind raced with questions: Why the royal insignia? Why the ritualistic elements? And why here, at Amber Fort?

He leaned back in his chair, rubbing his temples. He needed expertise beyond his department's resources. Someone who could understand the deeper layers of this crime. Someone well versed in Jaipur's history and culture and could see beyond the surface of the crime and uncover the truth buried beneath.

He opened his drawer and dug up a business card he was given a couple of months ago during a training seminar on historical crimes. The name printed in bold letters read: **Dr Anika Thakur, Forensic Psychologist.**

Singh hesitated only a moment before dialling the number.

'Dr Anika Thakur speaking,' a crisp, professional voice answered on the third ring.

'Dr Thakur, this is Inspector Rajesh Singh with the Rajasthan Police. I attended your seminar on historical crimes at the University of Delhi a few months ago. We briefly met after your seminar.'

'Yes, I remember,' she replied, her tone curious. 'What can I do for you, Inspector?'

Singh chose his words carefully. 'We have a case. A murder at Amber Fort. Its ritualistic nature makes me believe it could relate to Rajasthan's history. I believe your expertise could be invaluable.'

There was a pause on the line, and Singh braced himself for a refusal. Instead, Dr Thakur's voice returned, calm but resolute. 'Send me the details. I'll be there as soon as I can.'

Relief washed over Singh. He didn't know what answers Dr Thakur would bring, but he knew one thing for sure: This case was far more than it seemed.

CHAPTER 2

The lecture hall at the University of Udaipur was abuzz with anticipation. Students and faculty settled into their seats, their conversations fading as they turned their attention to the stage. The murmurs that had filled the large and airy room began to subside as everyone waited for the lecture to begin. At the front of the room, a large screen displayed the title of the day's lecture: **Historical Forensic Psychology: Uncovering the Mysteries from the Past.** Beneath it, in smaller letters, was the speaker's name: **Dr Anika Thakur.**

When Dr Thakur stepped into the room, it fell silent. She was tall and slender, with dark hair swept neatly back, and her piercing brown eyes seemed to take in every detail of the audience. There was an air of command in her movements, an intensity that drew every eye in the room. Though she was in her midthirties, her reputation as India's leading forensic psychologist had preceded her. Anika was known for solving seemingly impossible cases, and her expertise lay in the intersection of human behaviour, cultural history, and crime.

'Good morning,' she began, her clear voice cutting through the stillness. 'Forensic psychology is often seen as a modern tool—a science of analysing criminal minds. But its roots run deeper, connecting us to history, culture, and the stories that define us. Today, we'll explore not just the psychology of crime but the way time and culture weave into criminal behaviour, leaving clues not just in the present but in the past.'

She paused, scanning the room as her words settled. 'Every crime tells a story,' she continued. 'It's not just about motives or methods. It's about context—the threads of history, trauma, and human nature that lead to action. By identifying these threads, we don't just solve crimes. We resurrect forgotten voices, give life to untold stories, and uncover truths buried in time.'

Anika guided her audience through the evolution of forensic psychology, beginning with ancient civilisations. She described how the Babylonians interpreted dreams to judge guilt, how Chinese judges in the 13th century used forensic techniques to solve murder cases, and how the Enlightenment spurred the scientific study of criminal minds.

To bring her points to life, she referenced groundbreaking cases, such as that of the Mad Bomber of New York, whose capture was aided by a psychological profile predicting even his eccentric clothing; the Boston Strangler, whose behavioural patterns revealed his identity; and

Jack the Ripper, whose crimes, though unsolved, laid the foundation for modern criminal profiling.

Each example painted a picture of how psychology, history, and deduction converged to unlock secrets others failed to see.

'Forensic psychology,' she said, her voice calm but commanding, 'isn't just about reading minds or motives. It's about seeing the bigger picture—the historical and cultural patterns that shape every criminal act. Sometimes, it's a clue left in the present. Other times, it's something forgotten in the past.'

The audience hung on her every word, their curiosity palpable. A hand shot up from the middle row.

'Dr Thakur,' a young woman asked eagerly, 'how do you tell the difference between genuine historical clues and red herrings planted by a killer?'

Anika's lips curled into a faint smile. 'A great question. The answer lies in context and patterns. Criminals often leave deliberate distractions to mislead investigators. But history leaves its own patterns—clues hidden in traditions, behaviours, or language. When we combine psychology with historical knowledge, the red herrings become noise, and the truth emerges.'

As she continued, her attention flicked to a man seated at the back of the hall. His presence was unremarkable, but his intense gaze felt almost familiar. Her hand instinctively brushed the small antique compass in her pocket, a reminder of her brother, Yuvraj. As she took other questions from the audience, she couldn't help but think about her brother's disappearance. Anika took a deep breath and put aside the intrusive thoughts to focus on the boy in the fourth row, asking her about the consequences of overlooking a crime's historical and cultural references.

Twenty-five minutes later, as the lecture drew to a close, the room erupted into applause. Students and faculty rose, faces beaming with admiration and respect. Anika took a slight bow, her gaze steady and unflinching, though a flicker of weariness crossed her eyes. She carried the burden of personal loss for all her accolades, a void she had never filled.

As the crowd filtered out, Anika gathered her notes and gave herself time to think about Yuvraj. Her brother was kidnapped almost 20 years ago, right in front of her eyes, but no matter what she and her mother tried, the culprits were never caught. They were never given closure as the police miserably failed to find her brother, dead or alive. Yuvraj's cold case had shaped the entire graph of her career. She wanted to solve the impossible crimes, just like her brother's. She wanted to make a difference in the lives of people who had lost all hope, and somewhere, in her heart, she hoped, against her better judgment, to finally figure out what became of her brother.

Anika was stubborn, a trait she had inherited from her mother, who had raised her and her brother alone. She might have accepted Yuvraj's kidnapping as a random act had she not heard her mother's words, which still burn bright in her psyche: *'Leave him alone. It's not his fault.'* She had tried to question her mother several times about what it had meant and if she knew who those rowdy men were, but her mother had completely shut down and refused to say anything, not just to her, but to anyone. Shaking off her mother's desperate words, she made a beeline for her black Honda Civic. Little did she know, the past that haunted her was about to collide with her own present.

The sun was setting over the lively streets of Jaipur as Anika made her way back to her office, her mind still buzzing from the energy of the lecture. When she stepped into her office—a cosy space lined with books and artefacts from her many cases—she was greeted by the familiar face of her assistant, Rhea, who greeted her with a steaming cup of tea and a cheerful smile. 'How was the lecture?'

Anika smiled, setting down her bag and sinking into her chair. 'It was good. Quite engaging, I'd say, but . . . something felt different.'

Before Rhea could ask, Anika's phone buzzed. She glanced at the screen: an unknown number.

'Dr Anika Thakur speaking.'

'Dr Thakur, this is Inspector Rajesh Singh with the Rajasthan Police,' came a deep voice. 'I attended your seminar on historical crimes at the University of Delhi a few months ago. We briefly met after your seminar.'

'Yes, I think I remember. What can I do for you, Inspector?' she replied, intrigued.

'We have a case. A murder at Amber Fort. Its ritualistic nature makes me believe it could relate to Rajasthan's history. I believe your expertise could be invaluable.'

Anika caught her breath. Amber Fort. Her chest tightened as unbridled memories resurfaced: her childhood home in Jaipur, her brother's laughter echoing through the empty corridors of Amber Fort, and the night her world fractured. 'Send me the details. I'll be there as soon as I can,' she said, her voice steady despite the sudden rush of emotion.

Anika leaned back and took out Yuvraj's compass. Her heart raced with the faint hope that this case might bring her closer to answers she had long sought. 'Book me on the first flight to Jaipur,' she told Rhea.

Anika had left Jaipur behind because of how heavily his brother's presence weighed on her soul. It had been a decade since she last visited her home and her mother. Although they often kept in touch over the phone, Anika and her mother, Lata, had grown apart since that unfortunate night. Her mother's silence over the matter made Anika resent her in a way she could never understand. She'd avoided visiting Jaipur all these years so she wouldn't have to see her mother. After completing college, Anika took the first job she was offered out of the city. Since then, she'd been transferred to many places, including Delhi, Nagpur, Mumbai, Bangalore, Chennai, and now Udaipur, the closest she was ready to come to her home.

But now she'd be visiting Jaipur, her home.

That night, Anika dreamed of the dreadful evening when her world changed forever. The sun was setting over the dusty streets of Jaipur, casting long shadows across the crumbling walls of Thakur Niwas. Inside, the air was thick with the scent of spices and the sweet sound of laughter as the Thakur family gathered around the dinner table. Young Anika sat between her older brother, Yuvraj, and her mother, Lata. She was a bright-eyed and curious teen pulling her brother's leg over some fact he'd been quizzing her on. Yuvraj, a tall and lanky teen, had a glint of mischief in his eyes as he pretended to be annoyed by his younger sister. He was a good brother, and Anika always felt safe and happy around him.

Their mother, a beautiful woman with a regal bearing, chided Anika for not seriously answering her brother's question. Although they were happy, Anika couldn't help but notice an unmistakable sadness in her mother's grey eyes. Lata loved her children fiercely, but a part of her always seemed closed to the entire world, including her children. Despite being in her late thirties, Lata's shoulders seemed burdened by the weight of something she refused to share. She was a single mother and worked as a history teacher at a local government school. As far as her children knew, their father, Rajendra Thakur, had left them soon after the birth of Anika without saying a word and had been absent from their lives since. Being just two years older than Anika, Yuvraj did not remember his father any more than she did. Because of their mother's reluctance to talk about him or his family, the children knew better than to ask her about anything related to their father. It was a topic never discussed or even acknowledged in their house.

As the family enjoyed the delicious meal of *dal-bati-churma* prepared by Lata after a long day at school, the blissful atmosphere was rudely interrupted by loud banging on their front door. As Anika looked at her mother, she noted how her mother got up from the table and went to the window to see who it was. Yuvraj froze midbite, and he, too, just like Anika, followed his mother's movements. As the banging continued, Lata ran to the children. 'Go to your room and lock it from inside. Do not come out. No matter what.'

Anika and Yuvraj stared at her in confusion.

'Now!' she shouted.

But just as Yuvraj took Anika's hand and was about to run to their room upstairs, the door burst open, and a group of rowdy men stormed into their house.

Yuvraj stopped in his tracks and stared at the angry men as they started yelling loudly at Lata, waving pistols and rifles at her. One of them spotted Yuvraj and yelled, 'There he is!'

Anika let out a scream, and her small hands refused to let go of her brother as the men grabbed Yuvraj by his arms and started dragging him away from her. They shoved Lata into the wall when she tried to stop them. Anika ran to her mother, whose head was now bleeding profusely. She heard her mother pleading with the men to leave Yuvraj alone.

'Please, don't take him! Please . . . he is just a child! It's not his fault.'

Yuvraj tried to break free, but he was beaten badly by the goons as they dragged him out of the front door.

'No . . . !' Lata cried, getting up from the floor and running behind the men as they got into their cars and drove off into the dark night. 'Leave my son alone. It's not his fault . . .'

Anika ran to her mother's side, her body shaking with sobs, but Lata stood frozen, her eyes fixed on the road and her face a mask of anguish and despair.

Days passed without any news of Yuvraj. The police came and went, investigating with no genuine leads. For the following weeks, the police asked Anika, Lata, and their neighbours many questions, but after about a month, they stopped asking. Weeks turned into months, and the hope of seeing Yuvraj began to fade, replaced by an aching grief that seeped into every corner of their lives.

Anika watched her mother disintegrate, barely speaking or eating. She became a shell of herself, consumed by the loss of her son. Anika felt the weight of her brother's absence like a constant ache in her chest. She lay awake at night, wondering where he was and why those men had taken him. But more than anything else, she tried to answer the question that haunted her the most: What did her mother know about Yuvraj's disappearance? She remembered the words that her mother had said repeatedly the night Yuvraj was kidnapped: *'It's not his fault.'* What did it mean?

Anika had tried to ask Lata about this a hundred times but was always met with silence. Once, Lata even denied having said anything at all. She knew her mother was hiding something, just like she hid things about her father and his family. But this time, Anika was desperate for answers. As the years passed and Lata's silence remained, Anika started feeling resentment towards her mother. By the time Anika enrolled in college, they were barely talking to each other. Once Anika finished college, she left her mother and Jaipur behind to build a new life, swearing to find whatever she could about her lost brother.

In the last decade, Anika has found many promising leads, but they all proved dead ends. She even managed to track down the men who had kidnapped her brother, but they were just paid goons who did what they did for some money and booze. Still, she never gave up hope. She knew someday, some case would lead her on the path that would take her to her brother.

ॐ

Anika sat up in bed, sweating heavily. It wasn't a dream; it was the memory she tried to keep buried. She got up, washed her face with cold water, and went to her home office. It was the only place that made her feel calm. She sat in the soft glow of the desk lamp. The room was quiet, except for the gentle ticking of the clock and the distant hum of the city outside. But Anika barely noticed, lost as she was in her thoughts. Her mind drifted back to that night when Yuvraj was kidnapped. Even now, after all these years, the pain of her loss was still too raw, a wound that had never healed. It was a scar she carried everywhere.

Her eyes fell on the framed photograph on her desk. It was a picture of Yuvraj and her as children posing outside their home, their faces bright with laughter and happiness. She picked it up and traced her brother's face with her fingers, the familiar ache stirring in her heart.

She picked up another framed photograph in which her mother stood beside her. She looked at her mother's face with longing. Anika hated admitting it to herself, but she missed her mother terribly. There were times when she'd hated her mother for being the way she was, especially after Yuvraj was gone. Looking back now, she appreciated everything her mother had done for her. She was particularly grateful to her mother for instilling her love for history. Being a history teacher, Lata would share the stories of Rajasthan's past with her children, and it was only because of her that Anika and Yuvraj would spend hours at the local library finding clues and connections between these different stories.

After Yuvraj's case turned cold, Anika knew why she had chosen to be in law enforcement. She wanted to find out what had become of her brother and, if she was honest with herself, whether he was even alive. But when she came across a field that made it possible for her to pursue her love for history while chasing criminals, she took it without a second thought. She completed her studies in historical forensic psychology and devoted her life to learn everything she could about the mysteries of the past to catch criminals in the present. She knew first-hand how the unsolved cases wreaked devastation on families—the way unanswered questions could eat away at the soul, leaving only emptiness and despair behind. So she had vowed to herself to solve all the cases she was handed, no matter the cost.

So she had thrown herself into her work with a passion that bordered on obsession, poring over ancient texts and artefacts, and studying how history and psychology intersected to create patterns of behaviour that could be used to solve even the most complex crimes.

But the thought of finding Yuvraj always lingered in her mind like a dark shadow.

Anika set the photograph down and leaned back in her chair, her eyes drifting to the window and the city's twinkling lights. Anika took a deep breath, feeling a sense of calm settle over her. She took a long breath and held it in for ten seconds before releasing it slowly. She knew the call from Inspector Singh had unsettled her in such a way that she could not control her thoughts from spiralling back to the past. She shook her head and, taking a deep breath, resolved to be strong and face whatever lay ahead at Amber Fort.

She went back to bed to catch a couple of hours of sleep before her flight and fell back into a fitful sleep, dreaming, yet again, about the night Yuvraj went missing.

꣠

Anika boarded the plane to Jaipur early that morning, her heart racing with excitement that she felt before every new case, though this time it was laced with a sense of foreboding because of her ties with the city. Amber Fort was a place she had visited as a child with her mother and Yuvraj several times, so the thought of going there again to investigate a murder made her feel a little odd. As the flight took off, she closed her eyes and whispered, 'I'm coming back home, Yuvraj.'

In the uneventful flight, Anika tried to catch up on some sleep but felt restless. She dismissed her growing sense of unease as anxiety about the new case but couldn't resist thinking if somehow it would lead to her brother. Dismissing her thoughts, she loosened the collar of her shirt and counted backwards from 100.

The sun had just risen over the horizon as Anika's plane touched the tarmac at Jaipur International Airport. As she looked out the window, the city stretched before her, a sea of pink and gold buildings shimmering in the early morning light.

Anika quickly claimed her luggage, a sturdy black VIP suitcase, and made her way to the exit. The heat hit her like a physical force as she exited the airport. She reeled back from the blast of dry air that seemed to draw the moisture from her skin. But despite the sweat already forming on her brow, Anika also felt a surge of anticipation wash over her. After all these years, she felt she was where she was meant to be.

As she was weaving through the crowd, her eyes scanned for the driver who was supposed to be waiting for her right outside the airport. Before long, she spotted a tall lean man in a crisp police uniform holding a placard with her name.

'Dr Anika Thakur?' the policeman asked as she smiled at him, his accent thick with Rajasthani inflection.

Anika nodded. 'That's me,' she said, hoisting the backpack onto her shoulder.

'I am Constable Driver Rohit, Jaipur police.' The constable's face broke into a wide grin. 'Welcome to Jaipur, Dr Thakur. Let me take your bags.' He bowed slightly before adding, 'I trust you had a pleasant journey?'

Anika laughed softly, shaking her head. 'As pleasant as it could be,' she replied, walking beside him to the waiting car.

'I'll be taking you to the hotel to freshen up and have some breakfast. After that, I'll drive you to the headquarters, where Inspector Singh is waiting for you,' Rohit said.

'Actually,' Anika replied, 'why don't we go straight to meet the inspector? I'm sure there'll be coffee at the headquarters.'

'Are you sure?' Rohit asked, surprised. 'But yes, there will definitely be coffee, and I'll arrange for some *kachoris* too.'

'Perfect. Then let's go.'

As they wound their way through the busy streets of Jaipur, Anika couldn't help but feel a sense of nostalgia wash over her. The city was a riot of colour and sound—street vendors called out over the traffic noise, and laughing women in bright *saris* carried bursting shopping bags. In the distance, Amber Fort rose like a mirage from the desert sands, like an ancient citadel that held the key to the mystery that had brought Anika to this place again.

As the car wound down through the narrow twisting streets of the old city, Anika felt the weight of Jaipur's royal history on her being. She knew she had already stepped out of her busy life and into a world that had remained unchanged for centuries. The weathered buildings lined the streets, a testament to the city's rich past—a patchwork of Mughal and Rajput architecture that seemed to hold secrets of the ages.

'Here we are, Dr Thakur,' Rohit said as the car pulled through the gates of Rajasthan Police Headquarters, a seven-storey building in Lalkothi, the heart of Jaipur. It was an imposing structure, designed to reflect modern and traditional architectural elements, featuring a blend of contemporary office spaces and traditional Rajasthani architectural motifs. The Central Administrative Office of the Rajasthan Police, overseeing law enforcement activities across the state, was situated here, as was the Special Crime Unit, led by Inspector of Police Rajesh Singh.

Anika stepped out of the car, shouldered her bag, and took a deep breath. The heat of the rising sun pressed against her skin, but so did the excitement of what lay ahead. She felt ready to follow the trail of clues that would lead her to the heart of yet another mystery.

Inside the police headquarters, the building buzzed with activity. Phones rang incessantly, and urgent conversations filled the air as Anika followed an assistant sub-inspector who had met her at the entrance.

As ASI Mohan guided her through the maze of corridors, Anika kept pace, feeling a sense of adventure. Her passion for her work surged within her, the passion that had governed her entire life. Rounding a corner, she caught sight of Inspector Rajesh Singh's office, and a flicker of trepidation crept in. She had spoken to him only briefly on the phone. Although he sounded sincere about enlisting her help, her past experiences with the local police had mostly led her to believe that her involvement in cases was not always appreciated. Especially given how she was (a) an outsider and (b) a woman in a male-dominated field of work. She despised internal bureaucratic politics; no matter how long she'd had to deal with it, she never felt apt at dealing with reluctant officers. She took a deep breath and braced herself to meet Inspector Singh.

'Here you go, ma'am,' ASI Mohan said, stopping at the reception area outside Singh's office. 'I'll leave you here.'

'Thank you,' Anika said, raising her hand to knock on the door.

'Come in,' answered a deep voice from inside.

Anika pushed the door open and winced when it creaked a little as she stepped inside. Instinctively, her sharp gaze took in the man who rose from behind the desk. Inspector Rajesh Singh was tall—taller than she'd expected—and broad-shouldered, his presence filling the room in a way that felt unintentional but undeniable. His neatly trimmed beard framed a face that looked like it had weathered both storms and the sun, the faint lines around his eyes hinting at long hours and sleepless nights.

He studied her in silence for a moment, his dark eyes assessing but not unkind. They weren't the eyes of a man who judged hastily. No, these eyes were calculating, weighing her against something unseen, though there was no hostility in his gaze—just curiosity tempered by a practised wariness.

Anika extended her hand, and when Singh shook it, his grip was firm but not crushing. His palm was calloused, a detail she noted with mild surprise; he wasn't the sort of officer who spent all his time behind a desk. His tone, when he spoke, was deep and deliberate, with an edge of authority that didn't need to be forced.

'Dr Thakur,' he said, his voice steady but tinged with genuine gratitude. 'Thank you for coming on such short notice.'

'Inspector Singh,' Anika replied, mirroring his formality. 'I appreciate the opportunity.'

As he gestured for her to sit, Anika couldn't help but observe the subtle contradictions in his demeanour. His frame and sharp features exuded strength, but his movements were surprisingly measured, almost careful, as though he were always mindful of the space he occupied. The small leather strap on his wrist—a child's handmade braid, she guessed—was a touch of softness that contrasted with his otherwise meticulous appearance. *A family man then*, she thought, despite the hardened exterior.

Her trained instincts noticed the little details: the faint scent of coffee lingering in the air, the neatly arranged files on his desk, and the absence of clutter. This man thrived on order, someone who didn't just solve puzzles but lived in their intricate arrangement.

As they began to talk, Anika found herself intrigued. Singh wasn't just capable; he was thoughtful. A quiet intensity about him reminded her of a chess master carefully positioning his pieces. She had worked with her share of officers who dismissed her methods, but something told her Singh wasn't one of them. He would listen—if only to figure out whether she was worth the gamble he'd taken by bringing her in.

'I've heard a lot about you, Dr Thakur,' Singh began, leaning back slightly. 'Your work on historical crimes is impressive. I was quite impressed by the way you solved the Peacock Throne case in Noida. Detective Rana, the lead on that case, is a good friend, and he was the one who'd praised your work. In fact, he's the reason why I attended your lecture in Delhi in January. And I must say, I wasn't disappointed. I think your unique perspective could be invaluable in this case.'

Anika nodded appreciatively, her mind going back to the case that had taken her well over seven months, too long in her opinion. The case involved the recovery of a priceless artefact—a fragment of the legendary Peacock Throne stolen from a private collector's estate in Delhi. 'I'm happy to help, but I'll need access to all the evidence and case files. Only then can I assess how I can assist you.'

'Of course.' He opened a desk drawer and pulled out a thick folder. 'Here's everything we have so far—crime scene photos, the autopsy report, and witness statements.'

He slid the folder across the desk, and Anika took it with a nod. She released a long breath, trying to hide the tension she'd been holding in her shoulders. She had half expected Singh to tell her he wouldn't be comfortable sharing *everything*.

As she was flipping through the pages briefly, her practised eye scanned the documents and photographs.

'The staging of the body points to a ritualistic practice suggesting that the killer wants to convey a message,' she said, looking up at Singh. 'Whoever did this had meticulously planned it. This isn't a random crime. There's a deeper meaning behind the killer's actions. And finding that could be the key to finding him.'

Singh's eyes darkened. 'That's what I had feared. But who is this message for? The police? Media? People of Jaipur? I'm not sure who the killer is targeting. After all, had it been for the police or the media or the people in general, why would the killer have used symbols and so many historical references? Why be cryptic? Doesn't the killer want everyone to understand the message?'

Anika gave Singh a patient smile. 'If only criminals thought like we did.' Anika spread the crime photos on the desk in front of Singh and said, 'It's a game for him. He doesn't want to send a message. He wants to do it while enjoying the game.'

'A game?'

'Yes, that's what it is for him. A game. A puzzle, if you will. And he is giving us clues to put it together.' Anika studied the crime scene photos for another minute. 'If I am right, we're going to have our hands full as this is just the beginning.'

'I have to admit, Dr Thakur, I was a bit hesitant to bring in an outsider at first. But the more I learned about your work, the more I realised we needed someone like you on this case.'

'I understand. And . . . I appreciate your honesty. I was a bit hesitant too. I appreciate your approach towards the case and your open-mindedness about involving me, but my experience has taught me to be wary. Many people in our field are sceptical of nontraditional approaches. Profiling is a very delicate aspect of finding a killer. If you add complex elements to the crime, like involving historical references to form an impossibly difficult pattern to break, well, to put it simply, it makes people nervous. They like to fall back on the more traditional ways of catching the killer, like DNA testing and interrogating witnesses and suspects. So I am impressed by your attitude.'

Inspector Singh looked visibly straightened, hearing the praise. He gave Anika a hesitant smile and said, 'Well, I must warn you, our department is not short of people you just referred to. When I proposed bringing you in, some of them openly protested. I had a long discussion about this case with the assistant commissioner of police, ACP Krishnan, and, thanks to her, I obtained her permission to involve you in this investigation completely.'

Anika gave him another knowing smile. 'It's kind of you to warn me, but trust me, Inspector, I've faced my fair share of criticism and scepticism and am well aware of how people can be cynical of forensic psychology, but in the end, results speak for themselves, don't they? Don't worry about me. I'm used to it.'

'Good to know. Hopefully, with your help, we stand a good chance of solving this case.'

'Thank you, Inspector. I'll do my best.'

They both stood up and shook hands.

'ASI Mohan will take you to the office we've set up for you. Let me know if you need anything else.'

'Thanks.'

As Anika stepped out of Singh's office, the weight of the case files pressed against her arm, but the weight of something intangible lingered in her mind. A quiet unease curled in the back of her thoughts, as though this case carried a significance she couldn't yet grasp. This wasn't just another investigation. It felt like the opening chapter of something far larger, something that would challenge her in ways she hadn't imagined.

CHAPTER 3

The afternoon sun filtered through the beautiful *jali* screens with marble inlays of Amber Fort's Diwan-i-Khas, the Hall of Private Audience, creating intricate patterns of light and shadow across the marble floor. The chamber, once a sanctum of royal power where Mughal Emperor Jahangir had honoured Raja Man Singh I with the title of Mirza Raja, now stood as a silent witness to an act of unspeakable violence. The grandeur of the Sheesh Mahal above, its delicate mirror work catching the sun's waning rays, only heightened the grotesque contrast of the crime scene below.

Anika stood motionless in the centre of the chamber, her sharp eyes taking in every detail. The killer had staged the scene with unnerving precision. The chalk outline on the patterned floor marked the body's placement, mimicking the position of a maharaja presiding over his court. A tableau of historical symbolism lay meticulously arranged around the outline of the dead body, each element placed with a deliberate hand. The sweet scent of marigold garlands, lingering from the morning rituals, mingled with the faint metallic tang of dried blood and created a cloying aroma that made her stomach churn.

The grandeur of the fort should have evoked nostalgia. Instead, it filled Anika with a deep sense of unease. She had spent countless childhood afternoons here, racing through these very halls with Yuvraj, laughing and playing as if the world couldn't touch them. But now, the killer had desecrated the sanctity of those memories. For the first time in years, she felt something akin to hatred for the person who had turned a place of such magnificence into a grotesque stage for their twisted message.

Inspector Rajesh Singh stood beside her, his broad frame casting a long shadow across the marble. His expression was stoic, but his tight jawline betrayed his frustration. 'Dr Thakur,' he began, his voice steady, 'the scene has been preserved since the initial documentation. We haven't touched anything beyond securing evidence. I thought it would be more helpful to discuss the case here, where it all happened.'

Anika nodded, her voice calm but thoughtful, appreciating the inspector's cooperation. Anika nodded. 'Thank you, Inspector. A scene like this has layers. It can only be understood by seeing it in context.' She glanced at the forensic team, moving with precision in their protective suits, but her focus returned to the symbols Singh had described. The faint lines etched into the wall drew her closer.

As she moved towards the alcove, her fingers instinctively brushed against the small locket around her neck. It was a family heirloom passed down through generations, and its intricate engravings had always been a mystery to her. Yet wearing it grounded her, serving as a reminder of her roots as she stood amid the echoes of a shared past.

Taking a deep breath to brace herself, Anika stepped into the chamber. From somewhere deep within the fort, the mournful call of a peacock echoed, and it sent shivers down her spine, bringing up a surge of memories she tried to push aside. She laid a hand on the wall beside her to steady herself and felt the stone walls, cool and rough beneath her fingertips, seeming to pulse with centuries of secrets. From somewhere within the fort, the mournful call of a peacock echoed, a haunting counterpoint to the grim scene before her.

Walking behind her, Singh took the lead and pointed her to the stone where the symbols were engraved. She took one look and declared, 'It's a fusion of the royal emblems.' Her breath hitched at the end. She had come across references to it in her research—a unified crest tied to a legend of betrayal and a curse that had allegedly haunted Rajasthan's royal lineage. Could the killer be invoking that legend? Or was this an elaborate misdirection? Anika's mind raced as she examined the details, her fingers trailing the cool carved stone.

The chamber was thick with the musty scent of age and something sharper, metallic. The peacock's cry echoed again, louder this time, and despite herself, tugged at the memory buried deep within her.

Anika was ten years old, crouched in the shadowy corners of this very chamber during a game of hide-and-seek with Yuvraj. Anika's mother worked in the school close to Amber Fort and would often leave them there to play whenever she had to spend extra hours there. The chamber had smelled of sandalwood and time, the air heavy with stories whispered across generations. 'Come out, come out, wherever you are!' Yuvraj's voice rang out, teasing and playful. She had stifled a giggle, only to freeze as her hand brushed against a loose stone. Behind it lay a small medallion, marked with strange intertwining symbols . . .

The memory dissolved as quickly as it had surfaced, leaving Anika staring at the carved wall before her. A bitter pang of longing rippled through her chest, but she pushed it aside. The past would have to wait.

Singh's voice cut through her thoughts. 'The body's removal followed a strict protocol,' he said, gesturing towards the chalk outline. 'We documented everything before transportation. The positioning, the state of the body. The forensic team, headed by Dr Dilip Malhotra, is cataloguing every single detail. We'll have all the necessary information by tonight, and that's where your work begins.'

Anika nodded, her gaze still fixed on the alcove. 'The killer's precision speaks volumes,' she murmured. 'This isn't just a murder. It's a performance. The killer is inviting us to decode it.'

The forensic team worked silently in the background, cataloguing evidence with practised efficiency. Every detail had been preserved: photographs and videos documenting the position of the body and its surroundings, samples taken from the intricate marble floor, and the faint traces of blood that had been meticulously analysed.

Anika's eyes drifted back to the chalk outline, her mind filling in the gaps that the body's absence left behind. She could almost see the victim—a man forced into the posture of a ruler, his position a mockery of authority. *But why was the killer trying to recreate a historical scene? And what was the significance of the unified crest carved in the stone?*

Anika turned to Singh, her tone sharp with realisation. 'The symbols, the positioning of the body, the objects found by the body, and the location—I think the killer is pointing to a specific incident in history. The killer isn't just leaving clues. They're creating, or *recreating*, a narrative. We just have to figure out which incident, and I think I know where we should start digging.'

Singh's gaze lingered on the etched crest, his expression grim but resolute. 'A story written in blood,' he muttered. 'But one way or another, it needs to end here.'

ॐ

The afternoon sunlight poured through jali screens, its golden beams dancing across the chamber's marble floor. Anika crouched near the chalk outline, her gaze falling on a small metallic object glinting faintly near where the victim's right hand had rested. Her pulse quickened. The placement wasn't arbitrary; it was precise, deliberate. And disturbingly familiar.

She leaned in, catching her breath. The object's position mirrored exactly where she'd once discovered the medallion as a child, hidden in the dusty alcove during a game of hide-and-seek with Yuvraj. The memory flared to life, intense and unsettling, but before she could dwell on it, a sudden gust swept through the chamber. The flimsy crime scene markers trembled, a few scattering across the floor.

'Careful!' a voice cut through the stillness, his tone sharp as he moved to secure the disturbed evidence.

In the brief commotion, Anika's fingers brushed against the metallic object. A strange jolt shot through her, as if static electricity had passed between her and the artefact. But it wasn't just physical. Something else flickered at the edges of her consciousness. A fleeting image, almost a vision: a crowded court, its air heavy with tension, and a figure kneeling before a throne. She drew back sharply, blinking, the phantom scene vanishing as quickly as it had appeared.

'Dr Thakur?' Singh's voice was closer now, edged with concern. 'Are you all right?'

Anika straightened, shaking her head as if to clear the lingering image. 'Yes, I'm fine,' she replied, her voice steadying. She gestured to the object. 'What can you tell me about this?'

Singh consulted his notes, his expression thoughtful. 'It's a replica of a 16th-century Rajput seal ring. The craftsmanship is exceptional, but our team confirmed it's modern.'

Anika frowned, picking up the ring with gloved fingers. Its weight felt oddly significant in her hand. 'This pattern—it's tied to Maharaja Bhagwant Das, a ruler of Amber in the late 16th century. He was known for his diplomacy, particularly in forging alliances through marriage and treaty.'

She traced the engravings with her thumb, her brow furrowing. 'But there's something unusual about this design. Look here, these symbols.' She tilted the ring to catch the light, revealing faint markings etched along the band. 'They're a fusion of emblems from different royal houses. This isn't a replica. It's a reference to the unified crest.'

Singh's brows knitted. 'Unified crest?'

Anika nodded, her thoughts racing. 'There are mentions of it in obscure historical texts—a supposed emblem created to symbolise the unity of rival Rajput clans. Most historians dismiss it as a myth. But if this ring is real, it changes everything we know about Rajput history.' She paused, excitement flickering in her voice. 'This could be evidence of something long thought to be a legend.'

She squinted at the surface, noting faint scratches that seemed too deliberate to be random. 'And these marks? They're not imperfections from manufacturing.' She glanced at the forensic technician nearby. 'You said this might be a defect?'

The technician nodded. 'That's what we thought. Could be from wear or damage during production.'

'No,' Anika said firmly, her voice sharp with certainty. 'The variations in thickness and depth—they're intentional. These weren't caused by a blunt tool. They were carved using different implements with careful precision.' She leaned back, her expression contemplative. 'It's an inscription. Ancient *Devanagari* script, if I'm not mistaken. But it's not a dialect used today. We'll need a historical linguistics expert to translate it.'

Singh's eyes narrowed, his gaze fixed on the ring. 'You're saying the killer left us a message in an ancient script?'

'It seems so,' Anika replied, her tone grim. 'The question is why.'

As Singh stepped out of the chamber to call ASI Mohan to contact their department's linguistics expert, Anika continued examining the crime scene. After carefully examining the area around the chalk outline, she turned her gaze towards the surrounding elements. She started studying every corner of the place for details that stood out. She was dealing with an intelligent killer and was sure of it now. She knew he might have left more clues hidden in plain sight. Her breath caught in her throat right then, when her attention shifted to a nearby pillar, her eye catching a faint carving almost hidden among the elaborate detailing. She stepped closer, her breath hitching as she recognised it: another unified crest. This one, however, was far older, weathered by centuries but still unmistakable. A chill crept up her spine as fragments of a legend resurfaced in her mind.

She started as Singh returned. 'Inspector,' she murmured, 'have you ever heard of the curse of Chandravati?'

Singh folded his arms, his brow furrowing. 'The name sounds familiar. Folklore, isn't it?'

'More than that,' Anika said, her voice barely above a whisper. 'Chandravati was a mystic in the court of Amber during the late 16th century. Renowned for her foresight, she fell out of favour and was accused of treason. Legend has it, she cursed the royal lineage before her execution.'

Singh gave her a sceptical look, but she cut him off before he could protest. 'It's not about whether the curse is real, Inspector. What matters is that the killer chose to evoke it. That means it holds significance to him, and *that's* what matters.'

As they continued examining the crime scene, Anika was reminded of her grandmother's stories of courtly intrigue and royal secrets. She had always dismissed them as the fanciful imaginings of an old woman. But now, standing amid this historical recreation, she couldn't help but wonder if there had been more truth in them than she'd realised. Or is the killer trying to create their own imagined version of history?

She was lost in thought when her gaze fell on the wall behind the body's outline. A vibrant tapestry hung there, its colours vivid against the chamber's sombre tones. She moved closer, noting the scene it depicted: a royal court in session and a ruler presiding over the trial of a kneeling figure. Her heart quickened.

'This tapestry,' she said aloud, 'it's not part of the fort's original decor, is it?'

'No,' Singh confirmed. 'It was recently brought here, about a week or so ago. It was donated by someone. We're still trying to trace its origins.'

Anika's eyes lingered on the woven scene. 'This isn't just any trial,' she said softly. 'It's the Trial of Chandravati.'

The room fell silent as everyone turned towards her. Anika continued, 'According to the legend, Chandravati was accused of treason and sentenced to death. This tapestry shows her final moments.' Her voice dropped. 'If the killer brought this here, it means something. This crime is more than a statement. It's a recreation of history, possibly with deliberate alterations.'

Singh regarded her for a long moment. 'But why this specific event? What is the killer trying to say?'

Anika turned to the array of items near the chalk outline: a tarnished goblet, prayer beads, and a ceremonial dagger. Her gaze narrowed on the dagger, its jewelled hilt catching the light. 'Everything here is symbolic,' she said. 'Power, spirituality, protection. The dagger's placement, pointing away from the body, isn't random. It suggests the killer sees themselves not as an attacker, but as a defender.'

She met Singh's gaze, her voice steady but grave. 'This isn't just murder. It's a performance. A message. And until we decipher it, we won't understand what the killer is truly after.'

'But here's the real question: Why go to such extraordinary lengths? Why recreate an entire scene, stage a murder, and leave behind all these elaborate symbols? Why not just write a manifesto, send an anonymous letter to the press, or even scrawl the message on these very walls?'

As she opened her mouth to reply to Singh, her gaze was drawn to a small alcove in the far corner of the chamber. It tugged at her subconscious, an itch she couldn't quite place. She moved towards it slowly, her eyes narrowing as they scanned the intricate carvings that adorned its surface. Something about it didn't sit right.

'Inspector,' she called out, 'was anything found in this alcove?'

Singh flipped through his notes, his brow furrowing. 'Nothing. There's no mention of it in the initial documentation. I believe it was empty.'

Anika leaned in, her breath shallow, as her fingertips hovered over the cool carved stone. There, nearly invisible unless you knew exactly where to look, was a tiny symbol etched into the surface—a stylised eye, rays of sunlight radiating from its centre, so delicately inscribed that it could easily be mistaken for a weathered detail in the ancient design.

'This wasn't here originally,' she murmured, her voice barely audible over the faint rustle of the forensic team at work. 'It's new. Recently carved but made to mimic the fort's ancient aesthetic.' Straightening, she turned to the nearest technician. 'I need detailed photographs of this—macro shots. And if possible, create a cast of the carving.'

As the technicians scrambled to comply, Anika stepped back, her thoughts racing. The symbol wasn't unfamiliar; she had encountered it before, buried in the pages of obscure historical texts and whispered legends. The Eye of Chandravati was a mythical artefact believed to grant its possessor the ability to see hidden truths, both past and present.

She turned towards the room, her voice calm but heavy with meaning. 'Our killer isn't just recreating an event from history. They're weaving together a larger narrative that blends historical fact, myth, and symbolism into a single, cohesive story. And for some reason, they've chosen to tell it to us through blood.'

Inspector Singh's face darkened, the weight of the revelation settling over him. 'And what do you think that story is, Doctor?' he asked, his voice low but firm.

Anika met his gaze, her own eyes fierce with determination. 'I don't know the full story yet. But I suspect it's tied to righting what they see as historical wrongs. The killer may believe they're an agent of justice or vengeance. They could be reaching across centuries, attempting to settle scores left unresolved long ago.'

A heavy silence fell over the room, the implications of her words rippling through the air like a tangible force. If Anika was right, this was more than a simple murder investigation. It was a descent into the dark tangled web of Rajasthan's royal history—a place where betrayal, power, and secrets had festered for generations. Somewhere in that labyrinth lay the truth, buried beneath centuries of myth and shadow.

The sun dipped lower on the horizon, casting the chamber into a deepening gloom. Shadows stretched across the marble floor, their shifting shapes lending an almost spectral quality to the space. Anika shivered, though the air remained warm. The chill was something else entirely—a premonition, a sense of foreboding she couldn't shake.

She had come to Amber Fort searching for answers. Instead, she had stumbled into a maze of riddles. One thing, however, was becoming painfully clear: This case would demand every ounce of her knowledge, intuition, and resolve. It wasn't just a test of skill. It was a battle against the weight of history itself.

Anika let out a slow, steady breath, her gaze returning to the faintly etched Eye of Chandravati. 'Whoever this killer is,' she said softly, almost to herself, 'he's playing a long game. And I'm not sure we're ready for all the rules.'

Inspector Singh, standing beside her, studied her expression carefully. 'Then we'd better catch up fast,' he replied. But there was a shadow in his voice. They both shared a look of shared acknowledgement that they were walking into something far larger than either of them had anticipated.

ॐ

A profound silence blanketed the ancient walls as night settled over Amber Fort. The forensic team had packed up, their work done for the day, and Inspector Singh had reluctantly agreed to give Anika a few more minutes at the crime scene. She had insisted, driven by a nagging feeling that the room still held secrets waiting to be uncovered.

Standing in the centre of the grand chamber, Anika swung her flashlight in slow arcs, its beam slicing through the oppressive darkness. The air hung heavy, thick with the weight of centuries of history and the lingering chill of violence. She turned in place, her intuition tugging her gaze in one direction after another.

'What are you trying to tell me?' she murmured, her voice a whisper lost in the vast stillness.

A faint glimmer in the far corner caught her attention. Had she not examined that area thoroughly earlier? Something about it called to her, an inexplicable pull she couldn't ignore.

With each step closer, her pulse quickened. The flashlight's beam revealed a portion of the wall adorned with intricate carvings that seemed almost hypnotic in their complexity. Anika leaned in, her breath fogging the cool surface as she studied the patterns.

Her fingers paused over a slight irregularity—a barely noticeable indentation that disrupted the otherwise flawless design. Hands trembling, she pressed the anomaly.

A muted click broke the silence, and a segment of the wall shifted inwards, revealing a hidden compartment. Anika's breath hitched. She knelt, her flashlight casting long shadows as she peered into the concealed recess. Dust swirled in the beam, disturbed for the first time in centuries. Nestled inside, resting on a bed of decayed velvet, was a tarnished object.

Carefully, she reached in with gloved hands. Her training told her to call the team, but a stronger, more personal instinct whispered that this moment was hers alone. Slowly, she lifted the object into the light.

It was a medallion, small and worn, but its craftsmanship was undeniable. Despite the tarnish of age, its carved surface still gleamed faintly, its design delicate and deliberate. She caught her breath as she turned it over in her palm.

'The unified crest,' she whispered, her voice trembling. 'But that's impossible . . .'

The medallion bore symbols from multiple Rajput dynasties, seamlessly merged into a single design. According to every historical record she'd studied, such unity had never existed. The royal houses had fiercely guarded their independence, their identities remaining distinct for centuries.

Yet here it was, evidence of a vision—or perhaps an achievement— that defied the historical narrative.

A chill swept over her, prickling her skin as the enormity of the discovery settled in. If this medallion were genuine, it could rewrite centuries of Rajasthan's history. But if the killer had known about it, well . . .

A faint scrape, like stone brushing against stone, broke her thoughts. Anika froze, heart pounding as she spun around, the flashlight beam darting through the shadows. The room appeared empty, but her instincts screamed otherwise. Her skin prickled with the unmistakable sensation of being watched.

She forced herself to breathe and turned back to the medallion, her mind racing. Then something tugged at the edge of her memory. The design on the back of the medallion—intricate swirls radiating outwards from a central sunburst—looked hauntingly familiar.

Her hand darted into her satchel, fingers closing around the worn brass compass that Yuvraj had left her. She flipped it over, her heart pounding.

There it was—the exact same pattern etched on the back of the compass, albeit slightly weathered.

Anika's breath hitched. A cold shiver ran through her. What were the odds? The symbol wasn't just unique; it was unmistakable, unlike anything she'd seen elsewhere in her research. A deliberate design meant to stand out, the kind of mark that carried significance.

She ran her thumb over the matching patterns, her thoughts spiralling. Was this Yuvraj's way of leaving her a clue? A message he couldn't deliver himself?

The logical choice was to report the medallion immediately. But this connection felt deeply personal, almost as though it had been waiting for her, meant for her. The matching designs couldn't be a coincidence.

Anika slipped the medallion into her pocket, its weight now heavier with meaning. She decided she wouldn't report it just yet. Not until she understood what it meant.

She stepped back from the alcove, her mind racing. This medallion wasn't just a relic. It was a key. But to what? And at what cost?

As she left the chamber, the air seemed heavier and the shadows darker. She quickened her pace, her steps echoing in the silence. Outside, the cool night air hit her like a shock, but the medallion burned in her pocket like a live ember.

What she couldn't yet know was that her choice had set events into motion—events that would plunge her into the depths of a centuries-old mystery. The lines between past and present, justice and vengeance, would soon blur beyond recognition.

The game had begun. And Anika Thakur had just taken her first move.

The conference room at the Rajasthan Police Headquarters stood in stark contrast to the vibrant chaos of the city outside. Whiteboards and maps lined the walls, their surface covered with notes, timelines, and arrows of a case already spiralling in complexity. The long table at the centre was cluttered with files, photographs, and empty coffee cups, a testament to the relentless pace of the investigation.

Anika sat at the table, her gaze moving from the case materials to the faces around her. Inspector Singh was beside her, his brow furrowed as he flipped through a sheaf of papers. Across the table sat SP Jagjit Verma, his sharp features unreadable as his fingers steepled beneath his chin. Senior officers from Crime, Forensics, and other departments flanked him, their expressions a mix of tension and expectation. This was no ordinary investigation; it demanded an unprecedented level of collaboration.

Anika had heard of Verma's reputation—his meteoric rise through the ranks, being a shrewd political operator who knew how to handle the delicate intersection of law and power. Now, as she watched him lean back in his chair, she couldn't help but feel that his presence was as much about optics as it was about solving the case.

'Dr Thakur,' Verma began, his voice polished but tinged with authority. 'Thank you for joining us on such short notice. I trust your journey here was uneventful?'

Anika gave a polite nod. 'Yes, Superintendent. I was eager to begin.' She noted how Verma exuded the polished demeanour of a man who thrived in the corridors of power. His sharp eyes missed nothing, and his every word seemed carefully measured, like a chess player anticipating his opponent's next move. Beneath the courteous exterior, Anika sensed a quiet intensity—an unspoken warning that Verma was not a man to be underestimated.

Verma's eyes shifted to the files scattered across the table. 'Good. Because this case demands nothing less than our full attention.' His voice dropped slightly, a subtle warning beneath the veneer of professionalism. 'The murder at Amber Fort has significant implications. The fort is not just a historical landmark. It's a cornerstone of our city's identity.' He paused, letting the gravity of his words settle. 'The murder at Amber Fort has already created ripples. If we don't handle this carefully, the economic, political, and cultural fallout could be devastating.'

Anika straightened, meeting his gaze with calm resolve. 'I understand, Superintendent. But with all due respect, my priority is uncovering the truth, not the consequences.'

Verma's smile was thin, calculated. 'Naturally. I wouldn't expect anything less. But I also expect discretion. Inform me immediately if you find out anything that could impact the city's reputation. Especially if it so much as points towards the city's royals.'

Anika smiled inwardly. She had known what Verma had been hinting at all along. The precious royals of this town. To Verma he said, 'Of course, sir,' her tone neutral. 'I have no intention of causing unnecessary disruptions.'

Verma nodded, apparently satisfied, and rose to his feet. 'Good, Inspector Singh and his team will provide you with all necessary resources. ACP Krishnan has spoken highly of you, and I trust her judgment.'

Anika gave ACP Krishnan an appreciative smile.

As Verma left the room, the tension seemed to lift, though the weight of the investigation still weighed heavily on everyone in the room. For a moment, no one spoke. Then Singh let out a sigh, his expression softening.

'The SP means well,' he said, 'but his priorities . . . well, they can complicate things. Don't let it rattle you.'

Anika allowed a wry smile. 'It's all right. I've dealt with bureaucrats before.' She turned to ACP Krishnan. ACP Jyothi Krishnan had an air of quiet authority that commanded attention without demanding it. Her sharp almond-shaped eyes missed nothing, and her no-nonsense demeanour was offset by a warmth that surfaced when she smiled. She was dressed impeccably in her uniform, and her poise reflected years of dealing adeptly with crime and bureaucracy. 'Thank you for your confidence, ma'am. I won't let you down.'

Krishnan nodded. 'I'm sure you won't. If you need anything, just ask. We're all in this together.'

Singh leaned forward, his tone serious. 'This case is bigger than it looks, Dr Thakur. The political pressure will only get worse, especially if the royal families are involved. But I trust you. If anyone can help us crack this, it's you.'

Anika's fingers brushed against the medallion in her pocket, its weight grounding her. She forced herself to focus on the task ahead. 'Let's get to work,' she said, her voice steady. 'We have a killer to catch.'

ॐ

The Rambagh Palace loomed before her. It was a sight to behold, a living testament to Rajasthani grandeur. Its domed pavilions and sprawling courtyards shimmered in the evening light, exuding an opulence that seemed almost otherworldly. As Anika approached the gates, a young guard straightened abruptly, hastily tucking something behind his back.

'Your ID, please,' he said, clearing his throat, his voice slightly gruff.

Anika noticed the faint smell of bidi smoke lingering in the air. She arched an eyebrow but handed over her credentials without comment.

The guard glanced at them quickly, avoiding her gaze as he fidgeted with the collar of his uniform. 'All clear,' he muttered, stepping aside.

Anika suppressed a smile as she walked past. The faint red tinge on his ears and his nervous shuffling made it obvious he'd been caught indulging in a forbidden habit on duty. A minor transgression, but enough to make him jittery.

Inside, her footsteps echoed on the marble floor, the grandeur of the palace feeling overwhelming. The pristine white floors gleamed under towering chandeliers, and ornate tapestries adorned the walls. Anika followed a secretary, Naveen, through a series of winding corridors, the grandeur pressing in on her. As they walked, she couldn't shake the sensation of being watched. The shadows seemed alive, as though hidden eyes tracked her every step.

She had come to meet Vikram Singh Rathore, a descendant of the royal family and a key figure in Jaipur's elite social circles. Given the case's historical connections, Inspector Singh had arranged the meeting, hoping that Vikram could provide some insight into the case, especially the unified crest.

Finally, she reached a small sitting room where Prince Vikram Singh Rathore awaited her. He stood as she entered, his height and regal bearing instantly commanding attention. Anika couldn't help but notice the effortless magnetism he carried. Tall and broad-shouldered, he had the kind of looks that belonged on magazine covers—sharp, symmetrical features framed by a perfectly groomed beard and a hint of rakish stubble. His tailored suit fit him like a second skin, accentuating a physique that spoke of both discipline and indulgence.

'Dr Thakur,' he greeted, his voice smooth. 'Thank you for coming.'

Anika smiled politely, noting the way he moved—with the easy confidence of someone who had never questioned his place in the world. His smile was disarming, a deft mix of warmth and mischief that could set anyone at ease or on edge, depending on his intention.

Anika regarded him with a practised detachment, though she couldn't deny the subtle allure of his charisma. Princes, she reminded herself, were often trained in the art of charm as much as politics. Vikram was no exception. Yet, beneath the polished exterior, she detected something more—a flicker of calculation in his dark eyes, a guardedness that hinted at layers he wasn't ready to reveal.

He greeted her with a voice as smooth as silk, his tone light and conversational. But as Anika extended her hand to meet his, she couldn't shake the sense that Vikram Singh Rathore was a man who thrived on being underestimated.

'Thank you for meeting me on such short notice, Mr Rathore,' Anika replied, extending her hand. Vikram had greeted her in a light, conversational tone, but as she extended her hand to meet his, she couldn't shake the sense that Vikram Singh Rathore was a man who thrived on being underestimated.

'Please, call me Vikram,' he said, his handshake firm. 'And no need for formalities. I'm always happy to help, especially in such . . . intriguing circumstances.'

As Vikram gestured for her to follow him into a smaller elegantly decorated sitting room, his voice dropped as he turned to his assistant,

Naveen. 'Don't forget to confirm my meeting with the commissioner of heritage tomorrow,' he said, his tone brisk.

Anika's ears perked up at the mention, but she kept her expression neutral as she followed Vikram into the room. She made a mental note of the exchange. The commissioner of heritage wasn't a name that came up often in casual conversation. What business could Vikram Singh Rathore have with the commissioner?

He gestured for her to sit, then settled into the chair opposite her. 'I understand this concerns the murder at Amber Fort. A terrible thing, and most unusual for Jaipur.'

She settled into the plush armchair he offered, her mind momentarily split between the case and the threads of intrigue surrounding this man. Whatever role Vikram was playing—helpful ally or something more ambiguous—she resolved to keep her guard up. 'Unusual, yes,' Anika said, studying him. 'But perhaps not unrelated to the fort's history. You seem well versed in Jaipur's past.'

Vikram's expression darkened, a shadow passing over his features. 'Amber Fort has always been a part of my family's history. My father used to tell me of bravery, betrayal, and secrets best left untouched.'

Anika tilted her head, catching the faint shift in his expression. 'Secrets?'

He hesitated, the lightness in his voice dimming. 'Once, I walked into his office without knocking and saw him burning old family documents and photographs. When I asked why, he looked at me like I'd walked in on something I wasn't meant to see. He made me swear never to speak of it again. That it was an important secret.'

There was a pause, his words hanging in the air like smoke. Vikram offered a faint rueful smile, but his eyes betrayed a deeper weight. 'After that, he never talked about our family's past. Not once.'

Anika studied him for a moment, noting the way he deflected just enough to reveal without fully exposing himself. Certainly trained in the art of disclosure. She decided to tread carefully. 'Do you think those secrets have anything to do with what's happening now?'

Vikram's smile widened, but it didn't reach his eyes. 'That's for you to find out, isn't it, Dr Thakur?'

'Call me Anika,' she replied, her voice soft but firm.

'Very well, Anika,' he said. He leaned forward, elbows resting on his knees and his sharp gaze never leaving Anika. 'You see,' he said, his voice low but deliberate, 'when a crime like this happens—a crime that seems to echo some dark chapter of our past—there are always those who will stop at nothing to uncover the truth.' He let the words hang in the air before continuing, 'I may be able to help you. I have access to resources, connections, and knowledge that could prove invaluable to your investigation. But . . .' He paused, his tone shifting ever so slightly. 'I need to know if this case might affect my family. I trust you understand why that's important to me.'

Anika hesitated. The medallion in her pocket felt heavier, its implications more profound with each passing moment. Vikram's offer was tempting. His influence and resources could untangle threads she might struggle with alone. Yet something about his demeanour, the veiled intensity behind his charm, made her wary.

'I appreciate the offer, Vikram,' she said carefully, her voice steady. 'But you understand that I have to maintain impartiality and confidentiality in my work. I can't promise to share everything or involve outside parties unless it's necessary to the investigation.'

His smile didn't falter, though his eyes gleamed with something unreadable. 'Of course. I wouldn't expect anything less from you. Still,' he added, his tone lighter, 'keep my offer in mind. You never know when you might need a friend in high places.'

Anika felt her breath quicken, but she pushed the reaction aside, focusing instead on his words.

Vikram rose, his height and presence seeming to fill the room. 'Now, if you'll excuse me, I have other matters to attend to. But if you need anything, don't hesitate to reach out. I'll be watching your progress with great interest.'

As he led her towards the exit, they passed an ornate tapestry adorning the wall. Anika's eye caught on a familiar motif woven into its intricate design—a triangular eye surrounded by radiating lines.

'Vikram,' she asked, keeping her tone casual, 'what's the significance of that symbol?'

He glanced at it briefly, his expression carefully neutral. 'Oh, that? It's an old family crest. Nothing of importance,' he said smoothly, steering the conversation elsewhere. But the deliberate way he brushed it off only heightened Anika's suspicion.

As she stepped out into the cool night air, the sensation of being watched prickled at her neck. Were there unseen eyes following her movements, or was it her imagination? Either way, she made a mental note: Trust would have to be earned in this city of secrets.

Anika reminded herself of the task ahead; she had a killer to catch.

At the Rajasthan Police Headquarters, the sterile glow of the forensic lab cast on the steel counters and glass cabinets. Anika stood at her workstation, her dark hair pulled back in a tight ponytail, the crime scene photos splayed out meticulously. Each image pulled her deeper into the killer's world, whispering of ritual, precision, and purpose. Yet the motive, a key to the truth, remained maddeningly out of reach.

She leaned closer to one photo, her brows furrowing as she studied an unusual pattern in the victim's clothing. Before she could examine it further, the door swung open with a forceful push, slamming into the wall behind.

Dr Dilip Malhotra strode in, his crisp white coat pristine and his presence filling the room like an unwelcome gust of wind. Malhotra carried himself with the air of a man accustomed to being the most intelligent person in the room. With its chiselled jawline and perpetually furrowed brows, his face bore the intensity of a man who lived for precision. Behind his wire-rimmed glasses, his sharp, analytical eyes seemed to size up everything and everyone in the room.

Malhotra had built a reputation as one of India's leading forensic scientists, known for his sharp intellect and uncompromising methods. But he was also infamous for his disdain towards newer approaches, particularly anything he deemed unscientific, like forensic psychology.

'Dr Thakur,' he said, his tone a careful balance of forced politeness and thinly veiled disdain. 'I understand you've been . . . consulting on this case.' His eyes flicked over the crime scene photos on the table, lingering briefly before locking on to hers. 'Odd that Inspector Singh didn't think to involve me sooner.'

Anika straightened, refusing to be intimidated. 'Dr Malhotra,' she began evenly, 'the superintendent authorised my involvement because of the historical and cultural dimensions of this case. It was a chaotic start, and I apologise for the delay in meeting you.'

Malhotra's lips curved into a smile that was more cutting than cordial. 'Hectic, no doubt. While you've been pursuing your "historical context", my team has been focused on tangible forensic evidence. We're investigating a murder, Dr Thakur, not curating a museum exhibit on Rajasthani folklore.'

The tension in the room thickened, but Anika kept her composure. 'The historical elements *are* tangible evidence, Dr Malhotra. The killer's choice of location and the precise details of the crime scene suggest intentional symbolism. Ignoring that would be like solving a puzzle with half the pieces missing.'

Malhotra crossed his arms, his scepticism unmistakable. 'Symbolism, puzzle? This isn't a dissertation, Dr Thakur. It's a homicide investigation. Our job is to follow hard evidence, not indulge in speculative storytelling.'

Her jaw tightened, but she pressed on. 'The symbols and staging are hard evidence, Dr Malhotra. The killer chose the location and the details with purpose.' She gestured to a photo of the etched crest near the victim. 'This isn't just a flourish. It's a calculated choice. Whoever did this has a deep understanding of Rajasthan's royal history.'

Malhotra leaned over the photo, his gaze sharp. 'Or they did a quick search on Google or Wikipedia,' he said dryly. 'Killers are often far more mundane than you imagine. This elaborate staging? It's attention-seeking behaviour. Narcissistic, likely male, midthirties, escalating from minor crimes. Textbook stuff.'

Anika raised an eyebrow, her patience wearing thin. 'Textbook, perhaps, but incomplete.' She gestured to the photos spread across the workstation and continued, her voice measured but firm, 'This isn't just narcissism at play, Dr Malhotra. The killer exhibits traits of obsessive-compulsive tendencies. Notice the precision in the staging, the symmetry in the placement of objects around the body. This isn't random. It's ritualistic. The choice of location—the Amber Fort, a symbol of Rajasthani heritage—suggests someone who feels deeply connected to its historical significance. Likely educated, with access to resources that provide a detailed understanding of royal history.'

She picked up a close-up of the crest etched near the victim and pointed to it. 'This variant of the Rathore emblem is obscure. It hasn't been in use for centuries and isn't something the average person would recognise, let alone reproduce accurately. That tells us the killer is not only knowledgeable but meticulous, with a very specific intent.'

Malhotra's lips pressed into a thin line, but Anika pressed on, sensing the room's attention shifting to her. 'The narcissism is there, yes,' she conceded. 'But it's not the driving force. This is someone who views themselves as an arbiter of justice, possibly avenging what they perceive as historical wrongs. They're theatrical, yes, but also methodical. Likely in their late thirties to early forties, male, with a background in history or archaeology, or someone with access to those circles. The attention to detail suggests they're comfortable with planning over extended periods and confident enough to execute without fear of being caught. This isn't someone escalating from petty crimes. They've likely been operating under the radar for a long time.'

She placed the photo down and met Malhotra's gaze. 'The killer isn't just sending a message. They believe they're part of something much larger—a mission, if you will. Dismissing this as mere attention-seeking behaviour ignores the deeper psychological complexities at play. And in my experience, ignoring those complexities is how investigations hit dead ends.'

For a moment, Malhotra said nothing, his sharp features betraying no reaction. But there was a flicker of something in his eyes— recognition, perhaps, or grudging respect. When he finally spoke, his tone was clipped. 'An interesting theory, Dr Thakur. Let's hope it holds up under the weight of actual evidence.'

Anika didn't miss the dismissive undertone, but she allowed herself a small private smile. The seed of doubt was planted. She turned back to the photos, ready to keep building her case and confident that her expertise would speak louder than Malhotra's scepticism.

Right then, the lab door opened, cutting the tension in the room, and a young technician stepped in, holding a file. 'Excuse me, Dr Malhotra,' she said nervously, sensing the tension. 'Preliminary DNA results are in. And . . . there's something else you need to see.'

Malhotra snatched the file, flipping through its contents. His frown deepened. 'The DNA is inconclusive,' he said, his voice clipped. 'No matches in the database.'

He hesitated before continuing, clearly reluctant, 'There's also an unidentified substance on the victim's clothing. Early tests suggest it's a pigment. Very old—possibly centuries.'

Anika's pulse quickened, though she kept her tone neutral. 'Centuries-old pigment? That aligns with the historical angle, wouldn't you say?'

Malhotra glared, his expression thunderous. 'It's an anomaly, nothing more. We'll identify it soon enough, and it will have a perfectly logical explanation.'

'Logical, yes,' Anika replied, pressing her advantage. 'But that doesn't exclude the possibility that it ties back to the killer's knowledge of history. If they're using genuine historical materials, that tells us something critical about their resources and intent.'

The technician lingered uncertainly. 'Dr Thakur might have a point,' she ventured cautiously. 'This isn't . . . normal.'

'That will be all,' Malhotra snapped. The technician retreated hastily, leaving the room heavy with unspoken tension.

He turned back to Anika, his tone cold and measured. 'Listen carefully, Thakur. I've built my career on facts and results, not flights of fancy. Your . . . approach may amuse the superintendent, but it has no place in a real investigation.'

Anika met his gaze unflinchingly. 'Extraordinary crimes sometimes demand extraordinary methods, Dr Malhotra. This case requires collaboration, not division.'

Malhotra snorted derisively, gathering the file. 'Collaboration?' he repeated. 'I suggest you stick to your historical musings and leave the actual investigation to professionals.'

He paused at the door, turning back with a cold smile. 'Oh, and, Dr Thakur? Be careful spreading your theories around. We wouldn't want to alarm anyone unnecessarily—or waste precious time chasing false leads.'

As the door closed behind him, Anika exhaled slowly, the tension in her chest easing. Malhotra's dismissal stung, but it also fuelled her determination. The medallion in her pocket felt heavier, a reminder of the layers yet to be uncovered.

She looked back at the photos, her resolve hardening. The killer had left a trail that blended history with horror. If solving this case meant digging into Rajasthan's royal past, so be it.

Adjusting her notes, she left the lab with purpose in her stride. This wasn't just a murder investigation. It was a battle to uncover truths buried under centuries of history.

CHAPTER 4

The City Palace's library was a vault of secrets, its air steeped in the scent of old parchment and weathered leather. Sunlight filtering through the latticework of jali screens cast shifting patterns across the rows of towering shelves. Dust motes hung suspended in golden beams, dancing to the rhythm of the faintest breeze.

Dr Anika Thakur sat at a massive teak desk, surrounded by a fortress of ancient manuscripts and scrolls. Her gloved hands carefully turned fragile pages of a centuries-old royal chronicle. Each word she read carried the weight of history, its ink a testament to lives lived, ambitions forged, and promises broken.

She paused over a section detailing the ancient rituals of Jauhar and Saka—the final acts of defiance in the face of defeat. 'To preserve honour in the shadow of capture,' she read, her voice tinged with unease. Could the killer's motivations be rooted in such devotion to legacy and sacrifice?

Her eyes flicked to another manuscript, its miniature paintings capturing the centuries-old depictions of court life. She traced a depiction of a royal procession, recognising the celebration. 'Gangaur,' she whispered. Even now, centuries later, the festival still lit up Jaipur's streets. The past was alive in this city as much as the present.

The medallion she had discovered at Amber Fort felt heavy in her pocket, a constant reminder of questions still unanswered. When her gaze fell on a photograph of Jaipur's royal family, one image stopped her cold—a young prince with a face that stirred a memory.

'Look, Anika!' Yuvraj's voice echoed in her mind, bright with excitement. 'This prince looks just like me!'

Twelve-year-old Anika had laughed, rolling her eyes at her brother's childish claim. 'Don't be silly, Yuvraj. We're not royalty.'

'But what if we are?' His voice, unusually earnest, carried a spark of conviction. 'What if there's a big secret about our family too?'

Anika's pulse quickened. Had Yuvraj, even as a child, sensed something she had dismissed? She shook off the thought, refocusing on the photograph.

'More *chai*, Dr Thakur?' the warm voice of Mr Gupta, the elderly librarian, interrupted her reverie. He stood at her side, holding out a steaming cup of masala chai. His eyes, magnified behind thick glasses, sparkled with a kind of joy only a lifelong love of books could bring.

'Thank you, Mr Gupta,' Anika said, accepting the cup gratefully. 'I don't know how I'd manage without you.'

Gupta chuckled, his lined face crinkling into a smile. 'It's rare to see someone so dedicated to history these days. Most visitors here are more interested in taking selfies than delving into the treasures of the past.'

Anika smiled. 'I'm not most people. This history'—she gestured to the stacks of manuscripts—'it's vital to my investigation and my work.'

Gupta's expression grew serious. 'You're investigating the murder at Amber Fort, aren't you?'

Anika hesitated, then nodded. 'Yes. I believe the key to solving it is hidden in these records. Have you ever come across references to a unified royal crest? A symbol combining elements from multiple Rajput dynasties?'

Gupta frowned thoughtfully, clearly intrigued. 'A unified crest?' He shook his head, muttering, 'That's unheard of. The royal houses were fiercely independent. But . . . there have been some mentions of it, in very rare texts and mostly dismissed as the fancy of writers, about attempts at unification. But . . .' He trailed off, considering something. 'There have been rumours about attempts at unification, though it never materialised, at least not enough to have a dedicated crest for it.'

Anika's hand instinctively brushed against her pocket, feeling the outline of the medallion. 'What if history isn't what we think it is? What if it's hiding inconvenient facts?'

The librarian's eyes sharpened. 'You've already found something, haven't you, Doctor?'

Anika made a split-second decision and pulled the medallion from her pocket, placing it on the table for him to see.

Gupta leaned in, catching his breath as he examined it. 'Extraordinary . . . These symbols . . . shouldn't be together. Where did you find this?'

'At the crime scene,' she said quietly. 'It was hidden in a secret compartment.' She met his gaze. 'We are the only two who know about this. Can I count on your discretion, Mr Gupta? I need help figuring out its origin, why it was hidden, and how it connects to the murder.'

Gupta straightened, his earlier calm replaced by excitement. 'Yes, yes, of course.' His eyes widened, and he said, 'Wait a minute, let me check something.' He shuffled away, muttering under his breath, 'Extraordinary . . . Where did I see . . . Oh, yes, here!'

As he vanished into the stacks, Anika returned to her research. A passage in a 17th-century manuscript caught her attention:

> *And in those dark days, when brother turned against brother and the very foundations of Rajput honour trembled, there arose a secret council, bearing a symbol of unity that was both hope and heresy.*

Anika's heart began to race. This was it—the first reference to something that could explain the medallion. The council was real. She read on, her fingers trembling:

> *The council, composed of members from each great house, sought to end the bloodshed through a grand unification. But their efforts were deemed treasonous by those who clung to the old ways. The council was denounced, and its members hunted. Their symbol of unity became a mark of*

shame, hidden away lest it rekindle the flames of forbidden ambition.

'Dr Thakur!' Gupta returned with a stack of old journals. 'These private records aren't part of official histories but may have what you're looking for.'

Anika pointed to the manuscript she'd been reading. 'Mr Gupta, this council—they were real. And the crest on this medallion? It's their symbol.'

The librarian's eyes widened as he read. 'If this is true, Doctor, it changes what we know about Rajput history. But be careful. If these secrets were buried, it was for a reason. Digging them up could be dangerous and might upset the higher-ups in the royal echelons.'

As if on cue, a gust of wind rattled the jali screens, shadows flickering like spectres across the walls. Anika suppressed a shiver.

'Thank you, Mr Gupta. I'll be careful, but I can't pretend not to know this. Lives are at stake. I think we finally have a solid lead.'

Turning to the desk, Anika opened another journal. Mr Gupta quietly shuffled away, leaving Anika immersed in her research. Anika's eyes strained in the dim light as she pored over another ancient text. Suddenly, a name caught her attention: Chandravati. Her heart skipped a beat as she read:

> *The curse of Chandravati lives on. Though the council is long dead, their descendants carry the weight of their ambition. The medallion, the last remnant of that doomed dream, only brings sorrow to those possessing it. It is said that the curse will be lifted only when the great houses are truly united in blood and spirit. But the price of such unity . . . it is too terrible to contemplate.*

A loud crash shattered the stillness of the library.

Anika jolted upright, her pulse pounding in her ears. The sound had originated from somewhere within the library, reverberating off the stone walls like a sharp reprimand. Mr Gupta, who had been leafing through a stack of journals, froze midmotion, his fingers poised over a page.

'What was that?' he whispered, his voice barely audible.

Anika was already on her feet, her instincts guiding her. 'Stay here,' she said firmly, though her own unease was growing.

She moved cautiously towards the sound, the weight of the medallion in her pocket like a constant reminder of the danger she might be courting. The library seemed darker now, the light from the yellow lamps overhead casting shadows that clung to the edges of the shelves.

Rounding a corner, she found the source of the noise—a shelf of scrolls and books had toppled, its contents scattered across the floor. The air was thick with the scent of dust and parchment.

Mr Gupta hurried up behind her, his face pale. 'How did this happen? These shelves have stood firm for decades.' He crouched down, carefully gathering the scattered scrolls.

Anika's sharp eyes scanned the area, searching for signs of an intruder. A window nearby was slightly ajar, its screen swaying gently in the breeze. 'The wind?' she said aloud, though her tone was uncertain.

Gupta looked up at her. 'Perhaps. Or perhaps . . .' He hesitated, his expression darkening. 'As I said, some things are better left undisturbed.'

Anika turned back to the fallen shelf, her gaze narrowing. She felt an inexplicable certainty that this wasn't an accident. Someone, or something, didn't want her looking into these secrets.

She got on the floor to help Mr Gupta pick up the scrolls. As she picked up the ancient scrolls, she noticed a scroll lying nearer to the window than the toppled shelf. She quickly got up and picked it up. It was a particularly old scroll, its edges singed as if it had been rescued from a fire. Carefully unrolling it, she noticed that the faded script was barely legible, but one of the symbols mirrored what was etched onto the medallion in her pocket.

'Mr Gupta,' she said slowly, 'did you notice this before?'

He leaned closer, squinting at the scroll. 'No . . . but this is extraordinary. This crest . . .' He trailed off, visibly unnerved.

The faintest creak echoed through the library, and both whipped around. The shelves loomed like silent sentinels, and the air was heavy with an oppressive stillness.

Anika straightened, tucking the scroll under her arm. 'We need to secure these texts,' she said firmly. 'This isn't just history anymore. It's evidence.'

Gupta nodded, though his hands trembled slightly as he resumed collecting the fallen journals and scrolls. 'Be careful, Miss Anika,' he murmured. 'The deeper you dig, the dangerous it's going to be.'

Thanking Mr Gupta, she left the library. The cool night air did little to calm her racing thoughts. As she walked through the palace grounds, the ancient stones seemed to whisper secrets, and every shadow seemed to come alive with potential for hidden danger.

Was she being followed? Was someone keeping a tab on her moves? Anika thought back to the texts she'd come across. Retribution, revenge, redemption—what was the killer after?

Somewhere in the distance, a peacock's cry broke the silence, its haunting echo sending a shiver down her spine. Anika paused, turning her gaze to the looming silhouette of the Amber Fort in the distance. Its presence seemed to challenge her, beckoning and foreboding all at once.

She tightened her grip on her notes and walked on, her mind a storm of possibilities and fears. She took out her phone and sent a quick text. She made her way to the courtyard, where she planned to meet with the only person who could give her concrete answers. Whatever lay ahead, she knew one thing for certain: This case wasn't just about solving a murder; it was about uncovering an untold story about Rajput history.

The City Palace lay cloaked in the velvet of night, its sandstone walls shimmering faintly under the glow of scattered lanterns. The sky stretched vast and inky above, studded with stars that seemed brighter against Jaipur's quiet grandeur. In a secluded courtyard, far from the palace's bright interiors, Dr Anika Thakur paced by a softly murmuring fountain, her shadow stretching long under the flickering light of a hanging brass lantern.

The chill of the night air brushed against her skin, but Anika barely noticed. Her mind churned with the secrets she had uncovered in the Royal Archives—truths that felt too immense to contain.

The sound of measured footsteps echoed softly across the cobbled courtyard, and Anika turned sharply. Vikram Singh Rathore emerged from the shadows, his tall frame commanding as he stepped into the lantern's glow. His midnight blue *bandhgala* blended seamlessly with the night, the polished silver buttons catching the light like stars themselves.

'Dr Thakur,' he said, his voice smooth and low, carrying a warmth that was almost out of place in the cool stillness. Then, with a hint of a smile that curved his lips, he continued, 'Anika. I got here as soon as I could.'

Anika nodded, suddenly conscious of how dishevelled she must look after having spent hours in the dusty library. She quickly ran a hand through her hair and said, 'Thank you for coming, Mr Vik . . . I mean, Vikram,' gesturing towards a stone bench by the fountain. 'I've found something important and wasn't sure if you'd believe me without seeing it yourself.'

They sat, the stillness of the night broken only by the soft splash of water from the fountain. The lantern's flicker painted shifting patterns across Vikram's face, highlighting the sharp angles of his jaw and the intent in his eyes. She mentally reprimanded herself and pushed away the thoughts, focusing on the task at hand.

'Vikram,' Anika began, keeping her voice low, 'what do you know about a unified royal crest? A symbol that combines emblems from multiple Rajput dynasties?'

Vikram's brow furrowed. 'A unified crest? That's unheard of. The royal houses of Rajasthan have always fiercely protected their individuality. Such a symbol would defy everything we've been taught.'

Anika took a deep breath and reached into her pocket, her fingers brushing against the cold metal of her discovery. 'That's what I thought too,' she said, pulling out the medallion and holding it out to him. 'Until I found this.'

Vikram took the medallion with the care of someone handling a relic. The faint light caught the etchings on its surface, and his expression shifted from curiosity to astonishment. 'Where . . . did you find this?' His voice was almost reverent.

'At the crime scene,' Anika explained. 'It was hidden in a secret compartment.' She recounted her discovery and the details from the archives. As she spoke, she saw Vikram's expression turn from surprise to curiosity, his grip on the medallion tightening.

'A secret council seeking unification . . .' Vikram's voice trailed off as he turned the medallion over in his hands. 'If this is real . . . Anika, do you know what this could mean?'

'Yes,' she said, her tone growing sharper. 'It means this murder isn't just about revenge or personal vendettas. The killer is trying to bring the truth, this version of history, to light, and to justify their actions.'

Vikram leaned back, his shoulders stiff with tension. The lantern light caught in his dark eyes, making them gleam with an intensity that matched Anika's own. 'I grew up hearing different versions of this story,' he admitted. 'Rumours of a council that tried to unify the royal houses during a time of chaos. But supposedly they were betrayed, hunted, and their dream of unification was buried with them.'

'And Chandravati?' Anika pressed. 'Did you hear anything about her curse?'

His expression darkened. 'The curse of Chandravati was the stuff of nightmares for us as children,' he said softly. 'She was said to have cursed the royal bloodlines, condemning them to centuries of strife unless true unification was achieved. But the cost . . .' He hesitated, his voice dropping to a whisper. 'The cost was blood. The curse could only be lifted through the spilling of *royal* blood.'

The weight of his words sent a chill through Anika, colder than the night air. 'So . . . is the killer trying to lift the curse somehow? But wait a minute. You said royal blood. That would mean the victim has to have royal lineage . . .' Anika took out her cell phone and quickly sent a message to Singh.

'Check if the victim has any tie to the royal bloodline.'

Vikram stood abruptly and walked towards the edge of the courtyard. His silhouette cut an imposing figure against the distant glow of the palace walls. 'It's possible,' he said finally. 'If the killer believes in this version of history, he might be trying to fulfil the prophecy . . .' He trailed off, the implications too heavy to voice.

Before Anika could respond, a faint rustle drew their attention. Both turned sharply towards the shadows at the courtyard's edge. Vikram moved instinctively, placing himself between Anika and the source of the sound.

'Stay back,' he hissed, his tone leaving no room for argument. He stepped silently towards the shadows, his movements precise and deliberate. Anika watched as he disappeared into the darkness, her heart pounding.

A tense silence followed, broken only by the fountain's steady murmur. When Vikram reappeared, his expression was grim. 'Whoever it was, they're gone. But someone was watching us.'

Anika's breath hitched as her suspicion was confirmed. 'This isn't just about the murder, is it?' she said quietly. 'If someone's watching us, he knows I'm getting closer to the truth.'

Vikram's jaw tightened as he handed her the medallion. 'This isn't just a medallion, Anika. It's a key to secrets that were buried for a reason. If you're not careful, uncovering them could cost you more than you realise.'

The weight of his words hung heavy in the air as they made their way out of the courtyard. Anika gripped the medallion tightly, its cold surface grounding her amid the storm of questions swirling in her mind.

As they walked back towards the palace, the night seemed darker and the shadows deeper. Anika glanced at Vikram, his profile sharp and unyielding. She felt the gravity of the moment, the unspoken understanding that they were no longer just solving a murder. They were untangling a history steeped in blood and betrayal.

When they reached the palace doors, Vikram paused, his hand brushing against hers briefly. 'Be careful, Anika,' he said, his voice low. 'This isn't just about the past. It's about the future—and everything it could change.'

Anika met his gaze, her resolve hardening. 'I know. And I'm not stopping until I find the truth.'

Vikram nodded, his expression a mix of admiration and concern. 'Then I'll be beside you every step of the way.'

She nodded, trying to hide the colour rising to her cheeks. She was good at expressing her emotions, but in that moment, under his intense gaze, she could feel herself losing control. But the moment passed, and as she stepped through the doors, Anika couldn't help but feel the weight of eyes on her back. Somewhere in the depths of history and the present, a killer was watching her, waiting for her to make her next move.

⚛

The faint glow of a desk lamp illuminated the organised chaos of Anika's temporary apartment in Jaipur. Inspector Singh had arranged for a centrally located apartment that was close to the police headquarters. Anika had transformed the space into a war room of research. Papers and photographs were strewn across every surface, ancient texts balanced precariously on the edge of the bed, and a corkboard on the wall was covered in a web of red string connecting various photos and notes. In the centre of this whirlwind sat Dr Anika Thakur, her hair dishevelled and eyes bloodshot from hours of intense study.

The digital clock on the nightstand blinked 2.37 a.m., but Anika barely noticed. She was lost in a world of centuries-old secrets and royal intrigue, chasing down every lead and whispered legend that might shed light on the killer's motive and their next move.

'It has to connect somehow,' she muttered, rubbing her temples. The medallion lay before her, its tarnished surface catching the lamplight. Anika had been staring at it for hours, willing it to reveal its secrets.

The bitter taste of cold coffee pulled her back to the present as she took a sip from her neglected mug. Grimacing, she set it down and turned her attention to a stack of notes from the Royal Archives. One page stood out, detailing an execution.

'Raja Ajit Singh,' she read aloud, her voice hoarse. 'Accused of treason against the Mughal emperor Aurangzeb in 1679. Publicly executed to set an example . . .' Her words trailed off as her eyes darted to the crime scene photos pinned to the corkboard.

Anika stood abruptly, scattering papers to the floor. She crossed the room in a few quick steps, her gaze narrowing on the positioning of the victim's body and the placement of the objects at the Amber Fort crime scene. There was something familiar, something that had been nagging at the edge of her memory.

Grabbing a thick historical text from the shelf, she flipped through the pages with feverish intensity. When her eyes fell on an artist's rendering of Raja Ajit Singh's execution, her breath caught.

'Oh my God,' she whispered, comparing the illustration to the photos. The similarities were uncanny—the exact positioning of the body, every single object and their arrangement around the body, and even the chosen location. It wasn't just a staged scene but a meticulous recreation of Raja Ajit Singh's death.

Her heart raced as the implications hit her. Ajit Singh's crime had been an attempt to unite Rajput houses against the Mughals—an early push for unification that ended in betrayal and bloodshed.

She picked up the medallion and held it under the light. The unified crest gleamed faintly, its symbols suddenly taking on new significance.

'It's not just an artefact,' Anika murmured. 'It's a key.' The killer had recreated Raja Ajit Singh's execution, which meant she needed to investigate other similar executions and try to identify patterns from the period when unification was attempted and failed.

She sank onto the bed, her mind whirling. The curse of Chandravati resurfaced in her thoughts. The legend spoke of shame and failure repeating through generations unless true unification was achieved. But for the killer, these recreations seem to be about righting the wrongs. The killer was either attempting to reunify the royal house or break Chandravati's curse. It would depend on which side of the fence they were on.

Rising again, she paced the room. 'The victims must represent the royal houses involved in these historical betrayals.' She paused, staring at the web of connections on the corkboard. 'And if I'm right . . . I might be able to predict the next target.'

The excitement of her breakthrough was quickly tempered by dread. The killer's methods were meticulous, and their purpose unwavering. How many more lives would they take in their quest for what they believed was justice?

Anika's gaze drifted to the open book on her desk, her fingers tracing the sketch of Ajit Singh's execution. 'The curse of Chandravati,' she whispered, recalling Vikram's words. 'Doomed to repeat their shame unless unification is achieved. But at what cost?'

She turned to the window, pulling back the curtain to reveal the sleeping city of Jaipur. The moonlight bathed the ancient streets, making them seem deceptively tranquil. Somewhere out there, the killer was planning his next move, weaving another deadly tableau from Rajasthan's past.

'I have to stop them,' Anika said softly, her reflection in the glass staring back at her with determination. 'But how do you fight someone who believes they're fulfilling destiny?'

She returned to the corkboard, pinning new connections and refining her theories. Her fingers lingered on the execution photo, her thoughts shifting between the present and the past.

When the first light of dawn crept into the room, Anika was still working, her exhaustion overshadowed by resolve. She had peeled back one layer of the mystery, but the answers she had uncovered only led to more questions.

⚘

CHAPTER 5

The predawn streets of Jaipur lay shrouded in silence, the air still and cool beneath the fading night. A figure moved through the narrow alleys with deliberate stealth, his nondescript bag slung casually over one shoulder. He paused in the shadow of the Hawa Mahal, its towering façade rising like a honeycomb, the intricate latticework blending into the darkness.

Eyes scanning the deserted area, the figure slipped into a hidden entrance, an access point known only to those who understood the palace's labyrinthine secrets. Inside, the faint scent of aged stone filled the air as the figure began his grim task.

He withdrew certain items from the bag, including a coiled rope, an ornate dagger, and a crown of pearls. He arranged each item with a precision that bordered on reverence. As he worked, his lips moved silently, reciting an ancient mantra of cleansing and justice.

'Soon,' he whispered, his fingers brushing against the cold stone of the palace walls. 'Soon, the sins of the past will be washed clean with blood.'

🦂

The first rays of sunlight kissed the pink sandstone façade of Hawa Mahal, making its intricate latticework gleam in a warm glow. Hawa Mahal or the Palace of Winds, one of Jaipur's most iconic landmarks, stands as a testament to the city's rich architectural heritage. Its honeycomb of 953 small windows, referred to as a marvel of design, captivates visitors from all over the world.

As the city of Jaipur stirred to life, a steady stream of tourists gathered at Hawa Mahal's entrance. Tour guides, identifiable by their crisp uniforms, corralled their groups, their voices rising above the general murmur as they began their well-rehearsed spiels.

'Ladies and gentlemen, welcome to Hawa Mahal, one of Jaipur's most beloved attractions,' one guide announced proudly. 'Built in 1799 by Maharaja Sawai Pratap Singh, this palace allowed the women of the royal household to observe street festivals without being seen by anyone.'

Visitors marvelled at the coloured glass windows that cast kaleidoscopic patterns onto the stone floors. Cameras clicked as tourists posed against intricately carved jali screens. Among them, a figure lingered near the palace's eastern wing, his attire of faded jeans, a loose shirt, and a camera around his neck ensuring he blended seamlessly into the crowd. But his dark sunglasses masked eyes that moved with unsettling precision, scanning the palace and its occupants with predatory focus.

Cameras clicked, and tourists jostled to capture the best angles, their excited chatter filling the air in a dozen languages. A group of college students posed for selfies, their laughter echoing off the ancient stones. Nearby, an elderly couple pored over a guidebook, enthusiastically pointing out details to each other.

On the upper levels, a young tour guide led a group through the narrow corridors and up the steep staircase. Her voice was lively as she recounted tales of the palace's architectural marvels.

'If you follow me to the next level, you'll see some of the best-preserved examples of . . .' Her voice faltered as she reached the landing, her smile turning into a frown. A faint acrid smell hung in the air. It was subtle, nearly lost in the musty scent of the old palace, but enough to make her hesitate.

'Everything all right?' one of the tourists asked, noticing the guide's hesitation.

The guide forced a smile. 'Just . . . catching my breath. These stairs can be quite a workout!' she said, waving off their concern, although her laugh was strained. She led the group onward.

Meanwhile, an American couple had wandered away from their group, eager to explore on their own. Cameras at the ready, they pushed open a wooden door leading to a secluded chamber.

'Oh my God, look at this view!' the woman exclaimed, rushing to one of the small windows. 'You can see the whole city from here!'

Her husband raised his camera, following her inside to capture the panorama, but as he stepped into the room, his foot caught on something. Stumbling, he looked down and froze.

The scream that tore from his throat shattered the tranquil morning, echoing through the ancient halls like a thunderclap.

The chaos outside began instantly. Conversations halted midsentence, and heads turned towards the palace as the scream echoed again. Guides, tourists, and vendors froze, confusion and fear spreading like wildfire.

The figure loitering near the eastern wing tilted his head slightly, his lips curling into the faintest smile. Without drawing attention, he moved into the crowd, slipping away unnoticed as panic erupted.

The American couple stumbled out of the chamber, the woman sobbing uncontrollably and her husband shouting incoherently. 'There's . . . there's a dead body in there!' he managed to shout as other tourists and guides rushed to see what was happening.

The young guide, who'd just reached the same level where the American couple were, fumbled with her phone to call the authorities. 'There's . . . there's been a murder,' she stammered, her voice shaking as she described the scene.

Tourists fled the palace, some crying and others shouting in confusion. Those waiting to enter surged forward in morbid curiosity, jostling against guards who struggled to hold the line.

Local vendors and shopkeepers who had been setting up their stalls watched in bewilderment as the usual tourist crowd turned into a roiling mass of fear and confusion. Within minutes, the distinct wail of sirens cut through the noise, and police cars screeched to a halt outside.

Inspector Rajesh Singh emerged, his usual composed demeanour strained by the urgency of the situation.

'Clear the area!' he barked at his officers. 'No one gets in or out without clearance. Lock it down now!'

As officers pushed back the growing crowd, Singh's phone buzzed. A message from Dr Anika Thakur flashed on the screen: *Heard the news. On my way.*

Singh's jaw tightened. He had hoped they had more time before the killer's next move. But he had struck again, and this time, it was the Pink City's most iconic landmark.

Inside the Hawa Mahal, the crime scene was a haunting echo of the murder at Amber Fort. The victim lay posed with unnerving precision, their body surrounded by symbolic objects: a dagger, a rope, and the crown of pearls, each item steeped in historical significance.

Forensic photographers moved methodically through the chamber, the harsh flash of their cameras briefly illuminating the ancient walls. The faint acrid smell lingered, a sinister reminder of the staged scene.

Singh surveyed the crime scene grimly, noting every detail. His heart sank deeper in his chest the more details he observed. It was the work of the Amber Fort killer without any doubt. His intention was clear. He was forcing the entire city to confront some injustice committed in the past, one carefully orchestrated crime at a time.

Outside, the palace's façade, so often a symbol of beauty and grandeur, now stood as a silent witness to the unfolding horror. Yellow police tape fluttered in the morning breeze, sealing off the entrance as news vans arrived and reporters jostled for position.

Somewhere in the heart of the city, the killer smiled to himself. His message had been delivered, another piece placed on the board of his twisted game, a game that had escalated with chilling precision.

࿇

The secluded courtyard of Hawa Mahal, typically a serene refuge nestled within the palace's grandeur, now thrummed with chaos. Its delicately carved jali screens and faded frescoes stood in stark contrast to the grim reality that had overtaken the space. Police officers in khaki uniforms moved urgently, their purposeful strides clashing with the courtyard's timeless tranquillity. Yellow crime scene tape fluttered in the morning breeze, cutting jagged lines across the soft pink sandstone walls, as tourists huddled in tense, frightened clusters.

Inspector Rajesh Singh stood at the heart of the maelstrom, barking orders that carried across the courtyard. His voice, sharp with urgency, matched the tension in his posture, his usual composure fractured by the weight of the scene.

'Every tourist needs to be accounted for,' Singh commanded, gesturing to a group of junior officers. 'Check their photos and videos. I want every frame scrutinised for anything suspicious.'

The officers nodded, dispersing into the crowd of tourists corralled into one corner of the courtyard. Their faces reflected an array of emotions from confusion to fear, and anger to disbelief.

'This is outrageous!' bellowed a red-faced man in a Hawaiian shirt, jabbing a finger at a young constable. 'You can't just keep us here like prisoners!'

'Sir, please,' the officer replied, his voice strained. 'We need your cooperation. We'll take your statement and let you go as soon as possible.'

Nearby, a group of backpackers huddled together, their earlier excitement now replaced by wide-eyed dread.

'I can't get a signal,' a young woman with dreadlocks said, her voice rising in panic as she waved her phone. 'Why can't I get a signal?'

'We've temporarily blocked cell service,' an officer explained as he passed by. 'It's standard procedure for a crime scene.'

The murmurs in the crowd grew louder. Words like *murder* and *crime scene* rippled through the huddled tourists, each repetition heightening the collective unease.

At the far end of the courtyard, the forensic team moved with clinical precision. Their white protective suits and slow, deliberate movements created a stark juxtaposition against the surrounding turmoil. Flashbulbs lit the area as they documented the scene, each click of the camera adding to the mounting tension.

A commotion at the entrance drew the crowd's attention. Dr Anika Thakur ducked under the yellow tape, her stride purposeful and her expression resolute.

'Dr Thakur,' Singh called out, relief evident in his voice as he approached her. His face was lined with fatigue, his tone softer than usual. 'Thank you for coming so quickly.'

Anika nodded briskly. 'What do we know so far?'

Singh began briefing her, but her eyes wandered over the scene. Her gaze fixed on the group of forensic technicians, and an uneasy chill crept down her spine. Singh guided Anika to the dead body.

It was a woman, probably in her midtwenties. Anika felt a pang of sadness looking at the woman's face. Another life lost, another family destroyed. Yuvraj's smiling young face flashed in front of her eyes, and she shook her head to clear her thoughts. She was awake all night, and the exhaustion was catching up with her. She looked at the crime scene closely. The body was positioned differently from the one at Amber Fort, but it was the handiwork of the same killer. It was yet another historical scene brought to life with blood and rituals.

'Do we have an ID of the victim?'

Singh shook his head. 'Not yet.'

'And what about the Amber Fort victim?'

'I received a call from Dr Malhotra last night. He said there was a malware attack on the lab computers last night and that his assistants have lost the file with the victim's details.'

'What? That's ridiculous.'

Singh looked like he agreed with her but said, 'Well, it is what it is. Dr Malhotra is a senior, so I can't really reprimand him. Anyway, he has already fired two of his assistants and asked the cybersecurity team to retrieve all the data on the forensic lab computers, so we'll have those details by tomorrow.'

'You think the killer had something to do with it?'

Singh opened his mouth to reply, but a sudden cry from behind stopped him.

'That's my sister!' A young man broke free from the crowd, running towards the scene with anguished screams. 'Oh God, that's my sister!'

Two officers intercepted him before he reached the body, holding him back as he fought to break free. His raw grief filled the air, thick and suffocating. The entire place broke into chaos again as people started panicking.

Anika's chest tightened. She could see her own grief from decades past reflected on the young man's face.

'Yadav.' Singh moved to one of the inspectors on his team and instructed him to take the man to the courtyard where a workstation had been set up and take his statement.

When he returned, Anika turned to him and said, 'We need to move these people,' pointing to the increasingly restless crowd outside the main chamber. 'This isn't helping anyone.'

Singh raked a hand through his hair, exhaling heavily. 'I know, but we can't let them leave until we've processed every witness. We could lose valuable information.'

Anika thought quickly. 'What about Jantar Mantar? It's nearby, enclosed, and can accommodate a crowd this size.'

Singh's eyes lit up. 'That could work. I'll make the arrangements.'

As Singh went outside the chamber to make the call, Anika moved towards the body, mindful of the technicians working the scene of the crime. The young woman lay posed on the ground, her arms outstretched, palms facing upward, with symbolic objects carefully arranged around her. A broken spinning wheel lay at her feet, and a string of pearls formed a makeshift crown atop her head.

Anika's breath caught. 'This . . . this is a re-enactment of Rani Padmini's execution,' she said to no one in particular.

One of the technicians glanced at her sharply. 'The legendary queen?'

Anika nodded grimly.

'But didn't she commit suicide?'

Anika shook her head. 'That's the widely known story of her Jauhar, her self-immolation. However, this also references a lesser-known tale of betrayal and an execution orchestrated by her own court.'

A heavy silence fell over the forensic team as they absorbed her words and looked at each other in bewilderment.

Meanwhile, the streets surrounding Hawa Mahal churned with restless energy, a chaotic sea of flashing cameras, hurried voices, and jostling crowds pressing against makeshift barricades. Where the iconic monument once welcomed throngs of eager visitors, it now played host to a spectacle drenched in fear and morbid curiosity.

Manoj Dutta, the sharp-suited anchor whose name had become synonymous with Rajasthan's current affairs, stood at the epicentre of this media frenzy. Dutta was a man who carried himself with poise, and his every movement was deliberate and confident. His neatly pressed shirt gleamed under the harsh sun, and his hair—dark, thick, and impeccably styled—remained perfectly in place despite the commotion around him. His angular face and the faintest hint of a five o'clock shadow lent him an edge that complemented his polished demeanour. With his commanding voice and piercing eyes, Manoj Dutta had the kind of presence that made people stop and listen, even in the noisiest of crowds.

'Two minutes to air,' his producer called, barely glancing up from her tablet as she juggled studio instructions and live feed logistics.

Manoj gave a brisk nod, his expression a mask of composed professionalism. Inwardly, he was rehearsing the opening lines that he would deliver with authority and empathy, the style that had made him Jaipur's most trusted news anchor. Yet beneath his veneer of calm lay a simmering ambition. He knew that this story, this shocking convergence of murder, history, and mystery, could be his ticket to national prominence. Still, a genuine unease gnawed at him even as he savoured the opportunity. These killings were more than a headline; they were a dark cloud over his beloved city.

'Thirty seconds!'

Manoj tuned out the surrounding chaos, focusing instead on the camera's blinking red light as his producer began the countdown.

'This is Manoj Dutta, reporting live from Hawa Mahal, where tragedy has once again struck the heart of Jaipur,' he began as the broadcast went live, his deep, resonant voice cutting through the noise. 'Just hours ago, a body was discovered here, at one of our city's most cherished landmarks, marking the second brutal murder in as many weeks.'

The camera panned to the historic façade of Hawa Mahal, its grandeur now overshadowed by yellow crime tape and the frantic movements of law enforcement.

'Though police have yet to release an official statement,' Manoj continued, 'sources close to the investigation have confirmed chilling parallels between this crime and the recent murder at Amber Fort. Both appear to be staged with historical precision. Could this be the work of a serial killer with a sinister obsession with Rajasthan's royal past?'

As he spoke, the crowd behind him grew restless, the weight of his words rippling through the onlookers. Local shopkeepers shouted their frustrations, while tourists huddled together, some whispering and others wide-eyed with fear.

Manoj's practised gaze remained fixed on the camera, his tone steady. 'Eyewitnesses report a heavy police presence, including forensic teams and senior officials. Inspector Rajesh Singh, who is leading the investigation, and Dr Anika Thakur, the forensic psychologist and historical consultant, were seen entering the crime scene earlier this morning.'

As if on cue, the camera shifted to capture Dr Thakur emerging from the palace, flanked by officers who shielded her from the surging press.

'Dr Thakur!' Manoj called out, his voice cutting through the din. 'Can you confirm if this murder is connected to the Amber Fort case?'

Dr Thakur glanced briefly in his direction, her exhaustion evident in her drawn features. But she didn't stop, slipping into a waiting police vehicle that sped off, leaving a trail of disappointed reporters in its wake.

Unfazed, Manoj turned back to the camera, his expression serious. 'While officials remain tight-lipped, the similarities between these heinous crimes are impossible to ignore. Both victims were posed in ways reminiscent of historical events, both murders took place at iconic landmarks, and both have sent shockwaves through Jaipur's tourism industry.'

Behind him, the crowd's growing unrest was unmistakable. Shopkeepers argued with officers, their livelihoods disrupted. Uncertain and unsettled tourists clustered near barricades, some demanding refunds and others begging for information.

'The economic impact of these crimes cannot be overstated,' Manoj continued, gesturing to the chaos. 'Hotels are reporting cancellations.

Tour operators are struggling to reassure their clients. The very lifeblood of Jaipur, its tourism industry, is under siege.'

Lowering his voice for dramatic effect, he added, 'And perhaps most unsettling of all are the rumours spreading amongst Jaipur's older residents. Stories of curses and vengeful spirits, dismissed by many as superstition, are beginning to take hold in the public imagination.'

Just then, his producer waved frantically, signalling breaking news. Manoj transitioned smoothly.

'We're receiving word that city officials have called an emergency press conference for this evening,' he said, his voice imbued with urgency. 'There are unconfirmed reports that the chief minister himself may address the public, underscoring the gravity of the situation.'

Manoj's closing lines were delivered with the gravitas of a seasoned anchor. 'As night falls on the Pink City, fear and uncertainty hang over Jaipur's residents. Citizens are urged to remain vigilant and report any suspicious activity. This is Manoj Dutta, reporting live from Hawa Mahal. Back to you in the studio.'

As the red light on the camera blinked off, Manoj allowed himself a moment of relief. He ran a hand through his hair, his usually composed façade slipping as he surveyed the simmering tensions around him.

'Good job, Dutta,' his producer remarked, reviewing the footage on her tablet. 'We'll need you to stay on-site for extended coverage tonight.'

Manoj nodded but said nothing, his attention drawn to an elderly woman standing near the barricades. Her face, lined with age and wisdom, held a peculiar stillness amid the chaos. She stared at him with an intensity that sent an involuntary shiver down his spine. For a fleeting moment, Manoj felt as though she was trying to warn him of something.

He pushed the thought aside. Stories needed telling, and he was the one to tell them.

Far away, in a shadowed room, the killer watched Manoj's broadcast with great interest, his lips curling into a satisfied grin. Everything was proceeding exactly as planned.

The secluded courtyard within Hawa Mahal had been transformed into a hub of activity. Police officers moved swiftly with purpose, their voices clipped as they relayed orders and managed the scene. Forensic technicians in white protective suits knelt near the victim, meticulously documenting every detail. The air, thick with the lingering heat of the day, carried a weight that pressed heavily on everyone present.

Dr Anika Thakur stood near the outline of the victim's body, her expression one of intense focus. The initial shock of the murder had faded, replaced by the cold clarity of an investigator who knew the stakes. Her dark hair, loosely tied back, glinted in the fading sunlight as her sharp gaze scanned the crime scene.

Inspector Rajesh Singh approached her, his appearance slightly rumpled, his shirt collar open, and his sleeves rolled up. His exhaustion was evident in the lines etched deeply around his eyes.

'Long day?' Anika asked.

'Very . . . So, what do you make of it?'

Anika took a deep breath, centring herself. She hadn't had a chance to tell Singh about her discovery, as she had to leave for the lab at the headquarters, and Singh had to oversee the processing of witnesses. Returning to the crime scene felt like a relief after the cold treatment she'd received from Dr Malhotra and his staff. She studied Singh and realised she liked his company better than anyone else's. He understood her in a way that others could not. She stopped her thoughts from getting the best of her and cleared her throat before saying, 'The similarities to the Amber Fort case are undeniable. But this one . . . it's more elaborate. The killer's approach has intensified. As you can see'—she pointed to the markings on the floor—'the staging of the scene is more elaborate.'

She crouched near the midsection of the body's outline, her gloved hand pointing to the place where there had been a red silk cord that bound the victim's wrists. 'This positioning of hands and the pearl necklace symbolising the crown and the broken spinning wheel at the foot are all a direct reference to the legend of Rani Padmini. But not the version most people know.'

Inspector Singh frowned. 'I thought Rani Padmini committed Jauhar to avoid capture by Alauddin Khilji. Isn't that what happened?'

Anika nodded. 'That's the popular narrative, yes. But there is a lesser-known account of betrayal within her own court, of accusations and an execution carried out as an act of punishment rather than sacrifice.' She gestured to the broken spinning wheel. 'This is significant, Inspector. In Rajput culture, the spinning wheel symbolised domestic duty and loyalty. By breaking it, the killer is implying betrayal.'

Her fingers hovered above the area where the pearls on the victim's forehead were marked. 'And this is placed like a crown of thorns. Pearls are symbols of nobility and purity, but here they've been weaponised. The legend of Padmini describes her being forced to wear her royal pearls as a mockery of her status before her death. The killer is drawing from these obscure versions of history to construct their narrative.'

Singh's jaw tightened. 'So, what exactly is the killer trying to say here?'

Anika rose to her feet, her mind racing. 'He's trying to tell the alternate histories. The killer is engaging with contested versions of the past, ones that challenge the sanitised narratives we're comfortable with.'

Nearby, a forensic technician called out, holding up a tarnished medallion. Singh motioned for the item to be brought to them, and Anika examined it closely. Her pulse quickened as she recognised the unified crest—a fusion of Rajput dynasty symbols, just like the medallion found at Amber Fort.

'It's another signature,' she said quietly, her voice laced with urgency. 'The medallion is central to the killer's message. He's not just targeting individuals. He's targeting Rajasthan's collective memory, rewriting the past to fit the vision he believes in.'

Singh's brow furrowed. 'And the victims? Why them?'

Anika's gaze turned distant. 'The victims represent something specific, maybe their lineage ties to these historical events, somehow. We need to cross-reference their backgrounds with royal genealogies. This victim likely has a distant connection to the Chittor lineage associated with Padmini. She has to.'

As Singh radioed instructions to his team, Anika's eyes drifted to an alcove in the far corner of the courtyard. The faintest discolouration on the sandstone caught her attention. She moved towards it, her instincts prickling.

'Inspector,' she called over her shoulder. 'I need a UV light here.'

A technician hurried over and handed her the device. Anika switched it on and ran the beam across the wall. Slowly, symbols began to glow, an inscription hidden in photosensitive ink.

Singh joined her. 'What does it say?'

Anika squinted, translating the ancient Rajasthani script. 'The sins of the old have tainted generations. Only through fire can the impurities be burned away.'

A heavy silence fell over the courtyard. Singh exhaled sharply, his voice taut. 'What the hell are we dealing with, Dr Thakur?'

Anika turned to him, her expression grave. 'Someone who believes they're on a mission to cleanse Rajasthan's royal lineage. These murders aren't random. They're calculated rituals designed to bring about a reckoning with the past.'

Singh rubbed the back of his neck, the weight of the case pressing down on him. 'How do we stop someone like this? How many more will they kill before we figure it out?'

'We need to look deeper into Rajasthan's alternate histories,' Anika said, her voice firm. 'Identify the events the killer is referencing, trace the connections, and predict who might fit his twisted narrative. And most importantly, we need to understand what unification really means to him.'

Singh's gaze lingered on her. 'I'll get you whatever resources you need, Dr Thakur. We can't afford to miss anything.'

Anika nodded, her resolve hardening. 'We're dealing with more than a killer, Inspector. We're dealing with a crusader attempting to rewrite Rajput history. If we don't stop him in time, this won't just be about loss of life. It may be a loss of truth as we know it.'

The sun dipped below the horizon, casting the courtyard in deepening shadows. As the forensic team resumed their work and Singh moved to coordinate the next steps, Anika remained rooted in place, her eyes scanning the scene one last time.

In the dim light, the symbols on the wall seemed to shimmer, as if taunting her. Anika took a deep breath, steeling herself. The game was escalating, and the next move would have to be hers.

>‌‌❧

The sun had set fully over Jaipur, plunging Hawa Mahal into an ominous darkness. Where it once dazzled under golden floodlights, its façade now loomed against the twilight, a shadow of its former glory. The palace's extraordinary architecture, which had charmed millions, now seemed to be brimming with secrets of a darker past. In their harsh stead, the police floodlights illuminated the courtyard in stark white, casting long eerie shadows.

The courtyard itself was a whirlwind of controlled chaos. Officers barked orders, reporters shouted over one another, and forensic technicians worked under the heavy burden of urgency. The murder had shaken Jaipur to its core, the implications of its staging far outstripping the immediate horror of death.

Manoj Dutta stood beside his makeshift broadcast station at the edge of the scene. Even after hours of coverage, his tailored blazer remained immaculate, and his hair had been tousled into what his producer called the 'perfect imperfection' for live TV. Yet there was genuine concern in his eyes. For all his polished exterior, Dutta was a man who believed that stories had the power to change the world.

'Ready in five,' his producer called.

Dutta nodded, and when the red light blinked on, he straightened, stepping into the persona the city knew well: authoritative, poised, and unrelenting in pursuit of the truth.

'This is Manoj Dutta reporting live from Hawa Mahal, where the air of fear thickens by the hour,' he began, his voice steady and the cadence practised. 'After the brutal murder at one of our city's most iconic landmarks, quite similar to the murder at Amber Fort just two weeks ago, we are left with the terrifying question: Who is behind these gruesome crimes, and why?'

A ripple of movement caught his eye, and he saw a petite woman in a faded cotton saree being escorted towards the broadcast station. The camera shifted to frame her pale, nervous face that was lined with barely contained fear.

'Joining me now is Mrs Neetu Jairaj, a local shopkeeper who claims to have seen something important on the morning of the murder.'

The camera zoomed in as Manoj gestured for her to step forward. 'Mrs Jairaj,' he said, his voice softening to coax her testimony, 'thank you for speaking with us tonight. Can you tell us what you saw?'

Neetu hugged herself, her gaze darting between Manoj and the camera. 'It was early,' she began haltingly. 'Around 6:30 in the morning. I was setting up my shop near the palace when I saw . . . someone . . . unusual.'

'And why did you think it was unusual?' Manoj prompted gently.

Neetu's voice strengthened, and she replied, 'He wore a hooded robe. At first, I thought it was part of some tourist performance. But something felt . . . off. He moved too carefully, too deliberately, and kept looking around nervously.'

Manoj leaned in slightly, his eyes locked on hers. 'And where exactly did you see him?'

'Near one of the side entrances,' she replied, pointing towards a door partially obscured by scaffolding. 'It creaked loudly when he slipped in.'

'Did you see his face?'

'No, the hood covered it,' Neetu said, shaking her head. 'But his hands . . . his hands were stained dark red. At first, I thought it was *mehendi*, but it wasn't a design. It felt like his hands had been dipped in red colour.'

A collective gasp rippled through the gathering reporters and bystanders. Manoj didn't let the moment slip.

'You're saying his hands were stained with red liquid, possibly with blood?' His tone carried just the right mix of shock and professionalism.

'I think so, maybe,' Neetu said firmly. 'And he was carrying something. It looked like an old book or maybe a box. I couldn't tell for sure.'

Manoj turned back to the camera, his voice dropping to a grave timbre. 'Viewers, we may have just heard a crucial lead. A hooded figure, seen entering Hawa Mahal, his hands stained with what could be blood. This sighting could represent a breakthrough in the investigation.'

Just then, police officers pushed through the crowd, clearly intent on reaching Manoj's station. Their stern expressions betrayed irritation, and the commotion added urgency to the broadcast.

'Mrs Jairaj,' Manoj said quickly, 'did you report this to the authorities?'

'Yes,' she answered, her voice trembling. 'I told them everything.'

Before Manoj could ask another question, a senior officer stepped into the camera's frame. 'Mr Dutta, Mrs Jairaj,' he said, his tone firm but controlled, 'I need you both to accompany us to the police station.'

Manoj smoothly transitioned, addressing the camera one final time. 'It seems our testimony has caught the attention of law enforcement. We will cooperate fully and bring you updates as they come. This is Manoj Dutta, live from Hawa Mahal.'

The camera's red light blinked off, and Manoj immediately turned to the officer, his tone now direct and assertive. 'Inspector, I've complied with every legal protocol in my reporting. Are we being detained?'

The officer glared at him. 'Detained? No. But your broadcast could jeopardise our investigation. Next time, inform the police before you go live.'

As Neetu was led away, Manoj adjusted his jacket, exuding calm professionalism despite the tension. 'The public has a right to know, Inspector,' he said, his tone firm but respectful. 'If my work can help catch this killer, then I consider it a service to Jaipur.'

The officer muttered something under his breath and turned away, leaving Manoj to consider his next move.

❧

In a dim room elsewhere in the city, the killer sat in front of a flickering television, watching Manoj's broadcast. His hood, pulled low over his face, cast his features in shadow. The stained hand that Neetu had described reached out, tracing the reporter's image on the screen.

'You talk too much, Dutta,' the figure murmured, their voice soft and chilling. 'But do you truly understand the story you're telling?'

He turned to a nearby table, where an open book displayed an illustration of a royal execution. Beside it lay tools for his next act.

'The stage is all set,' he whispered, his voice filled with dark satisfaction. 'And soon, the curtain will rise again.'

As Jaipur slept fitfully under the weight of fear, the killer's game continued, the next chapter of their twisted historical saga already in motion.

Night had fully descended on Jaipur, casting its streets and landmarks into an uneasy silence. The shadows seemed longer, the streets darker, and every distant sound carried the weight of suspicion.

An unnatural stillness reigned at Johari Bazaar, where the day usually ended in a cacophony of haggling and laughter. Lal Chand, a jeweller whose family had run a shop here for generations, stood at his doorway, arms crossed, staring at the nearly deserted street.

'Two murders at the city's most famous sites,' he muttered to Amira, the textile merchant next door, who clutched a shawl as though for comfort. 'How long before people stop visiting Jaipur altogether? How long before we close our shops for good?'

Amira nodded, her brow furrowed with worry. 'Three tour groups cancelled orders today alone. One minute, people are admiring your work, praising Jaipur's heritage, and the next, they're too scared to step outside.' She lowered her voice. 'Do you think the rumours are true? About the curse? The royal history?'

Lal Chand sighed, his weathered face a portrait of frustration. 'Curse or not, something needs to be done. If the police don't catch this murderer soon, it'll destroy everything we've built over generations.'

In the sleek confines of City Centre Mall, a group of teenagers huddled around a smartphone, the glow of the screen reflecting off their anxious faces. Manoj Dutta's live report from Hawa Mahal played on repeat, his grave voice narrating the grim events.

'A hooded figure with bloody hands,' a girl whispered, her eyes wide. 'It's like something out of a horror movie.'

Her lanky friend adjusted his glasses. 'It's not a movie, Asha. People are dying.' His voice wavered. 'My parents are already talking about sending me to stay with my cousins in Delhi until this is over.'

'What if it's never over?' another boy said, his voice tinged with paranoia. 'What if this killer keeps going until every famous spot in Jaipur is a crime scene?'

Nearby, a security guard overheard the conversation and stepped closer, his voice gruff but concerned. 'That's enough, kids. Stop spreading rumours. Let the police do their job.'

But even as he spoke, the guard's eyes flicked nervously towards the mall's entrances, and his hand hovered near his walkie-talkie. The usual evening buzz was absent, and the food court and shops were emptier than they had been in years.

⁂

In Malviya Nagar, an emergency meeting of the residents' association erupted into chaos.

'We need extra security!' a middle-aged man shouted, slamming his fist on the table. 'If the police can't protect us, we'll have to protect ourselves.'

A woman in her fifties stood, her voice trembling. 'My daughter works as a guide at City Palace. What am I supposed to do? Tell her to quit? How are we supposed to live with this fear hanging over us?'

The association president, a retired colonel, raised his hands to silence everyone. 'We mustn't panic,' he said, his tone measured. 'Yes, we'll explore security options, but remember, the killer's targets have been historical sites, not neighbourhoods. We need to stay vigilant but not paralyse ourselves with fear.'

His words were met with reluctant nods, though the unease in the room was palpable.

At Maharani Gayatri Devi Girls' School, an emergency parent–teacher meeting mirrored the same anxieties.

'We've increased security at all entrances,' the principal assured the gathered parents, though the worry in her eyes betrayed her words. 'All school trips to historical sites are suspended until further notice.'

A father stood, his voice rising with anger. 'That's not enough! This killer is clearly obsessed with royal history. Our school is funded by the royal family. It could be a target!'

The room buzzed with murmurs of agreement until a history professor, another parent, spoke up. 'Shutting down institutions is exactly what this killer wants,' she said firmly. 'To disrupt our lives, to make us doubt our heritage. We must be cautious, but we cannot give in to fear.'

In the narrow lanes of the old city, elderly residents sat on stoops, their voices low as they shared tales of curses and vengeance.

'I always believed those palaces were haunted,' one old woman insisted, clutching a string of prayer beads. 'The sins of the past don't stay buried forever.'

Her neighbour, a retired professor, scoffed, 'Ghosts and curses? Ridiculous. This is the work of someone dangerous, someone who knows our history and is using it for their own twisted ends.'

At a dimly lit cybercafé, a group of college students scoured conspiracy forums, diving into alternative histories and lesser-known royal scandals.

'Look at this,' one boy said, pointing at the screen. 'This site says there were secret councils formed to unite the royal houses, alliances that ended in betrayal.'

'Maybe the killer is trying to expose a hidden truth,' his friend mused, her expression a mix of fascination and fear.

'Or maybe they're just using these stories to justify murder,' another student interjected. 'Either way, it's terrifying.'

❧

By midnight, Jaipur's otherwise active nightlife was in complete lockdown. Restaurants and bars that usually thrummed with energy were eerily quiet. A popular hookah lounge prepared to close early when a group of foreign tourists walked in.

'Sorry, we're closing,' the owner said apologetically.

'But it's not even midnight,' a young woman protested, guidebook in hand. 'The book says you're open until 2.00 a.m.'

'Not anymore,' the owner replied, glancing towards the darkened street. 'It's not safe. You tourists should think about leaving Jaipur.'

He locked the door behind them, his hands trembling as he turned the key.

❧

In a dim apartment on the city's outskirts, the killer sat before an old television, watching Manoj Dutta's report with quiet satisfaction.

'Your fear feeds the cleansing fire,' he whispered, his stained fingers brushing over an ancient book filled with sketches of executions and cryptic notes.

On a nearby table lay the tools for his next act: a replica of an ancient garrotte and a small vial of poison.

'Every death brings us closer to absolution,' the figure murmured, his voice a chilling blend of reverence and resolve.

He turned to the window, gazing at the city below. Smoke from impromptu protests rose in the distance, mingling with the glow of street lights. The killer's lips curved into a smile. Everything was unfolding exactly as planned.

As dawn approached, the once-proud Pink City found itself shrouded in fear and suspicion. In homes across Jaipur, parents double-checked locks, children lay awake imagining hooded figures in every shadow, and the streets echoed with the murmurs of a city on edge.

The questions on everyone's mind were the same: Who would be next? Which beloved landmark would be the stage for the next act of this twisted historical drama?

And somewhere, hidden in the shadows, the killer prepared to write the next chapter.

CHAPTER 6

The atmosphere in Commissioner Verma's office felt heavy, the kind of oppressive weight that only unsolved murders and public outcry could bring. The room's once-pristine order was disrupted by hastily assembled case files, maps, and crime scene photos spread across the mahogany desk. Even Verma, known for his stoic composure, showed cracks in his usually imperturbable demeanour. His sharp eyes swept over the team one by one. Dr Anika Thakur, whose urgency shone through her exhaustion; Inspector Rajesh Singh, visibly haggard from sleepless nights; and Dr Dilip Malhotra, his body language stiff with barely contained disdain.

Verma's gruff voice broke the tense silence. 'We have two high-profile murders, a city on the brink of panic, and a killer who seems to be pulling strings from the shadows. I need answers, not excuses.'

Anika leaned forward, her voice steady despite the weight of the room. 'Commissioner, I've identified a pattern. The killer isn't acting randomly. In both instances, his choice of locations and methods points to a specific narrative: bringing the alternate and lesser-known versions of Rajasthan's royal history to light.'

Malhotra scoffed, crossing his arms, 'With all due respect, Commissioner, this is absurd. We're chasing ghosts and folklore while a murderer runs loose. What we need is solid, evidence-based forensics, not wild speculation.'

Anika's eyes flashed with frustration, her tone sharpening. 'This isn't speculation, Dr Malhotra. The evidence is clear if you look at it without bias. The crime scenes, symbolic objects, and even the medallion all point to a killer deeply versed in alternative histories of Rajasthan.'

Singh straightened and nodded. 'I agree. There's too much consistency in the murders for this to be a coincidence. The killer's re-enacting specific historical events.'

Malhotra sneered, 'And what's next? Are we going to start summoning mediums to solve the case?'

'Enough,' Verma said in a tight voice, cutting through the tension. His gaze fixed on Anika. 'Dr Thakur, explain this pattern. Why are you so certain the killer is following a historical narrative?'

Taking a deep breath, Anika stood and gestured to the map of Jaipur pinned to the wall. 'The first murder at Amber Fort recreated the execution of Raja Ajit Singh in 1679. The second murder at Hawa Mahal referenced a lesser-known account of Rani Padmini's story—an alternative version where betrayal, not self-sacrifice, is central. Both events represent moments of fractured alliances or failed unification among Rajasthan's royal houses.'

She traced a finger along the map, marking the sites. 'The killer is following a sequence. Each location has significance. Raja Ajit Singh was involved in the construction of Amber Fort, and even though Hawa Mahal is not directly connected to Rani Padmini, her Jauhar and the construction of the Hawa Mahal reflect the strict adherence to *purdah* and the safeguarding of women's dignity in Rajput society. I need more time to find deeper connections between the two murders, but on the surface, it seems like the killer is trying to expose what they see as the sins of the past.'

Malhotra's scepticism was apparent. 'And you expect us to base the entire investigation on your interpretation of the folklore?'

'This is more than folklore,' Anika snapped, her frustration spilling over. 'The killer is re-enacting these events with surgical precision. Understanding their motivations is the key to stopping them.'

Verma, who had been listening intently, leaned back in his chair, his expression thoughtful. 'If this pattern is correct, how do we use it to stop them?'

Anika's tone grew more urgent. 'We need to identify the killer's endgame. They're targeting people connected to these historical betrayals. We are yet to confirm it, but I am sure that the two victims might have distant ties to royal bloodlines. If we can confirm this connection and cross-reference genealogies, we might predict who's next.'

Singh added, 'We also need to increase security at other historical sites. If they're working through a sequence, those sites could be next.'

Malhotra interjected, his tone biting, 'And spread our resources even thinner? We're barely managing the chaos as it is.'

Anika turned on him, her voice firm. 'People are dying, Dr Malhotra. Ignoring the evidence because it doesn't fit your methods won't bring us closer to catching this killer. We need to think beyond traditional boundaries.'

Verma stood abruptly, silencing the room. 'Enough. Dr Thakur, I want you to continue investigating this historical angle. Collaborate with our historians and genealogists to identify potential targets. Dr Malhotra, focus on forensic evidence. We'll need every tool at our disposal to solve this.'

He fixed Singh with a pointed look. 'Inspector, use your judgment wisely to allocate resources where they're needed most.'

The tension in the room hung like a storm cloud as Verma surveyed his team. 'This isn't about egos or methodologies. It's about stopping a killer before they strike again. Am I clear?'

A chorus of 'Yes, sir' followed, though the underlying friction remained.

After the meeting ended, Anika found herself face to face with Malhotra in the hallway. His glare was ice-cold. 'If this wild theory of yours wastes our time and another murder happens, that blood will be on your hands.'

Anika met his gaze unflinchingly. 'I understand the stakes better than you think, Dr Malhotra.'

She walked away, her mind already racing with the implications of her theory.

ॐ

The fluorescent lights in Anika's makeshift office cast harsh shadows across the cluttered space. The walls were plastered with maps of Jaipur, photographs of the murder scenes, and pages of notes scrawled with connections. Her desk, strewn with open manuscripts, old texts, and her laptop, was a testament to the frantic pace of her investigation.

Anika stared at the map pinned to the wall, her eyes darting between the marked locations: Amber Fort and Hawa Mahal. Two dots connected by a faint pencil line she had drawn earlier.

She leaned closer, her fingers brushing against the edge of the map as if the answers might materialise through touch. 'There has to be more to this,' she muttered, reaching for her notes.

Two sites, two executions, both tied to acts of betrayal. But what was the connection between them?

A thought struck her, and she grabbed a ruler and a pencil and measured the approximate distance between the two locations. She jotted down the result: 12 kilometres.

'Could the distance mean something?' she whispered, tapping the pencil against her lips.

She opened her laptop and typed quickly, searching for historical routes between the two landmarks. Jaipur's ancient pathways, used by royal processions and messengers, criss-crossed the city in an intricate web. A faint line on an old map caught her attention—an ancient procession route once used by the Kachwaha rulers to connect Amber Fort to their palaces in the city.

Anika leaned back, staring at the screen. 'Is that what the killer is following? A royal route?'

She picked up her phone and called someone she thought might be able to help her with the details not accessible to others.

'Vikram,' she said, her voice tinged with excitement. 'Do you have a minute?'

'Anika? Sure . . .'

'Do you know about the old procession routes connecting Amber Fort and Hawa Mahal?'

Vikram's voice was thoughtful. 'Yes, the royals used them for ceremonies and to transport treasures. But those routes aren't widely known anymore, but they must be mentioned in old records. Why?'

'That's confidential. But I'd really appreciate it if you could help me with the information.'

Without skipping a beat, Vikram replied, 'Give me a day or two, and I'll look into it.'

'Thanks.' She hung up, turning back to her research. If the killer was retracing history, then these two locations were part of a larger narrative. But what?

Anika was running out of time. And the next chapter of Jaipur's bloody history was about to be written.

჻

The City Palace stood resplendent under the moonlight, its ivory walls shimmering like a ghostly beacon against the deep indigo of the Jaipur night. The day's clamour of tourists had long since faded, leaving only the faint rustle of leaves and the rhythmic chirping of crickets to fill the stillness.

Abdul, the night sweeper, moved through the palace grounds with his broom, the soft scrape of bristles against stone the only sound accompanying him. He had worked these grounds for almost three decades and knew every corner of the sprawling palace. But tonight, something felt . . . off.

The air was heavier than usual, the familiar pathways bathed in an eerie glow from the palace's decorative lights. His lantern cast elongated shadows that seemed to shift with a life of their own.

As he approached the inner courtyard, a secluded area flanked by intricately carved arches, Abdul's steps faltered. The lantern in his hand trembled slightly as a strange metallic tang reached his nose.

At first he thought it was a trick of the light, but as he edged closer, his heart leaped into his throat. There, in the centre of the courtyard, lay a body.

It was a young man, dressed in an elaborate golden *sherwani* that gleamed under the moonlight. His arms were outstretched, palms facing upward. Around him lay a carefully arranged tableau: a broken royal sceptre, an upturned throne, and a shattered crown placed near his head. His neck bore a deep, deliberate slash, and beneath him, the ground was darkened with blood.

Abdul's scream tore through the silence, echoing off the ancient walls and waking the palace guards. Within minutes, the courtyard was flooded with light and activity as the police arrived to cordon off the area.

⚜

Dr Anika Thakur arrived shortly after, the police jeep screeching to a halt outside the palace gates. Inspector Rajesh Singh was already there, his face grim as he directed officers and spoke into his radio.

'Rajesh,' Anika called out as she hurried towards him, clutching her satchel.

Singh turned, his expression softening briefly. 'Anika, you were right.' He paused, running a hand through his hair. 'It's worse than the others.'

Anika nodded, bracing herself as they walked into the courtyard. The scene was eerily quiet, save for the clicking of cameras and the hushed murmurs of forensic technicians.

When Anika saw the body, she froze. The meticulous staging and symbolic objects were unmistakably the work of the same killer, but this time, there was an added layer of intricacy.

She crouched near the victim, her trained eyes scanning every detail. The positioning of the body, the shattered crown and the sceptre, and the deliberate placement of the throne all screamed of a historical re-enactment.

'Do we know who he is?' she asked, her voice steady despite the roiling unease in her chest.

Singh nodded. 'Rajeev Talwar. Twenty-six years old. He worked as a historian and guide here at the palace.'

Anika's heart sank. She knew what the genealogists would find: another victim with ties to Rajasthan's royal lineage.

She turned her attention back to the scene. 'The sceptre, the throne, the crown—this is a representation of a royal deposition.'

Singh frowned. 'Deposition? As in a king being dethroned?'

Anika nodded. 'There's a legend tied to this courtyard. In 1732, Maharaja Kishan Singh's younger brother, Virendra Singh, attempted to usurp the throne. The coup failed, and Virendra was captured and brought here to face punishment.'

She gestured to the shattered objects. 'The maharaja ordered a public humiliation before his execution. Virendra was stripped of his regalia, his sceptre broken to symbolise his failed rebellion. He was then executed by garrotte in front of the court.'

Singh's jaw tightened. 'That's why you said this place was going to be next.'

Anika nodded. If only she had fought harder with Dr Malhotra just hours ago. But then it was too late anyway.

'So, this murder is recreating that execution?' Rajesh's voice interrupted her thoughts.

'Yes,' Anika said, her voice thick with emotion. 'The killer is following the same pattern—a symbolic stripping of power, the instruments of royalty broken, and finally, the execution itself.'

Singh's voice was laced with frustration. 'And they managed to do all this undetected, right here in the heart of the City Palace.'

She examined the victim's neck, noting the precision of the wound. 'This wasn't done in a struggle, so no, the murder wasn't committed here. I think they performed the ritual elsewhere and then brought the body here. The killer likely used a garrotte or something similar. The act was deliberate, controlled.'

Singh rubbed his temples, his exhaustion evident. 'Do you think they'll strike again?'

Anika hesitated, glancing at the shattered sceptre. 'Yes,' she said quietly. 'This isn't the end. The killer is methodical, and their pattern is far from complete. They believe they're fulfilling a prophecy that won't be satisfied until they've recreated every critical event tied to the curse of Chandravati.'

Singh's eyes darkened. 'Then you need to figure out where they'll strike next. And this time, trust me, nothing and no one is going to stop me from listening to you.'

Anika nodded, determination hardening in her gaze. 'I will, Inspector. Now we know what the killer is after. And I'll do you one better—I'm going to figure out his endgame too and put an end to the bastard for good.'

As the forensic team worked tirelessly to document the scene, Anika took out her phone and called Vikram.

The air in Commissioner Verma's office was thick with tension. The sun had just risen, but the morning air felt heavy with fatigue. The usual polished order of the room, a gleaming mahogany desk, neatly stacked files, and the faint scent of leather polish, felt at odds with the anger simmering under Verma's red face.

Behind his desk, the commissioner sat rigid, his expression thunderous as he stared down Dr Dilip Malhotra, who stood stiffly before him. The forensics expert's usually unshakable confidence was notably absent, his eyes darting anywhere but the commissioner's unforgiving gaze.

Anika Thakur and Inspector Rajesh Singh stood near the door, silent observers to the unfolding scene. While Singh maintained his professional composure, Anika's crossed arms and narrowed eyes betrayed her frustration.

'I warned you,' Verma began, his voice deceptively calm, like the stillness before a storm. 'Dr Thakur came to you with a clear theory, supported by evidence, and you dismissed it out of hand. Is that correct, Dr Malhotra?'

Malhotra's jaw tightened, his pride warring with the obvious consequences of his actions. 'Commissioner Verma, with all due respect, her theory lacked the kind of hard evidence we base investigations on—'

'Stop,' Verma's voice cut through the air like a whip. He leaned forward, his hands flat on the desk. 'Do you know what I base my decisions on, Dr Malhotra? Results. And right now, all I'm seeing are failures. Three victims. Three crime scenes. And a killer who's mocking us at every turn.'

Malhotra opened his mouth to respond, but Verma wasn't finished. 'When Dr Thakur came to you with her findings, you had a responsibility—to listen, to investigate, to explore every possible lead. Instead, you dismissed her theory outright, didn't you?'

Malhotra's silence spoke volumes.

Verma rose to his feet, his imposing figure towering over the smaller man. 'Your arrogance has cost us, Doctor. A man is dead because we were unprepared. Because we failed to act on actionable intelligence. Do you understand the gravity of that failure?'

Malhotra's face flushed with a mix of anger and shame. 'I was following procedure—'

'Procedure?' Verma barked, his patience snapping. 'Don't talk to me about procedure when there's blood on the ground! Procedure doesn't save lives. Action does! And right now, we're in a crisis. One more murder like this, and I'll have to explain to the chief minister why my team can't catch a killer parading historical re-enactments across Jaipur!'

The room fell into a tense silence, broken only by the ticking of the clock on the wall.

Finally, the commissioner straightened, his voice cooling to a steely calm. 'Dr Malhotra, effective immediately, you are removed from this investigation. I'll expect a full handover of all forensic reports and evidence by the end of the day.'

Malhotra's eyes widened in disbelief. 'Commissioner, you can't be serious! My expertise is vital to this case!'

'Your expertise has led us to a dead end,' Verma snapped. 'This case requires someone who can think outside the box and adapt to the complexity of what we're dealing with. That person is not you.'

He turned his gaze to Anika, who straightened under his scrutiny. 'Dr Thakur, you've demonstrated not only your knowledge but your commitment to this case. From this moment forward, you will serve as co–lead investigator alongside Inspector Singh.'

The weight of his words hung in the air. Even Singh, usually unflappable, blinked in surprise.

'Commissioner,' Anika began cautiously, 'I'm honoured, but are you sure—'

'I'm sure,' Verma interrupted firmly. 'You've earned it, Dr Thakur. Your insights have been invaluable, and this team needs your expertise to move forward.'

He glanced at Singh. 'Inspector, you'll work closely with Dr Thakur to integrate her historical findings with your tactical approach. I expect full cooperation between the two of you.'

'Yes, sir,' Singh replied, his tone respectful but tinged with a newfound determination.

Verma's eyes returned to Malhotra, who stood frozen in disbelief. 'Doctor, you're a brilliant forensic scientist. But brilliance means nothing if it's undermined by ego. Take this as a lesson, one I hope you'll learn from.'

Malhotra's lips pressed into a thin line, his face pale as he nodded curtly. 'Understood, Commissioner.'

'Good,' Verma said, his tone final. 'You're dismissed.'

Malhotra strode from the room without another word, his back stiff with indignation.

As the door closed behind him, Verma turned back to Anika and Singh. 'We're running out of time. The killer is escalating, and we need to be one step ahead. Use every resource at your disposal—officers, archives, forensics, whatever it takes. I want results.'

Anika nodded, her resolve hardening. 'We'll catch them, Commissioner. I promise.'

Verma studied her for a moment, then nodded. 'See that you do. Jaipur can't afford another failure.'

As she and Singh left the office, for the first time, Anika felt like she had the authority to make real progress and the support she needed to see it through.

Singh fell into step beside her, his voice low and sincere, a hint of a smile playing at the corner of his lips. 'Looks like you're in charge now, Dr Thakur. Congratulations.'

'Let's just hope I can live up to it,' Anika replied, her tone wry but tinged with nervousness.

'You will,' Singh said confidently. 'You've got a knack for this. And now, you've got a team that believes in you.'

Anika glanced at him, a small smile playing at her lips. 'Thanks, Rajesh. That means a lot.'

As they walked down the busy corridor, Anika felt a glimmer of hope. They were making progress. And together, they would bring this killer to justice.

⁂

The late afternoon sun cast elongated shadows across the Royal Archives of Jaipur, its imposing sandstone façade standing as a stoic witness to centuries of history. The air was heavy with the weight of the past, a past that seemed poised to reach out and entangle those daring to uncover it.

Dr Anika Thakur stood at the base of the wide stone steps, her gaze fixed on the grand structure. The building exuded an aura of reverence and foreboding, as if guarding its secrets fiercely. Standing beside her, Vikram Singh Rathore was every bit the embodiment of his heritage— poised, authoritative, and visibly tense.

'Are you sure about finding the answers here?' Vikram asked, his voice low and measured, betraying the internal conflict he was trying to mask.

Anika nodded. 'It's the only place I can think of. We're out of time, and these archives might hold the answers we need to stop the killer.'

They ascended the steps, their movements brisk but weighed down by the urgency of their mission. Anika's heart thudded with anticipation, but she kept her expression calm. The events of the last 24 hours replayed in her mind—the body at City Palace, meeting with Commissioner Verma, and her promotion that entailed a great deal of responsibility.

A uniformed guard stationed at the entrance regarded them with suspicion, his stance rigid. 'The archives are closed today,' he said curtly, barring their way.

Vikram produced an ornate seal from his pocket, holding it up with the ease of someone well accustomed to its power. 'I'm Vikram Singh Rathore,' he said, his tone calm but commanding. 'This is Dr Anika Thakur. We're here on urgent business concerning the royal family's history.'

The guard hesitated, his eyes darting to the seal before snapping to attention. 'Of course, Your Highness. Please, go ahead.'

As the massive carved doors swung open, a wave of musty air greeted them—a mixture of aged parchment, leather bindings, and the faint metallic tang of history itself. The grand hall of the archives stretched before them, a labyrinth of knowledge and secrets hidden within shelves that reached for the vaulted ceiling.

An elderly archivist shuffled towards them, his movements slow but precise. His sharp eyes scanned Vikram with recognition, then lingered on Anika. 'Prince Rathore,' he said, his voice quavering but respectful. 'And . . . your guest?'

'This is Dr Anika Thakur,' Vikram explained. 'She's assisting with an investigation that involves certain elements of our family's history.'

'Thakur, you say?' the archivist repeated, his expression momentarily clouded. 'A familiar name, though not one I've heard in these halls for many years.'

Anika tilted her head, curiosity piqued. 'Is there a reason my name might be significant?'

The old man gave a cryptic smile. 'Perhaps. But the past is full of surprises, Doctor. What is it you seek?'

'Records of royal executions, especially the ones expunged from public archives,' Anika said without hesitation. 'And anything related to the curse of Chandravati.'

At the mention of the curse, the archivist's demeanour shifted, unease flickering in his eyes. 'Those are restricted documents,' he said carefully. 'Accessible only with express permission from the royal family.'

Vikram stepped forward, his voice steady. 'You have my permission. It's a matter of life and death, Dr Patel. We don't have much time.'

The archivist hesitated, then sighed, his shoulders slumping as if burdened by the weight of the request. 'Very well. Follow me.'

They trailed behind him as he led them through winding corridors and past rows of shelves stacked with fragile tomes and delicate scrolls. The air grew cooler and heavier, as though even the building understood the gravity of the knowledge housed within.

At last they reached a heavy iron door at the back of the archives. Dr Patel produced an ancient key from his pocket, fitting it into the lock with a practised hand. The door groaned as it swung open, revealing a smaller dimly lit chamber lined with glass cases and weathered books bound in cracked leather.

'These are the restricted archives,' Patel said quietly. 'What lies within has been kept from the public for generations. Handle everything with care.'

'Can you bring anything, whether it is a document, a book or whatever, that is related to royal executions? And these could be from any period,' Vikram said with a quiet authority that reflected his centuries of inherited royal culture.

Anika stepped inside, catching her breath as she took in the shelves brimming with centuries of suppressed history. The gravity of the moment settled over her, a potent mix of excitement and dread. She moved between the shelves, observing the arrangement of the books into various categories and stopping now and then to check a document or a book.

Beyond the shelves, there was a space with tables and chairs, an area for archives users to read and research. As Dr Patel started bringing various books and documents, Anika took a seat at the corner table near a window overlooking one of the courtyards.

Soon the table had an array of open books, yellowing manuscripts, and carefully preserved scrolls. Her fingers moved deftly through the brittle pages of a centuries-old account as she went about looking for clues for the next murder, her mind racing to connect fragments of information. Across from her, Vikram methodically sifted through genealogical records, his usually composed features tight with concentration.

Moving confidently between the shelves, the elderly archivist walked with surprising agility for his age, pulling down volumes and offering nuggets of commentary as the pair worked. His knowledge of Rajasthan's royal history proved invaluable to their investigation.

Anika's phone buzzed on the table, a jarring interruption in the stillness. She glanced at the screen to see a message from Inspector Rajesh Singh:

'I have given the names to my team. An update from the forensic team: Trace elements found on the second victim match 16th-century embalming practices. He wants an immediate conference call to discuss implications. Looks like your theory is gaining traction.'

Anika replied to the text message and returned to the delicate script in the book before her. The manuscript was a first-hand account of Chandravati's trial, penned by a court scribe.

'Look at this,' she said, her voice barely above a whisper but brimming with excitement. 'It's an eyewitness account of Chandravati's final moments.'

Her hand trembled slightly as she read aloud:

And as the blade fell, Chandravati's voice rang out, not in anger but with unshakable clarity. She spoke of reckoning, foretelling that the bloodlines of those who betrayed justice would wither under the weight of their sins. Her words chilled all who heard them, and none present could meet her gaze as she fell.

The room fell silent, the words hanging heavy in the air around them. Vikram leaned in, the lines on his face deepening as he scanned the text.

'So, it wasn't just a curse,' he murmured. 'It was a reckoning, a prophecy tied to their own actions.'

Dr Patel, who had been quietly observing, spoke up. 'It aligns with oral traditions. Chandravati wasn't just a mystic. She was a voice for the oppressed, a reformer in her own right. Her execution was as much about silencing her as it was about her alleged treason.'

'This view changes things,' Anika said, her mind racing. 'Our killer isn't just re-enacting historical executions. They're continuing Chandravati's work, fulfilling her prophecy of justice.'

Patel nodded gravely. 'There are even accounts of . . . strange deaths among the royal family in the years following her execution. Mysterious illnesses, unexplained accidents.'

Vikram's hand froze on the pages of a genealogical journal. 'My great-great-grandfather,' he said quietly. 'I was always told he died peacefully in his sleep, but this account . . .' He trailed off, staring at the text as if willing it to change. 'It says his body was found posed exactly like Chandravati at her execution.'

Anika inhaled sharply. 'That confirms it. The killer isn't just picking any descendants. They're targeting those connected to Chandravati's trial and execution. And this is not new. This has been happening for centuries. It means only one thing. We are not dealing with a killer who is working alone. He has help. I think it is, in fact, a secret society of some sort that has been operational for centuries.'

'It would explain how the killer is gaining access to such critical information,' Vikram added thoughtfully.

'Yes, and how he is able to perform the rituals without anyone noticing. He is not working alone.'

She rose from her seat, pacing as her thoughts coalesced. 'The staged murders aren't random. They're part of a pattern within a pattern. The historical re-enactments are the surface layer, but the real narrative lies in the victims themselves. Each one represents a link in the chain that led to Chandravati's death.'

Vikram set the book down, his expression troubled. 'If that's true, we need to understand where all this is leading. What happens when the killer reaches the last link?'

Anika's gaze drifted to the scattered papers and maps around them. 'I don't know,' she admitted. 'But if the curse was a reckoning, the final act might not just be a murder. It could be a statement, a way to unearth the truth that was buried with Chandravati.'

Patel returned with a bundle of aged documents, placing them gently on the table. 'These are records of incidents tied to Chandravati's curse. Some are clearly natural, but others . . .' He shook his head. 'Let's just say there were enough strange occurrences to fuel fear for fear.'

As Anika sifted through the records, her pulse quickened. The entries painted a grim picture: heirs struck down in their prime, scandals erupting over forged alliances, and hints of betrayal among the nobility. Each incident felt like a continuation of the prophecy, each a step closer to the reckoning that Chandravati had foretold.

But the question that most taunted Anika was why, after all these centuries, the killer was deviating from the set pattern of murdering and had started this spree of killing people one after the other? Why now? Was the end nearer than she had thought?

Vikram received a call and returned with the family record keepers' volumes he had requested. The table became covered with cross-referenced documents and notes. 'They're sending over more detailed genealogies, right up to the present. Let us see if any of those names of the visitors to the library turn up,' he said, his tone grim. 'But Anika . . . these connections go deep. If the killer intends to expose every injustice tied to Chandravati's execution, we could be looking at a much larger web than we imagined.'

Anika nodded, her expression set with determination. 'Then we'll untangle it one thread at a time. But we need to move quickly. The killer isn't waiting for us to catch up.'

As they delved back into the research, the room seemed to hum with a shared sense of urgency. Each discovery brought them closer to understanding the killer's logic, but with that understanding came a dreadful awareness of the stakes.

The past was no longer a distant memory. It was alive, woven into the present in blood and shadow. And with every second that ticked by, the next act in the killer's twisted re-enactment drew closer.

अत

CHAPTER 7

The light in Anika Thakur's temporary office at the police headquarters hummed softly, casting a bright glow over the wall that had become her canvas for extricating the killer's pattern. Maps, photographs, and hastily scribbled notes covered nearly every inch, connected by a web of red strings. The City Palace was now circled in bold red, the fresh ink standing out like a wound on the map of Jaipur.

The afternoon warmth seeped into the room, stifling it, but Anika paid it no mind. She stood before the wall, her arms crossed and her eyes scanning the patterns in the chaos before her. Her mind worked tirelessly, sifting through the fragments of information she had uncovered at the Royal Archives. She'd be meeting Vikram again in the evening to cross-check genealogical research to try and figure out their next potential victims. But for now, she had other pressing issues.

She reached for her notebook, flipping through pages of observations, and paused at the timeline she had constructed. The first murder at Amber Fort had been followed by a second two weeks later at Hawa Mahal. But the third murder at City Palace had occurred just a week after the second.

Her pen tapped against the notebook as she murmured, 'The killer's pace is speeding up. If they stick to this pattern, the next murder could happen in the next three or four days.'

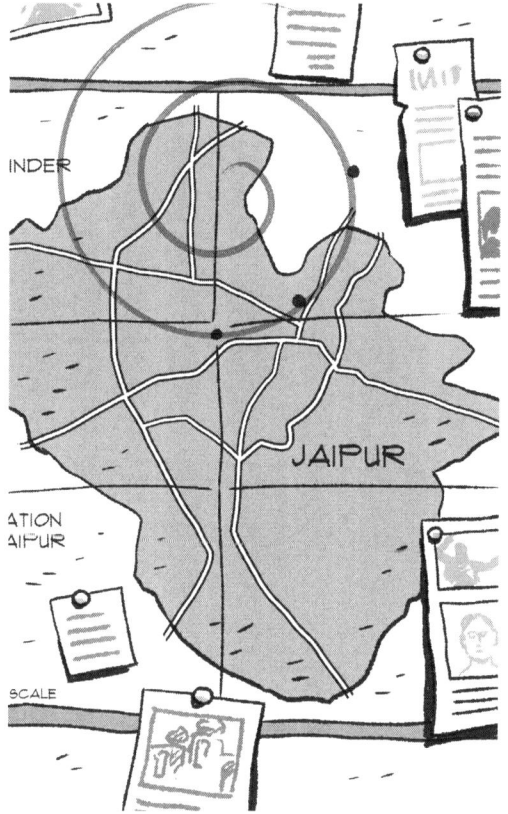

Her gaze shifted to the map again, where she had scrawled different potential patterns. The pattern that looked most promising to her was the spiral going inwards. The spiral pattern she had created with City Palace as one of the points should, by all logic, move inwards towards the heart of Jaipur's historical and royal sites. But where?

Her finger traced the trajectory between Amber Fort, Hawa Mahal, and City Palace. The line wasn't perfect, but it had a discernible direction. The next location would have to align with both the historical executions that the killer was re-enacting and the spiral's progression.

She referred to her notes and then circled two names on the map: Nahargarh Fort, Govind Dev Ji Temple, Albert Hall, and Sisodia Rani Garden.

Now Anika needed to dig deeper to determine the next location the killer would choose.

Anika's hand paused mid-air as a troubling thought surfaced. The killer's baffling knowledge of Rajasthan's history and his access to sites like City Palace, Amber Fort, and Hawa Mahal pointed to someone with privilege, possibly even royal connections. She felt increasingly sure that he was not working alone.

The possibility chilled her. The killer could have an ally, someone with access to the inner circles of Jaipur's royal descendants. This was the only explanation for how he was able to access the restricted sections of the archives and obtain confidential information.

Her thoughts turned to the heirs and heiresses of Rajasthan's noble houses, those who had grown up steeped in the traditions of their lineage—people like Vikram Singh Rathore, whose royal status opened doors that were otherwise sealed shut.

But unlike Vikram, not all of them would have wanted to protect Jaipur's heritage. Some could easily have had a motive to use their historical knowledge for darker purposes.

Anika jotted down a list of potential suspects, heirs, and descendants whose names she had come across during her research. She underlined three of them, based on proximity to the murder sites and their connections to Chandravati's prophecy:

- Samar Singh Shekhawat, who was well known in the royal circles for his fiery speeches about restoring Rajasthan's royal pride.
- Alka Devi Chundawat, who was a recluse with a known obsession for ancient texts and artefacts.
- Devendra Singh Rathore, a distant cousin of Vikram, with a reputation for courting controversy over disputed family histories.

Anika frowned. If the killer wasn't one of them, they might still be aiding the killer knowingly—or unwittingly.

She picked up her phone and dialled Inspector Rajesh Singh's number. He answered after a few rings, his voice rough with exhaustion.

'Dr Thakur,' he greeted. 'Tell me you've found something.'

'I'm working on it,' Anika replied, her tone brisk. 'But I need your help. I've identified a pattern in the timing of the murders. The killer is accelerating—City Palace happened just a week after Hawa Mahal. I think the next murder will happen in three, maybe four days.'

Singh swore under his breath. 'That doesn't give us much time. Do you have any idea where they'll strike next?'

'I'm narrowing it down. I have a couple of potential locations, but I have yet to make the connection with Chandravati's curse. So, I can't yet be sure which one it will be,' Anika admitted. 'But there's something else. The killer's knowledge of history and their access to these sites— it's too specific. I think they're either a royal or working with someone who is.'

There was a pause on the other end of the line. 'That's a bold theory, Dr Thakur.'

'But it fits,' Anika insisted. 'Think about it. The medallions, the staged murders, the locations—all of it points to someone with insider knowledge. I've compiled a list of potential suspects, heirs and heiresses who might have access or motives. I need you to question them.'

'Who are we talking about?' Singh asked, his tone wary but interested.

Anika read off the names, adding her reasoning for each. Singh listened intently, occasionally grunting in agreement.

'I'll handle it,' he said finally. 'But this kind of inquiry will need to be discreet. Royals don't take kindly to being interrogated, even indirectly.'

'I understand,' Anika said. 'But it's crucial, Rajesh. If one of them is aiding the killer, or worse, if one of them is the killer, we can't afford to wait until they strike again.'

Singh sighed heavily. 'All right, I'll start making calls. But you need to focus on pinpointing that next location. If we can get ahead of them for once, it'll save lives.'

'I'm on it,' Anika promised.

After ending the call, Anika returned to her whiteboard. She circled the key locations again: Amber Fort, Hawa Mahal, and City Palace. The line connecting them suggested a trajectory moving deeper into the heart of Jaipur.

Her mind churned over the possible options: Nahargarh Fort, Govind Dev Ji Temple, Albert Hall, and Thakur Rani Temple. Each held historical significance, but which one aligned with the executions tied to Chandravati's prophecy?

Anika stared at the map until her vision blurred. The killer's pattern, the accelerating timeline, and the potential royal connection—they were all there, but the pieces hadn't fully clicked into place.

She glanced at the list of names she'd given Singh, her gaze lingering on one in particular: Devendra Singh Rathore. A historian himself, Devendra had access to archives and artefacts that could help the killer piece together their gruesome re-enactments.

But was Devendra the killer or just a pawn?

Anika closed her eyes and took a deep breath. The answers were near; she could feel them, just out of reach.

The room seemed to close in around her as the weight of the case pressed down. Somewhere in Jaipur, the killer was preparing for their next act. And with the clock ticking faster than ever, Anika knew she had to stay ahead of them, no matter the cost.

ॐ

The small café nestled in the shadow of the Royal Archives was a haven of quiet, its warm, earthy interior providing a brief reprieve from the relentless weight of Anika Thakur's investigation. Sunlight filtered through intricately carved wooden screens, casting delicate patterns on the stone walls, and the aroma of spiced tea and freshly baked bread mingled with the faint buzz of low conversation.

Anika and Vikram sat at a corner table, their plates laden with local delicacies: dal-bati-churma, stuffed *parathas*, and bowls of thick, tangy chutneys. A small pot of masala chai sat between them, its steam curling in the afternoon light.

'I'd forgotten how much I love this place,' Vikram said, his voice tinged with nostalgia. 'My father used to bring me here when we visited the archives. Back then, I'd only come for the food. The books were just an excuse.'

Anika smiled as she stirred her tea. 'And now here you are, poring over records like a true historian. Life has a funny way of coming full circle.'

Vikram chuckled, leaning back in his chair. 'True. Though I have to admit, seeing our family's history laid bare like this isn't what I imagined. It's unsettling to realise how much of what I grew up believing might be . . . carefully curated stories.'

Anika set her cup down, her expression softening. 'I can understand that. History is often manipulated to serve those in power. But uncovering the truth, no matter how uncomfortable, is the only way to truly understand where we come from.'

Vikram nodded, his gaze thoughtful. 'You're right. But it's not just history, is it? This case . . . it's forcing all of us to confront uncomfortable truths. About ourselves, our families, our city.'

As the conversation eased into silence, Anika hesitated before broaching something she'd had on her mind since morning. 'Vikram, can I ask you something about your family?'

'Of course,' Vikram said, setting down his fork. 'What's on your mind?'

'Devendra Singh Rathore,' Anika said carefully, watching his reaction. 'Your cousin. I came across his name while researching the genealogy records. What can you tell me about him?'

Vikram's brow furrowed, but his tone remained even. 'Dev? He's . . . an interesting character. Brilliant, no doubt, but always walked his own path. He studied history at Cambridge and became somewhat of a recluse after returning to India. He spends most of his time in his library, surrounded by the ancient manuscripts.'

Anika raised an eyebrow. 'Sounds like he'd be very familiar with the kind of history our killer is obsessed with.'

Vikram shrugged. 'Possibly. But Dev's obsession with history is more academic than anything else. He's fascinated by the mythology of our family, but I can't imagine him involved in something like this.'

He hesitated, then added, 'His family's had its share of tragedy though. His sister's son, Arjun, left the family years ago. They had a falling-out over some dispute, and from what I've heard, he's been living in exile ever since.'

'Exile?' Anika asked, intrigued.

'It's not as dramatic as it sounds,' Vikram clarified. 'He left voluntarily, renouncing his claim to any family assets or titles. Last I heard, he was living a quiet life somewhere in the hills.'

Anika's mind buzzed with possibilities. 'Do you think Devendra might still be in contact with him?'

Vikram frowned. 'I doubt it. They were never particularly close. But if you think there's something worth exploring, I can arrange for you to meet Dev.'

'That would be helpful,' Anika said. 'Thank you, Vikram.'

As the conversation shifted, Anika leaned back, allowing herself a rare moment of curiosity. 'What's it like, Vikram? Being part of the royal family, especially now, when the princely states are a thing of the past?'

Vikram smiled wryly. 'Complicated. We're not rulers anymore, but we're not exactly ordinary citizens either. There's a certain . . . weight that comes with the name. People expect us to embody tradition while being modern, representing Rajasthan while staying relevant in the wider world.'

'That sounds exhausting,' Anika said, her tone light but sincere.

'It can be,' Vikram admitted. 'But it's also rewarding. I've always believed that our influence, limited as it is now, should be used for something meaningful. That's why I've supported initiatives to preserve our heritage, restore old monuments, and promote Rajasthan's culture. It's a way to honour the past while ensuring it has a place in the future.'

Anika nodded, impressed. 'It must be difficult though, balancing all that while confronting the darker parts of that history. Like Chandravati's story.'

Vikram's expression turned sombre. 'It's more than difficult. It's . . . humbling. To realise that my ancestors may have committed terrible acts to secure their power. But isn't that the story of every ruling family? Power and blood have always gone hand in hand.'

Anika tilted her head, her curiosity unabated. 'If you hadn't been born into royalty, what do you think you'd be doing?'

Vikram laughed, his mood lightening. 'Probably something far less dramatic. Maybe a chef. I've always loved experimenting with flavours.'

'A chef?' Anika smiled. 'I wouldn't have guessed that.'

He leaned forward, a playful glint in his eye. 'Cooking is a lot like history, you know. Taking raw ingredients, combining them in just the right way to create something meaningful.'

Anika laughed softly. 'I think that might be the most poetic take on cooking I've ever heard.'

As their lunch wound down, the light-heartedness of their conversation faded, replaced by the load of the task ahead.

'We should head back,' Anika said, her tone resolute. 'There's still so much to go through, and time isn't on our side.'

Vikram nodded, his expression mirroring hers.

As Anika and Vikram stepped out into the Jaipur afternoon, the sun bathed the Royal Archives in golden light. The tranquillity of the scene was a stark contrast to the chaos that greeted them. A loud commotion filled the air, and Anika's heart sank as she saw the gathered crowd outside the grand building.

Protesters packed the space in front of the archives, their faces a mix of anger and desperation. Police officers formed a tense barricade, their expressions unreadable as they held back the surging tide. Hand-painted signs waved in the air, their messages stark and urgent: *'No More Secrets!'* *'The Truth Will Set Us Free!'* *'Blood on the Hands of Silence!'*

The chants were loud and insistent, a rhythmic pounding against the fragile peace of the city.

'What's going on here?' Anika asked, her voice tinged with apprehension as she scanned the scene.

Inspector Singh emerged from the throng, his jaw tight and his uniform dusted with the debris of the restless crowd. He approached them with hurried steps, his tone sharp and weary. 'The situation's escalating, Anika. The protests have spread across the city. There's serious talk of a citywide strike unless we make significant progress.'

Anika's stomach churned at the implication. 'A strike? Over the case?'

Singh nodded, his eyes darting to the crowd as an officer radioed him for instructions. 'They're demanding the release of all historical records related to royal crimes. They think the murders are connected to some long-buried scandal, and they're not wrong. But opening up the archives to everyone . . . it'll only cause panic.'

Vikram's brows knitted. 'And it could tip off the killer, giving them exactly what they want—a city in chaos.'

'Exactly,' Singh said, rubbing the bridge of his nose. 'If we don't show results soon, this powder keg will explode.'

Before Anika could respond, a rock sailed through the air, shattering one of the tall stained-glass windows of the archives. The crowd roared in approval as shards rained onto the stone steps.

Singh's head snapped to the side, his voice a bark of authority. 'Secure the perimeter! No one else gets through!'

As officers rushed to contain the growing unrest, Anika felt the weight of the situation settle on her shoulders. The pressure to find answers had been immense before, but now it felt suffocating. Every second they spent chasing leads was another second closer to the city erupting into complete chaos.

'Let's get inside,' Singh said, jerking his head towards the doors. 'We need to figure this out as soon as possible.'

Anika and Vikram followed him up the stone steps and into the archives, the angry chants of the crowd still audible even as the heavy doors closed behind them. The atmosphere inside was a jarring contrast to the chaos outside—quiet and heavy with the scent of aged paper and time-worn stone.

But that quiet was deceptive.

Singh turned to Anika, his tone laced with urgency. 'We can't afford to waste any more time. Whatever you need—resources, people, access—tell me now. This city won't hold together much longer without answers.'

Anika met his gaze, her own resolve hardening. 'We'll find him, Inspector. Whatever it takes.'

Outside, the protesters continued their chants, their voices a stark reminder that the clock was ticking. Anika knew that the stakes had never been higher. The next few days would determine not just the case's outcome but Jaipur's fragile stability.

❧

The main archive room of the Royal Archives had taken on an ethereal quality as evening descended. Pools of lamplight illuminated scattered research materials on the expansive oak tables, while towering bookshelves dissolved into shadow, their contents waiting silently to divulge their secrets. The quiet hum of activity from earlier in the day had ebbed into a solemn stillness, broken only by the occasional shuffle of papers.

Singh left soon after escorting Anika and Vikram safely inside the ancient building. And soon Anika and Vikram were back at their stations, sifting through the texts that could shed light on the killer's next move.

'I think we should start with the records from the late 18th century,' Anika suggested as they approached their desks. 'That seems to be when the pattern of these executions really began to take shape.'

Vikram nodded, already loosening his jacket and rolling up his sleeves. 'I'll look through my family's personal accounts from that time. If something was deemed too sensitive for the official records, there's a chance it's buried in the private journals.'

Without further ado, they dove back into the sprawling mess of documents that had consumed their day. Piles of papers, charts, and notes accumulated steadily, the lines of their focus etched deeply into their features as hours bled into one another.

It wasn't until a gentle knock echoed from the door that they looked up, startled by the intrusion.

'Excuse me,' a security guard said, poking his head into the room. His voice was polite but firm. 'It's well past closing time. Do you need anything else for the night?'

Anika exchanged a glance with Vikram, both of them momentarily disoriented by how quickly the day had slipped away. The scattered papers around them bore testament to their progress—or obsession.

'Do you think we can stay a little longer?' Anika asked, a spark of determination still bright in her tired eyes. 'We're making headway, and it's crucial.'

The guard hesitated, his gaze flitting to the chaotic desk. After a moment, he relented with a small nod. 'I'll let the night staff know. Just be sure to check out with security before you leave.'

As he stepped out, Vikram leaned back in his chair, giving her a small grin. 'Looks like we're going to be here for the entire night. I'll order coffee.'

Anika laughed softly, already reaching for another stack of notes. 'Make it strong. We have a long night ahead of us.'

ॐ

Hours later, the quiet intimacy of the room seemed to close in around them. The muted scratch of pen against paper and the occasional rustling of documents were the only sounds, punctuating the intense focus etched on their faces.

'Anika,' Vikram called softly, breaking the silence. His voice carried a note of urgency, enough to make her look up from her charts. 'I think I've found something.'

She rose from her chair, crossing to his side of the table. Vikram held out a genealogical chart, his finger tracing a specific line. 'Look at this branch,' he said, his voice steady. 'It connects both our victims. And if you follow it back . . .' He moved his finger farther up the chart, pausing dramatically.

Anika leaned in, her eyes scanning the connection he'd outlined. 'It leads to one of Chandravati's supporters,' she finished.

'Exactly,' Vikram said, his voice low but intense. 'The killer is targeting descendants of those *directly* involved in her trial and execution.'

Anika nodded, although she already knew about this particular aspect of the investigation. 'Vikram,' Anika said carefully, her voice quieter than before, 'you mentioned earlier that your family has access to all the genealogical records of all the Rajput lineages, right?'

He nodded, leaning against the table as if bracing himself for whatever she was about to ask. 'Yes, the royal families kept detailed records. Even after the princely states were abolished, those records were preserved. Why?'

Anika hesitated. It felt like a strange thing to ask, like she was tugging at a thread she wasn't sure she wanted to untangle. 'Could you . . . look into my genealogy? I know we're Rajputs, but my family was never particularly wealthy or prominent. Still, if this case is about bloodlines . . .'

Vikram's brow furrowed in thought. 'It's possible your family could be connected to the lesser branches, distant relatives of a royal lineage that didn't inherit titles or lands but still carried the name and bloodline.' He straightened, his gaze serious. 'I can check, Anika. It might take some time to trace, but if there's any connection, I'll find it.'

Anika nodded, the room's lamplight casting soft shadows on her tense features. 'Thanks, Vikram. It's probably nothing, but . . .' She trailed off, her thoughts drifting to Yuvraj, his curious nature, and his passion for historical research.

'But you think it might be connected to your brother's disappearance,' Vikram finished for her, his voice gentle but perceptive.

She sighed, running a hand through her hair. She wasn't surprised Vikram knew about her brother. Most people in Jaipur did. 'Yuvraj was obsessed with history, especially Jaipur's royal past. He would spend hours poring over old texts, always searching for something. I used to tease him about it, calling him a treasure hunter without a map.' Her voice softened, tinged with guilt. 'What if he found something? What if, in his innocent curiosity, he stumbled onto something he wasn't supposed to see?'

Vikram's expression darkened. 'You think the killer, or someone connected to this, might have targeted him because of what he discovered?'

'I don't know.' Anika's hands tightened into fists, the frustration of unanswered questions gnawing at her. 'It's just a feeling, but I can't shake it. If this is all connected—Chandravati, the executions, the medallions—it's possible Yuvraj came across a piece of the puzzle before anyone else. And if he did . . .' She swallowed hard, her voice faltering.

Vikram moved to where she sat, his calm presence steadying her. 'If he did, then I'll help you find out what happened to him, Anika. Whatever he discovered, we'll uncover it too. And if it's connected to this case, it'll help us stop the killer.'

Anika nodded, her resolve hardening once more. 'Start with my family records please. If there's any link to the people involved in Chandravati's execution, or even just the royal bloodlines, I need to know.'

'I will,' Vikram promised. 'And Anika . . . if there's anything else you remember about Yuvraj's research, anything he might have mentioned, it could be important.'

She exhaled slowly, searching her memory. 'He used to talk about wanting to find out the truth behind the brightly presented stories. He wanted to "solve" the crimes committed by nobility, that kind of childish stuff.'

Vikram's expression tightened, his jaw clenching. 'It sounds like there is a chance he might have been on to something bigger than even he realised. We'll figure it out, Anika.'

As they turned back to their respective piles of documents, the weight of their task felt heavier than ever. The threads of history were tangled with personal pain, drawing Anika deeper into a case that was no longer just about stopping a killer. It was about uncovering the truth that Yuvraj might have even died for.

But with each revelation, the stakes grew higher, and the shadows of the past loomed ever closer.

Around 4.00 a.m., as Anika and Vikram nursed their sixth cup of coffee, the heavy silence of the Royal Archives was shattered by a loud crash echoing through the labyrinthine corridors, sharp and jarring against the stillness of the predawn hour.

When Vikram and Anika went to inspect the crash that had shattered the stillness, it turned out to be a precariously stacked pile of books succumbing to gravity. Though harmless, the noise left Anika and Vikram on edge, their nerves frayed after hours of poring over haunting connections.

'We should probably call it a night,' Vikram suggested, running a hand through his hair, which was now more tousled than regal. 'But there's something I need to check in my office first. An old family heirloom. It might help us understand what we're dealing with.'

Anika nodded, impressed by the fact that he had his own office in such a significant place. 'Lead the way.'

Vikram's office, tucked into a quiet corner of the archives, was as elegant as it was functional. Antique furniture filled the small space, with shelves crammed full of books and objects that reflected both his royal lineage and his personal tastes. A heavy desk bore a mix of modern paperwork and relics of the past, its surface cluttered yet meticulously arranged.

As Vikram crossed the room to a carved wooden cabinet, Anika's gaze fell on a framed photograph on the desk. It showed a younger Vikram standing proudly beside an older man with a striking resemblance.

'My father,' Vikram said, noticing her interest. His voice carried a mix of pride and nostalgia. 'That was taken when I formally took on my responsibilities as the family's representative in Jaipur's civic affairs.'

Anika detected a tinge of sadness beneath his composed tone. 'Were you close?'

Vikram nodded, a wistful smile flickering on his lips. 'Yes. He taught me everything he thought I needed to know about our family, its history, its responsibilities, its place in Jaipur. But sometimes I wonder what he didn't tell me.'

Anika glanced at the photograph again, understanding the gravity of a legacy passed down from one generation to the next.

Before the conversation could deepen, Vikram opened the cabinet and pulled out an ornately carved wooden box. He placed it carefully on the desk. 'This has been in my family for generations,' he said, his tone reverent. 'It contains documents and objects tied to our most significant moments, both triumphs and tragedies.'

Anika exhaled slowly. *Rahasya-Lekh.* Her anticipation quickened as Vikram unlatched the box. Inside were bundles of yellowed papers, faded letters bound with ribbon, and small artefacts that bore the patina of centuries.

Vikram reached for a bundle of letters, untying the ribbon with steady hands. As he unfolded the first letter, his expression shifted, disbelief etched across his features.

'This can't be,' he murmured, his voice heavy with shock.

Anika leaned in. 'What is it?'

Vikram scanned the letter, his eyes darting over the ancient handwriting. 'It's from my great-great-grandfather. He writes about being part of a secret society, a group dedicated to breaking Chandravati's curse.'

Anika's breath hitched. 'The same society we've been theorising about?'

Vikram nodded slowly. 'Yes. And according to this letter . . . he wasn't just a member. He was the leader.'

Anika stared at him, the weight of the revelation sinking in. 'Leader?'

Vikram's voice grew quieter as he read further. 'He orchestrated the first wave of "cleansing executions" in an attempt to lift the curse. The staging, the symbols, even the sequence—it's all here. Whoever the killer is, they're using this manifesto as a guide.'

The implications struck Anika like a thunderclap. 'So, your family was not only connected to the curse, but your ancestors *started* the rituals that the killer is now re-enacting.'

Vikram sat heavily in his chair, the full weight of history crashing down on him. 'If the killer has access to this, or even knows about it . . .' He trailed off, his eyes clouded with guilt and unease.

Before either of them could process further, Anika's phone buzzed sharply, breaking the tense silence. It was Inspector Singh.

'Anika.' Singh's tone was brisk, all business. 'We've had a breakthrough. The forensics team recovered DNA from the last crime scene. It's degraded but viable. They've narrowed it down to a specific family line, one tied directly to the royal court.'

Anika's pulse quickened as she locked eyes with Vikram, the pieces clicking into place. 'That's incredible news, Rajesh,' she said, her voice steady despite her racing thoughts.

Singh's voice softened slightly. 'We need to move fast. The public is growing restless, and if this killer strikes again, we're looking at a city in chaos. How's your end?'

Anika glanced at the letter in Vikram's hand. 'We've uncovered something significant here too. I think it ties directly to the murders, and possibly to who the killer is targeting next.'

'Good,' Singh replied. 'Let's regroup at headquarters. And bring Rathore. If this involves his family history, we need him in the room.'

As the call ended, Anika turned back to Vikram, who was still staring at the letter, lost in thought.

'Vikram,' she said gently, placing a hand on his arm. 'We'll figure this out. Your family's past may be part of the puzzle, but it's not the whole picture. We're close to something big, I can feel it.'

He looked up at her, his eyes conflicted but resolute. 'I'll do whatever it takes, Anika. If this is the legacy my family left behind, I have to help fix it.'

Together they gathered the documents, their shared determination cutting through the heaviness of the moment. And they left the building that provided them with many answers but also a whole lot of different questions.

Anika stood at her bedroom window, staring out at the dimly lit streets of Jaipur. The city, usually alive with energy, seemed unnervingly quiet tonight. She wrapped a shawl around her shoulders to ward off the morning chill and glanced at the clock. It was just past 6.00 a.m. She had managed to get home an hour ago, and though exhaustion weighed heavily on her, her mind buzzed with everything they'd uncovered.

Stacks of notes and photocopies from the archives lay on her desk, taunting her. Every piece of evidence felt like a step closer to unmasking the killer, but the picture was still incomplete. She rubbed her temples, exhaustion gnawing at her resolve.

'Two hours,' she murmured to herself. 'Two hours of sleep, then back to the headquarters.'

Changing into a loose kurta and tying her hair into a messy bun, she slid under the covers, her body aching for rest. The adrenaline of the day had waned, replaced by a bone-deep fatigue. Closing her eyes, she willed her racing mind to quiet. The shrill ring of her phone cut through the silence. Anika groaned, fumbling for it on the bedside table. She squinted at the screen. Vikram's name flashed across it.

'Vikram?' she answered, sitting upright, her exhaustion evaporating in an instant. 'Is everything all right?'

His voice on the other end was strained, anger and disbelief lacing his words. 'Anika, it's out. The press—everything about my family's connection to the secret society. It's all over the news.'

Her stomach dropped. 'What? How? We only just found out about it!'

'I don't know,' Vikram said, his frustration apparent. 'But there are reporters outside my house, calling it the Curse Chronicles. They're spinning wild theories, talking about Chandravati's curse and my family's role in perpetuating it.' He paused, his voice lowering to a near whisper. 'They're even naming me as a possible suspect, Anika.'

Anika felt her pulse quicken. 'This doesn't make sense. We've barely discovered this information. No one else knows about it except you and me.'

'And the killer.' Vikram's voice hardened. 'Look, I don't know how this happened. But this changes things. My family's reputation is being dragged through the mud, and now the killer knows we're on to him.'

Anika swung her legs over the side of the bed, her mind racing. 'It's deliberate, Vikram. Someone's trying to turn the city against you or distract us.'

'It is the killer then?'

'I wouldn't rule it out,' she said, pacing the room. 'The timing is too perfect. The backlash could stall our investigation. Worse, it might provoke him to escalate his plans.'

Vikram sighed heavily. 'What do we do now?'

Anika paused, forcing herself to focus. 'First, you need to stay out of sight for a while. Let the press storm pass. I'll call Singh to see if he can handle the pressure of the media. But, Vikram, this could also work to our advantage.'

'How?'

'If the killer thinks the heat is on you and your family, they might let their guard down. We can use this to narrow down suspects or force them to make mistakes.'

'That's a dangerous gamble, Anika,' Vikram said.

'Maybe,' she admitted, her voice firm, 'but it's our best shot. You've been brave enough to face these truths, Vikram. Now we can use them to stop this madness.'

There was a long pause before Vikram spoke again, his voice tinged with a mix of resignation. 'All right. Do what you need to do . . . but just keep me in the loop. I don't want to sit on the sidelines.'

'You won't,' Anika promised. 'I'll call Singh now and meet you at the headquarters in a few hours. We'll figure this out.'

As she ended the call, Anika sat on the edge of her bed, staring at her phone. The leak had again shifted the game, raising the stakes to dangerous new heights. Anika's jaw set with resolve. They might be closer to the truth, but the cost grew by the minute. She couldn't let the pressure derail their mission, not when they were so close to unearthing centuries-old secrets.

Grabbing her notepad, she jotted down a new list of priorities before throwing on a jacket. Sleep would have to wait. The race against the killer—and time—was now a battle on two fronts.

Jaipur's history, present, and future hung in the balance.

CHAPTER 8

The first blush of dawn painted the sky in pale hues as Suraj Sharma jogged through Sisodia Rani Garden. The garden's tranquil beauty, with its blooming marigolds and intricately carved pavilions, usually provided a moment of solace in his morning routine. The scent of damp earth mingled with the delicate fragrance of flowers, carried on the crisp morning air.

As he rounded a corner near the serene central fountain, Suraj faltered. Something was out of place—a flash of bright colour caught his eye, incongruous against the muted tones of the early morning landscape. He slowed, squinting to make out the shape sprawled near a bed of marigolds. His pulse quickened as he approached, unease coiling tightly in his chest.

There, splayed amid a bed of marigolds, lay a woman's body, her bright sari pooling around her like a grotesque flower. Her lifeless eyes stared unblinkingly at the sky, and her hands were crossed on her chest.

Suraj stumbled back, his breath coming in short, panicked gasps. His trembling fingers fumbled for his phone as he dialled 100.

⁂

Within minutes, the tranquil garden transformed into a hive of activity. Police vehicles screeched to a halt outside the gates, their sirens shattering the morning calm. Officers swarmed the area, their voices terse as they cordoned off the crime scene with yellow tape.

Sub-Inspector Pradeep Kumar took command, his sharp voice slicing through the gathering chaos. 'Secure the perimeter! No one in or out without clearance!'

Yellow tape snaked its way around the scene as curious onlookers clustered at the gates, their hushed murmurs adding to the tense atmosphere. Camera flashes lit up the area, capturing every detail of the crime scene.

Pradeep crouched by the body, his trained eyes scanning for clues. The early sunlight glinted off an ornate medallion clutched in the woman's hand, with an intricate design on its surface.

A young constable approached hesitantly, his face pale. 'Sir . . . this—it matches the other murders.'

Pradeep stood slowly, the weight of recognition pressing on him like a mountain.

'Get me Inspector Singh and Dr Anika Thakur,' he said, his voice low but resolute. 'Tell them it's happened again.'

As the garden fell under the shadow of the investigation, its once-pristine beauty seemed tarnished, overtaken by a sinister presence. Sisodia Rani Garden, a symbol of Jaipur's regal elegance, now bore the mark of the darkness stalking the Pink City.

⁂

The sun hovered just below the horizon, a thin line of gold spreading across the sky as Anika Thakur stepped into the Sisodia Rani Garden. The tranquil beauty of the place—its ornate pavilions, carefully arranged flower beds, and tiered fountains—was now marred by the yellow crime scene tape fluttering in the morning breeze. Police officers moved purposefully, their voices low but urgent, as the burden of another murder settled over the once-idyllic space.

Anika adjusted the strap of her satchel, her steps brisk as she crossed the cordoned area. The faint scent of jasmine mixed with the metallic hint of tension in the air. Near the fountain, Inspector Rajesh Singh stood waiting, his sharp gaze scanning the scene before resting on her.

'Dr Thakur,' he called out.

'How is this possible? We had men here, right?'

Singh nodded. 'I had men placed at all the four locations you told me about, including here. I think we were stretched too thin.'

Anika shook her head. 'What do we know so far?'

Singh motioned her to follow him towards the body, his tone clipped with urgency. 'The victim was found just after 5:30 this morning by a jogger. It's a female in her midthirties, no ID on her. Her positioning and the objects around her, well, it's our killer.'

They reached the victim, who lay in a meticulously staged tableau. Her sari's *pallu*, deep blue with intricate silver embroidery, fanned out in a near-perfect circle around her. White jasmine blossoms were woven into her long unbound hair, their pristine beauty grotesquely contrasting with the lifelessness of her pale face. Around her, objects had been arranged with ritualistic precision—a small figurine of Maha Sati, a thorny branch, and a brass oil lamp still faintly warm.

'What are we looking at here?' Singh asked, fidgeting with his watch.

Anika's fingers hovered over the intricate placement of the objects. 'This is a recreation of the execution of Rani Padmavati's handmaiden, circa 1576. According to legend, the handmaiden sacrificed herself to protect her mistress's honour, clutching an idol of Maha Sati to her chest as she died. The killer is mimicking this moment, down to the smallest detail.'

Singh's jaw tightened.

Before Singh could respond, an officer approached, holding an evidence bag. 'Inspector, this was found near the victim's left hand.'

Inside the bag was a tattered scrap of paper, its edges singed. Anika squinted at the faded text, murmuring as she deciphered it. 'It's Old Rajasthani . . . a poem or a fragment of one.' She translated aloud:

> *The stones remember what men forget,*
> *In blood and tears, a debt yet unpaid.*

Three by three, the past awakens,
Till justice blooms in the garden of time.

Singh's expression darkened. 'Three by three? Do you think that means nine victims?'

Anika nodded, her mind already fitting the pieces together. 'It's possible. I'll have to cross-reference it with the texts I've been studying.'

A commotion at the edge of the garden drew their attention. A group of reporters, led by Manoj Dutta, had gathered at the gates, their cameras flashing and their voices raised in an aggressive chorus of questions.

Singh sighed heavily. 'The press here already? My God! I swear they get to know about the murders even before we do.'

Anika's phone buzzed in her pocket. She pulled it out to find a message from Dr Malhotra. Anika frowned, not sure what the forensic expert wanted from her.

Anika, we need to talk. I want to help. Call me when you can.'

Anika's lips pressed into a thin line. Malhotra's scepticism had been a thorn in her side since the beginning of the investigation, but his willingness to extend an olive branch hinted at the gravity of their situation.

Singh touched her elbow lightly, drawing her attention back. 'Commissioner Verma is out of the city. He has asked me to talk to the press. You're coming with me too.'

Anika hesitated, but before she could protest, Singh added, 'You're the co-lead, Anika. It's part of the job description.'

Anika nodded reluctantly. 'Fine, but what do we say?'

Singh looked at the reporters, who seemed like a mob of angry hyenas looking at their prey. 'Let's stick to the facts and keep the focus on the investigation. If we lose control of the narrative, the killer could use the chaos to their advantage.'

As they approached the press barrier, Anika could see the reporters surging forward, questions firing like bullets.

'Inspector Singh, how many more murders will it take for the police to catch this killer finally?' one reporter asked.

'Dr Thakur, is it true Dr Malhotra wanted you off the case?' another one shouted.

'Inspector Rajesh, do you think the killer is a royal?' a woman questioned.

Inspector Rajesh Singh stepped forward, his imposing presence commanding immediate attention. The press, momentarily silenced, turned their cameras and microphones towards him. His crisp uniform, marked with the insignia of his rank, caught the morning light as he raised a hand to quiet the murmurs.

'Listen to me,' Singh began, his voice steady but firm. 'First and foremost, let me assure the people of Jaipur that this investigation is our highest priority. Early this morning, a tragic incident occurred at Sisodia Rani Garden. A woman lost her life under circumstances that are both troubling and highly unusual.'

The journalists leaned in, their pens poised. Singh continued, his tone measured, ensuring every word conveyed both authority and calm.

'We are actively investigating this case and are working with a dedicated team of forensic and historical experts to uncover every detail. At this time, while we cannot divulge specifics, we can confirm that certain elements of this crime share similarities with two previous cases currently under investigation.

'However, I want to be absolutely clear, this is not the time for speculation or fearmongering. We are pursuing strong leads, and every available resource is being deployed to ensure the safety of our citizens.'

A reporter from the back raised a hand, but Singh held firm. 'We understand your need for answers, but remember this is an active investigation. Premature conclusions or sensationalised reporting can jeopardise our efforts and mislead the public.'

He gestured towards Anika, who stood nearby. 'To clarify certain particulars of this case, I'd like to introduce Dr Anika Thakur, a historical forensic psychologist co-leading this investigation. Her expertise has been invaluable, and she will address some of your questions.'

Singh stepped aside, meeting Anika's gaze briefly. His nod was subtle but reassuring, reminding her that she had his full support as she faced the spotlight.

'Dr Thakur!' Dutta called out. 'Is it true this murder follows the same historical pattern as the others? Are we dealing with a serial killer obsessed with Rajasthan's royal history?'

Anika took a deep breath. 'While we cannot comment on specifics, the Jaipur Police Department is actively pursuing all leads. I assure you, we are working tirelessly to bring the perpetrator to justice. We urge the public to remain vigilant and report any suspicious activity.'

Anika answered some questions about the killer's profile, sharing only the bare minimum of information—nothing that would make the killer think they were on to him.

As the press continued shouting questions after Anika was done, Singh gestured for the officers to push them back. Anika turned away, her mind already spinning with possibilities.

Back at the crime scene, she knelt beside the victim once more, studying the intricate details of the tableau.

'Dr Thakur,' Gupta, one of the senior forensic technicians, approached Anika, his voice grave. 'We've completed the preliminary examination. There's something you need to see.'

He handed her the tablet, displaying close-up images of the victim's hands. Anika leaned in, her eyes narrowing. 'Ink stains,' she murmured, tracing the outline on the screen.

'The ink stains suggest she worked with documents. Maybe an archivist or librarian.'

'Have the genealogists check her connection to the royal bloodline.

Singh walked over to Anika as Dr Gupta left, rubbing his temples. 'Is everything okay?' Concern creased her forehead.

'It's Commissioner Verma. He had a meeting with the minister of tourism. He gave Verma a good dressing-down, and Verma, in turn, gave me one.'

'I'm sorry. I know how hard all this is for you. You have to deal with everyone, investigate the leads, question the witnesses, and handle the reports. I wish I could help out in some way.'

Singh shook his head. 'No . . . Whatever you're doing is going to help us catch the killer. I don't mind following the protocol. Someone has to, right? You just focus on decoding the killer's pattern and leave the rest to me.'

'Are you okay?' Anika asked.

Singh shook his head, sighing heavily. 'It just . . . I want this to be over. If we don't stop the killer soon, this bloodbath is going to consume each and every one of us.' He looked in the distance, his gaze far off. 'You know, I haven't seen my daughter since this investigation began.'

Anika's head shot up faster than she'd meant. 'Oh? You have a daughter?'

Singh nodded. 'She is five now. Very intelligent. Sometimes I feel I'm failing her by not catching this killer.'

Anika placed a hand on Singh's shoulder. 'Trust me, we will catch him. We are close, Rajesh. I can feel it.'

Singh gave her a thankful smile.

'So, you're married?' Anika felt annoyed that her heart beat a little faster while she waited for Singh's reply.

He nodded. 'And divorced. It took my wife two years to realise that I could never give her the time or the attention she deserved. This line of work makes it impossible.'

Anika nodded. Relief rushed through her. She smiled at Singh and said, 'It is a tough job.'

'Inspector Singh, the victim has been identified.' Singh and Anika turned around. It was Sub-Inspector Kumar.

'Already? That's fast.'

Kumar nodded grimly.

'Good work. Who is she?' Singh said, feeling proud of the work his team was putting in.

'Her name is Priya Mathur. She was a research assistant at the Maharaja Sawai Man Singh II Museum, specialising in Rajasthani miniature paintings and historical documents.'

'Maybe she came across some information that she wasn't supposed to,' Singh said.

'Or maybe the killer is simply following his pattern of killing people with royal lineage,' Anika added.

'Either way, we'll have to look into what Priya Mathur had been working on in the weeks leading up to her murder,' Singh concluded. He spoke to Kumar and instructed him and the other members of his team to start questioning the people at Priya Mathur's workplace.

Anika turned to the crime scene and started studying it closely. She took note of the poem left behind by the killer. It was a deviation from his usual pattern. Is he leaving a clue for the next crime, or is he taunting Anika?

Anika continued examining the scene as the body was picked up by four people from the autopsy team and hauled into a body bag placed on a gurney. The moment the body was picked up from the ground, Anika saw an envelope fall on the ground.

She quickly called a forensic technician and opened the envelope with her gloved hands after having the envelope photographed and logged. Her movements were precise and practised as she carefully extracted the yellowed paper from within the envelope.

The technician photographed the decaying paper, and once he was done, Anika studied the calligraphic text.

'What's that?' Singh approached Anika after having finished his discussion with his team.

'It's a letter dated 1576, the same year as the handmaiden's execution. It's the confession from a royal advisor who admits to falsely accusing the handmaiden of treason to cover up his own crimes.'

'And it was on the body?'

Anika nodded. 'It was concealed in the back pocket of the victim's jeans.'

'Something about this scene feels . . .'

'Different,' Anika completed. 'I was just thinking about that. This time it's too direct. As if the killer is trying hard to get the message across.'

'What if it's someone else?' Singh asked, curious.

'You mean a copycat killer? No . . . I don't think so, but something has definitely changed. I believe the killer is not working alone, so this could be the result of more than one mind at work.'

'Inspector Singh! Dr Thakur! We've found something in the water!'

Singh and Anika exchanged a look before they hurried over. A diver emerged from the fountain, holding a waterproof bag containing an intricately carved stone tablet.

'It was lodged in the fountain mechanism,' he explained.

Anika examined the tablet through the plastic. The carving on its surface depicted a scene of ritual sacrifice, with inscriptions in ancient script around the edges. 'This is incredible . . .,' she murmured. 'The artistry seems ancient, possibly from the 16th century. It's an original, but we'll need to authenticate it.'

Singh frowned. 'How did the killer get their hands on an artefact like this? And why plant it here?'

'I think the killer's endgame is near. That's why the dynamic of the crime scene has shifted. He's leaving a trail of breadcrumbs for us. Each piece of evidence is a clue to the final act.' She turned to the forensic team. 'I need a comprehensive analysis of all the historical artefacts left at all three crime scenes. Carbon dating, material composition, everything. If we can trace their origins, we might be able to track the killer's source. Also, start cross-referencing any fingerprints or DNA traces with the royal family's records and genealogical databases. Our killer might be closer to the royal families than we think.'

Anika turned to Singh, her voice urgent. 'Inspector, we need to compile a list of everyone with access to the Royal Archives and other restricted historical collections all over Jaipur and cross-reference it with individuals who have connections to the royal families.'

'I was afraid we'll have to begin looking into the royals sooner or later,' Singh said before turning around and gathering his team.

As the forensic team continued to process the scene, Anika felt a growing sense of unease. The killer's attention to detail, access to historical artefacts, and knowledge all pointed to someone with significant resources and a deep connection to Rajasthan's royal past.

※

The midday sun streamed through the blinds of the forensic lab, casting slatted shadows on the stainless steel countertops. Dr Anika

Thakur sat at a workstation, her eyes fixed on a digital display. The artefact retrieved from the crime scene, a delicately carved stone slab, spun slowly on the monitor as the computer processed its details. Next to her, another screen displayed a high-resolution scan of the letter fragment found near the victim. The lab buzzed softly with the hum of equipment and the murmurs of technicians in the background.

Anika's brow furrowed as she reviewed the initial findings. The artefact's material composition, stone from the 16th century, matched perfectly with known items from Rajasthan's royal collections. Its design was unmistakable, bearing the intricate craftsmanship of artisans employed exclusively by the Rajput royalty.

'Dr Thakur,' a voice interrupted her thoughts. She looked up to see Sub-Inspector Kumar entering the office, holding a file. His expression was hesitant, almost apologetic.

'We've traced the registration of the artefact found in the fountain,' Arjun said, sliding the file across the table to her. 'It's registered under Vikram Singh Rathore's name.'

Anika's heart sank. She flipped open the file, scanning the details. There it was in black and white, Vikram's name, along with documentation that linked the artefact to his family's private collection.

For a moment, her thoughts spiralled. Could Vikram have withheld this information? Was his connection to the case deeper than he'd let on? Shaking off her doubts, she took a deep breath. Vikram had been nothing but helpful so far. If there was an explanation, she needed to hear it from him directly.

'Thanks, Kumar,' she said, closing the file. 'Keep this under wraps for now. I'll follow up on this.'

Kumar nodded and left, leaving Anika to grapple with the implications.

Anika returned to her small office, the clutter of notes, photographs, and timelines growing by the day. She added the high-resolution photograph of the letter fragment from the crime scene. She sat down and studied the lines of Old Rajasthani poetry, muttering translations under her breath. 'Three by three . . . the past awakens . . . garden of time.' The cryptic phrasing gnawed at her.

A soft knock at the door broke her concentration. She looked up to see Dr Dilip Malhotra standing in the doorway, his usually smug demeanour replaced by something bordering on . . . humility?

'Dr Malhotra,' Anika greeted, unable to keep the surprise from her tone. She remembered the message she had received from Malhotra that morning, but she never got around to replying to it.

He stepped inside, his hands tucked into the pockets of his tailored trousers. 'Dr Thakur, I know I've been removed from the case,' he began, his voice measured, 'but I wanted to let you know, I'm still available if you need help. No strings attached.'

Anika's eyes narrowed slightly, her instincts prickling at the unexpected offer. 'That's . . . generous of you, Dr Malhotra. But I thought you didn't put much stock in my theories.'

Malhotra shrugged, offering a self-deprecating smile. 'I'll admit, I was sceptical at first. But it's clear you're on to something. If my expertise can contribute in any way, I'd like to be of service.'

Anika considered his words carefully. His sudden change in attitude was strange, but rejecting his offer outright might alienate him, and despite her wariness, Malhotra's forensic expertise could still be helpful.

'Thank you, Dr Malhotra,' she said finally. 'I'll keep that in mind.'

Malhotra nodded, lingering for a moment before heading towards the door. 'Good luck, Dr Thakur. I have a feeling this case is going to make history.'

Anika couldn't shake a sense of unease as the door closed behind him.

Later that afternoon, Anika dialled Vikram's number, the file from the forensic lab open on her desk. He picked up after the second ring, his voice warm despite the tension she could hear beneath it.

'Anika, I saw the news. What's going on?'

'I need to ask you something,' she said, diving straight into the heart of the matter. 'The artefact from the crime scene, the stone slab. It's registered under your name.'

There was a pause, then Vikram exhaled sharply. 'I was afraid of this. Anika, a stone slab was stolen from my family's collection about a month ago. I filed an FIR as soon as we realised it was missing.'

Anika's grip on the phone tightened. 'Stolen? And you didn't think to tell me earlier?'

'I didn't even remember the artefact until you mentioned it,' Vikram admitted. 'Honestly, I assumed it was an isolated theft, maybe even an inside job. I never imagined it could be linked to the murders. I'll send you a copy of the FIR right away.'

Anika absorbed the information, her mind racing with possibilities. 'Thanks for clarifying. And, Vikram, I need to give you a heads-up about something else.'

'Go on,' he said, his tone cautious.

She hesitated, knowing her next words wouldn't sit well with him. 'We're going to begin investigating the royals more closely. Your family and others with ties to Rajasthan's history. We'll be cross-referencing access to artefacts, archives, and other restricted materials. It's a standard procedure given the killer's apparent knowledge and resources.'

There was a pause before Vikram spoke, his voice heavy with disappointment. 'I understand why you must do it, Anika, but it still stings. My family has always tried to uphold our legacy responsibly. To think we might even be tangentially involved in something so horrific . . .' He trailed off, his frustration evident.

Anika softened her tone. 'Vikram, I know this isn't easy. But I promise you, this isn't personal. We're following the evidence, and I have to be thorough. Your cooperation means a lot, and it's not something I take for granted.'

'I know you're just doing your job,' he said after a moment. 'And I appreciate your honesty. If there's anything I can do to help, you only have to ask.'

'Thank you,' she said sincerely. 'And, Vikram, for what it's worth, I don't think you or your family is involved in this directly. But we need to explore every angle if we're going to stop this killer.'

His voice softened. 'Thanks, Anika. Just . . . be careful. Rajasthan's royals are a complex group of people, and investigating them will only upset them.'

'I'll keep that in mind,' Anika assured him. 'And send over that FIR when you get a chance. It might help us figure out how the artefact ended up at the crime scene.'

'Of course. I'll send it over right away,' Vikram said. 'And, Anika . . . thank you. For keeping me in the loop.'

After the call ended, Anika leaned back in her chair, the weight of the investigation pressing down on her. Her eyes drifted back to the letter fragment. 'Three by three,' she murmured again, the words heavy with ominous possibility.

Time was running out, and the past was closing in on the present faster than she could keep up.

❧

The press room at Jaipur's local government building was a hive of activity. Journalists from regional and national media outlets jostled for position, cameras perched on tripods and microphones thrust forward like spears. The low hum of murmured conversations mingled with the occasional click of a pen and the faint whirr of air conditioning.

At exactly 2.00 p.m., the door opened, and Tourism Minister Raghuveer Shekhawat entered. Dressed impeccably in a crisp white kurta and his gold-rimmed glasses glinting under the overhead lights, he exuded a composed authority. He moved to the podium with measured steps, his expression carefully neutral.

'Good afternoon, ladies and gentlemen,' Shekhawat began, his voice calm and practised, carrying over the rustle of last-minute notes. 'Thank you for joining us. I understand the recent tragic incidents have raised many concerns, and I am here to address them.'

The room quieted, pens poised mid-air. In the front row, Manoj Dutta leaned forward, his sharp gaze fixed on the minister.

Shekhawat continued, his tone reassuring, 'First, I want to emphasise that Jaipur remains one of the world's safest and most welcoming destinations. While tragic, the unfortunate incidents we've seen are isolated and do not reflect the spirit of our city.'

The journalists exchanged quick glances, a ripple of murmurs passing through the room.

'Let me assure you,' Shekhawat said, his voice firm now, 'our police force, under the capable leadership of Commissioner Verma, is working tirelessly to solve these cases. We've also enlisted the expertise of professionals like forensic psychologist Dr Anika Thakur to aid in the investigation.'

At the mention of Anika, Manoj Dutta's pen scratched across his notepad, his interest piqued.

'Minister Shekhawat,' a reporter from a national news channel called out, 'rumours suggest these murders are tied to Jaipur's royal history. Can you confirm or deny this connection?'

A flicker of annoyance crossed Shekhawat's face before he replaced it with a diplomatic smile. 'I would caution against spreading such unfounded rumours. Jaipur's royal heritage is a source of pride and fascination for millions. Tying it to these crimes without evidence is speculative and harmful.'

Manoj Dutta was next, his voice sharp and direct. 'Minister, sources close to the investigation indicate that these crime scenes bear similarities to historical executions. Is the government prepared to address the possibility of a serial killer fixated on Rajasthan's past?'

Shekhawat's smile tightened imperceptibly. 'Mr Dutta, I understand your concern, but I urge caution. Speculation does not serve the public interest. The police are exploring every lead, and we have full confidence in their ability to solve these cases.'

Another hand shot up. 'Minister,' a younger journalist asked tentatively, 'with the Jaipur Literature Festival approaching, are there plans to increase security? Or might events be postponed?'

Shekhawat's expression softened at this. 'An excellent question. We will enhance security measures to ensure the safety of all participants and visitors. However, let me be clear: The festival and other events will proceed as planned. Jaipur's cultural legacy will not be overshadowed by fear.'

Despite Shekhawat's measured responses, the tension in the room was palpable now. The journalists sensed the undercurrent of unease behind his words, and their questions became sharper.

Dutta pressed on. 'Minister, you've assured us these are isolated incidents. But with four murders following a clear pattern, can you truly rule out the possibility of more? What message does this send to tourists reconsidering their visits?'

A brief shadow passed over Shekhawat's face. He drew a breath, his tone sharpening. 'Mr Dutta, while these crimes are serious, Jaipur is a city of over three million people. Statistically, it remains one of the safest places in the country. To our tourists, I say this: Come and experience the wonders of Jaipur. Its beauty, history, and hospitality remain unaffected.'

The questions continued, probing deeper into the investigation's implications for Jaipur's reputation and tourism economy. Shekhawat deflected the more pointed inquiries with polished ease, but the slight tension in his jaw betrayed the pressure mounting behind his composed exterior.

After nearly an hour, he raised a hand. 'That will be all for today. Thank you for your questions and for helping us communicate the facts. Rest assured, the safety and well-being of our citizens and visitors remain our highest priorities.'

As he stepped away from the podium, ignoring the flurry of follow-ups, the room erupted into murmurs. Journalists hurried to file their reports, the buzz of conversation rising as they dissected the minister's statements.

Manoj Dutta lingered in his seat, tapping his pen against his notepad. Something about Shekhawat's polished reassurances rang hollow. If a specialist like Dr Thakur had been brought in, and still the killer is at large, the situation was far more worrisome than the minister was letting on. He decided it was time to dig deeper.

Outside the building, the late afternoon sunlight bathed Jaipur's iconic pink façades. Inside a black SUV pulling away from the building, Shekhawat loosened his collar, his composed mask slipping.

His phone buzzed, and he glanced at the message from Commissioner Verma: *'Urgent developments. We need to meet immediately.'*

Shekhawat sighed, staring at the sprawling city he had sworn to protect. The Amber Fort loomed in the distance, a silent sentinel of Jaipur's history. As the SUV wound through the crowded streets, the minister allowed himself a rare moment of reflection. The past, it seemed, was no longer content to remain buried.

The lights in Anika's temporary office at the Jaipur police station buzzed softly, casting a harsh glow over her haggard face. It was well past midnight, but she hardly noticed the time. Her mind was racing, fuelled by caffeine and the thrill of an impending breakthrough.

Crime scene photos from all four murders were spread before her on the worn wooden desk, their gruesome details a stark contrast to the richly illustrated art books open beside them. Anika's tablet displayed a rotating 3D model of the latest crime scene, while her laptop showed a live feed of data being processed by the forensics team.

She leaned back in her chair, her fingers steepled under her chin, and studied the profiles spread across her desk. Four lives. Four untimely deaths.

> **Victim 1:** *A historian who specialised in 16th-century royal power struggles.*

> **Victim 2:** *An archivist who had been cataloguing royal documents related to Chandravati's curse.*

> **Victim 3:** *A curator at the City Palace Museum, focused on royal jewellery and artefacts.*

> **Victim 4:** *A researcher at the Maharaja Sawai Man Singh II Museum, who worked on Rajasthani miniature paintings.*

Something nagged at her unconscious mind: a remark that one of the constables had made the other day at the crime scene, which confirmed that the last victim was indeed connected to the royal lineage. Here, every second person seemed to be connected to the royal families. If someone were to run a gene test on her DNA, she might even be related to some long-forgotten maharaja.

It was just a thought that seeped into consciousness, but Anika couldn't stop wondering if the statement had a grain of truth. What if royalty is not something that connects just the victims? If that's the case, then were they not overlooking other connections? Or maybe the killer misled them to distract them from the real connection between the victims.

Anika took a deep breath and focused on the other connections the victims might have. But after hours of examining their lives for a unifying thread, the connections felt tenuous. The historian and the archivist shared a focus on written records; the curator and the researcher leaned more towards tangible artefacts.

'Why these people?' she muttered, tapping her pen against the edge of her desk. 'What connects them, beyond their work?'

Her eyes flitted back to the board, drawn to the victim from the Maharaja Sawai Man Singh II Museum. The note beneath her photo read: *Miniature Paintings Expert.*

Anika frowned. Her mind began to churn, combing through everything she knew about miniature paintings. They were not just art but storytelling tools, chronicling events, rituals, and legends. Stories immortalised in intricate brushstrokes.

She turned back to the profiles. Her pen hovered over the curator's photo: *Royal Jewellery.* Jewellery often featured prominently in miniature paintings as symbols of power or divine favour. The focus on power struggles also appeared as a key theme in many miniatures. And the archivist, whose work dealt with Chandravati's curse, a narrative that had inspired countless artworks in its time.

It was there, just out of reach. Anika scribbled notes furiously, her mind racing to connect the dots. Then, suddenly, it clicked.

Her hand froze midword as her pulse quickened. 'They're not just random experts in royal history,' she whispered, sitting up straight. 'They're all connected to the stories told in miniature paintings.'

Her gaze darted to the latest victim's profile. She flipped through her notes, zeroing in on a description of the victim's last project: cataloguing a series of rare miniatures recently acquired by the museum.

Grabbing her tablet, she pulled up the museum's online archive. Her fingers flew across the keyboard as she searched for information about the collection. When the results loaded, she felt a chill run down her spine.

The paintings depicted scenes from Chandravati's curse, the power struggles within Jaipur's royal courts, and ritual sacrifices tied to royal scandals.

She flipped through the pages with trembling fingers, stopping at a particular painting. It depicted a royal garden strikingly similar to the Sisodia Rani Garden, where the latest victim had been found. In the painting, a woman lay on the ground, posed almost identically to that of their latest victim.

Anika's heart raced as she quickly pulled up the crime scene photos on her tablet and compared them to the miniature painting. The similarities were undeniable, from the body's positioning to the clothing's arrangement, and even the placement of nearby objects.

The killer had recreated this specific painting. She quickly pulled up the other crime scene photos and checked the archives for similar paintings. Before long, she found the remaining three paintings replicated by the killer.

Her voice trembled as she spoke aloud, 'The killer is using these miniature paintings as the blueprint for murders.'

She quickly dialled Singh's number. 'Rajesh, I've found something. Can you come to my office?'

'I'll be there in 15 minutes.'

After ending the call, Anika studied the photo of the victim of the last murder on her laptop screen. She zoomed in on the victim's hands. The forensic technician at the scene had catalogued the pinpricks of thorn on the victim's hands, but as Anika stared at them, a pattern emerged from the seemingly random pricks.

She took a notepad and drew the design on the paper. Then she opened another window and searched for what she thought was a constellation. And there it was. The pinpricks formed a constellation: Ursa Major, the Great Bear. The equivalent in *Jyotish Shastra*, Indian astrology, is the *Saptarishi Mandal*, a highly spiritual representation significant for symbolising Hindu mythology's seven great sages (rishis). This must have a connection with the killer and the murder victims somehow.

When she did more research, she discovered that the current position of the stars was not the same, but it matched the sky in 1576. Yet another clue!

'The year of the handmaiden's execution,' Anika whispered.

The sound of footsteps in the hallway announced Inspector Singh's arrival. He burst into her office, still adjusting his hastily donned jacket.

'Show me what you've found, Anika,' he said without preamble.

Anika quickly walked him through her discovery, pointing out the similarities between the crime scenes, the miniature paintings, and the hidden diagram of the constellation she had just discovered.

Singh's face grew increasingly grave as he absorbed the information. 'This is turning into a living nightmare,' he said finally. 'So, we're not just dealing with a killer. We're dealing with someone who considers themselves an artist, using murder as the medium.'

Anika nodded, her expression sombre.

Singh ran a hand through his hair, his exhaustion evident. 'How do we go about solving this now?'

'We can start by focusing on the specific style and period of the paintings that have been recreated up to this point. I'll need the team of our art historians working with me on these miniature paintings.'

'Consider it done. I'll ask Kumar to have the team gathered by tomorrow morning.'

Anika thanked Singh and, after he left, turned back to her research. A thought struck her: The paintings themselves might hold clues to the killer's next move.

She dove back into her work with renewed focus, flipping through digital archives and historical texts. The pieces of the puzzle were falling into place, but the whole picture was still shrouded in shadows.

For the first time, Anika felt she was truly seeing through the killer's eyes, an artist wielding murder as their brush, crafting a dark masterpiece on the canvas of Jaipur's history.

※

The conference room at the Jaipur police station buzzed with nervous energy as the investigative team filed in, clutching coffee cups and notepads. Their tired eyes were a testament to the relentless pace of the investigation. Early sunlight spilled through the tall windows, its warmth doing little to soften the tension in the air.

Anika stood at the head of the table, a screen glowing with the opening slide of her presentation behind her. Her laptop and notes were meticulously arranged, a sharp contrast to her mind's chaotic tangle of ideas. She waited until Commissioner Verma, flanked by Singh and Kumar, entered, his firm step quieting the room, and the door clicked shut.

'Thank you all for coming in early,' Anika began, her voice steady despite the fatigue evident in her face. 'Last night, I made a significant breakthrough that could shift our understanding of the case entirely.'

She tapped her keyboard, and the screen behind her flickered to life, displaying a series of images: the crime scenes juxtaposed with bright Rajasthani miniature paintings. A ripple of shock spread through the room as the team absorbed the parallels—the positioning of the bodies, the intricate details, and even the surrounding props.

Verma leaned forward, his brows furrowed. 'The resemblance is . . . uncanny. How did we miss this?'

Anika looked at Singh, who offered her a small nod of acknowledgement. 'These paintings aren't widely known outside of art and history circles. I noticed similarities while reviewing the victims' profiles, but it wasn't until I tried to find a connection between the victims outside of the royal lineage connection we've already established. The killer is replicating specific Rajasthani miniature paintings.'

Commissioner Verma's expression darkened. 'What does this tell us about the killer, Dr Thakur?'

'It tells us he's more than a killer and historian,' Anika replied, her tone measured. 'He is also an artist, someone with deep knowledge of Rajasthani history *and* art. It is now obvious that this isn't some random violence. It's a calculated series of re-enactments, possibly driven by a sense of justice, vengeance, or even ritualistic purpose.'

The room was silent, the weight of her words settling over the team.

'These paintings,' Anika continued, 'were not just decorative. They chronicled historical events, stories of betrayal, punishment, and power struggles. The killer is using them to craft a narrative. To understand their next move, we need to decode the story he's telling.'

She continued, 'The use of historical artefacts and symbols in the murders reveals a killer with a ritualistic mindset. They view these killings not just as art but also as a form of ceremonial justice or even sacrifice. This could indicate someone with a spiritual or mystical vein, possibly influenced by ancient Rajasthani religious practices. The killer likely sees themselves as an agent of cosmic justice or karmic realignment.'

A young detective, Shilpa Nair, raised her hand. 'You think we should compile a database of miniature paintings that depict scenes of violence or justice and cross-reference those with Jaipur's history and locations that could be tied to future murders?'

'Good thinking, Officer Shilpa,' Anika said, a flicker of relief crossing her face. 'We also need to involve art historians to help interpret the hidden symbols and paintings. They could hold clues about the killer's endgame.'

Kumar raised his hand and, when Anika nodded for him to go ahead, asked, 'What about the timeline, Dr Thakur? The first murder and the second had a two-week gap. The second and third, exactly one week apart. But this last one? Four days.' He leaned on the table, his expression grim. 'It's inconsistent. Why would the killer suddenly shorten the timeline?'

Everyone straightened in their chairs. Anika took a deep breath and gathered her thoughts. She'd wanted to discuss this with the team and was glad for the opportunity. 'It's a good point, Sub-Inspector. It's what we call a deviation. I had suspected it. Frankly, it was either that or the killer would have struck the next day, which somehow didn't happen. So, it is a deviation. Deviations like this can indicate several things, especially in cases where we're dealing with a ritualistic or pattern-driven killer.'

She picked up a marker, approached a whiteboard, and sketched a simple timeline. 'Look here,' she said, marking the dates of the murders. 'Killers like this often operate on what we call a *stress–relief cycle*. The time between their crimes can give us clues about their psychological state. A shorter interval usually means an escalation. They might feel an increasing need to complete their "mission", or they might be experiencing external pressures—someone close to them growing suspicious, or fears of being caught.'

Singh frowned. 'So, you think the killer is panicking?'

'Not quite,' Anika replied, shaking her head. 'This doesn't feel like desperation. It feels deliberate. The sudden reduction in the timeline suggests they're recalibrating, adjusting their schedule to align with something important to them. It could mean they're moving towards a climactic act.'

Singh studied her expression. 'Are you saying this might be the endgame?'

'Possibly,' Anika said, her tone measured. 'But not necessarily. In cases like this, we often see a *restorative escalation*. The killer accelerates their actions to regain control of their narrative, especially if they believe their message is being diluted or misunderstood.'

'Restorative escalation,' Verma repeated thoughtfully. 'So, they're speeding up to stay ahead of us or to ensure the story they're trying to tell remains intact?'

'Exactly,' Anika confirmed. 'And here's the critical part: Killers who escalate this way often recalibrate before their final steps. They pause, regroup, and refine their plan. It's not uncommon for there to be a longer gap after an acceleration like this.'

Singh leaned back, his hand on his chin. 'So, we might have more time before the next strike?'

'Yes,' Anika replied, 'but we can't grow complacent. The killer's recalibration could mean one of two things. Either they're planning something significantly larger than what we've seen so far, or they're preparing for the final step in their plan. Either way, the next move will be crucial.'

Singh sighed, his shoulders relaxing slightly. 'That's a relief in a way, but it also raises the stakes.'

Anika nodded. 'Exactly. This recalibration period is both an opportunity and a danger. It gives us a window to disrupt their process, but it also gives them time to perfect whatever comes next. We need to use this time wisely—anticipate their next step, understand their narrative, and identify their endgame.'

Singh asked, 'Is there any way to narrow down their next move? Something about the paintings or the historical narratives that points to what they're building towards? Like you did in the last two crime scenes?'

'That's what I'm hoping for,' Anika replied. 'Each murder corresponds to a specific historical painting and event. If we can map out the sequence of those events and the themes they represent, we might get a clearer picture of where they're heading.'

Singh nodded, and the meeting shifted to logistics. Anika was assigned tasks: building a comprehensive database of paintings, decoding the symbols, and analysing the victims' connections to the killer's narrative.

Anika turned back to the photos and notes, her mind racing. The recalibration meant the killer was entering the most dangerous phase of their plan, and every second counted. Whatever their narrative, their 'masterpiece' was nearing completion, and it was up to her to decipher it before the final act unfolded.

As the team dispersed, Singh lingered, his expression clouded with concern. 'Anika,' he said softly, 'you're doing incredible work, but . . . are you okay? This case seems like it's getting to you.'

Anika offered a tired smile. 'I'm fine, Rajesh. Just . . . this case feels different. It's not just the complexity. It's like the past is demanding to be heard. I can't shake the feeling that there's even more to this than we're seeing.'

Singh rested a hand on her shoulder, his voice steady. 'We'll figure it out, Anika. Just don't push yourself too hard. We need you sharp.' Anika felt the warmth of his touch, and with that came a feeling of connection and reassurance. She quickly dispelled these thoughts from her mind. She needed to focus. Time was running out.

As he left, Anika turned back to the board, the painted figures staring back at her with unspoken secrets. The past was whispering, and she was determined to listen.

With her notes in hand, Anika returned to her office, ready to uncover the killer's narrative before he painted their next masterpiece in blood.

※

CHAPTER 9

The late afternoon sun cast an oppressive glow through the half-drawn venetian blinds of Commissioner Verma's office, cutting harsh lines across the polished wooden desk. The air was heavy with unease, the weight of three unsolved murders pressing down on the room's occupants. Commissioner Verma sat behind his desk, shoulders squared, his expression carefully composed despite the political storm brewing around him.

Anika and Singh had been summoned to the commissioner's office not half an hour after the team meeting at the police headquarters. Anika knew it was something important and felt nervous as she stood near the window, arms crossed, her mind churning as she replayed the morning's discoveries. Singh stood across from her, his arms crossed. The sound of hurried footsteps in the hallway broke the silence, followed by the sharp click of the door opening. Tourism Minister Raghuveer Shekhawat strode in, his gold-rimmed glasses glinting in the slanted sunlight.

'Commissioner Verma. Inspector Singh. Dr Thakur.' Shekhawat's voice was clipped, his usual calm veneer showing cracks. He didn't sit, looming instead as a commanding presence in the room. 'We need to talk.'

'Minister Shekhawat, good to see you, sir,' Verma greeted, gesturing towards a chair.

Shekhawat ignored the invitation to sit, fixing Verma with a steely glare. 'I'm not here for pleasantries, Commissioner. We're four murders in, and what do we have to show for it? Speculations about historical recreations? The city's patience is wearing thin, and so is mine.'

Anika, leaning against the windowsill, met his gaze evenly. 'Minister, I understand your frustration, but we're making progress. The connection to Rajasthani miniature paintings isn't speculation. It's evidence. It's helping us narrow down the killer's methodology and motives.'

Shekhawat's lips pressed into a thin line. 'Evidence that ties us in knots, Dr Thakur. The press is having a field day, the tourism board is in chaos, and the Literature Festival is threatening to pull out if we can't guarantee safety. The optics of this are disastrous. I need arrests, not art analysis.'

Anika's tone remained steady. 'Minister, rushing this investigation would be a mistake. The killer is methodical, precise. If we act without fully understanding their endgame, we risk not only failing but escalating their actions. Every step we take must be calculated.'

Shekhawat's gaze narrowed, and he turned his attention to Verma. 'Commissioner, this isn't the time for academic exercises. Singh, I need Dr Malhotra reinstated on this case immediately. His expertise is . . . practical. And frankly, we need someone who understands the importance of discretion.'

Singh's jaw tightened. 'Dr Malhotra's methods have proven less effective in this particular case. Dr Thakur's insights have brought us closer to understanding the killer's mindset and patterns—'

'Enough, Inspector,' Shekhawat snapped, his voice rising. He turned back to Anika, his tone softening but gaining a veiled edge. 'Dr Thakur, I'm going to give you some advice. This investigation is already treading dangerous ground. I suggest you avoid involving certain . . . circles in your inquiries. Stirring up old royal matters is unnecessary and could complicate things in ways you don't fully understand.'

Anika caught the implication immediately. He looked at Singh, who shook his head imperceptibly, telling her to take it easy. She took a deep breath and said, 'Minister, the evidence dictates the course of this investigation. If it leads us to sensitive areas, then that's where we'll go. The truth is our priority.'

Shekhawat's expression darkened, but he forced a thin smile. 'Be careful, Dr Thakur. The truth is rarely as clear-cut as you think, and pursuing it without considering the consequences can be dangerous for everyone involved.'

Anika didn't flinch. 'Understood, Minister. But I hope I can count on your support when those truths come to light.'

Shekhawat ignored the comment, his focus shifting back to Verma and Singh. 'One week. That's all I can give you to show tangible results. After that, we'll need to reassess leadership for this investigation.'

With that, he turned on his heel and strode out, leaving the room heavy with tension.

Verma exhaled slowly, running a hand over his face. 'He's not a man to be trifled with, Dr Thakur.'

'I'm aware,' Anika said quietly, her arms still crossed. 'But we can't afford to tiptoe around political sensitivities. There's too much at stake.'

Singh shook his head, a smile playing at his lips as Verma nodded reluctantly. 'You truly believe this case is tied to the royal families?'

Anika hesitated, choosing her words carefully. 'The level of detail in these murders, the historical precision, suggests access to knowledge and resources that aren't available to just anyone. We'd be negligent if we didn't investigate that angle.'

'Fair point,' Verma conceded. 'But Shekhawat isn't wrong about the risks. Poking around in royal matters has a way of . . . unearthing things better left buried.'

Anika moved closer, her voice firm. 'But that's our job, Commissioner, to unearth the truth, no matter how uncomfortable it is.'

Verma studied her for a moment, then nodded. 'Agreed. But be careful, Dr Thakur. As Shekhawat said, the deeper we dig, the more dangerous this will become for all of us.'

As Anika and Singh left Verma's office, Anika turned to Singh and said, 'You were quiet in there.'

Singh smiled at her and said, 'I'm used to their bickering and mud-slinging.'

'So, you are with me on questioning the royals?'

'My father always said being a good cop means knowing when to play the game and when to break the rules.'

'Your father was a cop?' Anika asked, intrigued.

'No, a state legislator,' Singh said with a wry smile. 'Taught me a lot about bureaucracy. I just chose a different path.'

Anika smiled faintly. 'It's a good skill to have. We'll need it if we're going to get through this mess.'

Singh nodded. 'So, what's next?'

'Next,' Anika said, her voice firm, 'we meet with the curator of the museum where our last victim worked. If there's a connection to the paintings, we need to find it.'

As they stepped into the busy corridors of the police station, Anika felt the weight of the investigation settle more heavily on her shoulders. The stakes were higher than ever, but she refused to back down. Somewhere in the layers of Jaipur's past lay the key to the killer's motives, and she was determined to uncover it, no matter who tried to stop her.

The Maharaja Sawai Man Singh II Museum, an opulent blend of regal history and architectural grandeur, was cloaked in an uneasy stillness as Anika and Singh made their way through its labyrinthine halls. The usual chatter of tourists was absent, the museum being closed to the public for their investigation. Their footsteps, soft yet deliberate, echoed faintly against the cool marble floors.

Dr Anjali Krishnan, the museum's curator and a renowned scholar in Rajasthani art, led them through the cool, winding corridors. Her composed demeanour was marred by subtle worry lines, the weight of the murders casting a long shadow over her life's work.

'The paintings you're interested in are kept in a special climate-controlled gallery,' Dr Krishnan explained, her soft voice echoing around the centuries-old artefacts adorning the walls. 'They are among the rarest in our collection, and we've taken every precaution to preserve them. We don't often allow close examination, but given the circumstances . . . It's really unfathomable to think they've inspired such atrocities.'

Anika offered a reassuring nod. 'We appreciate your cooperation, Dr Krishnan. Your expertise could help us understand the killer's motives and predict their next move.'

The gallery's temperature shifted as they entered, the air cool and meticulously controlled. Exquisite miniature paintings, displayed under soft, calibrated lights, adorned the walls, their vibrant hues and intricate details seeming to defy time.

Dr Krishnan stopped before a particular section, motioning to four paintings. 'These works correspond to the . . . the events you're investigating,' she said, her voice faltering slightly.

Anika and Singh approached, their eyes taking in the details. Each painting told a story, its details stunningly precise, down to the very elements replicated at the crime scenes.

'It's remarkable,' Singh murmured, his eyes scanning the artwork. 'The killer's knowledge of these paintings and his ability to replicate such intricate details. It's beyond obsession. This is expertise.'

Anika's frown deepened. 'Dr Krishnan, could you walk us through the historical significance of these pieces? What stories are they telling?'

The curator stepped closer, her hands clasped in front of her. 'This first painting depicts the execution of Maharaja Bijal Singh in 1537,' she began, pointing to a delicate image of a ruler struck down in his garden. 'It marked the fall of one dynasty and the rise of another, a moment of immense power shifts in Rajasthan's history.'

She moved to the second piece, its palette alive with saffron flames licking stone battlements. 'Here we have the ritual sacrifice of a handmaiden during the siege of Chittorgarh in 1568. Legend says her death was both a plea for victory and a curse on those who betrayed the fort.'

Dr Krishnan led them farther along the gallery, pausing before another intricate painting. Her expression grew solemn. 'This is one of the most unsettling—*The Silencing of the Palace Rose*, 1735. A royal concubine, Mehrunissa, was executed in the City Palace courtyard for alleged treason that many believe was fabricated.'

Anika leaned closer to the third painting, studying it closely. The concubine, dressed in opulent silks, was shown kneeling in a courtyard surrounded by courtiers. Her expression, one of defiance, contrasted sharply with the dour faces of her onlookers. In the background, the faint outline of the City Palace loomed, unmistakable in its grandeur.

'Dr Krishnan, can you tell me more about this work?' Anika asked.

'The story goes,' Dr Krishnan continued, 'that the concubine, Mehrunissa, was accused of plotting against the then queen and engaging in treasonous correspondence with rival factions. She was condemned without trial and executed publicly to set an example. However, there were rumours that the accusations were fabricated—an elaborate ploy to eliminate a politically inconvenient figure.'

Anika's jaw tightened. 'So, another injustice. A life taken to maintain power and silence dissent.'

Dr Krishnan nodded. 'Yes. This painting has always been controversial. Some historians argue that it romanticises Mehrunissa's final moments, portraying her as a tragic heroine. Others see it as an indictment of the court's hypocrisy and brutality.'

Singh pointed to the corner of the painting, where a small figure stood apart from the crowd, half shrouded in shadow. 'Who's that?'

'Ah,' Dr Krishnan said, her voice dropping slightly. 'That's believed to be the court scribe who recorded the execution. His inclusion in the painting is rare, almost as if the artist suggested that even those tasked with preserving history were complicit in its darker moments.'

Anika's mind raced as she absorbed the parallels to the third murder. 'The killer mirrored this scene almost exactly. The victim's pose, the use of ceremonial ornaments, the setting, it's all here. And this shadowed figure . . .'

Dr Krishnan appeared to hesitate, then crossed to a narrow flat file beneath the wall mounts. A key clicked, and velvet-lined drawers slid out to reveal a palm-sized panel swathed in acid-free tissue.

'This last miniature was considered too disturbing to display,' she murmured, unveiling a midnight blue scene of a stone stepwell. '*The Descent of Dewan Girdhar*, 1615. The court lowered the minister alive into Panna Meena Kund after he exposed corruption. His body was never recovered.'

Anika caught her breath. 'The rope pulley . . . the burning lantern on the ninth stair—exactly what CSI logged at the stepwell murder. The four murders correspond almost perfectly to the depictions in the miniatures. The Amber Fort blood pool, royal dagger, mock-regal posture. The Hawa Mahal victim shamed with a pearl crown and rope—objects linked to public punishment in the zenana. The City Palace staging: sceptre snapped, throne upended, jewels shattered around a kneeling figure. And the most recent victim with the rope pulley and the burning lantern.'

Singh frowned. 'So far, we have four events where power was abused, voices were silenced, and justice was subverted. It's not random. The killer is building towards something.'

Dr Krishnan hesitated before speaking again. 'There's something else you should see,' she said, leading them to a locked cabinet at the back of the gallery. She retrieved a leather-bound volume, its edges worn with age.

'This is a rare collection of miniatures commissioned by a lesser-known Rajput prince in the early 18th century,' she explained, opening the book with careful gloved hands. 'These works were considered too politically sensitive and were never displayed publicly.'

As the pages turned, Anika and Arjun leaned in, catching their breath. Unlike the serene depictions in other miniatures, these paintings chronicled assassinations, betrayals, and cycles of revenge.

'This collection . . .,' Anika said, her eyes scanning the intricate brushwork, 'has all four scenes from those miniatures but in greater detail. Look here.' She pointed to the corner of the second image.

'A string of pearls.'

'That's it! This is the collection the killer is using as a blueprint for the murders,' Anika said, her head reeling.

Dr Krishnan looked stunned. She said, 'The prince who commissioned these paintings wanted to expose the hidden truths of royal politics—the betrayals, the injustices. It's said he had pledged to document what others sought to erase.'

Singh's face grew grim as he turned to Dr Krishnan. 'If the killer is following this particular collection as the guide, then can it tell us where the killer is headed with all this?'

Dr Krishnan carefully turned the collection pages and paused on a particularly elaborate painting. 'This one,' she said softly, 'is called the *Day of Reckoning*. It depicts a public gathering where all secrets are laid bare and justice is served to both the powerful and the powerless.'

Anika felt a chill run down her spine. 'The killer is building towards this,' she said, her voice tight. 'A grand spectacle. Something big. And it won't have just one victim.'

'These paintings,' Anika said, her voice breaking the silence, 'are incredible. I imagine a collection like this must be one of a kind.'

Dr Krishnan nodded solemnly. 'They are. There are no copies, no reproductions. These works are unique, commissioned centuries ago by a lesser-known Rajput prince. They've been in institutional or private care ever since.'

Anika exchanged a glance with Singh, who stepped closer to the case, his expression grim. 'So, to use these paintings as a reference,' he asked, 'someone would need direct access? There are no photographs, no digital records?'

'Correct,' Dr Krishnan said, glancing nervously at the glass case. 'Given their fragility, they've never been fully digitised. Even scholars must go through an extensive approval process to view them. Access is extremely restricted.'

Singh turned to face her fully, his voice carrying a sharper edge. 'Restricted to whom, exactly? Who has that kind of access?'

Dr Krishnan hesitated, shifting on her feet. 'Generally, only approved researchers. But . . . there are exceptions. Members of Jaipur's royal families and certain high-ranking officials have standing permissions. Their ties to Rajasthan's cultural heritage afford them privileges that others don't have.'

Anika stepped closer, her tone careful but insistent. 'Dr Krishnan, we need to know exactly who has accessed this collection in the past few months. If you have visitor logs, we need to see them.'

Her eyes darted to the locked cabinet containing the records. 'This collection is rare,' she said softly. 'Revealing access logs could . . . It could cause a lot of problems, especially if high-profile individuals are involved.'

'We understand the risks,' Anika said, her voice gentle but resolute. 'But we're dealing with a killer who's using these works to commit murder. If we don't act quickly, more lives could be lost. Please, Dr Krishnan.'

The curator hesitated, her hands trembling slightly, before she gave a small nod. 'Very well. Give me a moment.'

Anika and Singh watched as she moved to her desk, unlocking a drawer and pulling out a leather-bound logbook. She carefully opened it, her finger trailing down the neatly written entries.

The room was silent for a moment except for the faint rustle of paper. Then Dr Krishnan stopped, her face going pale. She stared at the page as if it might burn her.

'What is it?' Singh asked, stepping forward. 'Who was it?'

Dr Krishnan slowly lifted her gaze, meeting their eyes with visible reluctance. 'Vikram Singh Rathore,' she said finally, her voice barely above a whisper. 'His name is in the log. He visited about six weeks ago.'

Anika froze, her mind reeling. 'Vikram?' she said, barely able to form the words. 'Are you sure?'

'I remember it clearly,' Dr Krishnan said, wringing her hands. 'His name carries weight. He didn't need to go through the usual process. He said he was researching a personal project on Rajasthani art and history. He spent days here, taking notes, studying the paintings.'

Anika felt as though the air had been knocked out of her lungs. Vikram? Had he been lying to her?

Singh crossed his arms, his expression dark. 'Why would someone like Vikram need to study these paintings so thoroughly? It doesn't make sense.'

'It doesn't add up,' Anika murmured, half to herself. Her voice sharpened as she looked back at the curator. 'Could someone have used his name to gain access? Is there any chance this was a mistake?'

Dr Krishnan shook her head. 'I don't think so. He is a public figure, and I have seen him in the media. He introduced himself personally. He even spoke about his family's contributions to preserving Rajasthan's cultural heritage. It seemed entirely legitimate.'

Anika turned away, pacing as her thoughts churned. 'This doesn't fit. If Vikram had legitimate reasons, why not tell me?'

Singh's voice was low but firm. 'It's one of two things, Dr Thakur. Either it was him, and he's the guy we're after, or someone managed to fool everyone here into thinking he was Vikram, but I think it's doubtful.'

Dr Krishnan spoke hesitantly. 'You must be careful. Accusing someone of Vikram Singh Rathore's stature without solid proof could create a political storm like you can't imagine.'

Anika nodded, her face set with resolve. 'We're not jumping to any conclusions. But we'll need to bring in Vikram for this. Thank you, Dr Krishnan.'

As they left the gallery, Anika's mind raced. How could Vikram be involved? Could he be the killer? Or was someone trying to frame him, but why? The pieces didn't align, but she knew one thing for sure: She was running out of time.

⁂

The late afternoon sun painted long golden streaks across the stone steps of the Jaipur police station. As Anika stepped outside, a cacophony erupted from the waiting crowd. Journalists surged forward, their microphones and cameras thrust into the air, while worried citizens pressed against barricades, their faces etched with fear and desperate curiosity.

'Dr Thakur!' voices clamoured from all directions, each one vying for her attention. Camera flashes popped like staccato gunfire, momentarily blinding her.

She paused, took a measured breath, and stepped forward, her expression calm but resolute.

'Dr Thakur, is it true the killer is recreating historical paintings?' Manoj Dutta's sharp voice cut through the din, his notebook poised for the next scoop. 'Are we dealing with an artistic serial killer?'

Another voice followed quickly. 'And what about the rumours of royal involvement? Is there any truth to the talk of centuries-old curses?'

Anika raised her hands, and the chaotic noise ebbed to a tense murmur. Her voice, clear and steady, carried across the restless crowd. 'I understand your concerns, and I know how frightening this is for all of us. Let me assure you: We are pursuing every lead with the utmost urgency. Our priority is to bring this killer to justice.'

A woman near the front, her voice trembling, called out, 'We don't feel safe in our own house! Should we keep our kids at home from now on?'

Anika locked eyes with her, her tone softening. 'We believe the public at large is not at immediate risk. However, I urge everyone to remain vigilant and report any unusual activity to the police immediately. Together, we can help keep Jaipur safe.'

Dutta pressed forward again. 'Dr Thakur, there are reports that you've identified the killer's methods and motives. Can you elaborate?'

Anika hesitated for a fraction of a second, her mind weighing the balance between public reassurance and the integrity of the investigation. 'We've identified significant patterns in the killer's actions, including connections to Rajasthani history and art. These insights are helping us narrow our focus and anticipate their next move.'

The crowd erupted in a frenzy of questions. 'What kind of art?' 'Are they targeting specific people?' 'Will there be another attack?'

Anika's voice rose above the clamour. 'Please! Speculation and rumours will only help the killer. What we need now is to stay calm, be vigilant, and cooperate with one another. Jaipur has faced challenges before, and we've overcome them through unity. This is no different. Together, we will face this and prevail.'

For a moment, the crowd quieted, her words sinking in. But then, from the back, an accusatory voice rang out: 'How do we know you're not covering for someone powerful? Maybe it's a royal, and you're protecting them!'

Murmurs of agreement rippled through the crowd, and Anika felt the precarious balance tipping. She stepped forward, her tone firm but measured. 'Let me be clear: No one is above the law. Our investigation is impartial, and we follow the evidence wherever it leads. Rest assured, we will uncover the truth.'

Manoj Dutta fired another question. 'Dr Thakur, is political interference slowing down the investigation?'

Singh, who had been busy talking on the phone and directing Kumar to prepare a team to tail Vikram, came running to Anika's aid, seeing how the media was closing in on her like vultures, and interjected with practised care, 'Our team has the full backing of city officials. We're working collaboratively to bring this case to a swift and just resolution.'

A thoughtful voice broke through the noise—a professor, judging by his jacket and scholarly demeanour. 'Dr Thakur, given the historical connections, are you consulting historians or cultural experts?'

'Absolutely,' Anika replied, grateful for the thoughtful question. 'We're working with some of the most knowledgeable experts on Rajasthani history and art to deepen our understanding of the killer's motivations.'

The crowd's tone shifted, curiosity replacing outright fear. Singh sensed an opportunity to bridge the gap between public concern and trust and quickly took it before Anika could be attacked again. 'We are making progress, but this is a complex case. I urge you all to stay vigilant but also to trust that our team is doing everything in its power to bring this killer to justice.'

Commissioner Verma appeared at the top of the steps, motioning for him to wrap up. As Anika and Singh turned to leave, a small voice from the front stopped her in her tracks.

'Dr Thakur!' A young girl, no more than seven, stood clutching her mother's hand. Her wide eyes reflected a mix of fear and hope. 'Are you going to catch the bad person?'

Anika went to the child and crouched to her level, her voice gentle but firm. 'We're doing everything we can, and yes, we will catch the bad person. But we also need your help. Be brave. Look after your friends and family. And remember, there's more good in the world than bad.'

The girl nodded solemnly, her small smile igniting a flicker of warmth in the crowd. Anika stood, sensing that the moment had struck a chord. The press had their sound bite, and the citizens had received a glimmer of reassurance.

As Anika re-entered the station with Singh behind her, Verma fell into step beside her. 'You handled that well, but it's a minefield out there. One wrong word and . . .'

'I know,' Anika replied wearily. 'But they deserve to know the truth. Even if it's hard.'

Verma nodded. 'Let's hope we can give them something solid soon. This city's running out of patience and time.'

As Anika entered the makeshift war room, the conference room in normal times, she glanced at the faces waiting for her brief. The time was running out, and the stakes were growing higher by the day. Somewhere out there, the killer was preparing their next move.

The clock on the wall ticked relentlessly towards 6.00 p.m., its sound barely audible over the hum of computers and the tense voices of the core investigation team. Whiteboards covered in timelines, suspect profiles, and crime scene diagrams dominated one wall, while screens displaying data analysis and surveillance feeds flickered on another.

Anika went to stand at the head of the long table, her eyes scanning the tired but determined faces of her team. Commissioner Verma took a seat to her right, his usual stoic demeanour showing cracks of fatigue and worry. At the same time, Singh sat to her left, opening his laptop before furiously typing on it, cross-referencing the latest data. Other key members of the investigative team—forensics experts, profilers, and senior detectives—filled the remaining seats, their attention focused intently on Anika.

'All right, everyone,' Anika said, her voice steady despite her fatigue. 'We're in a race against time. The killer is escalating. Based on the pattern we've uncovered, their next move isn't far off, and it's going to be big.'

She gestured towards the large screen behind her, which displayed a timeline of the murders overlaid with images of the corresponding Rajasthani miniature paintings. 'Thanks to our work with Dr Krishnan, we've uncovered a specific narrative arc. The killer isn't just recreating art. They're following the storyline depicted in a rare collection of paintings.'

Singh stood, taking over the presentation with a nod from Anika. He tapped the screen, zooming in on the final image, a chilling tableau titled *Day of Reckoning*. 'This painting portrays a mythical event where centuries of wrongs are exposed, and justice is delivered in a grand, public spectacle. We believe the killer is building towards their own version of this, something large-scale and symbolic.

'We've identified the objects and artefacts seen in this particular painting, and Dr Anika and the team of historians and art curators will begin by tracking those. Hopefully, one of the items will give us a strong lead. In the meantime, Kumar has formed a small team of officers who will be tailing Vikram Singh Rathore, whose name has come up a couple of times in this investigation. Dr Thakur has some ideas about the possible locations for the next crime, which she will share with you shortly.'

Singh looked at her and gave her a small troubled smile before saying, 'And Dr Malhotra has been reinstated as the forensic lead on this investigation. We need his expertise to catch this killer.' Singh averted Anika's eyes.

A senior detective leaned forward, his brow furrowed. 'So, what is the location of the next crime? And when?'

Anika adjusted her glasses and stepped towards the screen, pointing to the timeline. 'Let's address the locations first. The Jaipur Literature Festival is an obvious choice. It's public, symbolic, and internationally significant. If the killer wants maximum attention, it's the ideal stage for their so-called Day of Reckoning. But,' she paused, glancing at the team, 'if they're following the curse of Chandravati narrative, the Temple of Chandravati becomes critical. It ties directly to the historical context of the paintings and could provide them with a secluded yet dramatically symbolic venue.'

Commissioner Verma, who had been silently listening, interjected, 'Anika, how do we split resources between two such different locations? We can't stretch ourselves too thin. We risk losing the killer entirely.'

Anika nodded. 'I agree, Commissioner. That's why we need a tiered approach. Team One focuses on securing the Literature Festival. They'll work closely with event organisers to vet every participant and establish discreet surveillance. We must treat every corner of the venue as a potential crime scene.'

Singh leaned forward. 'And what about the temple?'

'Team Two will handle that,' Anika said. 'It's a remote location, and we can position a smaller unit there under the guise of a routine security drill. It will also serve as a fallback if the killer changes their pattern or tries to misdirect us. I'll need Officers Kumar and Shilpa to coordinate efforts on both fronts.'

Kumar, who had been scribbling notes furiously, looked up. 'What about tracking the artefacts? If we locate even one from the painting, it might give us a clearer picture of their plans or, at least, confirm the location.'

'Exactly,' Anika replied. 'I'll oversee that personally, working with Dr Krishnan and other historians. If the killer needs these items to complete their narrative, they're either already in possession or planning to acquire them soon. That gives us a window of opportunity to intercept.'

Verma tapped his foot against the leg of the table. 'And Vikram Singh Rathore? What's the approach there?'

Anika hesitated for a fraction of a second before answering. 'We treat him as a person of interest. Surveillance only. He's cooperative and has been assisting us so far, but we can't ignore the connections that have come up. If he's involved, this will either confirm it or eliminate him from suspicion.'

A murmur of agreement rippled through the room, though Anika could feel the weight of Verma's gaze on her. She met his eyes briefly, understanding the unspoken message: Treading carefully around someone of Vikram's status was as much about politics as it was about evidence.

Dr Malhotra, freshly reinstated, cleared his throat. 'I'll ensure forensic teams are on standby for both locations. If we're lucky, the killer will leave behind traceable evidence during their preparations.'

Anika's jaw tightened slightly, but she pushed aside her personal reservations. 'Thank you, Dr Malhotra. Your team's quick response will be critical.'

A senior detective broke the brief silence. 'Dr Thakur, how confident are you that this lead will narrow down the timing about the constellations?'

Anika exhaled, glancing at the intricate patterns on the screen. 'It's a complex lead, but promising. The killer is meticulous, even ritualistic, in his methods. If he's following astrological patterns as they align with historical events, we can use that to predict their next move. But it's not foolproof.'

Singh, sensing the room's growing tension, leaned forward. 'We're working with incomplete information, but this team has achieved remarkable breakthroughs. Let's stay focused. The stakes couldn't be higher, and we can't afford to overlook any detail.'

The room fell quiet, the gravity of his words settling over the team. Anika glanced at her watch, the ticking seconds a reminder of how little time they had. She straightened, her voice firm. 'We're running out of time, but we're not out of options. We'll work in parallel, securing the festival, monitoring the temple, tracking the artefacts, and digging into Vikram's connections. Every piece of this puzzle matters, and the killer is counting on us missing something. Let's prove him wrong.'

The room erupted into motion as team members filed out to their respective tasks, a renewed sense of urgency driving them. Verma lingered by the table, his expression unreadable.

'You're certain about tailing Vikram?' he asked quietly, his tone almost wary.

'I am,' Anika replied with conviction.

Verma nodded slowly, then walked towards the door. 'Let's hope we catch the killer before anyone else gets hurt.'

As he left, Anika turned back to the screen, the chilling image of the *Day of Reckoning* painting still glowing faintly. The answers they needed lay somewhere in its intricate details, and the countdown to a deadly climax.

⚘

The *Jaipur Chronicle* newsroom hummed with the familiar chaos of an approaching deadline. The rapid-fire clicking of keyboards mingled with hurried conversations and the occasional bark of an editor demanding rewrites. Fluorescent lights cast a harsh glow below, accentuating the tired eyes and coffee-stained desks of journalists racing against the clock.

Manoj Dutta sat hunched over his computer, fingers flying across the keyboard as he fine-tuned his latest article on the city's water conservation efforts. Despite the pressing deadline, his mind wandered back to the serial killer case gripping Jaipur. As the *Chronicle*'s star investigative reporter, Manoj had been covering the murders from the beginning, but he knew in his gut that there was a lot more to the story than what the police were revealing.

His phone buzzed, displaying an unknown number. Manoj hesitated momentarily before answering, his journalistic instincts on high alert. 'Manoj Dutta speaking.'

'Mr Dutta . . .,' came a raspy voice, distorted as if by a voice modulator. 'I have information about the Jaipur killer case, information the police don't want the public to know.'

Manoj's heart raced, but he kept his tone measured. 'I'm listening. But I'll need to verify any information you provide.'

'Check your email in two minutes. You'll receive all the proof you need. But act fast, Mr Dutta. Lives depend on this information.'

The line went dead. Manoj stared at his phone, mind whirling with possibilities. '*Who the hell was that?*'

Two minutes later, on the dot, his email pinged. Manoj opened the message, his eyes widening as he scanned its contents. Attached were photographs of crime scene evidence, internal police memos, and, most shockingly, a detailed analysis linking the murders to specific historical paintings.

As he studied the documents, Manoj felt an excitement tinged with dread. This was explosive information, the kind of scoop that could make a career. But if it was genuine, it also meant the killer was operating on a level far more complex and dangerous than they had realised. The documents didn't just reference well-known historical events; they touched on the shadowy corners of Jaipur's past. There were mentions of secret treaties between rival Rajput clans, coded messages hidden in seemingly innocuous court poetry, and ritual practices that blended Hindu traditions with Mughal influences. This syncretism had been carefully erased from official historical records. This wasn't just a killer with a history fetish; this was someone with access to information that had been suppressed from the masses for centuries.

'Dutta! Where's that water conservation piece?' his editor's voice boomed across the newsroom.

Manoj looked up, momentarily disoriented. 'Coming, sir. Just . . . just doing a final proofread.'

He quickly sent off the completed article, his mind already racing ahead to the story that now demanded to be written. But a nagging doubt crept in as he began to organise his thoughts. How had his caller obtained this information? Could publishing it jeopardise the investigation or, worse, play into the killer's hands?

Manoj pushed back from his desk, needing to clear his head. He made his way to the small break room, pouring himself a cup of stale coffee. As he sipped the bitter liquid, he weighed his options. On one hand, the public had a right to know the true nature of the threat they faced. If the killer was indeed recreating historical scenes, it could help the public be more vigilant. Moreover, the documents hinted at possible connections to Jaipur's royal families, a bombshell that could shake the city's power structures to the core.

On the other hand, revealing this information could cause panic, impede the police investigation, and potentially provoke the killer into accelerating their plans. There was also the question of the caller's motive. Was this a whistle-blower trying to force the police into action, or could it be the killer himself, playing some twisted game with the media?

Lost in thought, Manoj didn't notice his editor, Girish Kumar Gupta, enter the break room until the older man spoke. 'You look like you're carrying the weight of all Rajasthan on your shoulders, Dutta. Everything okay?'

Manoj hesitated, then made a split-second decision. For all his gruffness, Gupta was one of the most ethical journalists he knew. Who better to consult with regarding such a delicate matter?

Dutta leaned closer to Gupta and said in a low voice, 'I've received some . . . sensitive information about the multiple murder case.' Dutta continued cautiously, 'Game-changing stuff, if it's legitimate. But publishing it could have serious consequences.'

Gupta's bushy eyebrows rose. 'How sensitive are we talking?'

Manoj outlined the contents of the email, watching his editor's expression shift from scepticism to shock. 'Wow, Dutta,' Gupta muttered when Manoj finished. 'This is . . . If it's true, it's the biggest story to hit Jaipur in decades.'

'I know,' Manoj agreed. 'But is it really our place to release this information? What if it does more harm than good?'

Gupta was quiet for a long moment, absently stirring his coffee. When he spoke, his voice was uncharacteristically soft. 'You know, Dutta, in all my years in this business, I've learned one thing: The truth always has consequences. Sometimes good, sometimes bad, often both. Our job isn't to manage those consequences. Our job is to uncover the truth and present it to the public.' He fixed Manoj with a stern gaze. 'But—and this is a big but—we have to be damn sure it is the truth. Have you verified any of this information?'

Manoj shook his head. 'Not yet. I was planning to reach out to some contacts in the police department, maybe try to corroborate some details with art historians as well.'

Gupta nodded approvingly. 'Good. Do that. And, Dutta? Be careful. You'll be kicking a hornet's nest if there's any truth to the royal family connection. Make sure you're prepared for the sting.'

As Manoj returned to his desk, he made up his mind. He would pursue the story methodically, verifying every detail before even considering publication. He began making calls, carefully framing his questions so that they wouldn't reveal the full scope of what he knew.

As the clock ticked away, Manoj's phone buzzed incessantly as confirmation after confirmation rolled in. A breathless junior officer spilled information about art historian consultations. Minutes later, a City Palace Museum assistant confirmed frantic police interest in specific paintings. With each verification, Vikram's pulse quickened, and the story's weight on him grew heavier by the second.

The newsroom emptied, and darkness fell, but Manoj barely noticed. His fingers flew over his keyboard, cross-referencing leaked documents with historical records at a frenzied pace. Each connection sparked a jolt of adrenaline, the story's explosive potential building to a fever pitch.

Finally, as midnight approached, Manoj began to write. His fingers flew across the keyboard, bringing together the complex threads of his groundbreaking piece on ancient art that was the blueprint to the modern-day murders. He wrote of a killer obsessed with righting historical wrongs, of a police force struggling to decipher centuries-old clues, and of dark secrets lurking in the shadows of Jaipur's majestic palaces.

As he neared the end of his draft, Manoj paused, his cursor hovering over the section that hinted at the royal family's involvement in this macabre tale. This was the most incendiary part of the story, the claim that could upend Jaipur's social and political canvas. Did he dare include it without more concrete proof?

A memory flashed through his mind. Dr Anika Thakur, with her careful words and guarded expressions, was at the press conference. She knew more than she was letting on, and Manoj was certain, and it was to be expected. The police were not going to give everything away; it would put the investigation and even the public at risk.

Perhaps it was time to force Thakur's hand, to push the investigation into the open where the truth couldn't be buried. Of course, there will be consequences. But could he completely accept what Gupta told him earlier? 'Our work is not to manage the consequences but to present the truth.'

With a deep breath, Manoj made his decision. He left the royal family connection in, carefully worded to imply rather than accuse. As he typed the final sentence, he felt a mix of exhilaration and fear. This story could either make or end his career.

The sky was now lit with a predawn glow as Manoj sent the finished article to Gupta's inbox. He sat back, exhausted but wired, knowing that Jaipur would wake up to a story that would change everything in a few short hours.

As he gathered his things to head home to catch a few hours of sleep, Manoj's phone buzzed with a text from an unknown number: 'Well done, Mr Dutta. The truth will set us all free.'

A chill ran down Manoj's spine. How did the caller know about Manoj's story? It hasn't even been published yet. Had he just done exactly what the killer wanted?

As he stepped out into the quiet streets of early morning Jaipur, Manoj couldn't shake the feeling that he had just set in motion events that would have far-reaching and possibly tragic consequences. Had he made the right decision to publish the story? Little tendrils of doubt began to creep into his mind.

The Pink City was still sleeping, unaware of the bombshell about to drop. But soon, very soon, the quiet would be shattered. And Manoj Dutta, for better or worse, would be at the centre of the storm.

CHAPTER 10

The early morning calm of Jaipur was shattered to bits as the city awoke to Manoj Dutta's explosive article. The story spread like wildfire, igniting conversations and speculation in every corner of the Pink City.

The usual morning bustle took on a frantic edge at Tapri Central, a popular coffee shop near Statue Circle. Gautam, a young IT professional, burst through the door, waving his smartphone.

'Have you guys seen this?' he exclaimed to his friends, who were already huddled over their own devices. 'The killer is recreating historical paintings! And there might be a connection to the royal families!'

Shripriya, a local artist, looked up from her latte, her eyes wide. 'I can't believe it. I've studied those miniature paintings. They're so beautiful, so innocent. To think someone's using them as inspiration for murder . . .' She shuddered.

An older man at the next table scoffed, 'Nonsense. It's just sensationalism. The *Chronicle*'s always stirring up trouble. Especially Manoj Dutta.'

'But the article has photographs, Uncle,' Gautam argued. 'Crime scene images that match those paintings exactly. How do you explain that?'

As the debate heated up, the cafe owner, Joshi, watched with growing concern. He'd seen Jaipur weather many storms, but this felt different. The fear was palpable, seeping into the very air of his beloved cafe.

Across town at the bustling Johari Bazaar, the news spread from stall to stall, mixed with equal parts fascination and terror.

'They say the next attack might happen at the Literature Festival,' whispered Mrs Chitti to her long-time jewellery vendor, Fareed.

Fareed shook his head grimly. 'My cousin works security at the City Palace. He says the police have been swarming the place, looking at old paintings. It must be true.'

A group of foreign tourists, oblivious to the local gossip, approached a nearby stall. The shopkeeper, usually eager for business, hesitated before plastering on a smile. As he haggled over prices for colourful textiles, he couldn't help but wonder: Could one of these outsiders be the killer, hiding in plain sight?

Meanwhile, in a trendy apartment in C-Scheme, social media influencer Zara Hussain was live-streaming her reaction to the news to her thousands of followers.

'Okay, guys, this is insane,' she said, her usually perfectly composed face etched with worry. 'I've always promoted Jaipur as this magical, safe destination. But now? I don't know what to tell my followers. Should people still come to the Lit Fest? Are we all in danger?'

Comments flooded in, ranging from support to scepticism to outright panic. Zara read a few:

'OMG, I'm supposed to visit next week. Should I cancel?'

'This has to be fake news. No way the royals are involved.'

'I bet it's a publicity stunt for some new Netflix series.'

Zara sighed, running a hand through her hair. 'I don't know what to believe, you guys. But please, let's not spread rumours. Stick to verified information.' Even as she said it, Zara knew her words would do little to stem the tide of speculation. She could already see hashtags trending: #JaipurKiller, #RoyalConspiracy, #ArtfulMurderer.

At Jaipur's Central Park, morning walkers gathered in small groups, their usual exercise routines forgotten as they debated the news.

'I always knew those old paintings were cursed,' declared Mrs Saxena, a retired schoolteacher. 'All that violence and betrayal, it was bound to attract dark energies.'

Her walking partner, Dr Reddy, rolled his eyes. 'Don't be superstitious, Roushika. This is clearly the work of a very disturbed individual. The question is, how did they get access to all this historical information?'

A young jogger slowed to join the conversation. 'My sister Heeral works at a museum. She says the police have been asking weird questions about visitor logs and restricted archives. What if the killer is someone known, someone with special access?'

The idea sent a ripple of unease through the group. Suddenly, the familiar faces of fellow park-goers seemed tinged with suspicion. Who could be trusted when the killer might be someone hiding behind a veneer of respectability?

As the morning wore on, the reaction spread beyond Jaipur's physical spaces and exploded online. Local Facebook groups, usually filled with event announcements and restaurant recommendations, became hotbeds of speculation.

On the Jaipur Heritage Lovers group, a heated debate broke out:

> **Moderator**: *Let's please keep discussions factual and avoid naming specific individuals or families.*

> **User1**: *How can we ignore the royal connection? If they're involved, the public has a right to know!*

> **User2**: *My neighbour's brother is a cop. He says they're bringing in special forces to protect the royal family. Why would they need protection if they're not targets?*

> **User 3**: *Or maybe they need protection because they're suspects! Wake up, people!*

> **Moderator**: *Final warning. Any more unsubstantiated accusations and I'll have to lock this thread.*

The moderator's plea did little to quell the frenzy. Within hours, amateur sleuths were combing through historical records, posting side-by-side comparisons of paintings and crime scene photos (some genuine, many fake), and constructing elaborate theories connecting centuries-old events to the present-day murders.

At the luxury Rambagh Palace Hotel, the staff struggled to maintain an air of calm as worried guests approached the concierge desk.

'Is it safe to go sightseeing today?' asked a nervous European couple.

The concierge, Ishaan, smiled reassuringly. 'Of course, sir, madam. Jaipur remains one of India's safest tourist destinations. Perhaps you'd like a guided tour of City Palace? I can arrange for one of our best guides.'

As the couple walked away, still looking uncertain, Ishaan's colleague leaned in. 'Should we really be sending them to City Palace? What if . . . you know . . .'

Ishaan sighed. 'We can't let fear paralyse the whole city. But maybe call Yashraj and tell him to stick to the main tourist areas for now.'

By midday, the panic had reached a fever pitch. Schools reported record absenteeism as parents kept children home. The Amber Fort, usually teeming with tourists, saw visitor numbers plummet. Local tour guides found themselves fielding more questions about the murders than about Jaipur's architectural marvels.

At the Ganesh Temple in Moti Dungri, the line of devotees seeking blessings stretched around the block. Many clutched copies of the *Jaipur Chronicle*, praying for protection against the evil that seemed to have descended upon their city.

As evening approached, Jaipur's famous rooftop restaurants, typically filled with tourists watching the sunset, sat eerily empty. A heated argument broke out at Bar Palladio, known for its stylish clientele.

'This is ridiculous,' declared Aarti, a well-known socialite. 'I've known the royal families my whole life. There's no way they're involved in something so . . . so sordid.'

Her companion, a visiting Delhi businessman, wasn't convinced. 'Money and power can hide all sorts of sins, darling. Haven't you read your history?'

As glasses clinked and voices rose, the bartender glanced at the manager worriedly. The fear and suspicion infecting the city seemed to be seeping even into its most exclusive spaces.

Meanwhile, in the narrow lanes of the old city, long-time residents gathered on stoops and in small shops, sharing worried whispers.

'They say the killer is trying to right old wrongs,' murmured Murli Dadi, the neighbourhood's eldest resident. 'But who are we to judge the sins of our ancestors? This will only bring more pain, mark my words.'

As night fell, an uneasy quiet settled over Jaipur. Streets that were usually lively with evening shoppers and diners lay quiet. Those who dared to venture out walked quickly, glancing over their shoulders and seeing potential threats in every shadow.

In homes across the city, families huddled around television sets, watching as talking heads debated the implications of Dutta's article. Phones buzzed constantly with messages from concerned relatives in other cities, asking if the news was really true.

On a popular late-night radio show, the host tried to calm fears: 'Let's remember, Jaipur has faced challenges before. We are a city of resilience, of beauty, of history. We cannot let fear divide us or blind us to the truth. Stay vigilant, yes, but also stay united.'

But as midnight approached and the city tried to sleep, the words of reassurance felt hollow to many. In the darkness, imaginations ran wild. Every unexplained noise and every passing shadow seemed to carry the threat of danger.

Jaipur, the beloved Pink City, had always proudly displayed its history. But now, that history seemed to have come alive in the most terrifying way possible. As the night wore on, these questions reverberated in the minds of its sleepless citizens: Where would the killer strike next? And could anyone truly be safe when the past itself seemed to be seeking vengeance?

✿

The war room at the Jaipur police station buzzed with tense energy, the usual focus fractured by the fallout of Manoj Dutta's article. Phones rang incessantly, and officers whispered urgently as they scrambled to assess the damage. Commissioner Verma paced at the head of the room, his jaw clenched.

'How did this happen?' Verma demanded, his voice slicing through the murmur of activity. 'I want to know who leaked this information, and I want answers now!'

Anika stood nearby, her fingers tightening around the edge of the table. 'Sir, while we investigate the source of the leak, our priority should be reassessing our strategy and mitigating the fallout,' she said, her voice steady but urgent.

Verma exhaled sharply, nodding. 'Agreed. Sinha, coordinate with cybercrime to trace the breach. Shukla, prepare a statement for the media. And I want updates on our Literature Festival security plans immediately.'

Singh approached Anika, lowering his voice. 'This complicates things. Do we bring Vikram in for questioning now that the article has tied the royal families to the case?'

Anika shook her head. 'Not yet. We don't have enough evidence, and we can't risk drawing unnecessary attention or creating panic. Let's keep the surveillance in place and discreet.'

Before Singh could respond, an officer handed Verma a note. His expression darkened as he read it. 'We've received a message from the killer,' he said grimly, passing the note to Anika.

She scanned the elegant calligraphy script:

The stage is set. The actors are in place. Jaipur will be my canvas, history my palette. Solve the riddle before the final brushstroke falls.

The room fell silent as the weight of the words sank in.

'Run a full analysis on this message,' Singh ordered. 'Handwriting, paper, any trace evidence. We also need to reassess other public venues tied to historical events. The killer is taunting us, and we need to stay ahead.'

Anika nodded, her tone resolute. 'No more mistakes. We've been outmanoeuvred once, but it won't happen again. Let's get to work.'

As the team dispersed, Anika studied the killer's message again, her mind racing. The leak had thrown the investigation into chaos, but it also presented an opportunity. If the killer wanted a spectacle, they were making themselves vulnerable. This time, Anika vowed, they would be ready.

⁂

The harsh lights of the television studio bore down on Anika as she sat in the make-up chair, the rushed activity around her a blur. The air was heavy with the chemical tang of hairspray and the unspoken tension of the moment. She had protested against this appearance, arguing that it would only complicate the investigation. Still, Commissioner Verma had insisted it was time to take control of the narrative and calm the city's growing unease.

'Almost done,' the make-up artist murmured, patting Anika's forehead with a brush. 'The lights can be brutal.'

Anika offered a distracted nod, her mind racing through the carefully crafted points she intended to make. There was no room for missteps. She needed to project calm and competence while revealing as little as possible about the investigation's progress.

A production assistant appeared beside her. 'Dr Thakur, we're ready.'

Straightening her shoulders, Anika followed the assistant onto the brightly lit set of *Jaipur Tonight*. Designed to look warm and inviting, the studio's cosy façade was betrayed by the cold precision of cameras, cables, and monitors. Kiran Kapoor, the show's sharp-eyed host, greeted her with a practised smile.

'Dr Sharma, thank you for being here,' Kiran said, her tone smooth. 'I know this is a challenging time for you and the city.'

'Thank you for having me,' Anika replied, shaking Kiran's hand with a firm grip. 'It's important to address the public's concerns.'

As she sat down, Anika spotted the other guest: Manoj Dutta. The journalist responsible for the recent leak lounged in his chair with an air of triumph. Their eyes met briefly, and Anika suppressed a surge of irritation. Of course, they would invite him.

'Two minutes to air,' the floor manager called out.

Kiran leaned closer, lowering her voice. 'I know you're not thrilled about this, Dr Thakur, but I hope we can have an honest discussion. The public deserves transparency.'

Anika's expression remained neutral. 'I understand, but I will not compromise the investigation.'

The countdown began, and as the red light blinked on, Anika pushed aside her unease, ready for the battle ahead.

'Good evening, Jaipur,' Kiran began, her tone authoritative. 'Tonight, we address the ongoing investigation into the murders that have shaken our city. With us are Dr Anika Thakur, the forensic psychologist leading the case, and journalist Manoj Dutta, whose recent article has sparked intense public debate. Dr Thakur, let's begin with you. How close are the police to catching the killer?'

Anika leaned forward slightly, her voice steady. 'I want to reassure the public that we are making significant progress. While I can't share specific details, I can say that we are following strong leads and using every resource available to bring this case to a resolution.'

Kiran nodded, turning to Dutta. 'Mr Dutta, your article revealed connections between the murders and historical paintings. Can you elaborate?'

Dutta's eyes gleamed with satisfaction. 'Thank you, Kiran. Yes, my sources revealed that each crime scene mirrors a specific Rajasthani miniature painting, suggesting the killer is deeply knowledgeable about the city's artistic and cultural history.'

Anika felt her jaw tighten at his casual disclosure of sensitive information. 'While we are examining every potential motive and methodology,' she interjected, her tone professional but firm, 'releasing incomplete information without context risks creating confusion and could even endanger lives.'

Kiran seized the tension. 'Dr Thakur, are you saying Mr Dutta's report is inaccurate?'

'I'm saying that complex investigations require discretion,' Anika replied evenly. 'Prematurely publicising details can provoke unintended consequences, including giving the killer insight into our methods or spurring them to act more recklessly.'

Dutta leaned forward, undeterred. 'Surely the public has a right to know if these murders follow a pattern, especially if it helps them protect themselves?'

'The public's safety is our top priority,' Anika countered. 'That's why it's crucial to release information responsibly. Speculation and panic only make our job harder and put people at greater risk.'

Kiran shifted gears. 'What about the suggestion of a connection to Jaipur's royal families? Can you address those rumours?'

Anika took a steadying breath. 'We're investigating every angle, including historical and contemporary ties. But I must emphasise that we cannot draw conclusions without evidence. Speculating about specific individuals or groups is both irresponsible and counterproductive.'

Dutta leaned back, a faint smirk on his lips. 'So, you're saying the royals are above suspicion?'

'No one is above scrutiny,' Anika replied sharply. 'Our investigation is impartial. But baseless accusations only distract from the work of finding the killer.'

The exchange left the air in the studio taut with tension. Kiran, sensing an opportunity for drama, pressed further. 'Dr Thakur, how has the leaked information affected the investigation?'

Anika paused, choosing her words carefully. 'The leak has forced us to adapt our strategies. If the killer changes their behaviour in response to the publicity, it could complicate our efforts. However, I assure you, we remain undeterred. Our focus is on catching this individual and preventing further harm.'

Dutta interjected, 'Or perhaps the leak has cornered the killer, forcing them to make a mistake?'

'Or provoked them to escalate their plans,' Anika said coldly. 'This is not a game, Mr Dutta. Real lives are at stake.'

Kiran stepped in, her tone brisk. 'Dr Thakur, with the Literature Festival approaching, what security measures are in place?'

Anika welcomed the shift in focus. 'We've implemented increased security across the city, with special attention to high-profile events like the festival. We urge the public to remain vigilant but not let fear disrupt their daily lives.'

The interview continued, a delicate dance of managing public perception while protecting the integrity of the investigation. Finally, as the segment drew to a close, Kiran turned to Anika. 'Dr Thakur, any final words for our viewers?'

Anika met the camera's gaze directly. 'Jaipur is a resilient city, built on a foundation of strength and community. We are working tirelessly to resolve this case. I urge everyone to stay vigilant, support one another, and trust that justice will prevail. Together, we will overcome this dark chapter.'

As the cameras cut, Anika exhaled deeply, the burden of the interview pressing down on her. Rising from her seat, she brushed past Dutta, who called after her with a sly grin, 'You handled that well, Dr Thakur. But the truth has a way of coming out.'

She stopped, turning to meet his gaze. 'The truth is rarely simple, Mr Dutta. When it does come out, I hope you're prepared to face it.'

Exiting the studio into the warm Jaipur night, Anika felt both relief and fortitude. Somewhere out there, the killer was watching, possibly recalibrating their plans in response to the broadcast. But Anika had made her move. It was time to press forward and outmanoeuvre the darkness threatening her city.

The real battle, she knew, was beginning.

The first rays of dawn cast a soft glow over Jaipur as Anika strode into her office at the police station. Despite the early hour, the building hummed with activity. Her desk was cluttered with case files, news clippings, and books on Rajasthani history.

Anika had barely settled into her chair when a knock at the door signalled the arrival of her team. Singh entered first, followed by Dr Priya Sharma from forensics, Sub-Inspector Kumar, Assistant Sub-Inspector Shilpa Nair, and Kavita Mehta, the media consultant recently brought on board to manage the growing public scrutiny. Commissioner Verma joined them moments later, his presence immediately grounding the room.

'Good morning, everyone,' Anika greeted, gesturing for them to sit.

Commissioner Verma introduced Kavita to everyone and said, 'I've called in Kavita to help us contain the damage Dutta has caused. From now on, no one will engage with the media without consulting with Kavita first.' He turned to Kavita and nodded.

Kavita adjusted her glasses, her sharp gaze sweeping the room. 'As we all know, Jaipur police's reputation is on the line here, and we are not doing well at all. The public is still reeling from the leaked information. The royal family angle is dominating the headlines, and the narrative is spiralling out of control. People are speculating about everything from ancient curses to political cover-ups. If we don't control this, it will only get worse.'

Verma, seated at the head of the table, leaned forward. 'What do you suggest?'

Kavita tapped her pen against her notepad thoughtfully. 'We need a tangible shift in perception. At present, everyone's fixated on the killer's methods and the historical connections. We need to bring attention to the investigation itself, the progress made, and the measures taken to protect the city.'

Singh frowned. 'But revealing too much will compromise the investigation.'

'Agreed,' Kavita replied. 'But we can be strategic. Highlight the advanced forensic techniques we're using, the collaboration with historical experts, and the increased security measures. Give the public confidence without tipping our hand.'

Anika considered this. 'Priya, any updates from forensics we can safely share?'

Priya checked her notes. 'We've identified a rare type of silk fibre found at the last crime scene. It was historically used in royal garments but is almost non-existent today. We're tracing potential sources. And the mineral traces found at the Thakur Rani Garden don't match with the garden's soil composition. They match the composition of soil found in the Aravalli Hills.'

'So, the killer must have brought this soil from somewhere in the hill range,' Kumar muttered.

'Yes,' Priya confirmed. 'We've also found trace amounts of a specific pollen mixed with the soil. It's from the dhok tree, also native to the Aravalli region.'

Anika's mind whirled with the implications. 'The killer must be connected to the hills then.' She looked at Kavita and said, 'Is this good? It's specific enough to show progress but vague enough to avoid giving too much away.'

Kavita nodded thoughtfully before making a note in her pad.

'What about Dutta?' Shilpa asked. 'He's not going to back off. He'll keep digging for more dirt.'

Anika's lips curved into a smile. 'Then we give him something to dig for. We can arrange for a "confidential" briefing. Share details about increased patrols in historical areas and enhanced surveillance. Let him feel like he's getting an exclusive, but nothing that compromises the investigation.'

Kumar nodded, jotting down notes. 'It's a good idea.'

Verma nodded. 'That sounds good.' He turned to Kavita and added, 'And what about the royals?'

'Right now, it looks like the investigation is targeting the royals, whether intentionally or not. That's feeding into public mistrust. If we one of the royals, say someone as powerful as Vikram Singh Rathore, into the fold more visibly, we can counter this.'

Anika frowned, her expression sceptical. 'You want us to involve him publicly? Given the rumours, that could backfire.'

'Not necessarily,' Kavita countered. 'Vikram has already assisted with the investigation so far. Inspector Singh told me about how he let you access the restricted texts in the Royal Archives, the *Rahasya-Lekh*.

If we formalise his involvement, it sends a strong message: The police aren't targeting the royals. They're working with them. It also deflates a lot of the public speculation about a cover-up.'

Verma stroked his chin thoughtfully. 'That's an interesting angle. It could help shift the narrative away from a royal conspiracy.'

'And,' Kavita added, glancing at Anika and Singh, 'it gives you both a legitimate reason to keep him close. If there's even the slightest chance Vikram is connected to the case, directly or indirectly, it's easier to monitor him if he's part of the team. He'll have fewer reasons to hide anything, and any information he provides can be scrutinised in real time.'

Kumar, sitting next to Anika, raised an eyebrow. 'You're suggesting we bring him in as a collaborator to keep him in check?'

'Exactly,' Kavita said, her tone firm. 'It's a win-win. The public sees cooperation instead of conflict, and you get to keep a closer eye on him without it appearing adversarial.'

Singh leaned back in his chair, considering the proposal. 'And what happens if he *is* connected? If the killer is using his name, or worse, if Vikram himself is involved, we'll have handed him inside access to our investigation.'

'That's a risk,' Kavita admitted. 'But from a public perception standpoint, it's far better to involve him openly than to keep him at arm's length if he turns out to be a strong suspect. Right now, the lack of transparency is fuelling suspicion. By making him a visible ally, you're reframing the story.'

Verma looked at Anika, his expression serious. 'What do you think? You've worked with Vikram closely so far. Do you trust him?'

Anika hesitated. Vikram had been helpful, opening doors to resources she wouldn't have accessed otherwise. But the revelation that someone had used his name to study the controversial paintings had cast a shadow of doubt. Could she balance professional caution with the benefits of his involvement?

'I trust his commitment to protecting Jaipur's history,' she said finally. 'But I also think he may be hiding something.'

Kavita interjected, 'Then keep him close, Dr Thakur. This is the best way to find out if he's hiding something. And if he's innocent, his involvement strengthens our position.'

Anika turned to Singh. 'What do you think, Rajesh?'

Singh nodded slowly. 'It's a sound strategy. Vikram's influence could open doors we can't, and involving him publicly shifts the narrative in our favour. The royals will be more open to being investigated if Vikram is involved. But we need to set clear boundaries. If he's part of this, he can't have unrestricted access to the investigation.'

Verma sighed, the weight of the decision evident in his posture. 'All right. Anika, arrange a meeting with Vikram. Explain the situation and gauge his willingness to cooperate publicly. Make it clear that this isn't an invitation to meddle. It's a formal role, with defined parameters.'

Anika nodded. 'Understood.'

As the team began to disperse, Verma lingered behind. 'Dr Thakur,' he said quietly, 'I know this isn't ideal, but Kavita's right. Keeping him close is the best way to manage this situation, for the public and for us. Just . . . be careful. The stakes are high, and this could blow up in ways we can't predict.'

Anika met his gaze, her resolve firm. 'I'll handle it, Commissioner.'

As she returned to her desk, she picked up her phone and scrolled to Vikram's number. Kavita's reasoning was sound, and Verma's directive was clear. It was time to bring Vikram further into the fold, whether as an ally or under scrutiny remained to be seen.

She pressed *call*. Vikram answered on the fifth ring, his voice calm. 'Anika. I had a feeling I'd be hearing from you.'

'Vikram,' she began, keeping her tone neutral. 'Will you be open to being involved in the investigation openly? Commissioner Verma would like to formalise your role.'

There was a pause on the line, then Vikram spoke, his voice measured. 'I see. And this formal role comes with conditions, I assume?'

'It does,' Anika confirmed. 'Full transparency. Defined boundaries. And a willingness to collaborate publicly. Are you willing to work with us on these terms?'

Vikram's tone shifted slightly, a touch of wry amusement. 'Publicly, is it? Clever. You're making me part of the story to control it.'

'It's not just about control,' Anika said firmly. 'It's about ensuring transparency and trust. If you're serious about helping Jaipur, this is how you do it.'

There was a long silence. Finally, Vikram said, 'Very well. I'll do it. But, Anika, when this is over, I hope you'll understand why I've been cautious about certain truths.'

Anika's grip on the phone tightened. 'Just make sure those truths don't jeopardise the investigation, Vikram. We're playing with fire here.'

'I'll see you around,' he replied before hanging up.

As she set the phone down, Anika felt a mixture of relief and unease. Kavita's plan was in motion, and Vikram was now officially part of their strategy. But she couldn't shake the feeling that involving him had added another layer of complexity to an already precarious situation.

A knock at the door broke Anika's thoughts. It was Singh.

Anika smiled seeing Singh enter her office with a cup of steaming chai. 'Thanks, Rajesh. I just spoke to Vikram,' Anika said as he sat opposite her.

'He's in?' Singh asked before taking a sip of his tea.

Anika nodded.

'Congratulations. I bet Verma and Shekhawat will sleep better tonight.'

Anika couldn't help but laugh.

'I have a meeting with the cybercrime head in about 15 minutes.' Singh checked his watch. 'I wanted to check if there's anything you need from them.'

'Can we set up a data mining operation? We need to scrape social media, news archives, and even tourist photos for anything that matches the artefacts found at the crime scenes. The killer might have left a trail without realising it.'

'Consider it done. I'll have one of the assistants coordinate with you when they have the data.'

'Thanks. And thanks a lot for the tea. I needed a little boost.'

Singh rose and gave her a small salute. 'Anytime. I'll see you after the meeting.'

As Singh left her office, Anika looked out the window at the setting sun. She knew everyone was working around the clock and stretching themselves to their limit, especially Singh. She thought about how her team was working relentlessly and promised herself to beat the killer at his own game for all of their sakes.

The musty scent of parchment and ink clung to the air as Anika and Singh made their way through the labyrinthine corridors of the Jaipur City Archives. The dim glow of antique chandeliers overhead flickered against rows of towering wooden shelves, each laden with the fragile weight of history. Scrolls bound in silk, ancient ledgers, and brittle manuscripts stretched as far as the eye could see, each a silent witness to the legacies of the Pink City's past.

Anika's sandals clicked softly against the worn marble floor as she trailed a gloved hand along the spines of the archival records, her mind already deep in thought. Time was running out, and she was certain that the answer lay buried somewhere in the annals of the city's history.

'Anika,' Singh's voice called from a few shelves away. 'I think I've found the section on 18th-century court proceedings.'

Anika turned sharply, navigating her way through the shelves to where Singh stood beside a towering wooden cabinet. The leather-bound indexes he had retrieved were thick and musty with age, their pages filled with elaborate Devanagari script and Persian annotations, remnants of Jaipur's Mughal and Rajput heritage.

The soft shuffling of slippered feet announced the arrival of Mr Niranjan Gupta, the elderly archivist who had agreed to help them. He peered at them through thick spectacles, his weathered hands gripping a small collection of catalogues.

'Ah, Dr Thakur,' he greeted, his voice as brittle as the pages surrounding them. 'I've brought the indexes you requested. These should help narrow down your search.'

'Thank you, Mr Gupta.' Anika took the ledgers from him, glancing at the faded inscriptions. 'We're also looking for records related to paintings depicting historical injustices, anything involving the royal families, political betrayals, or power struggles between the 17th and 19th centuries.'

The old archivist's bushy eyebrows lifted slightly. 'Now *that* is an interesting request. You might want to look at records from the reign of Maharaja Jai Singh II. He was a visionary, but his court was rife with rivalries and intrigue. His reign saw both progress and treachery.'

As Mr Gupta shuffled away, Anika and Singh split the indexes between them, scanning rapidly for any mention of historical conflicts that aligned with their case.

The hours bled away as dust motes drifted in the thin beams of sunlight seeping through the high, arched windows. The silence was broken only by the rustle of parchment and the occasional murmur as they noted down promising leads.

Then something caught Anika's eye.

Her fingers paused over an entry in one of the meticulously kept ledgers:

*Thakur family implicated in the royal dispute—1734—
See Folio 2781.*

Anika frowned. 'Thakur?' she whispered, almost to herself.

Arjun looked up from his own index, immediately catching the change in her expression. 'Did you find something?'

She hesitated, then straightened. 'I think so. Help me find Folio 2781.'

Together, they combed the shelves until they found the correct volume. It was a massive tome bound in darkened leather, its cover embossed with the insignia of the Jaipur court. Anika carefully pried it open, the spine groaning in protest, and turned to the referenced folio.

What she saw sent a shiver down her spine.

The document detailed a scandal involving the Thakur family, a powerful noble lineage in Rajput history, known for their unwavering loyalty to the Kachwaha rulers. The record spoke of a Thakur nobleman who had been accused of conspiring against the Jaipur throne, a warrior-turned-adviser who had allegedly allied with a faction seeking to destabilise the royal court.

Singh leaned in, scanning the page. 'This is . . . weird. You think you belong to the original Thakur lineage?'

Anika nodded slowly, feeling unsure of what she'd just read.

'It looks like your family may have been involved in Jaipur's history.'

Anika barely heard him, her eyes locked on a faded notation in the margin. It had been written in a different hand and likely added years later.

Keeper of the Third Key.

A chill ran down her spine.

She turned to Singh and said, 'I knew the Thakurs had served as feudal lords and military strategists in Rajasthan for centuries. Many had been granted *jagirs*, lands in exchange for military service, under the rule of the Kachwahas. But this—an accusation of betrayal? A secret title? I've never heard of it.' She looked back at the text. 'This doesn't make sense,' she murmured, running a finger over the words. 'The Thakurs were *loyalists*. They fought *for* Jaipur's rulers, not against them.'

Singh gave her a searching look. 'You think this might be connected to the case? To the paintings? Or to Yuvraj's kidnapping?'

Anika exhaled sharply, her mind racing. 'I don't know. But if this record exists . . . it means the killer might know something about my family's past that even I don't.'

The realisation unsettled her deeply.

Was this why Yuvraj had been kidnapped? Was this the reason why she had been drawn into the case? Had the killer *chosen* Yuvraj all those years ago, and now her for a reason beyond just her expertise?

Singh kept a comforting hand on Anika's shoulder. 'We should document this and keep searching,' he said, his voice measured. 'There could be more references to your family.'

Anika nodded, forcing herself to focus. But as she resumed flipping through the brittle pages, she couldn't shake the feeling that she had just stumbled across a door never meant to be opened.

The Jaipur City Archives suddenly felt suffocating. If her family had been involved in Jaipur's royal history, if they had been *keepers of something*, what exactly had they been safeguarding?

And, more importantly, *who else knew?*

❧

CHAPTER 11

The fading sun cast a golden glow over Jaipur, its warm hues reflected in the dusty windshields of cars and the pink sandstone buildings of the old city. The burden of past memories settled in her chest, a familiar feeling of heaviness, as Anika manoeuvred through her childhood's familiar narrow streets.

The road to her mother's home was unchanged—winding, uneven, lined with bougainvillaea spilling over whitewashed walls. A house she had once called home stood at the end of it, nestled between two ancient neem trees. The modest bungalow looked unchanged with its faded yellow walls and meticulously tended jasmine plants. But to Anika, it felt like a troublesome relic from another life.

She had spent years avoiding this moment. Dreading it. Avoiding *her*.

Taking a deep breath, she stepped out of the car and walked towards the house. She hesitated at the door before knocking. There was a pause, then the sound of hurried footsteps.

The door swung open, revealing Lata Thakur, her mother, with her once-raven hair now streaked with silver, her sharp features softened by time, but her eyes just as piercing as Anika remembered.

For a moment, they simply stared at each other.

'Anu?' Lata's voice was thick with disbelief, her grip tightening on the edge of the door. 'You finally decided to come home?'

Anika forced herself to meet her mother's gaze, trying to push aside the familiar pang of guilt. 'I needed to talk to you.'

Lata studied her for a beat longer before stepping aside. 'Well then, come in.'

Anika stepped over the threshold and, with it, into a space that flooded her mind with memories. The scent of sandalwood lingered in the air, mingling with the fragrance of the jasmine plants outside. The living room was the same: bookshelves stacked with old volumes, hand-embroidered cushions on the worn sofa, and framed photographs of happier times.

Her eyes landed on a picture of her and Yuvraj, six and eight years old, frozen in time, smiling in the sunlit courtyard of this very home.

Lata followed her gaze. 'I tried calling you so many times, Anu. But you never answered.'

Anika inhaled sharply, bracing herself. 'I was busy.'

Her mother's lips pressed into a thin line. 'Too busy to visit your own home? Too busy to even return my calls?'

Tension coursed through her as she clenched her fists. 'Ma, don't—'

'Don't what, Anu?' Lata's voice rose, her frustration spilling over. 'I have been following the case. Ever since I heard your name mentioned, I knew it would only be a matter of time before—' She stopped herself, shaking her head. 'I have been *worried* about you. And you couldn't even bother to let me know if you were safe?'

Anika exhaled slowly. 'I'm fine, Ma.'

'No,' Lata said, crossing her arms. 'You're not.'

Anika looked away, unwilling to engage in another battle of emotions, especially when her mind was still caught in the whirlwind of the case. 'That's not why I came.'

Lata sighed, rubbing her temples. 'Then why are you here, Anu?'

Anika hesitated before finally meeting her mother's gaze. 'I was at the city archives today. I found something . . . something about *us*.'

Lata stilled, the lines on her face deepening. 'What do you mean?'

'There's a record,' Anika continued, stepping closer, her voice low but firm. 'From 1734. It mentions a Thakur, perhaps our ancestor, accused of treason against the Jaipur throne. A man named Devesh Thakur.'

Lata's breath hitched, her expression unreadable.

'He was a court noble, Ma.' Anika pressed on. 'And he was executed. But before he died, he swore that his descendants would clear his name. That would be us, wouldn't it?'

Lata turned abruptly, walking towards the window. The sky outside had darkened, the evening air heavy with the scent of storm and rain.

'You knew,' Anika said softly, realisation settling like a stone in her chest. 'You knew about our history, about the accusations. And you never told me.'

Lata remained silent, her gaze fixed on the street outside.

Anika took a step forward. 'Did Yuvraj know?'

At the mention of her son's name, Lata stiffened.

Anika's pulse quickened. 'Is that why he was taken? Was Yuvraj targeted because of *this*?'

Lata let out a shaky breath. 'Stop it, Anika.'

'No, Ma.' Anika's voice wavered with restrained anger. 'I need to know. I have spent *years* trying to understand why Yuvraj disappeared. You never gave me answers, and now I find out that we have a past tied to Jaipur's royalty? To a *betrayal*? And you want me to stop?'

Lata finally turned, her eyes wet with unshed tears. 'I did it to protect you.'

Anika scoffed, 'Protect me from what? From the truth? From our own history?'

'From the people who don't want the truth to come out!' Lata's voice cracked, her control slipping. 'From those who believe in debts that span centuries. From those who took Yuvraj.'

The words hit Anika like a punch to the gut.

She stepped back. 'You think Yuvraj's disappearance is connected to this?'

Lata closed her eyes for a long moment before nodding. 'I never had proof. But . . . the night he was taken, they said something about "settling old debts". I tried to put it out of my mind, but now, with these murders . . .' She trailed off, shaking her head, the worry line in her face deepening even more.

Anika swallowed hard, the weight of realisation settling in. 'You should have told me.'

Lata let out a hollow laugh. 'And what would you have done, Anika? Gone searching for answers like Yuvraj did? Gone digging into things that should have been left buried?'

Anika's jaw tightened. 'Yes.'

Her mother's shoulders slumped. 'I was afraid. That if I told you, you'd go down the same path. And I couldn't lose you as well. I was terrified.'

Silence stretched between them, heavy and suffocating.

Anika finally spoke, her voice softer. 'You keeping me in the dark didn't protect me, Ma. It only made me blind, frustrated, and angry.'

Lata sat down heavily on the sofa, her hands trembling. 'I thought if I buried it, if I pretended none of it mattered anymore, we could live normal lives.' She let out a shaky breath. 'But the past doesn't let go so easily.'

Anika hesitated before lowering herself onto the sofa beside her mother. The anger in her chest hadn't dissipated, but beneath it was something else—a quiet understanding.

'Tell me everything,' she said, her voice steady.

Lata turned to her, eyes searching. 'Are you really sure you want to know?'

Anika nodded. 'I have to. I can't walk away from this.'

Her mother exhaled deeply, her gaze distant, as if she were staring into the past. 'It started long before us, before even Devesh Thakur. Our family was never just another noble house. We were *keepers* of something, something that some wanted erased.'

Anika felt the hairs on her arms rise. 'What was it? What were we keeping?'

Lata looked at her, and in her eyes, Anika saw the weight of generations of secrets. 'The truth.'

A cold shiver ran down Anika's spine. The truth was dangerous. And it had already taken too much from her family. But she was no longer afraid. She was ready to face it.

Lata sat quietly for a long moment, staring down at her hands, as if weighing the price of finally speaking the truth. The only sounds in the dimly lit living room were the ticking of the old grandfather clock and the occasional rustle of the jasmine vines outside the window. The weight of years, of silence, and of secrets pressed down on them both.

Anika waited, her breath steady but her pulse erratic. She had spent years chasing answers about Yuvraj's disappearance, about the shadows that seemed to follow her family, and now, finally, she was on the precipice of something, an understanding she wasn't sure she was ready for.

Lata inhaled deeply before she began.

'Our family wasn't just another noble house, Anika. The Thakurs of Amber, our ancestors, were once among the most trusted advisors and warriors of the Kachwaha dynasty, long before Jaipur was built. But we weren't just warriors. We were *keepers*.'

Anika frowned. 'Keepers of what?'

Lata's lips pressed into a thin line. 'The *truth*. A truth that many wanted buried.'

Anika's stomach twisted. 'What kind of truth?'

Lata looked up, her expression shadowed by memories. 'Have you ever wondered why Jaipur was built the way it was? Why did Maharaja Jai Singh II move the capital from Amber to Jaipur? Historians say it was for strategic reasons, better trade, better water supply. But the truth is . . . there were other reasons: a power struggle within the royal court.'

Anika leaned in, hanging on to every word.

'In 1734, a faction within the royal court believed the move to Jaipur was a mistake. They would often talk of omens, of prophecies that claimed the throne would be cursed if Amber was abandoned. But it wasn't just superstition. It was politics. Some believed that the move weakened the legitimacy of certain noble houses, that their influence would fade if Jaipur became the new seat of power.'

Anika's brow furrowed. 'And how does our family fit into this?'

Lata exhaled. 'Devesh Thakur was one of the maharaja's most trusted men. He wasn't just a court noble. He was entrusted with a responsibility. Something called *the Third Key*.'

Anika felt a chill spread across her insides. 'I saw that phrase in the archive records.'

Lata nodded. 'It's a metaphor. The *Third Key* referred to a secret, one known only to three men in the entire kingdom. The Maharaja, his chief priest . . . and Devesh Thakur.'

Anika's heartbeat quickened. 'A secret about what?'

Lata hesitated before speaking. 'A secret about *the rightful heir to the throne*.'

The words settled heavily between them.

Anika's throat went dry. 'You're saying there was a dispute over succession?'

'There were rumours,' Lata confirmed, 'that the maharaja had fathered an heir through a woman who was never acknowledged publicly. If true, it would have changed everything—who ruled, who had power, who was allowed to exist in the shadows.'

Anika sat back, her mind reeling. 'And Devesh knew about this?'

Lata nodded. 'Not only did he know, but he was also the one entrusted to protect the truth. To keep it hidden until the right time. But as you can imagine, there were those who didn't want that truth to ever come to light.'

'So, they framed him,' Anika murmured.

'They accused him of treason,' Lata said bitterly. 'Said he was conspiring to overthrow the maharaja, that he had poisoned one of the court's powerful nobles. But the truth was, they feared what he knew. And they silenced him before he could ever speak.'

Anika ran a hand through her hair, trying to absorb it all. 'And this . . . this oath you mentioned . . . it was about clearing his name?'

'Yes,' Lata said softly. 'But as time passed, the truth became legend. And legends were forgotten.'

Anika let out a shaky breath. 'Until now.'

Lata looked at her, her eyes filled with something raw and painful. 'Until now.'

The pieces of the puzzle were beginning to fit together in Anika's mind. The murders were calculated. The killer was following a *pattern*, bringing to light forgotten betrayals and injustices. And her family—*her* bloodline—was tangled up in that very history.

'Ma . . .' She hesitated, her voice barely above a whisper. 'Did Yuvraj know?'

Lata's hands clenched into fists. She didn't answer immediately. But when she did, her voice was so quiet that Anika barely heard it.

'He found something.'

Anika felt her blood run cold. 'What do you mean?'

'Before he disappeared, he started looking into old records,' Lata said, her voice thick with emotion. 'My sweet boy. He was so young and naïve. He thought he was protecting me by not telling me what he was searching for, only that he *had to know* the truth. He became obsessed with the stories, the old manuscripts—he even spoke to scholars. And then . . . one day, he mentioned the *Third Key*.'

Anika's heart pounded against her ribs. 'He mentioned it? *To you?*'

Lata nodded, her face pale. 'He said he had found something. Something *big*. But before he could tell me what it was . . . they took him.'

A shudder ran through Anika. 'Oh my God.'

She had spent years looking for answers about Yuvraj's disappearance, never knowing it was connected to something far bigger than she had imagined.

She could see the straight line now, running like a hidden seam through every choice she'd ever made: the night she packed a single suitcase and walked out of the family home because its walls echoed with her mother's unanswered sobs, the way she gravitated towards ancient libraries and forensic labs as if facts and fingerprints could muffle the silence Yuvraj left behind, and the doctoral thesis that folded psychological autopsy into cultural history because she needed to understand how stories—and people—vanished.

Every credential on her CV, every city she moved to, and every relationship she abandoned before it could root—all of them orbited the black hole of her brother's disappearance and the questions her mother had never dared to voice aloud.

A storm of memories surged through Anika—long-ago evenings hunched over brittle archives, the taste of burned coffee in police station corridors, and every sleepless night spent chasing ghosts across Rajasthan's deserts and Delhi's alleyways.

She felt the sting of old guilt for the life her search had stolen from her mother, the raw ache of hope each time a lead collapsed into dust, and the flicker of pride in the woman she had become because she would not let her brother be forgotten.

Now, in this quiet room that smelled of turmeric and tears, the threads she'd clung to for years suddenly stretched into a single terrifying tapestry: Yuvraj's disappearance was not the random cruelty she had feared but a calculated move in a conspiracy older and darker than any nightmare.

The dread was suffocating, yet beneath it pulsed a fierce relief and an iron resolve.

At last, the labyrinth had a centre, and she would follow it, no matter where it twisted, until she found her brother or the truth—or both.

'And you think whoever took him did it because of what he found?' Anika asked, her voice barely steady as she emerged from the whirlpool of memories.

Lata swallowed. 'I don't know. But I've feared it every day since.'

The silence between them stretched long and heavy.

Anika's fists clenched tightly. She had started this investigation chasing a killer who was recreating historical paintings, but now she was staring at something even darker—*a centuries-old conspiracy* that might have cost her brother his life.

And the killer *knew*. The murders, the paintings, and the cryptic messages—they were all part of something bigger. A reckoning of sorts. Anika pushed back the rising fear and steadied herself. She would not let history repeat itself. She would not allow the past to consume her family any longer. She stood up. 'I need to go.'

Lata grabbed her wrist, her eyes desperate. 'Anika, please. Don't go there and dig more. Leave it alone, please. If this is all connected—'

'I know,' Anika said, her voice firm. 'But I can't stop now, Ma.'

She gently pulled away and headed for the door, her mind already racing through everything she had learned. As she stepped outside into the cool Jaipur night, she realised something with startling clarity.

The killer wasn't just targeting forgotten injustices. He was *finishing* something. And Anika herself was now part of his story.

The soft glow of Anika's laptop cast flickering shadows across her apartment, where stacks of books on Rajasthani history lay scattered across the coffee table, intermingled with case files and hastily scribbled notes. The ticking wall clock marked the passage of time, past midnight now, but Anika barely registered it. She was too deep in the tangled web of history, secrets, and now the unsettling realisation of her own place in it.

Her fingers hovered over the keyboard, her gaze shifting between the glowing screen and the fragile time-worn pages of a family journal, one her mother had handed over with great reluctance at the end of their conversation. Anika hadn't stopped reading it since she got home, poring over every faded-ink entry and every cryptic note scrawled in the margins.

'Devesh Thakur,' she murmured, scrolling through a digitised court record from the 18th century. 'Appointed a trusted diwan in 1729, accused of treason in 1734.' Her brow furrowed as she read on, the charges deliberately vague and the phrasing suggestive of something far more sinister than simple court politics.

She flipped through the brittle pages of the journal until she found the corresponding entry. The handwriting was faded, but the pain in the words remained sharp:

Grandfather speaks of Devesh Thakur with great sorrow. The accusations were lies, spread by those who feared his influence. The Maharaja's trust in him was poisoned by men who wished to erase him from history. Devesh went to his death swearing his innocence, vowing that one day, the truth would rise from the ashes.

Anika exhaled slowly, pressing her fingers against her temple. The more she read, the more she realised that her family's connection to Jaipur's royal court ran deeper than she had ever imagined. This case was not just history anymore. It was *personal*.

A notification appeared on her screen, another newly digitised record, this one from the early 19th century. Anika clicked on it, exhaustion momentarily forgotten.

Rohit Thakur, great-grandson of Devesh, petitions the court for a review of his ancestor's case. Petition denied.

Note: R. Thakur is to be watched closely. He exhibits the family's characteristic stubborn pursuit of 'justice'.

Anika let out a dry, humourless laugh. *Characteristic stubborn pursuit.* The words might as well have been written about her. She had inherited that same dogged determination, the same refusal to let history be written by the victors.

She scrolled further, piecing together a harrowing pattern, one that made her stomach twist. Each generation of the Thakurs had tried, in some way, to bring Devesh's story to light. And each time, swift retribution had followed. And then there was Yuvraj. His disappearance—had he unknowingly walked the same path? Had he discovered something about their family's past? Had someone been watching him, just as Rohit Thakur had been watched?

'Leave him alone,' her mother had sobbed that night, long ago. *'It's not his fault.'*

Anika's breath came in shallow bursts, her heart pounding as realisation dawned. Yuvraj had found out about Devesh and had been investigating it, trying to uncover the deeper conspiracies. She wondered if someone had taken him to silence him.

A chill ran through her, shuddering as realisation dawned. The killer's historical fixation and the meticulously staged crime scenes—he was sending a message. He was following a script that had begun centuries ago. And now, it was *her* turn in the story.

The next day, the fluorescent lights of the Jaipur Police Headquarters buzzed softly, casting their stark white glare over the crowded bullpen. The usual rhythm of controlled chaos hummed around her: officers moving from desk to desk, paperwork piling up, and phones ringing ceaselessly. But Anika sat still at her desk in her office, staring down at the stacks of case files, historical documents, and handwritten notes that threatened to consume every inch of space around her.

She barely noticed when Officer Paul cleared his throat beside her.

'Dr Thakur, there's someone here to see you,' he said hesitantly. 'An elderly woman. She says it's urgent. And . . . personal.'

Anika looked up sharply. 'Personal?' Her pulse quickened. 'Did she give a name?'

Paul shook his head. 'No. She just insisted on speaking with you. Said she's a distant relative.'

A strange unease settled in her chest. 'All right,' she said, standing. 'Send her in. But stay close, just in case.'

Moments later, a frail yet strikingly dignified woman entered her office. Her sari, faded with time, draped loosely over her thin frame. Despite her years, her eyes were keen, shrewd, and sharp, taking in her surroundings before finally settling on Anika.

'Anika Thakur,' the woman murmured, her voice steady despite its age. 'At last, we meet.'

Anika gestured towards a chair, masking her suspicion. 'Please, sit. You have me at a disadvantage. Who are you?'

The woman lowered herself into the seat with a careful grace. 'Names are dangerous things, child,' she said cryptically. 'Especially in times like these. Let's just say I am family. A *keeper* of old stories and even older debts.'

Anika's instincts sharpened at the mention of the word *keeper*. 'You said this was urgent. What can I do for you?'

The old woman leaned in, her voice barely above a whisper. 'It's not what you can do for me, child. It's what I must do for you. The past is stirring, and old shadows are creeping in. You are in danger.'

A chill ran down Anika's spine. 'Danger from what? Is this connected to the murders?'

The woman's expression darkened. 'The murders. The miniature paintings. Your family history. They are all threads in the same weave, strands of a story written long before you were born.'

Anika's throat tightened. 'How do you know about that? Who *are* you?'

A sad smile played on the woman's lips. 'I told you. A keeper of secrets. Your great-grandmother's sister was my grandmother. I've watched your family from afar for decades, waiting for the day when the old stories would demand to be told again.'

She reached into the folds of her sari and produced a small ornate key, placing it on the desk between them. 'This opens a lockbox in the old Thakur family home. The one where your mother lives. You will find documents in that box—proof of Devesh's innocence and the true culprits behind his downfall.'

Anika stared at the key, her heartbeat thudding against her ribs. 'Why now? Why not sooner?'

The old woman's face clouded. 'Because fear is a powerful thing, child. It has kept our family silent for generations. But now, the silence is breaking. The murders were never just random acts. They were a message. And if you do not act quickly, you may be next.'

A deep, wrenching unease coiled in Anika's gut. 'What do you mean?'

'The paintings the killer is recreating,' the woman whispered, 'are more than just stories. They are a map, a code. Each one points to something, a hidden archive of sorts. Devesh's story is only *one* piece of a much larger puzzle.'

Anika's mind raced. 'A map? To what?'

The woman's expression was unreadable. 'To the truth. A truth that could shake the very foundation of Jaipur's power.'

Then, gripping Anika's hand, her voice took on an urgent tone. 'Listen carefully, child. Trust no one. Not the police. Not the royals. Not even your friends. Old loyalties run deep, and not everyone is what they seem.'

A chill settled over Anika, her grip tightening on the key. 'Who's behind this?' she pressed.

The woman only shook her head. 'I've already said too much.'

She rose abruptly, her earlier frailty forgotten. 'Find the lockbox. Follow the clues. And whatever you do . . .' Her voice dropped to a whisper. 'Beware the man with the silver pocket watch. He is not what he seems to be.'

Before Anika could stop her, the woman slipped away swiftly, leaving the police station and disappearing into the streets.

As Anika stood frozen, her fingers tightening around the small weighty key, she received a call that made her leave the police headquarters immediately and go to the local hospital.

⅔

The antiseptic scent of the hospital stung Anika's nostrils as she strode through the automatic doors, her heart hammering in her chest. The call had come just as the mysterious old woman had vanished into the busy streets.

'Your mother has been admitted to the hospital,' the nurse had said. *'She was attacked in her home last night.'*

Anika's breath had caught in her throat. Attacked? Someone had broken into her mother's house—her mother, who had spent years living in fearful silence, protecting the very secrets that now seemed to be crumbling all around them.

The bright lights overhead cast a harsh glare as she rushed down the corridor, the walls appearing to close in around her. Nurses and patients hurried past, but Anika noticed none of them; her thoughts were fixated on discovering what had happened.

She reached the nurses' station, her voice sharper than she intended. 'I'm here for Lata Thakur. I'm her daughter, Dr Anika Thakur.'

The nurse looked up, recognition flickering in her eyes. 'Dr Thakur, your mother is in room 215. She's stable now, but the doctor will be with you shortly to discuss her condition.'

Anika nodded curtly and made her way down the hallway. Every step felt heavier, the weight of dread pressing down her shoulders. As she reached the door to room 215, she hesitated for a fraction of a second before pushing it open.

Inside, her mother lay in a hospital bed, looking impossibly small and frail against the white sheets. The bruises along her arms and the bandage on her forehead stood out against her pale skin. The sight sent a sharp pang of rage through Anika.

'Ma,' she whispered, stepping forward. 'Ma, what happened? Are you all right?'

Lata's eyes fluttered open, exhaustion and pain clouding their depths. But when they met Anika's, a flicker of relief softened her expression. 'Anika,' she breathed. 'You came.'

'Of course, I did,' Anika said firmly, taking her mother's cold hand in hers. 'Tell me everything. Who did this to you?'

Before Lata could answer, the door swung open, and a weary-looking doctor entered, clipboard in hand. 'Dr Thakur?' he addressed Anika. 'I'm Dr Mehra. Your mother was brought in with signs of a struggle—minor bruising, a small head wound, and acute shock. She's stable now, but it's clear she suffered severe distress. Her vitals have improved, but the psychological trauma is significant.'

Anika swallowed hard, nodding. 'Thank you, Doctor. Has she spoken about what happened?'

Dr Mehra shook his head. 'She's been reluctant. I was hoping she might open up to you,' he said and turned and left.

Anika turned back to her mother, a sinking feeling settling in her gut. 'Ma,' she said softly, brushing a stray hair from Lata's forehead. 'Who did this?'

Tears welled up in Lata's eyes. She tried to speak, but her breath hitched. 'Some men came in the night,' she whispered. 'I heard them . . . moving through the house. At first, I thought it was a dream. But then I saw them—huge men, their faces covered with black scarves. They must have been searching for something. They overturned everything and looked through all the cupboards and drawers.'

Anika's fingers tightened around her mother's hand. 'The lockbox,' she murmured, realisation hitting her like a bolt of lightning.

Lata's tearful gaze confirmed it. 'Yes, but . . . how do you know about it?' she asked, her eyes big with surprise.

'I'll tell you about it later, Ma. But tell me, is it safe? The lockbox?'

Lata shook her head. 'They found it.'

Anika inhaled sharply. The lockbox that the old woman had told her about just hours ago. The one supposedly contained documents proving Devesh's innocence, potentially exposing a secret powerful enough to shake the foundations of Jaipur's royalty.

A storm of fury and helplessness churned inside her. 'Who were they, Ma? Did you see their faces?'

Lata shook her head, her frail body trembling. 'No. They were careful. But . . . I *felt* it, Anika. The same presence from years ago. The same feeling I had the night they took Yuvraj.'

Anika's breath hitched. Something was falling into place in her mind. 'Did you see a man?' she whispered. 'The man with a silver pocket watch.'

Lata nodded, her eyes brimming with fear. 'How do you know? Yes . . . he was there. Watching, waiting, just like before.'

A deep, unsettling chill spread through Anika's veins. The old woman's warning rang in her ears: *Watch out for the man with the silver pocket watch.* The same man who had been seen before Yuvraj vanished. And although she had memories from that time, she could not remember a man with a silver pocket watch. But she somehow connected what the old woman had told her just an hour ago.

'Ma,' she pressed gently but urgently. 'You have to tell me everything. What did Yuvraj find? Why did they take him?'

Lata closed her eyes, as if summoning courage from the depths of her soul. When she opened them again, there was something steely in her gaze—a decision.

'Yuvraj was close,' she whispered. 'Closer than anyone had ever been. He found proof, Anika. Proof that Devesh was framed. That his execution wasn't about treason. It was about erasing him from history. He had royal blood, Anika. He wasn't just a *diwan*. He was the maharaja's half-brother.'

Anika sat frozen, the words reverberating through her mind. She had suspected something of the sort, but hearing it confirmed sent her world tilting on its axis.

'Are you saying,' she said slowly, 'that Devesh was taken, not because he was a threat to the throne, but because he *belonged* to it?'

Lata nodded gravely. 'Yes. And Yuvraj found something—something that could prove it beyond a doubt. I heard him rambling to himself one day about Devesh. He was saying, *"There's more . . . There's got to be. The truth is scattered, hidden in pieces. I have to find it before they do."* And then . . . he was gone.'

Anika clenched her jaw, her mind racing. 'The paintings,' she murmured. 'The recreations . . . they're part of the same message.'

Lata's grip tightened, her eyes pleading. 'Anika, listen to me. If these people took Yuvraj and broke into our home for that lockbox, they know you're close too. You have to be careful. If you keep digging, they *will* come for you.'

Anika exhaled sharply, anger thrumming beneath her skin. 'Let them,' she said darkly. 'They can't stop me.'

Lata's lip trembled, her fear for her daughter evident. 'Anika . . .'

Anika bent down, pressing a kiss to her mother's forehead. 'I swear to you, Ma. I will find out what happened to Yuvraj. I will expose the truth, no matter what it takes.'

Lata's eyes glistened with emotion. She nodded imperceptibly, understanding that there was no turning back now.

Outside the hospital room, the world carried on as usual, nurses rushing through corridors and patients waiting for their turn. But inside Anika, a storm had been unleashed. She stepped into the hallway, her hands curling into fists. The lockbox was gone, but that only meant one thing: Someone out there was desperate to keep its secrets buried.

But she wasn't afraid. The truth had been hidden long enough. It was time to bring it to light.

When Anika returned in mid-afternoon, the police station was unusually quiet. The usual hum of activity was reduced to the occasional shuffle of papers and the distant murmur of officers wrapping up for lunch. Anika strode through the hallways, her steps hurried and determined, heading straight for Singh's office.

She needed to tell him everything, about her mother's attack, about the stolen lockbox, and most importantly, about what she had learned about her own past. She had promised him she wouldn't hide anything from him.

When she entered, Singh was at his desk, flipping through a file with a deep frown creasing his brow. He looked up at her arrival, taking in her tense posture and the urgency in her expression. Without a word, he gestured to the chair across from him.

Anika remained standing, gripping the back of the chair instead. 'I need to talk to you,' she said, her voice steady but taut.

Singh studied her for a moment before nodding. 'Go on.'

She took a deep breath. 'My mother was attacked last night.'

Singh's expression darkened instantly. He sat forward. 'Attacked? By whom?'

Anika shook her head. 'I don't know. She didn't see their faces. But they weren't there to hurt her. They were searching for something.' She met his eyes. 'They stole a lockbox from our home. A lockbox that, until this morning, I didn't even know existed.'

Singh's frown deepened. 'What was in it?'

'I don't know yet,' Anika admitted. 'But I think it contained some important documents, proof that could clear my ancestor Devesh Thakur's name. I learned yesterday that he wasn't just a *diwan*. He was the maharaja's illegitimate half-brother.'

Singh exhaled sharply, leaning back in his chair. 'What? Are you sure? That's a dangerous revelation.'

Anika gave a humourless laugh. 'Yes, I am certain now. It all fits together. And I think Yuvraj found out too. That's why he was taken.'

Singh's gaze sharpened. 'You think your brother's disappearance is tied to all this?'

Anika nodded. 'My mother said Yuvraj had found something important. The same conspiracy that the killer is recreating through these murders.'

Singh was silent for a long moment, absorbing her words. Finally, he said, 'This isn't just about revenge anymore, is it? This is about justice, about rewriting history.'

Anika met his gaze. 'Yes. And the people behind this, the ones who took my brother, the ones who attacked my mother, they're still out there. They know I'm close.'

Singh exhaled slowly, rubbing his jaw. 'This changes things. We need to rethink our approach. If this killer is following a pattern, we might still have a chance to anticipate their next move.'

Anika moved closer, pulling out her notebook and flipping to a page filled with hastily scrawled connections. 'I've been mapping it out. Each murder corresponds to a historical injustice, right? But they're moving progressively forward in time.' She pointed to a date circled in red. 'The next murder will be some injustice in the 17th or the 18th century. I shall be going through the texts and trying to figure it out. In the meantime, could you try to locate the men who attacked my mother?'

Singh nodded. 'Will do.' Anika turned around to leave, but thinking better of it, she turned back to Singh and said, 'I need your help, Rajesh.'

Singh frowned. 'Sure, Anika.'

'You have a good idea of Jaipur's politics. I need to know who benefits from keeping these secrets buried? Who has the most to lose if Devesh's story is brought to light?'

Singh thought for a beat before answering, 'There are many answers to that question. But one thing is certain, the people who have protected these secrets for generations will not give them up without a fight.'

Anika took a deep breath, forcing herself to steady the whirlwind of thoughts racing through her mind. 'Then we give them a fight,' she said firmly. 'I won't stop until I find out the truth.'

Singh studied her for a long moment before nodding. 'All right, Anika. We do this together. But we do it carefully. No reckless moves. No rushing into the dark without a plan.'

Anika managed a small smile. 'I wouldn't dream of it.'

The steady tick of the clock on Anika's office wall marked the relentless passage of time, its rhythm a sharp contrast to the fevered energy crackling through the small space. The harsh glow of the desk lamp cast shadows across the sea of papers, maps, and photographs strewn across her desk. As the world around her slept, Anika remained caught in the throes of a revelation she could feel just beyond her grasp.

Dark circles framed her tired eyes, her usually sharp mind dulled by exhaustion yet still racing, unable to slow down. The past and present blurred before her, crime scene photos intermingling with ancient Rajasthani miniature paintings, and fragments of family history bleeding into police reports. The connections were there. She just needed to pull the right thread.

She had expected the killer to wait before he struck next, but it had been almost a week since the last murder, and there had been nothing so far. She knew the killer was recalibrating. The last crime scene felt different from the others. It wasn't apparent at first glance, but the more she thought about it, the more she could sense that the killer's sense of urgency had escalated. So, despite the deviation, she had expected him to strike within a week, but he hadn't. Was it possible that the killer knew she'd decoded his spiral pattern and altered his strategy? It was quite likely. In fact, it was the only logic that made sense. And if that was the case, then it meant only one thing: Someone in their department had informed the killer.

But who? She'll have to talk to Singh about it. She reached for her coffee mug, grimacing as she drank the last of the cold, bitter liquid. As she set it down, wondering if she should call him right then, her elbow clipped a stack of files, sending them cascading onto the floor.

'Damn it,' she muttered, dropping to her knees to gather the scattered pages.

Her fingers brushed against a photograph that had landed atop an old map of Jaipur, and for a moment, she stilled. The photo depicted one of the crime scenes—the carefully staged tableau and the deliberate placement of the body. But, juxtaposed against the faded lines of the city's historic layout, something clicked.

Her pulse quickened. She grabbed the map with shaking hands, smoothing it out on her desk. She placed the other crime scene photos around it, aligning them one by one. She caught her breath.

'It can't be,' she whispered.

It was another pattern.

Each murder site, when mapped onto the old city layout, corresponded with a significant historical location. More than that, the killer had chosen these places with a purpose. The way the bodies were positioned and the angles of the recreated crime scenes aligned with Jaipur's structure.

It was not just a pattern. It was a message.

Anika scrambled for a blank sheet of paper, her pen flying across its surface as she sketched out the connections. 'The murders were not isolated acts of vengeance. They were pieces of a grander design. The city is the canvas, the killings the brushstrokes,' she muttered as she hastily sketched. And as the shapes emerged beneath her pen, her breath caught in her throat.

The lines formed a symbol.

Anika stared, her mind reeling. She had seen this before. In the dusty pages of her family's journal. In the historical texts she had pored over. It was an ancient insignia, a crest that had been buried by time. *The Seal of Truth and Justice.*

A symbol long erased from Jaipur's history—a forgotten mark of legitimacy and of power. An emblem that had once signified those who sought to restore balance against corruption and injustice.

Her hands trembled as she flipped through her notes, finding Devesh Thakur's writings. *'The key to absolution lies in the seal. Follow its path, and the truth will no longer be buried.'*

Anika's heartbeat thundered in her ears. The killer was exposing injustices. And they were leaving a trail. A trail that led to the truth.

Her gaze snapped to the phrase she had written hours ago in the margins of her notes: *'Hidden archives—scattered throughout the city.'*

A realisation slammed into her with the force of a monsoon wind. The symbol wasn't just an emblem. It was a map. Anika's hands flew to her keyboard, pulling up Jaipur's architectural records. She overlaid her sketch onto historical blueprints of the city, aligning the murders with ancient structures, forgotten alleyways, and remnants of old tunnels. It was a fit.

The killer was reconstructing the symbol across Jaipur's very foundation. And at its centre . . . She inhaled sharply—the *final murder.*

She was right. The killer had been planning something big for his next strike. The next murder would complete the pattern, revealing the location of the lost archives—the ultimate repository of secrets—proof of the conspiracy her family had been entangled in for generations.

Anika got to her feet, nearly knocking over her chair. She needed to act. To tell someone. She grabbed her phone, her thumb hovering over Singh's number.

But then she hesitated. The old woman's warning echoed in her mind: *Trust no one.*

A cold wave of apprehension swept over her. This was no longer just about a serial killer. It was about history, legacy, and power. There were people, powerful people, who had buried these truths for centuries. And they would do anything to keep them buried.

Yuvraj had disappeared. Her mother had been attacked. The lockbox containing evidence had been stolen.

She couldn't afford to make a mistake. Slowly, she lowered the phone.

Instead, she methodically gathered the most crucial documents, sketches, maps, and historical notes. She secured them in a locked drawer, pulled out her phone again, and began photographing every piece of evidence.

Whatever happened next, there needed to be a record. The truth had to come out.

As the first light of dawn seeped through the window blinds, Anika exhaled, steadying herself. The pieces had fallen into place, but the real challenge lay ahead.

Stopping the killer. Uncovering the lost archives. And finally bringing to light the secrets that had shaped Jaipur's past and threatened its present.

She wasn't just investigating a crime anymore. She was unearthing a truth that had been buried for generations, and once she found it, she was not going to let it be buried again.

Locking her apartment door behind her, Anika stepped into the crisp morning air. The knowledge she had burdened her, but it also liberated her.

CHAPTER 12

The conference room at the Jaipur Police Headquarters buzzed with low murmurs as officers and forensic specialists shuffled into their seats. Morning sunlight filtered through the blinds, casting angular shadows across the long wooden table. The tension in the room was thick. Everyone knew this case was spiralling into something far bigger than they had imagined.

Anika stood at the front, hands gripping the edge of the table, exhaustion clear in the dark shadows under her eyes. Despite her fatigue, her presence commanded attention. Today wasn't just about presenting a theory. It was about exposing a hidden truth, one that had roots stretching deep into Jaipur's past.

Commissioner Verma entered last, his gaze sweeping across the gathered team before settling on Anika. 'All right, Dr Thakur,' he said, lowering himself into his chair with a measured sigh. 'You called us all in at dawn. I assume you have something big?'

Anika nodded, switching on the projector. The map of Jaipur filled the screen, dotted with red and black markers, the locations of the murders. With a click, she overlaid an older version of the map, its lines revealing something startling beneath the modern city's sprawl.

She turned back to the room, her voice steady. 'The killer has a pattern that has been hiding in plain sight.'

A few officers leaned forward, eyes narrowing as she switched to the next slide. A completed geometric shape emerged from the overlapping murder sites, forming a symbol that had been lost to time.

'The royal seal,' Anika announced. 'The mark of truth and justice.'

A murmur of shock rippled through the room. Even Verma's usual impassive expression tightened with intrigue.

'This symbol has been erased from history books, but I found references to it in old Thakur family records. It isn't just a decorative crest. It is a guide. A map to something buried beneath Jaipur.' She hesitated, her throat dry, before adding, 'Hidden archives.'

Commissioner Verma exhaled sharply. 'Are you saying the killer is leading us to these archives through murder?'

'Yes,' Anika replied. 'Each murder site is strategically chosen. The way the bodies have been positioned and the historical injustices being referenced align with the layout of ancient Jaipur. They're reconstructing a message that has been suppressed for centuries.'

Dr Malhotra, who had been silently flipping through crime scene reports, spoke up. 'And what exactly do you think is in these archives?'

Anika glanced at him, feeling the weight of her next words. 'Documents. Proof. Records of political assassinations, land disputes, betrayals, and hidden truths, truths that powerful people have worked hard to erase.' She paused before adding, 'And if I'm right, the next murder will complete the pattern, revealing the final location of the main archive.'

A tense silence fell over the room. Singh, seated near the back, folded his arms. 'And how do we know for sure that the killer will follow through with this?'

Anika met his gaze. 'We don't. But so far, they've followed this pattern with precise intent. The only way to stop them is to anticipate their next move.'

She clicked to the next slide, which featured three pinpointed locations on Jaipur's map, her best guess at where the killer would strike next: Chand Baori, Tripolia Gate, and Jantar Mantar.

'These are the possible locations where we need to focus our efforts. But I also think that we need to put patrols over the old murder sites.

There is a small chance that the killer could target those places again.' Anika moved the cursor and marked three more places. 'We need to cover these locations also, Amber Fort, Hawa Mahal, City Palace, and Sisodia Rani Garden.'

Commissioner Verma rubbed his temple. 'It's a hell of a theory, Dr Thakur.'

Anika's fingers curled around the table's edge. 'There's more.'

She took a deep breath, steadying herself. 'My family is connected to this history.'

The air in the room shifted. Eyes flickered towards her, surprise creeping into their expressions.

'My ancestor, Devesh Thakur, was executed as part of a fabricated treason plot. His story was one of the first injustices covered up and the documents placed in these archives.' She paused. 'My brother Yuvraj was looking into it before he disappeared.'

That revelation hung in the air like a storm cloud, soft murmurs beginning to emerge in the silence.

Commissioner Verma's jaw clenched. 'Dr Thakur, are you telling me you have a personal stake in this case?'

Anika straightened. 'I'm telling you that my family's history is tangled up in this, whether I like it or not. But it doesn't change my objective. The only thing that matters to me is stopping this killer.'

Silence stretched for a beat. Then Singh spoke, his voice firm. 'I've worked with Anika every step of the way, and I can vouch for her integrity.' He nodded in her direction and said, 'This breakthrough isn't mere speculation. It's based on solid historical and forensic analysis, Commissioner. I know Dr Anika's way of working, and she wouldn't have presented us with this theory if she didn't have a reason to believe it.'

Commissioner Verma exhaled sharply, his eyes scanning the room. 'All right. What's our next move?'

Anika nodded back to Singh gratefully and said, 'We set a trap.'

She gestured to the map. 'We increase surveillance around the predicted location. Undercover officers, CCTV sweeps, and heightened security in historical areas. We make sure we're ready when the killer makes their move.'

She turned to Sub-inspector Kumar. 'I also need a team digging into city records. A lockbox was stolen from my mother's house the night before. It contained documents linked to the archives. If we find it, we might get ahead of the killer.'

A few heads turned sharply at that revelation.

'Your mother's house was broken into?' Verma's voice dropped, laced with concern.

'Yes,' Anika confirmed, her tone steely. 'She was attacked. Whoever did it knew exactly what they were looking for.'

A heavy silence fell. The implications were clear.

Then she levelled a hard gaze around the room. 'And there's something else. Someone is leaking information to the killer.'

Murmurs erupted as everyone exchanged wary glances. Verma's face darkened. 'Are you certain?'

Anika nodded. 'Too many times, the killer has anticipated our moves. They're always one step ahead. I don't believe in coincidences anymore.'

Defensive murmurs rose around the table, a mix of indignation and denial.

'Who would do that?'

'Impossible. We're the ones investigating!'

Anika held up a hand. 'I'm not accusing anyone. But I *am* saying that the killer has access to information they shouldn't. And that means we have a leak.'

Dr Malhotra, silent until now, cleared his throat. 'We should conduct an internal review. Look at case files. See if there's been any unauthorised access.'

Verma's expression was unreadable. 'Fine. But until we have evidence, I don't want paranoia disrupting this team.' His gaze flicked towards Anika. 'Anything else, Dr Thakur?'

She hesitated for only a second before shaking her head. 'No, sir. That's all.'

Verma stood, his voice commanding. 'Then let's move. I want surveillance in place *immediately*. We stop this killer before he can strike again.'

The room stirred into motion, chairs scraping against the floor as officers rushed out. Anika stayed behind, watching their faces carefully. Who had looked too defensive? Who had refused to meet her eyes?

Someone in this room was feeding the killer information.

And she was going to find out who.

Singh lingered by the door as the last of their colleagues filtered out. 'Are you okay?'

Anika inhaled deeply. 'Not really. But we're too deep in now. I just hope we can get to the killer before they commit the murder.'

Singh nodded grimly. 'Then let's make sure we do.'

As they left the conference room, Anika's mind raced. The pieces of the puzzle were falling into place, but the picture was still incomplete. And until it was, no one, including her, was safe.

The secure room deep within the Jaipur police station was a sharp contrast to the chaos of the conference room a while back. There were no interruptions, ringing phones, or murmurs of officers exchanging updates here. Soundproofed walls muffled the heartbeat of the station, leaving only the low hum of the fluorescent lights overhead. The polished wooden table in the centre of the room gleamed beneath the stark lighting, while the high-backed chairs carried an air of authority.

Commissioner Verma sat at the head of the table, his expression as unyielding as stone. Around him were five of the highest-ranking officers in Jaipur's force, hand-picked for their discretion and expertise: Anika, Singh, Kumar, ASI Nair, and Dr Malhotra, who had been reinstated as the lead forensic expert. While Anika sat with her fingers resting on a thick dossier filled with dark revelations that could topple the city's most powerful figures, Dr Malhotra's sharp gaze scanned the room as if already assessing the implications of what was about to be said.

As the heavy door swung shut with a definitive click, Verma leaned forward, his voice a measured warning. 'What is discussed in this room does not leave these walls. Is that understood?'

A chorus of nods and murmured affirmations followed. But Anika could sense the tension crackling beneath the surface, an unspoken wariness of the bombshell she was about to drop.

She inhaled deeply, steeling herself before she began. 'We have a problem, bigger than we initially imagined.' She paused, letting the weight of those words settle. She flipped open the dossier and spread several documents across the table. The map of Jaipur was at the centre, marked with crime scene locations. 'Each murder site aligns with key historical events that were deliberately buried. Someone has been trying to erase these stories for centuries. But our killer? They're doing the opposite. They're bringing them back into the light.'

Anika's fingers skimmed over a set of carefully curated files. 'The deeper I've dug, the more I've realised that these crimes don't just point to history. They point to people. Jaipur's elite. We have reason to believe that members of at least three royal families and two of the city's most powerful business dynasties are connected to these cover-ups.'

A heavy silence descended over the room.

The commissioner's lips thinned. 'Are you suggesting our suspects include some of the most influential figures in Jaipur?'

Anika met his gaze evenly. 'I'm suggesting they are part of a history someone is trying to expose. Whether they are active players or mere inheritors of past crimes, I can't say yet. But the killer's pattern suggests that the final victim will be someone connected to these secrets.'

She pulled out a second set of documents: profiles of individuals linked to these historical injustices. 'Based on my analysis, these are the most likely targets for the next murder. Their deaths would complete the symbol the killer is carving across Jaipur.'

Commissioner Verma scanned the names, his jaw tightening. 'This is a powder keg, Dr Thakur. If word gets out before we have concrete evidence . . .'

'It will be chaos,' Anika finished grimly. 'Which is why we need to move carefully but decisively. If my predictions hold, we are running out of time.'

A tense murmur rippled through the room, but Anika wasn't done. She took a deep breath, steadying herself for what she had to say next.

'As I mentioned in the conference room, someone in this department is leaking information.'

A silence followed, eyes flickering around the table, shifting between scepticism and unease.

Commissioner Verma's expression darkened as he straightened in his chair. 'I hope you understand how serious this accusation is, Dr Thakur. What proof do you have?'

Anika didn't flinch. 'It's evident, sir. Every single time we get close, every time we identify a lead, the killer is one step ahead. They knew about our museum inquiries. They knew when we were tightening security around key locations. Dutta revealed things he should never have known. And most recently, my mother was attacked, and a lockbox containing historical documents was stolen from her home the same day that I visited her.'

The room fell silent. Singh's brows knitted together. 'So someone in our department is betraying us.'

'I'm saying that someone with access to our case files is feeding information to the other side,' Anika said, scanning the room for any flicker of guilt. 'I don't know their motives, but we can't ignore the pattern anymore.'

Singh exhaled, rubbing his temples. 'That explains how they stay ahead of us. But if there's a leak . . . how do we even move forward?'

'We compartmentalise,' Verma said sharply. His eyes swept across the table. 'From now on, all communications happen in person. No emails, no unsecured phone calls. If we must share details, it's through written memos that are destroyed after being read.'

He looked at Anika. 'You suspect someone in this room?'

Anika hesitated, then chose her words carefully. 'I suspect someone in this station, knowingly or not, is passing along key details. Until we identify the source, we assume that nothing is safe.'

Verma's fingers drummed against the table. 'Agreed. Now, Dr Thakur, what's the next move?'

Anika straightened, switching to the final slide of her presentation. 'We set a trap. The killer needs to strike one last time to complete their message. We predict where they'll go next, and we get there first.'

She pointed to the map with red-marked locations glowing under the dim light. 'I pointed out several places earlier. These are the potential places where I believe he could strike. We set up deep cover surveillance, with officers disguised as house staff, security personnel, and even journalists. The moment we get a lead, we move in.'

Dr Malhotra looked sceptical. 'And what if we're wrong?'

Anika met his gaze unflinchingly. 'If we're wrong, then someone else dies. And we lose our only chance to stop them before this escalates further.'

Another long silence. Then Verma sighed, his voice heavy with finality. 'All right. We go with your plan. But remember this, Dr Thakur, if at any point I suspect your personal connection is clouding your judgment, you're out. No arguments.'

Anika nodded. 'Understood, sir.'

As the meeting adjourned, the officers left one by one, their faces set with purpose. Anika remained seated, staring at the profiles in front of her. Each name was a potential victim, and each face was tied to a history she was only beginning to uncover.

Commissioner Verma lingered by the door. 'Are you sure you're ready for what can be revealed?'

Anika looked up, her resolve as hard as iron. 'I don't think I ever had a choice. This started long before me and won't end unless we make it end.'

Verma nodded, his features looking burdened. 'Then may God help us all. Because if you're right about this, we're about to shake the very foundations of Jaipur.'

As the door closed behind him, Anika exhaled slowly. She had crossed the threshold. There was no turning back now.

The tea shop was a sanctuary of stillness, tucked away in a quiet corner of Jaipur's labyrinthine streets. Here, the city's relentless energy softened, its honking rickshaws and hurried footsteps dulled to a distant murmur. The scent of spiced chai curled through the air, mingling with the faint sweetness of cardamom and rose petals.

Anika sat at a secluded table near the back, stirring her tea absently and watching the steam rise into the dim light. Her thoughts were a tangled web, strands of history, murder, and personal revelations intertwining so tightly that she could scarcely tell one from the other.

Then the doorbell chimed, and Vikram Singh Rathore entered.

Even in the simplest of kurtas, he carried himself with an elegance that couldn't be masked. There was an air of command in how he moved and the slight nod he gave to the elderly owner as he stepped inside. Anika studied him as he approached. There was something different about him today: a weight in his eyes and tension just below the surface of his composed expression.

Vikram had been unusually distant for the past few days, busy with the ever-shifting dynamics of royal politics. Anika knew that while she had been chasing ghosts from the past, he had been manoeuvring through the present, dealing with the rising tensions within Jaipur's aristocracy.

'Anika,' he greeted her as he slid into the chair across from her. His voice, though warm, carried a note of exhaustion.

She offered a small tired smile. 'You look like you've had a long week.'

His lips quirked in wry amusement. 'Let's just say palace intrigue is alive and well.'

Anika arched a brow. 'Trouble in paradise?'

'You have no idea.' He sighed, rubbing his temple. 'There have been . . . disagreements. Some of the older houses are growing restless. The past has a way of haunting us all, doesn't it?' He gave her a pointed look.

She didn't flinch from his gaze. Instead, she reached into her bag, retrieving a folded paper and sliding it across the table. 'That's exactly why I asked you here.'

Vikram unfolded the document, his eyes scanning the intricate overlay of crime scenes, historical landmarks, and patterns drawn across the map of Jaipur. Slowly, his fingers traced the markings, recognition flashing in his expression.

'This is extraordinary,' he murmured. 'You've linked the murder sites to form an ancient royal seal.'

Anika studied his reaction closely. 'You recognise it.'

Vikram looked up, his gaze intense. 'It's the Seal of Truth and Justice, an emblem known only to a select few within the royal families. It's an old insignia, thought to have been lost to time.' His voice dropped to a near whisper. 'How did you find this?'

She hesitated. 'A combination of research, instinct . . . and a few unexpected revelations about my own family's past.'

A flicker of understanding passed across Vikram's face. He leaned back slightly, his features unreadable. 'Ah. So, you've discovered the truth about your lineage.'

'You knew?' Her voice carried a sharp edge of accusation.

Vikram exhaled, tilting his head as if weighing his response. 'I had my suspicions. Some old records hinted at your family's past, but it wasn't my place to tell you. Some truths must be found, not given.'

Anika held his gaze, searching for deception. She found none.

'The seal is not just a pattern the killer is following. He is leaving a trail. It's a map, a guide to hidden archives.'

Vikram's expression darkened, his fingers curling around the paper. 'You truly don't let mysteries rest, do you, Dr Thakur?'

'No,' she said plainly.

A slow, reluctant smile ghosted across his lips. 'Yes, you're right. The seal is more than an emblem. It marks locations of deep significance— places where, according to legend, records of Jaipur's darkest secrets were hidden.'

He leaned in, lowering his voice. 'But, Anika, if those archives exist, they contain truths that could shake Jaipur's foundations. We're talking about murders disguised as accidents, betrayals that altered the course of Rajasthan's history, and evidence of corruption and abuse that spans generations. The kind of truths that have the power to ruin lives.'

She felt a chill run through her.

'That's exactly what I believe the killer is trying to expose,' she said. 'Every murder is a puzzle piece, leading to these hidden truths. But I need to know, Vikram, what kind of secrets are we dealing with?'

Vikram studied her, as if gauging how much she could handle. Finally, he spoke, his voice quieter than before.

'There was a time,' he began, 'when royal justice was not always decided in courtrooms. Secret decrees, covert trials, and sentences were carried out in the dark. Some of Jaipur's noblest families have blood on their hands that never saw the light of day. Not just royalty, but the wealthy merchant dynasties and the political elite were also a part of this. This city was built on alliances, and for centuries, those in power ensured their sins were buried.'

His fingers tapped the map lightly. 'If someone has been tracing this pattern, if they know about these archives, then they are unearthing something very, very dangerous.'

Anika inhaled sharply. 'And what about the man with the silver pocket watch? Who is he?'

Vikram's entire demeanour shifted. His easy charm faded, replaced by something colder, graver.

'He . . . he is someone we never speak about. When I was a child, I thought he was just another myth, but as I grew old, I learned that the less one knew about him, the better.'

'I need to know, Vikram, please.'

Vikram sighed deeply. 'He isn't just a keeper of secrets,' he said. 'He is part of something much older. An order of protectors, guardians of balance. Some say they exist to prevent dangerous truths from being revealed. Others say they decide which truths must never see the light of day.' He paused. 'If he is involved, it means you're treading on very thin ice.'

Anika's pulse quickened.

'I need to find the next location before the killer's finale,' she said. 'Can you help me?'

For a long moment, Vikram didn't answer. His eyes searched hers, as if trying to determine whether she truly understood the gravity of what she was asking.

Then he nodded.

'All right,' he said. 'But we must be discreet. You're asking me to unravel a history that men have died to protect. And if we do this . . . you have to be prepared for the consequences.'

Anika held his gaze. 'I don't have a choice, Vikram. People are dying. And I won't stop until I find out why.'

Vikram sighed, then gave her a wry smile. 'You do have a way of making things difficult, don't you?'

Anika smirked. 'So do you.'

The tension between them lingered. Anika saw something in Vikram's eyes that made her realise why he'd been helping her all along. He liked her in a way that she did not.

'Anika,' Vikram said after a pause, his voice softer. 'Be careful. I would be . . . deeply troubled if anything happened to you.'

Something in his tone made her throat tighten. She swallowed, nodding. 'I will.'

For a moment, neither of them moved. Then, with a final glance at the map, Vikram gathered his notes, his fingers brushing against hers briefly as he took the paper.

'Until next time, Dr Thakur,' he murmured.

As Vikram stepped out of the tea shop and into the fading light of the Jaipur evening, Anika sat still, absorbing everything they had just discussed.

The past was stirring. The pieces were aligning. And the secrets of history were waiting to be unearthed.

ॐ

A solitary desk lamp cast flickering light across a shadowed office, illuminating the gleam of sweat on the forehead of the figure hunched over a desktop. With trembling fingers, they attached a series of documents to an email, hesitating for just a moment before hitting the 'send' button.

ॐ

Across town, in the buzzing newsroom of the *Jaipur Chronicle*, Manoj Dutta's phone vibrated against his desk. Annoyed at the interruption, he glanced at the screen. The subject line jolted him upright:

EXCLUSIVE: SERIAL KILLER INVESTIGATION BREAKTHROUGH

His pulse spiked. He barely muttered an excuse before rushing out of the conference room and striding towards his desk. A quick tap of the screen, a flurry of clicks, and the email unfurled before him, spilling out confidential police reports, forensic findings, crime scene photos . . . and a list of potential future victims.

Dutta exhaled sharply, scanning the names—some of Jaipur's most powerful families. He didn't just have a story. He had a reckoning in his hands.

Across Jaipur, the fallout was immediate.

In the penthouse suite of the Singhania Mansion, Aditi Singhania, heiress to one of Jaipur's oldest business dynasties, reclined in her sunlit study, sipping her morning Darjeeling tea. The first notification made her frown. The second stole the breath from her lungs. The third sent her into action.

Prominent Jaipur Families Linked to Serial Killer
Investigation—Aditi Singhania Named as Potential Target

The headline scrolled across her screen in stark black letters.

She shot to her feet, dialling rapidly. 'I don't care what it takes,' she hissed to her security detail. 'I want increased personal security, and I want it now. And I want to find out who leaked this.'

Meanwhile, at the Jaipur Police Headquarters, chaos erupted.

Phones rang off the hook. Senior officers huddled over screens, their faces tight with shock and fury as the leak spread like wildfire. The controlled operation they had so meticulously crafted had just been blown apart.

Commissioner Verma burst into the war room, his expression thunderous. 'Who leaked this? I want answers, now!'

❧

The newsroom of the *Jaipur Chronicle* throbbed with chaos. Phones rang off the hook, printers sputtered headlines in real time, and the low hum of frantic typing filled the air like a war drum.

Manoj Dutta stood at the centre, calm amid the storm. Clutching a sheaf of documents in one hand and a half-drained coffee in the other, he barked orders with a general's precision.

'Priya, get the background on every name in that document—socials, family, past political donations, and the works. Amit, comb through the Royal Archives for patterns. This isn't random. There's history in this. And for God's sake, someone get me Dr Anika Thakur on the line. I want her on record before every other outlet wakes up.'

A ripple of energy passed through the room. Everyone knew what the leak had unleashed.

It wasn't just confidential files. It was a cultural earthquake.

❧

Anika's phone vibrated violently against her nightstand. Still tangled in her sheets, she groaned and reached for it with one arm.

'Anika,' Inspector Singh's voice boomed before she could say hello. 'We've got a problem. A big one.'

Her voice rasped with sleep, 'Rajesh? What's going on?'

'Turn on the news. Now.'

She reached blindly for the remote, blinking against the screen's sudden glare. The news anchor's expression was grim.

'We interrupt this broadcast with breaking news. Sensitive documents from the Jaipur serial killings have been leaked to the press, revealing

explosive connections between the murders and members of Jaipur's elite—business leaders, royals, and prominent politicians. A partial list of future potential targets was included. Among the names: Aditi Singhania and Rajesh Mathur.'

Her pulse stuttered. Just then, her phone buzzed again.

Vikram (text): *What the hell is going on? Call me. Now.*

Anika stared at the screen. Her mind raced as a single chilling thought took form:

Someone close had lit the match, and Jaipur was burning.

She sat up slowly, the weight of it all pressing on her chest. The enemy wasn't just outside anymore. They were on the inside.

By midday, the *Jaipur Chronicle* had become gospel and wildfire rolled into one.

The front page screamed scandal, its images looping on every television and every mobile screen. Outside the sprawling Singhania estate, guards formed a trembling line as reporters clawed at the gates, microphones raised like weapons.

Elsewhere, in the marbled halls of Jaipur's old money, tempers flared behind closed doors. Spokespersons issued sterile press releases: 'No comment at this time.' 'Unsubstantiated speculation.' But behind their stone-faced façades, dynasties were cracking. Legacy was bleeding.

And nowhere was the chaos more palpable than inside the Jaipur Police Headquarters.

The fluorescent lights buzzed overhead, matching the tension that vibrated through the walls of the conference room like static before a storm. The air was taut, stale with panic and resentment. A ring of faces—drawn, defensive, and silent—surrounded the long table.

Commissioner Verma slammed a thick file onto the table. The sound made everyone jump.

'Who the hell leaked this?' his voice ricocheted off the glass walls, a lash across the faces of everyone seated. 'I want names. I want a chain of custody. I want heads.'

No one spoke. The room held its breath.

At the far end of the table, Anika sat stiffly beside Inspector Singh. To her left were Kumar, Nair, Dr Malhotra, and two senior officers. They all looked everywhere but at each other.

The leak hadn't just ruptured the investigation. It had fractured trust.

Verma's fury simmered into something colder, more dangerous. He leaned forward, planting both fists on the polished wood with deliberate force. His voice dropped, deadly quiet.

'Dr Thakur,' he said. 'You've had access to sensitive data. You've operated with unusual autonomy. You've been . . . remarkably close to Vikram Singh Rathore, whose name, coincidentally, features prominently in the *Chronicle*'s exposé.'

Anika didn't flinch, but her eyes sharpened.

'And now,' Verma continued, 'just as we were piecing together a credible pattern, our entire strategy is compromised. The city is a circus. Our suspects are closing ranks. Our credibility is eroding by the hour.' He let the silence thicken before delivering the blow.

'Tell me, Doctor, why shouldn't I believe this leak came from you?'

The words landed like a gut punch.

Singh shifted in his seat, visibly bristling.

Anika met Verma's eyes without blinking. Her voice was calm, but her anger hummed beneath the surface like a struck wire.

'Because I've spent every waking hour trying to *solve* this case, not destroy it. Because I haven't taken a single step without briefing your office. And because I don't have a personal agenda to protect, unlike some people in this room.'

Verma arched a brow. 'Interesting deflection.'

'It's not a deflection. It's a fact,' Anika said, voice firmer now. 'You want to know who leaked this? Start with who benefits. It wasn't me. But someone wants this case gutted before we reach the truth.'

For a moment, the room fell into an uneasy silence.

Then Dr Malhotra coughed lightly, his tone acidic. 'Spoken like someone with something to hide.'

Anika turned towards him, her smile icy. 'If I wanted publicity, Dr Malhotra, I'd be writing op-eds about your lab's inconclusive forensics.'

Malhotra flushed crimson.

Verma straightened. 'Enough. This isn't a courtroom. This is a crisis. And unless we get our house in order, we'll be solving this case from inside a public inquiry panel.'

He let the silence hang, then pointed at Singh.

'Lock down all access logs. Audit communications—internal and external. I want a full trail on every file touched, downloaded, forwarded, printed—anything. Dr Thakur will continue her work, but under tighter protocol. Is that understood?'

Singh gave a curt nod. 'Understood, sir.'

Verma's gaze swept the room one last time. 'I want answers. And I want them yesterday.'

He turned and stalked out, the door slamming behind him like a final verdict.

Inside the room, nobody spoke. But the damage was done.

And for Anika, the hunt for a killer had just become a hunt for a traitor.

CHAPTER 13

The conference room at the Jaipur Police Headquarters simmered with tension as officers trickled in, the low thrum of their voices laced with uncertainty.

The recent leak had shattered whatever fragile unity the investigation once held, and now every glance carried weight, every silence suspicion. Commissioner Verma stood at the head of the long table, arms folded across his chest like a barricade. To his right, Inspector Singh held a thick dossier, his grip firm, knuckles pale. Farther down sat Dr Malhotra, his expression unreadable, the steady tap of his pen against the table the only movement from him.

Dr Anika Thakur remained seated at the periphery, her presence diminished not by posture but by designation.

Verma's earlier message had been unmistakable: She was no longer leading this investigation. The sting of it pressed like a bruise.

For weeks, she had been the engine driving this inquiry—decoding symbolism, reconstructing history, and risking everything. Now she was little more than an observer.

Verma rapped his knuckles against the table, silencing the remaining murmurs.

'This meeting concerns our next steps following the leak,' he said, voice clipped and emotionless. 'Effective immediately, Dr Thakur is no longer heading the investigation.'

A ripple passed through the room like a gust through dry leaves. Singh shot Anika a glance—controlled but tight with restraint. He said nothing.

'Inspector Singh will lead operations from this point forward,' Verma continued. 'We can't afford further breaches. Procedures are to be followed to the letter.'

The implication was clear: Someone had broken ranks, and Verma believed Anika to be the weak link.

Her nails dug into her palm, but she stayed quiet. A reaction would only vindicate their doubts.

Verma gestured at Singh. 'Take over.'

Singh stepped forward, cleared his throat, and nodded. 'Yes, sir.'

The projector flared to life, illuminating the screen with a tactical map and bullet-point updates. The plan had Anika's fingerprints all over it, but now she had no say in how it would be executed.

'As you're aware,' Singh began, his voice neutral but steady, 'the killer has been staging the murders in alignment with specific historical incidents. Dr Thakur's groundwork identified a clear progression. That pattern suggests a culminating act at a symbolic site.'

He didn't say 'her theory'. He said 'her groundwork'—a subtle reinforcement of her credibility.

Anika saw the flicker of tension in Verma's jaw.

'With the details now public,' Singh continued, 'there's a high chance the killer will alter their plan. We must be ready for a deviation—an earlier strike, or a new location.'

'If they change the venue, we lose the trail,' Kumar said, frowning.

'We're accounting for that,' Singh replied, clicking through to the next slide. 'We're expanding surveillance to additional historic sites. But we're also considering off-list targets—locations with symbolic weight but less public prominence.'

Then Singh turned slightly towards Anika. 'Dr Thakur, your analysis was instrumental. Do you believe there are additional sites we may have missed?'

A silence fell. Every head turned.

For a moment, Anika considered letting the silence stretch. If they didn't trust her, why should she offer insight?

But that wasn't who she was.

She cleared her throat. 'Yes,' she said, meeting Singh's gaze. 'There are two alternate sites the killer could exploit. Both bear historical relevance but haven't been prioritised due to lower visibility.'

She opened her folder, flipping precisely to the marked page. 'First, Haveli Jhaveri—a lesser-known noble residence abandoned after its family vanished in the 1800s. Second, an out-of-use temple outside Jaipur was once used covertly during colonial resistance. Both carry symbolic resonance.'

A hum of interest rose around the room. Verma's expression didn't change.

Assignments resumed. Voices overlapped. Anika remained silent, observing. Malhotra contributed little; his interjections were vague. If he was responsible for the leak, he was being cautious.

As the meeting drew to a close, Verma raised a hand. 'Dr Thakur. Stay back.'

The atmosphere tightened. Officers loitered, shuffling papers they'd already sorted.

Anika stood. 'Yes, sir?'

Verma's tone was low, but his words cut clean. 'I'm watching you. You've been meeting with Vikram Singh Rathore, one of the families now under public scrutiny. You're delving into your own family's past. And now, this information ends up in the press. You see how this looks?'

Anika met his stare. 'I've done nothing to compromise this case.'

'Intentions don't matter. Outcomes do,' Verma replied coldly. 'You're being retained only because your knowledge remains useful. But if I detect even a whisper of personal bias influencing your work, I will end your involvement—and your career in this field—without hesitation.'

Anika's pulse thundered, but her voice remained firm. 'Understood.'

Verma studied her for a beat longer, then turned away.

Singh waited outside. He exhaled through his nose. 'He's impossible when he's cornered.'

'I noticed,' Anika muttered.

He nodded, voice low. 'I've got your back. But watch yourself. If Malhotra's behind this, he's not done.'

Anika's jaw tightened. 'Then we stay two steps ahead.'

As they walked out, the eyes of colleagues tracked her—some curious, some cold, and most uncertain. The damage had been done. Trust had ruptured.

And maybe, just maybe, that had been the killer's true objective all along.

The police SUV screeched to a halt before the imposing Singhania Mansion, its red-and-blue lights splashing across the marble façade like a warning flare. The estate—a lavish relic of Jaipur's aristocratic past—stood tall, stately, and completely out of sync with the urgency crackling in the air.

Anika pushed the door open before the vehicle had stopped. Her boots hit the pavement hard. Beside her, Singh followed, his expression set in grim focus.

'Dr Thakur, Jaipur police,' she said sharply, flashing her ID at the startled butler. 'We need to speak with Aditi Singhania immediately. This is a matter of life and death.'

The butler—a man in a pristine uniform with the stoicism of someone trained to serve royalty—hesitated just a beat too long.

'I'm sorry, ma'am,' he said, voice measured. 'Ms Singhania left about an hour ago. She appeared . . . distressed.'

Anika felt her stomach clench.

'Where did she go?' Singh asked, his voice firm.

The butler glanced between them, uneasy. 'She didn't say. But she kept looking behind her. She was nervous.'

'Was she alone?'

Another hesitation. 'No. A man accompanied her. I didn't recognise him.'

Anika tensed. 'Describe him.'

'Tall. Well dressed. Not flashy, but . . . refined. He carried a pocket watch. Kept checking it.'

That did it.

'We need access to your security footage. Now,' Anika ordered.

The butler looked uncertain, but Singh stepped forward, eyes hard. 'If you delay, you risk obstructing a police investigation. Your call.'

That broke the impasse.

Minutes later, they crowded inside the mansion's security room, watching grainy footage roll across the screen. Aditi appeared first, visibly anxious, her handbag clutched tightly. She moved fast. Behind her, the man. His face remained obscured—deliberately—but the glint of the pocket watch under the chandelier was unmistakable.

'He knows exactly where the cameras are,' Singh said grimly.

'This wasn't an escape. It was orchestrated,' Anika replied.

Her phone buzzed. Vikram.

'Anika? What the hell is going on?'

'No time. Aditi left with a man. Possibly the killer. Do you know where she might go?'

A pause. Then, 'There's an old property—the Singhania family owned it years ago. Outskirts of Jaipur. I'll send the location.'

'Do it. Fast.'

A text pinged almost instantly.

Anika turned to Singh. 'We've got a lead.'

Singh keyed into his radio. 'All units, converge on the following coordinates. Possible target location. Proceed with caution.'

As they raced back to the SUV, Singh muttered, 'Something doesn't add up. Why would she go with him willingly?'

Anika stared out the windshield as Jaipur blurred past. 'What if she wasn't abducted? What if she ran, and he's helping her?'

'You think he's not the threat?'

'Not necessarily. But this could be a panic response. She was named in the leak. Maybe she trusted the wrong person. Or maybe . . . he's the only one she trusts.'

Singh swore under his breath. 'So, we're not walking into a rescue. We're walking into a negotiation.'

The estate emerged ahead, set like a forgotten jewel against the night. Lights blazed from within, and movement stirred behind high windows.

Singh grabbed his radio. 'All units, hold position. We approach on foot. Unknown situation.'

Anika exhaled. 'Let's find out.'

She was out of the vehicle before it came to a full stop, striding towards the gate. Singh flanked her, his hand hovering near his weapon.

Anika hit the intercom.

Silence.

Then a crackle.

'Dr Thakur,' came Aditi Singhania's voice—calm, composed, and unmistakable. 'Please. Come in. We have much to discuss.'

Anika went still.

Singh looked at her. 'Not the voice of a terrified victim.'

'No,' she said slowly. 'It isn't.'

The wrought-iron gates creaked open.

They walked the long drive in silence, the mansion looming ahead like a slumbering sentinel. The doors opened before they reached them.

Aditi stood framed in the entryway, calm and elegant. At her side: the man with the silver pocket watch.

'Welcome, Dr Thakur. Inspector Singh,' Aditi said. 'You've come far for the truth. Now it's time you heard it.'

A chill slid down Anika's spine.

This wasn't a stand-off.

It was a reveal.

And they were walking into the heart of it.

As they stepped into the grand hall, the heavy doors closed behind them with an ominous click. The chandelier above flickered slightly as if reacting to the shift in atmosphere. Anika scanned the foyer—ornate murals, echoing marble, and the hush of something sacred or secret. Aditi paused near the hearth, her posture regal, a wary edge softening her poise. Beside her, the man held the pocket watch loosely in one hand, its chain glinting faintly.

Anika didn't waste time. 'Who are you?' she demanded. 'What is this?'

The man inclined his head. 'I am Udayveer Ranawat,' he said, voice deep and deliberate. 'Grand master of the Custodians of the Seal.'

Singh raised a brow. 'The what?'

Aditi answered, her voice controlled but tense. 'The Custodians are a secret order. Their role is to protect knowledge—dangerous knowledge—that could destabilise what little order Jaipur has left.'

Singh folded his arms. 'Sounds a lot like sanctioned secrecy.'

'Not secrecy,' Udayveer said. 'Stewardship. There is a difference.'

Anika took a step forward, her voice steel. 'Where is my brother?'

Udayveer's expression darkened. 'We took him, yes. But only because he was getting too close. He uncovered things not meant for unguarded eyes. We meant to protect him.'

Anika's hands clenched. 'You abducted him. And then what? You lost him?'

Aditi glanced away. 'There's another faction. A radical offshoot. They call themselves the Wrathbearers.'

Udayveer nodded solemnly. 'They believe in vengeance. They turned away from preservation and chose blood.'

Singh let out a dry laugh. 'Of course they did.'

But Anika was already threading it together. 'So, you hid Yuvraj. And the Wrathbearers found him.'

Udayveer's voice dropped. 'Yes. Before we could move him again. We failed.'

Aditi's eyes glistened. 'And he never came back.'

Silence stretched, heavy as stone. The pieces clicked in Anika's mind: Wrathbearers orchestrating vengeance, the Custodians guarding legacy, and in the crossfire, her brother.

'And the killer?' she asked. 'He's not a rogue. He's your enemy. Your opposite.'

Udayveer nodded. 'He leads the Wrathbearers. And he is closer to his goal than ever.'

'Then this isn't just revenge,' Singh said grimly. 'This is a centuries-old war.'

Aditi turned to Anika. 'You were never outside this. You were always part of it. Our family . . . has always been part of it.'

Udayveer's eyes were unblinking. 'Your brother's fate is unknown. But the Wrathbearers are preparing their final act. One last killing. One that will break the last seal.'

Anika's voice was barely a whisper. 'And what is behind that seal?'

Udayveer answered without hesitation. 'Control. Of memory. Of history. Of Jaipur itself.'

A chill ran down Anika's spine.

And in that moment, she realised that truth could be just as dangerous as lies. And both were now in play.

✳

As Anika and Singh stepped out of the Singhania Mansion, the weight of Aditi's revelations pressed down on them like monsoon heat. The scent of rain-soaked earth filled the air, and distant thunder grumbled over the horizon. Jaipur shimmered in the haze of midnight stillness, but Anika's thoughts churned.

The Custodians. The Wrathbearers. Yuvraj.

The truth had splintered the investigation wide open, yet it felt like they were only beginning to understand the full shape of the storm. If the Wrathbearers' leader was indeed orchestrating the murders—and if he had once held Yuvraj—then the final piece of the puzzle was already in motion.

Was Yuvraj still alive?

Anika's phone buzzed in her hand, yanking her back. A message from Dr Malhotra: *'Interrogation Room 2. Asst. Sub-Inspector Shilpa Nair in custody. Possible connection to the leak. You need to come. Now.'*

She showed it to Singh. His jaw tensed.

'Malhotra's got Shilpa in custody,' she said quietly. 'He thinks she's the leak.'

Singh exhaled, the sound sharp. 'Shilpa? No way. But let's see what he's up to.'

Without another word, they moved. The mansion's lights faded behind them as their vehicle cut through the night, winding back towards the station.

Tension hung heavy inside the Jaipur Police Headquarters. Whispers curled through corridors. Glances lingered a second too long. The leak had shattered camaraderie. Suspicion bled into every interaction.

Anika and Singh moved through the fog of distrust, arriving at Interrogation Room 2. Malhotra stood inside, his arms folded, eyes fixed on the figure seated at the steel table.

Assistant Sub-Inspector Shilpa Nair.

When she looked up, Anika saw it immediately. Not just fear.

Guilt.

Commissioner Verma paced like a caged lion. His voice, when it came, was a low growl.

'Officer Nair. Last chance. Did you leak classified information from this investigation?'

Shilpa's throat bobbed. 'No, sir. I swear—I didn't send anything to the press.'

Malhotra stepped in, sharp as a scalpel. 'Your access card was used to enter the evidence room at 2.03 a.m. the night before the leak. Your login was used to access sealed files. Explain that.'

Shilpa's eyes flickered, panic breaking through. 'I . . . must have left my card somewhere. Someone could have—'

'And your home computer?' Verma barked. 'Also compromised?'

Her shoulders sagged. 'I don't know. Maybe my password was stolen.'

Singh's voice cut through. Calm. Cold.

'Shilpa, we've worked together for years. I want to believe you. But right now, I need the truth. Who did you give information to?'

She hesitated. Her lips parted, then closed. Then . . .

'I didn't leak anything to the media,' she said softly. 'But I did share some case details. With someone who said they were helping. Someone who claimed they wanted to stop the killings.'

Verma slammed both hands on the table. 'Who?'

She flinched. 'I . . . I can't say.'

Anika stepped closer, her tone steady. 'You're not protecting them, Shilpa. You're giving them more power. We can protect you, but only if you trust us.'

Shilpa raked trembling fingers through her hair. 'You don't understand. This goes deeper than any of us.'

Singh narrowed his eyes. 'You're talking about the secret societies.'

She blinked. Shocked. 'You know?'

Anika nodded. 'The Custodians. And the Wrathbearers. We know enough to be dangerous.'

Shilpa caught her breath. Her defences cracked.

'I thought I was helping the Custodians,' she whispered. 'He said he worked for them. That he was trying to expose corruption.'

Verma's tone dropped to ice. 'You fed our investigation to a man who now leads a deadly underground network.'

Shilpa recoiled, her face pale. 'No . . . no, that can't be right. He told me—'

'He lied,' Singh said, voice like flint. 'People are dead, Shilpa.'

Tears welled in her eyes. 'I didn't know. I swear.'

'That doesn't make it better,' Verma snapped.

Anika stepped back, arms folded. 'Did you tell him about the seal? The historical pattern?'

Shilpa nodded numbly. 'He already knew. He just needed to know how close we were.'

Anika and Singh exchanged grim looks.

'He knows we're closing in,' Singh muttered.

'And he's accelerating,' Anika added.

Verma pinched the bridge of his nose, furious and exhausted. 'We're running out of time.'

'Please,' Shilpa pleaded. 'I never meant to—'

'Save it,' Verma barked. 'You're suspended. Effective immediately. If you're holding back anything else, pray it doesn't cost another life.'

Singh grabbed her arm, steering her gently but firmly towards the door.

Verma turned to Anika. 'I want everything. All of it. No more shadows, no more riddles.'

Anika met his gaze. 'Understood. But first, we stop them.'

Verma gave a tight nod. 'Go.'

As Singh escorted Shilpa down the corridor, Anika tapped Vikram's contact.

He picked up instantly. 'Anika?'

'We have a name,' she said.

A pause.

Then, 'Aditi told you?'

'The Wrathbearers,' Anika said. 'It's real. And it's moving fast.'

Outside, the storm broke.

And the final act had begun.

As Singh returned from escorting Shilpa, the war room at the Jaipur Police Headquarters was already in motion. The walls were lined with pinned photographs, forensic reports, and maps of the city marked in red circles. The air thrummed with the urgency of an impending storm.

Phones rang. Radios crackled. Officers moved like pieces on a chessboard—deliberate, alert, and wary.

Commissioner Verma entered, his uniform creased from long hours, but his voice was razor-sharp. 'Dr Thakur, bring us up to speed.'

Anika stood beside the central table, her notes spread before her. Singh flanked her, arms crossed and his expression unreadable.

She began calmly, but her voice carried weight. 'We have confirmation of what we're dealing with. The murders, the symbols, the seal—it all connects back to two ancient factions: the Custodians of the Seal, and their rivals, the Wrathbearers.'

A murmur passed through the room.

'Our source,' she continued, 'is Aditi Singhania. She and Udayveer Ranawat, the Custodians' grand master, revealed the truth. The Custodians aren't behind the murders. They've spent centuries protecting sensitive knowledge, trying to prevent chaos. The Wrathbearers, however, seek vengeance. Their leader is orchestrating this bloodbath.'

Kumar sat up straighter. 'So, these Wrathbearers . . . what's their endgame?'

'To settle centuries-old scores,' Anika said. 'Their belief is simple: Royal blood must pay for ancestral sins. But it's not just revenge. The murders are calculated to expose secrets, break the social order, and reclaim the narrative of Jaipur's history.'

Verma leaned forward, elbows on the table. 'And your brother?'

Anika's jaw tightened. 'Yuvraj stumbled onto the truth. The Custodians took him to protect him, but they couldn't hide him forever. The Wrathbearers found him before he could resurface.'

Singh spoke up. 'We don't know if he's alive. But we know they're accelerating. Their final act is coming.'

Dr Malhotra cut in, impatient, 'So, who is our killer?'

'The current leader of the Wrathbearers,' Anika replied. 'He's not just a killer. He's a symbol. Few within even know his true identity. He uses the murders as ritual, messaging, and vengeance. I believe he's taken liberties the previous leaders never dared.'

Another wave of murmurs rippled through the room.

Malhotra raised his voice. 'So where does that leave us?'

'It leaves us with a chance to stop the next killing,' Anika said firmly. 'We've identified three likely targets for the final ritual: an abandoned stepwell on the city's edge, a long-forgotten mausoleum tied to an erased noble line, and a crumbling section of Jaipur's old walls once used for executions.'

Officer Priya Singh stepped forward. 'What about evidence from earlier scenes? Anything forensic?'

Anika nodded. 'Traces of a rare pollen found at each site. It's tied to a flower not native to Jaipur. Botanists are helping us trace its source.'

Singh added, 'This last murder will be symbolic—larger, bloodier, theatrical. We can't underestimate the staging.'

Verma straightened. 'Then this is how we proceed: Malhotra, Priya, you and your teams sweep all three locations. Anything suspicious, report immediately. Kumar, coordinate drone and traffic surveillance. If the killer's on the move, we track him.'

He turned to the media liaison. 'Kavita, manage the press. No leaks. No sensational headlines. Feed them a decoy story if you must.'

The room nodded as one.

Verma's voice hardened. 'We've lost ground before. Not this time. No more mistakes.'

The war room came alive. Officers darted to their assignments. Radios clicked. Orders flew.

Anika tapped out a message to Vikram: *What do you know about the Wrathbearers and the Custodians?*

She slipped her phone into her pocket and looked over at Singh, who was barking orders into his headset.

When he finished, he caught her eye. She nodded.

He stepped close and gripped her shoulder.

'Let's end this,' he said.

And they both knew—whatever happened in the next few hours would reshape not just the case but the very soul of the city.

The final chapter had already begun.

CHAPTER 14

The flickering glow of candlelight bathed the cavernous chamber in a restless shimmer, sending distorted shadows dancing along the ancient stone walls. The air was dense with scent—sandalwood, camphor, and beneath it all, the unmistakable tang of fresh blood. In the centre of the chamber, before a weathered altar, a solitary figure moved with ritualistic precision.

The golden pocket watch lay open atop the altar, its delicate hands ticking towards the fated hour. The man stared at it in silence, drawing in a slow breath. This moment had not simply been planned. It had been foreseen. It was the culmination of centuries of silence and betrayal and a debt written in the blood of the forgotten.

The city above was restless. The stars above watched without mercy. Everything was aligned.

He knelt, drawing symbols into the dust that coated the stone floor, each line etched with solemn care. They were ancient sigils, remnants of a language older than the fortresses they once adorned. They carried power—ancestral, unbroken.

Nearby, a low wooden table held an assembly of relics. They were not trophies. They were evidence—proof of every cruelty whitewashed by royal decrees. An oxidised dagger, once driven through the chest of a rebel noble. Letters sealed with broken insignias of dishonoured houses.

A silk sash, stained and faded, once worn by a concubine whose murder was erased from history.

Each object whispered the same truth: History had never been just.

A shadow stirred at the entrance.

'You're late,' the killer said, without looking up.

From the darkness, a second figure emerged, their face hidden beneath a deep cowl.

'Everything is in place,' the voice replied. 'The prince has been moved. The cycle will conclude as it was written.'

The killer nodded. 'And the police?'

'Scattered. The leak fractured their rhythm. They're chasing ghosts.'

'Good,' he murmured. With a final gesture, he completed the sigil and laid both hands upon the altar. 'We will not fail as our ancestors did. This time, the reckoning will be complete.'

The hooded figure hesitated. 'And if they find us before the seal is broken?'

The killer's smile was slow and cold. 'Then they will witness it. And when the moment comes, even Dr Anika Thakur will see the necessity of what we do.'

The other shifted. 'The Custodians—'

'Are irrelevant,' the killer interrupted, his voice now edged with disdain. 'They protect the oppressors. They mask atrocity with noble intent. Their time has passed.'

Silence hung between them.

The hooded figure bowed. 'We'll be ready. The altar awaits.'

As they vanished into the shadows once more, the killer turned his gaze back to the altar. The chamber felt alive now, pulsing with memory and anticipation.

He glanced once at the pocket watch. Then, with a swift movement, he extinguished the candles one by one, plunging the chamber into darkness.

The end had begun.

The pink hues of dawn stretched across Jaipur's skyline, casting a deceptive serenity over a city now clenched in the grip of a silent, high-stakes manhunt. Beneath the surface of tranquillity, the pulse of the city beat faster. Police officers moved with silent efficiency, plain-clothes agents blended into morning crowds, and unmarked vehicles prowled narrow alleys like predators.

Inside the central command centre, Anika stood at the helm before a sprawling digital map aglow with blinking dots, each one representing a unit on the ground. She clutched her coffee mug like a talisman, sleep-deprived but locked into the adrenaline-fueled rhythm of crisis.

She tapped her earpiece. 'Team Alpha, report status at Amber Fort.'

A brief crackle. 'Alpha here. No sign of the suspect. We're sweeping the underground chambers now.'

Anika scribbled a quick note. 'Copy that. Stay sharp and don't get trapped in blind zones. We need mobility.'

She changed frequencies. 'Bravo Team, status at Hawa Mahal?'

'All clear so far,' came the reply. 'But the place is a maze.'

'Use thermal scans if necessary. And remember, we're not just looking for the killer. Anything odd: footprints, displaced objects, blood traces—mark and report.'

Across Jaipur, the search unfolded like a coordinated military drill. Singh's coordination ensured the operation remained fluid.

At Chand Baori, Delta Team moved cautiously down the ancient stepwell's winding tiers, their boots silent against stone. Flashlights cut through fog as officers checked recesses and shadows.

'Watch those ledges,' a team lead muttered. 'One slip and you'll vanish into history.'

Near Tripolia Gate, an undercover officer whispered into his mic, 'Possible sighting. Male, midforties, sherwani, moving north, looks nervous.'

'Nearby units, shadow and intercept,' Singh ordered. 'Keep it quiet. We want him unaware.'

At Jantar Mantar, search teams traced every dial and carved surface.

'Inspector Singh,' a voice called. 'Unusual etchings on one of the sundials. Sending visuals now.'

'Forward to Dr Thakur immediately.'

Anika's heart quickened as the images arrived. Intricate markings—possibly a cipher. Clue or misdirection?

'Good work,' she responded. 'Flag the site, but don't touch anything. I'm sending this to the historical team.'

The hours dragged forward. Nerves frayed. Every silence on the radio grew heavier.

Then . . . static.

'Delta Team, report,' Anika said. Nothing.

She looked to Kumar, just entering.

'Delta Team, do you copy?'

Silence.

'I don't like this,' Kumar said.

Anika's gut twisted. 'Dispatch backup to their last coordinates.'

But before orders could be issued, the command room door burst open.

Commissioner Verma entered like a thunderclap, fury barely contained.

'Dr Thakur,' he snapped. 'We've got a situation.'

Anika stepped forward. 'What's happened?'

Verma's voice dropped. 'The chief minister's office just called. They want us to scale back the search. Immediately.'

The words hit like a slap.

'Why?'

'They say it's hurting Jaipur's image. Too much public tension. Political pressure is mounting.'

Anika's eyes hardened. 'Or someone doesn't want us finding the truth.'

'I agree,' Verma said. 'Which is why we're going to *appear* to scale back. Uniforms off the streets. Official search shut down. But we move underground.'

He turned to the room. 'All marked patrols return to standard duty. Plain-clothes teams only. Communications via encrypted channels. No chatter. If anyone asks, the operation has been wound down.'

A chorus of understanding.

Anika leaned towards Kumar. 'Vikram might have insight. But he's not answering.'

'I'll find him,' Kumar replied.

Anika faced the digital map again. The dots moved like fireflies across the city grid.

Somewhere in those shadows, the killer watched. Planned. Waited.

She pressed her earpiece.

'All teams, new protocol. Radio silence unless vital. Trust your instincts. Watch each other. And remember—'

Her voice cut through like steel.

'We are the only thing standing between this killer and their next victim. We end this. Today.'

A quiet chorus of affirmations followed.

The hunt was now invisible.

But far from over.

The citywide manhunt and the mounting tension of the last few days seemed distant as Anika shut the door to her office. The command centre still buzzed beyond the walls—radio chatter, clacking keyboards, and a constant low hum of urgency—but here, in the dim quiet, she allowed herself a single breath of stillness.

She lowered into her chair, pressing her fingers to her temples. The headache that had stalked her since dawn throbbed in earnest now. Just a moment, she told herself. Just enough to recalibrate.

A knock disrupted the silence.

She looked up sharply, shoulders tensing, then softened as the door opened and Udayveer Ranawat stepped inside. The silver pocket watch glinted faintly against his chest, swinging gently on its chain like a pendulum counting down to something inevitable.

'Dr Thakur,' he said, his voice low and composed.

'What are you doing here?' she asked, dispensing with formalities.

'I bring a message,' he replied, stepping fully into the room. 'Intercepted from a channel we've been monitoring. It's a warning—anonymous, but urgent.'

He extended a small folded note. The paper was old, its texture coarse, but the ink was fresh, the handwriting elegant and slanted. Anika unfolded it.

> *Where the water whispers secrets of the past,*
> *A queen's folly stands, not meant to last.*
> *In shadow and light, the truth will show,*
> *Hurry, hurry—the time runs low.*

A chill wrapped itself around her spine. The words were too precise, too poetic to be random. It was a riddle—and a threat.

Her eyes met Udayveer's. 'Where did this come from?'

'One of our contacts embedded in the Wrathbearers' network received it,' he said. 'We suspect it came from within their own ranks. Someone who doesn't want to see this end as it was intended.'

His expression darkened. 'Whatever they've planned is already under way.'

Without another word, he turned and left, the silver of his watch glinting once more before disappearing.

Anika stared at the note again. Her lips moved as she murmured the lines.

> *Where the water whispers secrets of the past . . .*

Stepwells. *Baolis.* Ancient structures where sound carried like secrets across stone.

> *A queen's folly stands, not meant to last.*

She stood abruptly, pacing towards the large city map pinned to the wall. She ran her finger across the outskirts of Jaipur, her thoughts racing.

The Queen's Folly.

A ruined stepwell—commissioned in the 18th century by a royal consort against her council's advice. Poorly constructed. Never functional. Abandoned within a decade. An architectural embarrassment. A forgotten monument.

'Kumar!' she called.

He appeared within moments, breathless. 'What is it?'

She showed him the note. 'It's pointing to this,' she said, tapping the map. 'This old stepwell—commissioned by Queen Amaravati. They called it the Queen's Folly.'

'That's where Delta Team was searching.'

'Were you able to re-establish contact with them?'

He shook his head. 'No. After Verma's new protocols, I tried recalling them but got nothing. Dead signal.'

Her voice dropped. 'Then we may already be too late.'

'We'll send backup,' Kumar said at once.

Anika nodded, her mind churning. Was this a trap? Or was it a cry for help? Something about the riddle—it didn't feel like a threat. It felt like a map.

In shadow and light, the truth will show . . .

Stepwells were built with intricate stonework, light playing off carvings at different hours. Perhaps something hidden could be seen only at a certain time of day.

'We have to move now,' she said, already pulling on her jacket and grabbing her phone.

She dialled Singh's number. The line clicked once, twice.

'Singh,' she said as soon as he answered, 'I know where the killer is going. Or already is.'

And with that, the final chase was under way.

ॐ

The police vehicle sped through the early morning streets of Jaipur, headlights cutting through the mist and sirens off but urgency humming in the taut silence within. Anika sat rigid in the front seat, the cryptic lines of the message playing on repeat in her mind.

Kumar gripped the steering wheel tightly, navigating through quiet back roads and ancient thoroughfares. In the back, two of their most trusted officers rode in silence, their weapons checked and eyes alert. Singh would meet them at the target site. Four backup units were on silent standby.

'Take a left,' Anika instructed, eyes scanning the GPS and the narrowing tree-lined road ahead. 'The stepwell's tucked into a grove just beyond this ridge. Hard to spot unless you know exactly what you're looking for.'

Kumar nodded grimly. 'Do you think this is it?'

Anika exhaled, her breath fogging the window. 'It has to be. Every clue leads here. The history, the message, the timing—this is the culmination.'

A pause stretched between them. Then Kumar spoke, his voice laced with unease. 'Something's been bothering me.'

Anika glanced at him, tension rippling through her shoulders. 'What?'

He tightened his grip on the wheel. 'You said every murder mirrors a historical injustice. Each tied to someone from the royal past. But Aditi Singhania doesn't fit. Her family weren't royals. They were merchant class. Powerful, yes, but not aristocracy.'

The observation struck Anika like a bolt of lightning.

Her fingers flew to her notes, flipping through the sequence of murders. The patterns. The victims. The timelines. She traced the lineage—traced the chronology.

Her pulse stumbled.

'The Queen's Folly was built in the late 1700s. If the killer is following chronology, this isn't about Aditi.'

Kumar's eyes widened. 'Then who is it?'

Anika stared ahead, her voice a whisper. 'It's Vikram.'

A beat of stunned silence.

'But you spoke to him, didn't you?' Kumar asked.

'I did. At Aditi's mansion,' she said. 'But since then, nothing. I've messaged, called—radio silence.'

'I tried too,' Kumar admitted. 'No answer.'

Anika's chest tightened. 'We need to move fast. Contact HQ. Quietly. No sirens. No lights. The killer can't be alerted.'

Kumar nodded, immediately tapping into the encrypted channel to dispatch orders to the backup teams.

Anika, meanwhile, dialled Singh's number. The moment he answered, she launched into an urgent report.

'Singh, it's not Aditi. It's Vikram. He's the final target. The symbolism, the timeline—it all fits.'

There was a pause on the line. Then Singh's voice, sharp with understanding: 'We're already en route. I'll reroute Bravo and Charlie teams.'

Anika ended the call, her heart hammering. This wasn't just another ritual. This was the final trial.

Justice—or vengeance—was about to be served.

'There!' Kumar pointed.

Through the trees, the broken silhouette of the Queen's Folly emerged. Crumbling arches and ancient stone—shrouded in mist.

Kumar killed the engine. The vehicle rolled to a silent stop. A moment of breathless stillness.

Anika turned to the team. 'Stay sharp. This could be a trap. But if Vikram's alive, we're his only shot.'

They stepped out, gravel crunching beneath their boots. The grove was eerily quiet. Even the birds had fallen silent.

The stepwell loomed before them like a relic from another time, its stones slick with dew and its shadows deep with memory.

And somewhere within, the truth waited.

Unforgiving. Unavoidable.

Final.

The ancient stones of the Queen's Folly stood hushed in reverent stillness, their weathered carvings bathed in the golden light of early morning. The ruined stepwell, long forgotten and hidden beneath a curtain of gnarled trees and creeping moss, seemed to breathe with the weight of waiting—centuries of silence bristling now with imminent consequence.

Sub-Inspector Kumar and the Delta Team had already taken position, their comms disabled by an unexplained glitch. Shadows concealed their silent vigil, weapons drawn and breaths measured. From high alcoves to narrow recesses, they watched, the old walls swallowing their presence.

Inspector Singh stood near the jagged threshold of the lower tier, one hand on his holstered weapon and his body rigid with anticipation. His eyes followed Anika as she descended the ancient staircase carved into the stone, each step echoing like a countdown.

The deeper they went, the more the world above seemed to vanish. Cool air clung to the walls, and the shifting light created dancing patterns across moss-covered columns. Anika moved with purpose, but her heart was pounding, the riddle's final verse whispering in her mind.

Then . . . a sound.

Soft. Ragged. A muffled groan.

She halted.

Singh caught her eye. She gave the slightest nod. 'We've got someone,' she whispered.

Carefully, weapon drawn, she followed the sound into a shadowed corridor of the stepwell. The air grew heavier with each step. And then—

She found him.

Slumped against the cold stone, bloodied, bruised, and wrists bound tight behind his back—Vikram Singh Rathore.

'Vikram,' she gasped, falling to her knees beside him.

Singh and Kumar fanned out, covering the perimeter. Anika checked his pulse—weak but there.

Vikram's eyes fluttered. 'Anika . . .,' he rasped.

'I'm here,' she said gently, untying his wrists. 'You're safe now. Who did this to you?'

Before he could answer, a low, deliberate chuckle rolled through the chamber like a blade drawn across stone.

Anika stood abruptly, her breath catching.

'Still asking the wrong questions, Dr Thakur.'

The voice came from the upper tiers.

A figure emerged from the shadows, descending with unnerving calm. Singh raised his weapon, tension snapping like a live wire. Kumar shifted his stance, eyes locked.

The figure stepped into the light, and Anika caught her breath.

Dr Dilip Malhotra.

A silence deeper than stone fell. Even the birds above seemed to hold their breath.

'You,' Singh growled.

Malhotra smiled—a face twisted with smug certainty. 'Surprised? You shouldn't be. I've been right here the whole time.'

Anika's voice was a razor. 'Feeding us misinformation. Manipulating the evidence. Steering the case.'

'And you followed the trail so faithfully,' he said, amused. 'Like a lamb chasing shadows.'

'Why?' Singh demanded. 'Why stage these killings?'

'I didn't stage all of them,' Malhotra replied. 'Only what I was told to. The true ritual—the final offering—belongs to someone greater. I serve the master of the Wrathbearers. I merely . . . prepared the altar.'

He gestured to Vikram's bruised form.

'And who is this master?' Anika pressed.

Malhotra tilted his head. 'Soon, you'll meet him.'

Kumar spat, 'You betrayed the badge. The oath.'

'Not betrayal,' Malhotra hissed. 'Restoration. My ancestors were silenced, their legacy buried beneath royal lies. Now, balance will return. The blood of Jaipur's golden heirs will be the ink with which we rewrite its history.'

'You murdered innocent people,' Anika said, voice shaking with fury.

'No,' he countered. 'We liberated truth through blood.'

He checked his watch, then smiled wider.

'You weren't meant to stop me. You were meant to witness.'

Anika's stomach dropped.

'You never meant to kill Vikram here,' she whispered.

He nodded. 'Clever. This was never the end—just a distraction. The true ritual has already begun.'

Then . . . he moved.

His hand shot skyward, throwing a small glass vial.

The explosion was instantaneous. A blinding flash. Smoke filled the chamber, choking and dense.

'MOVE!' Singh bellowed.

Shouts rang out, and boots scrambled. By the time the smoke cleared, Malhotra was gone. The upper ledge was empty. The shadows were still.

'Damn it!' Kumar growled, sweeping the area. 'He vanished.'

Anika turned back to Vikram, kneeling. 'What did he mean? Where's the real site?'

Vikram coughed, struggling to speak. 'The Maharaja's Tomb . . . He's going there. To finish it.'

Anika felt the blood drain from her face. The tomb—a sacred, protected site. History's heartbeat.

Singh's voice was ice. 'We move. Now.'

Anika stood, her jaw set. 'Kumar, get Vikram to medical. The rest of us—we head to the tomb. Full force.'

Kumar was already on the radio.

Singh met Anika's eyes. 'This ends tonight.'

Anika's fists clenched.

'No,' she said. 'It ends now.'

The night air thickened as Anika, Singh, and what remained of Delta Team tore through Jaipur's ancient streets in a fleet of black SUVs. Their headlights sliced through the darkness, illuminating the chaos left in Malhotra's wake. The sirens had been silenced, but the urgency screamed louder than any alarm.

'Faster!' Singh snapped from the passenger seat, eyes locked on the flickering tail light of a motorbike zigzagging ahead. Malhotra was clinging to the back of the rider—a blur of dark fabric and silver glint. The rider was skilled. Too skilled. They wondered if this was the master.

In the SUV ahead, Anika leaned forward in her seat, every nerve on fire. Her hand gripped the dashboard, the other clutching the radio.

'Target is mobile. Repeat—target is mobile, heading northeast!'

The motorbike sliced through traffic like a phantom, weaving through startled vendors and skimming past fruit carts. One sharp turn and a cascade of onions exploded across the road.

'Dammit!' Kumar shouted, jerking the wheel to avoid the wreckage.

Anika's voice rang out: 'He's heading towards the tombs!'

Singh's voice barked through the comms, 'All units, cut off the outer perimeter. Do not let him reach the tomb complex!'

But it was too late.

The rider skidded to a halt near the stone arches that led to the ancient mausoleums. Malhotra leaped from the bike. The rider tumbled, clutching his side, likely injured from the fall.

'Go!' Anika shouted, throwing open the SUV door before the wheels stopped. Boots hit the pavement.

'Detain the rider,' Singh ordered, already in motion with two officers.

Malhotra darted through the entrance of the Maharaja's Tomb complex. He ran with the desperation of a man with no other choice—and the determination of one with a mission to complete.

Anika ran after him, her heart hammering and her breath fogging the night air. She knew this place: the tombs, the underground network, and the crypts beneath.

She didn't chase blindly. She predicted.

She veered down a side passage. Flashlights bobbed in the corners of her vision as Delta Team fanned out. Singh's voice echoed: 'Seal the back! Don't let him double back!'

A blur of motion—a figure diving into the old servants' tunnel.

'I've got him!' Anika called into her comm.

She plunged into the tunnel, her flashlight beam carving through the suffocating dark. The air grew colder, damper. The walls seemed to close in.

Ahead, Malhotra's footfalls echoed unevenly. He was slowing.

She pressed forward.

He burst into a vaulted chamber, breathing hard. Anika wasn't far behind. She skidded to a halt, weapon drawn.

'It's over!' she shouted.

Malhotra turned to face her. He was breathing heavily, blood on his sleeve, but he smiled.

'Too late, Dr Thakur.'

His foot kicked a stone lever. The floor beneath Anika groaned.

She dove forward just as a trapdoor yawned open behind her. Stone rumbled. Dust exploded. The exit behind her slammed shut.

'Singh!' she shouted, but her voice bounced off the walls.

Malhotra was already fleeing again. Anika rose, ignoring the pain in her shoulder, and chased him deeper.

They emerged into a crypt vast as a cathedral, lit only by fractured moonlight. Stone pillars reached towards a cracked ceiling. At the far end was a weathered iron door, half open.

Malhotra made for it.

Anika lunged.

They collided.

They tumbled across the floor, limbs entangled. Malhotra thrashed, blade in hand. Anika gritted her teeth and landed a punch to his jaw.

He slashed, catching her arm.

Pain seared through her. She twisted away, blood dripping.

Malhotra lunged for the door. Anika snatched a rusted iron sconce from the wall and swung.

CRACK.

It hit his leg. He crumpled, screaming.

She tackled him, gun pressed to his temple.

'Game over.'

He laughed, blood in his teeth. 'You're too late.'

A rumble began. Behind them, a stone arch collapsed.

'RUN!' she yelled.

She hauled him to his feet, dragging him towards the light seeping through the falling dust.

'ANIKA!' Singh's voice cut through the chaos.

She saw it—a crack in the debris, a narrow escape.

She dove.

The tomb collapsed behind them.

Malhotra coughed, hands pinned by the Delta Team as cuffs snapped around his wrists.

Singh knelt beside her. 'You okay?'

She winced at her bleeding arm. 'I'll live.'

Singh turned to Malhotra. 'Enjoy your cell.'

Malhotra grinned. 'You think this is over?'

Anika stared at him. His words chilled her.

Because behind that smile, she saw it—

Malhotra wasn't the end.

He was the beginning.

CHAPTER 15

The interrogation room was small and airless, its only illumination a flickering fluorescent bulb that cast fractured shadows across the battered metal table. Inside, the air was thick with the stench of sweat, old stone, and unspoken dread. At the centre of the room sat Dr Dilip Malhotra—bloodied, bruised, and handcuffed—but somehow still wearing the faint smirk of a man who believed himself untouchable.

Across from him, Dr Anika Thakur sat like stone. Her gaze didn't waver, didn't soften. Her presence filled the room like a loaded gun. She wasn't here to negotiate. She was here to dismantle whatever mask Malhotra still wore.

Inspector Rajesh Singh sat to her right, every inch of him coiled with restrained fury. His fingers were laced, his expression carved from granite. And at the far end of the table sat Commissioner Verma, the embodiment of cool authority—still but ready to strike.

But it was Anika who commanded the room. Tonight it was her show.

Malhotra slouched in his chair, a sheen of dried blood at his temple. His lips curled upward in a slow, maddening smile. 'You look tired, Dr Thakur,' he rasped, voice rough with dust and defiance. 'Having trouble sleeping?'

Anika didn't respond. Her silence was the reply.

Singh exploded. He slammed his hands on the table, the sound cracking like gunfire. 'Cut the theatrics, Malhotra. Who is your master? Who's leading the Wrathbearers?'

Malhotra chuckled low, like a man amused by a private joke. 'You still don't see it. You think I lost. But I led you to me. Every step. Every clue. You played the part exactly as intended.'

Verma shifted his gaze to Anika, giving her the nod. She leaned in, voice quiet and cold. 'And why would your master want that?'

Malhotra stretched his wrists against the cuffs, as if savouring the sting. 'Because the Wrathbearers are patient. Because the ritual demands balance. Because the final act must be witnessed.'

Singh's voice cut in, a blade of contempt, 'You murdered innocent people. Do you think calling yourself a pawn absolves you?'

Malhotra ignored him. His eyes were fixed on Anika.

'Do you know why the master chose now?' he asked softly.

Anika didn't blink. She leaned back in her chair, exuding quiet power. 'Because of the alignment. The celestial convergence. Same as the one when Chandravati was executed. Six days from now.'

Malhotra's smile faded.

Silence rippled through the room.

Anika pressed on. 'Your master believes he's fulfilling a prophecy. That the blood spilled across generations will culminate in one final sacrifice. This isn't revenge. It's theatre. Ritual masquerading as justice.'

Malhotra blinked. His arrogance faltered.

'You understand,' he whispered.

'I understand delusion,' Anika replied. 'And I understand cults dressing their crimes in the language of destiny.'

Malhotra's voice sharpened. 'We are not a cult. We are historians. Heirs to truth. Chandravati's words were real. Her vision was clear. My master will cleanse this city of its ancestral lies.'

Verma's voice was like iron. 'Name him.'

Malhotra just grinned. 'You are not worthy to speak his name.'

Singh's fists clenched. 'We'll find him. And we'll tear down every secret you think keeps you safe.'

Malhotra laughed—a hollow, haunted sound. 'You still don't get it.'

His gaze returned to Anika, and something darker bloomed in his smile.

'You think you're chasing the killer. But he's been waiting for you.'

Then he leaned forward and whispered, 'Oh, and by the way . . . Yuvraj sends his regards.'

The air left the room.

Anika froze.

Singh turned sharply. 'What did you say?'

Malhotra's grin widened, blood on his teeth. 'Didn't expect that, did you? Some ghosts stay buried. Others . . . reach back.'

Anika's fists tightened. 'You're lying.'

'Maybe,' Malhotra said with a shrug. 'Or maybe your past isn't past at all. Maybe it's been following you all along.'

Verma leaned in. 'Where is he? Where is your master?'

Malhotra's voice dropped to a whisper. 'In six days, the Wrathbearers rise. And with them, the truth.'

Then he looked at Anika again.

'And you, Doctor . . . You will see what your brother has become. What you were meant to become.'

He leaned back, closed his eyes, and smiled.

The room fell into silence.

And for the first time in two decades, Anika Thakur felt fear she couldn't reason away.

The air in the conference room was suffocating. Too many people and too many unspoken words. Officers, forensic analysts, and intelligence personnel sat around the large mahogany table beneath the cold fluorescent lighting. A digital board at the front displayed images of the crime scenes, the victims, and the ancient symbols of the Wrathbearers and the Custodians.

Anika sat among them, her hands clasped together, still reeling from Malhotra's final words. Yuvraj.

She hadn't spoken to Singh about it yet. She couldn't. Not until she could wrap her own head around it.

Commissioner Verma stood at the head of the table, his dark gaze sweeping across the room. He looked haggard, his jaw set in a way that made it clear that what he was about to say wouldn't be pleasant.

Singh sat beside Anika, his fingers interlocked and jaw tight as if anticipating a blow.

The room quieted as Verma cleared his throat. 'Last night, we caught one of the key figures involved in these ritualistic murders, Dr Dilip Malhotra.'

A murmur ran through the room.

'He was the architect behind the staging of the murders, but as we suspected, he is not the mastermind. He refers to his leader as *the master*, the head of a centuries-old faction known as the Wrathbearers.'

Sub-Inspector Kumar leaned forward. 'And the Custodians of the Seal? They are real?'

Verma nodded. 'According to our intel, the Custodians have always existed as the counterbalance to the Wrathbearers. They were the keepers of secrets, meant to guard the history that the Wrathbearers wanted to expose.' His voice darkened. 'The war between these two factions has been happening for centuries, right under our noses.'

Another silence settled. Then Verma sighed, rubbing his temples. 'We have one more complication.'

Anika felt it before he even said it.

'Malhotra mentioned a name,' Verma continued, his gaze landing on Anika. 'Yuvraj Thakur.'

The weight of his name suffocated her. The room reacted instantly. A flicker of confusion. Suspicion. Doubt.

Verma didn't pause. 'Given the new information, I can't ignore a potential conflict of interest.' His voice was heavy. Final. 'Dr Anika Thakur, effective immediately, you are removed from your lead position in this case.'

It was a gut punch for Anika. The words sank in slowly, like an execution order. She blinked, as if trying to force reality to correct itself.

'Commissioner, you can't be serious—,' Singh started but was interrupted by the commissioner.

'This isn't personal,' Verma said, though his expression was unreadable. 'Dr Thakur is too close to this case now. If her brother is involved in any way, I cannot allow her to lead the investigation.'

'I am not compromised,' Anika snapped, standing so quickly that her chair scraped against the floor. 'I have worked harder than anyone else to solve this case. I was the one who figured out the pattern. I was the one who found Malhotra's trail—'

'And that's why I'm keeping you on the case,' Verma interrupted. 'But not as lead investigator.'

Anika felt her pulse hammer against her throat. 'You don't understand—'

Verma cut her off again, 'I understand perfectly. I know what it's like when the past reaches out to drag you under. But I cannot, will not, risk this operation further because if word gets out about your brother being involved in this case in any capacity, it will be a career suicide for not just you but everyone involved.'

Anika clenched her fists, breathing through the sting of humiliation, the sheer powerlessness.

'I am reassigning Inspector Singh as the sole lead,' Verma continued. 'Effective immediately.'

Singh stiffened beside her. 'Commissioner,' Singh began, his voice controlled, 'I understand the concerns, but Dr Thakur is our best resource. If we remove her from a decision-making position, we're weakening our own advantage.'

Verma sighed, pinching the bridge of his nose. 'I'm aware, which is why she'll remain on the team, but in a more limited capacity.' He turned back to the others. 'Which brings us to another pressing matter, Vikram Singh Rathore.'

Anika snapped to attention.

'He was attacked last night,' Verma continued. 'The Wrathbearers got to him before we could. He's in the hospital now, stable, but unconscious. We don't know what he found before they tried to silence him, but as soon as he wakes up, we'll question him about the Wrathbearers and the Custodians.'

A heavy silence settled.

Verma looked at Anika one last time. 'I'm sorry, Dr Thakur. But you're off the lead.'

And just like that, Anika was left feeling alone and distraught.

The cold morning air burned against Anika's skin as she stepped onto the rooftop terrace of the police headquarters. She leaned into the railing, arms crossed and jaw clenched tight. She wasn't angry—not in the usual way. She was devastated.

Everything she had uncovered, everything she had chased, had been swept away in a single bureaucratic decision. And the worst part? She couldn't even blame Verma. Not entirely.

Footsteps approached behind her, quiet and deliberate. She didn't need to turn to know who it was.

'It wasn't fair,' Singh said quietly, stepping up beside her. 'But you knew it was coming.'

Anika let out a low, humourless chuckle. 'You don't have to comfort me, Singh. You're the new lead. Congratulations.'

He didn't take the bait. Instead, he mirrored her stance, resting his forearms on the railing and staring out at the sleeping city. 'Don't do that.'

'Do what?'

'Pretend this doesn't matter to you.'

She exhaled, a sharp breath that fogged in the cold. 'Of course it matters.'

Singh reached into his pocket and withdrew a neatly folded handkerchief. He didn't say anything as he took her hand and pressed it into her palm.

She frowned. 'What's this for?'

He nodded at her clenched fists. 'Because you've been holding on so tight, you're hurting yourself.'

She looked down. Small crescent-shaped marks had begun to bruise on her skin. Damn him for noticing.

She eased her hands open but didn't pull away.

'You're not alone in this,' Singh said, his voice low. Steady.

Something in the way he said her name—Anika—made her throat tighten.

'I feel alone,' she admitted, barely above a whisper.

'You're not,' he said again. Then softer, more certain, he added, 'I won't let you be.'

Anika turned to face him. For a moment, her expression was unreadable. But in her eyes, something vulnerable flickered. A bridge between two people who had seen too much and trusted too little.

Then, as quickly as it had appeared, it vanished. She pulled her walls back up.

'Verma took me off the lead,' she said, voice hardening. 'But I'm not stepping back.'

Singh smiled, just slightly, as if he'd been waiting for that.

'I didn't think you would.'

Anika looked him square in the eye. 'We're going to end this, Rajesh. We're going to take them down.'

His smile widened. 'Damn right we are.

The hallway of Jaipur Memorial Hospital carried the sterile chill of too many endings. The sharp scent of antiseptic clung to the walls, mingling with the faint aroma of overbrewed tea in paper cups. Nurses moved quietly, their rubber-soled shoes squeaking against the pale tiles beneath the stark buzz of fluorescent lights.

Anika stood at the reception counter, her fingers trembling slightly as she completed the discharge paperwork. Her injured hand made her writing shaky, the pen pressing ink too heavily onto the page. It mirrored her state—strained, worn, and pushed to the edge.

Behind her, Lata Thakur sat in a wheelchair, her figure slight but composed, wrapped in the same soft shawl Anika remembered from her childhood. Its fabric was worn at the edges, just like the woman herself—resilient but threadbare from grief.

A nurse hovered nearby, watching Anika with gentle concern. 'She'll need rest, Dr Thakur. And fluids. No stress.'

Anika let out a breathless laugh—hollow. No stress.

She nodded distantly and turned back towards her mother. 'Ready to go home?'

Lata lifted her head, her eyes clouded but alert. 'I think I've been ready to leave this place since the day I came in.'

Anika offered a faint smile and gently wheeled her mother towards the exit.

Outside, the evening wrapped Jaipur in the afterglow of a recent storm. The scent of damp earth clung to the streets. Raindrops hung heavy on the *gulmohar* leaves, the city momentarily quieted in reverence to the storm's passing.

They drove in silence, the hum of the engine the only sound. The familiar roads passed in a blur, but Anika felt like a stranger moving through a dream. And all the while, one sentence echoed in her ears: *Yuvraj sends his regards.*

The Thakur residence emerged at the end of a tree-lined path. Nestled between two towering gulmohars, it stood unchanged, an old memory frozen in time. The iron gate groaned open as Anika pushed it. The creak hit her like a whisper from the past.

The walls still bore the soft ochre wash of years gone by. The balcony railing, chipped and rusted, still held the skeleton of a wind chime Yuvraj had once crafted from seashells. And through the front windows, the dim glow of yellow light spilled like something sacred.

Inside, the house breathed with the scents of dust, sandalwood, and time. Anika helped her mother onto the brown couch, adjusting the worn cushions and placing a pillow behind her back. The silence in the room was heavy but familiar.

They sat together for a long moment. No words. Just breath and memory.

Finally, Lata broke the silence. 'You're too quiet.'

Anika stared at her hands. 'I'm just tired, Ma.'

Her mother reached forward, fingers cool and steady, and took Anika's hand in hers. It was the same gesture from her childhood—when nightmares came or fever broke. Unshakeable. Present.

'Tell me,' Lata said softly.

Anika swallowed. Her lips parted, and the truth spilled out before she could stop it.

'I know who took Yuvraj.'

Lata froze. The room changed—grew heavier, stiller.

'The Wrathbearers,' Anika said, the name tasting like iron. 'They had him. Maybe still do. I should have found him sooner. I should have done more.'

Her voice cracked under the weight of it.

Lata didn't let go. Her thumb brushed slow circles across Anika's knuckles.

'You were a child, Anu,' she said gently. 'You did what you could. And now, you're doing what he would have wanted.'

Anika's defences crumbled. She leaned into her mother's embrace, her forehead resting against the familiar scent of the old shawl. Tears broke loose, unrelenting.

And for the first time in 20 years, she let her mother hold her.

Not as a police officer.

Not as a profiler.

But as a daughter.

※

Anika was running.

The corridors twisted and narrowed, the walls pressing in as she sprinted forward, her breath ragged. Ahead of her, a masked figure waited.

She raised her gun. Fired.

The bullet disintegrated into smoke.

She drew a blade, then swung.

It passed through the air.

She ran again, faster and harder, until her lungs burned. But every time she reached him, she failed. Again. And again. And again.

His voice echoed from the shadows.

'You think you're in control, Dr Thakur. But the future is already written.'

The ground cracked.

She fell.

Anika jolted awake, heart racing and chest tight. The nightmare clung to her like a second skin.

Outside her room, the house was silent save for the clinking of ceramic.

She found her mother in the courtyard, seated on the old bench under the mango tree, the same spot where she used to sip her morning chai.

Dawn light filtered through the canopy, turning the world gold and green. The air smelled of jasmine and wet soil.

Anika sat beside her, silent.

Lata handed her a warm cup. 'When you don't know which way to go,' she said softly, stirring her tea, 'start from the beginning.'

Anika blinked.

Her voice was barely above a whisper. 'Baba used to say that.'

Lata smiled, gaze distant. 'He believed the past holds the answers, if we're willing to listen.'

Anika stared into her tea. The ripples settled.

Start from the beginning.

She exhaled slowly. A seed of clarity took root.

'I need to go back,' she said aloud.

Lata turned, curious.

'The first crime scene,' Anika said. 'If this is a story . . . the first page holds the key.'

Lata nodded once. As if she had always known.

The air in the archives was thick with dust, each breath laced with the scent of old paper and rusted metal. Faint shafts of light fell from narrow windows high above, illuminating motes of dust that floated like forgotten memories. Long rows of metal filing cabinets stood silent and still, each drawer labelled, locked, and heavy with the weight of untold stories.

Anika walked through the dim corridor with quiet determination, her boots echoing against the cracked linoleum. Overhead, the fluorescent bulbs buzzed tiredly, barely bright enough to push back the shadows.

At the far end of the room, behind a fortress of stacked folders and brittle case files, sat Detective Bhaskar Iyer. Late fifties. Short-cropped salt-and-pepper hair. Reading glasses perpetually slipping down the bridge of his nose. His brown shirt was slightly rumpled, his sleeves rolled up to reveal ink-stained wrists. He looked like a man who had never left this place.

As Anika approached, he didn't look up.

'Dr Thakur,' he said, voice like gravel. 'Didn't expect to see you down here.'

'I need Yuvraj Thakur's case file.'

Iyer sighed. Not with surprise—more like expectation. He set his pen down, pinched the bridge of his nose, and nodded. 'That case is older than some of the cadets upstairs. We didn't find much back then.'

'That's because you didn't know where to look.'

That caught his attention. His eyes, dulled by years of bureaucracy and dead ends, sharpened just a little. He studied her, then gave a single nod and rose from his chair.

He moved to the nearest filing cabinet marked UNSOLVED (1980–2005), pulled the drawer open with a screech of metal, and rummaged through its contents. After a moment, he retrieved a thick weathered file with frayed edges and a rusted clip.

He dropped it on the desk with a thud.

'Everything we had.'

Anika hesitated for a second before flipping it open.

There he was.

Yuvraj's black-and-white photo clipped to the top corner. His eyes—her eyes—looked back at her across the years. Young. Hopeful. Unknowing.

Her throat constricted.

Iyer leaned in, voice softer. 'What are you expecting to find?'

Anika's jaw set. 'A pattern.'

'You think his disappearance is connected to the Wrathbearer murders?'

'I don't think. I know.' She pointed to the file. 'Yuvraj was taken. And the people who took him are still out there.'

There was a flicker in Iyer's eyes. Recognition. Fear.

'You've heard of them,' Anika said quietly. 'The Wrathbearers.'

He didn't deny it.

'Whispers,' he said. 'That's all we ever had. No names. No proof. Just . . . stories.'

'Well, stories are all we have left,' Anika said. 'And I intend to follow every one of them.'

For a long moment, Iyer said nothing. Then, with the weary resolve of a man revisiting old ghosts, he stood.

'All right, Dr Thakur.'

He pulled another stack of old case reports from a shelf behind him and laid them on the desk.

'Let's see what the past has been trying to tell us.'

༚

The soft glow of the desk lamp barely pushed back the darkness, casting long shadows across the sprawling mosaic of files before her. The room was quiet, save for the gentle scratch of her pen against paper. Anika sat alone in her office, surrounded by towers of case reports, crime scene photos, and archival records—an island of chaos in the dead of night.

The digital clock blinked 01:50 a.m.

Her desk, once cluttered with daily essentials, was now buried beneath layers of memory and grief. At the centre was Yuvraj's case file, worn at the corners. Around it sprawled police reports from the current serial murders, maps, timelines, and a disturbing collection of cold cases dating back over three decades.

Every one of them bore the same markers—missing persons with ties to royal history, each file echoing the same silence. And each one, like Yuvraj, had vanished while digging into the city's forgotten past.

A knock at the door cut through her focus.

Detective Bhaskar Iyer entered, another bundle of folders in his arms. He looked as tired as she felt, the lines around his eyes etched deeper than before.

'These are the rest,' he said, dropping the stack onto the overflowing desk. 'Disappearances stretching back 30 years. Mostly students, historians, and researchers. All vanished under conditions just like your brother.'

Anika's throat tightened. 'And no one connected the dots?'

Iyer shook his head, rubbing his temple. 'Not until now. They were spread out, years apart, across different cities. No one was looking for patterns.'

'Well, we are now.'

She rifled through the files, flipping pages with increasing urgency. She saw familiar names. Familiar details. Timelines that overlapped. Photos of faces frozen in time. They were all looking for the same thing: truth buried in royal history. And like Yuvraj, they'd all disappeared into thin air.

She pulled her brother's case file towards her. The black-and-white photo was still clipped to the top corner. But this time, it didn't feel like just his story. It was part of a much larger truth.

Then, from her bag, she retrieved a photo she had found at her mother's house—Yuvraj, standing outside a small obscure museum, holding the leather-bound journal of Devesh Thakur. That same journal now sat on her desk.

Iyer's eyes sharpened. 'Hold on.'

He pulled a cold case file from the new stack, flipping through a series of old black-and-white crime scene photos. Then he stopped.

'Does this symbol look familiar?'

He turned the file towards her. Anika leaned in—and froze.

Carved into the stone of an abandoned courtyard was a symbol.

The same one etched into Devesh Thakur's journal.

The same symbol was left at the crime scenes.

'Oh my God,' she whispered. 'This goes back further than we thought.'

Iyer nodded grimly. 'And it gets worse.'

He spread out a map of Jaipur, red dots marked across it. Each dot represented a disappearance. 'Every single one was last seen near a historical site—museums, estates, royal temples. Every one of them is connected to a royal family lineage.'

Anika's fingers flipped through the earliest file—1985. A young researcher vanished while reviewing royal court records.

A chill ran down her spine.

Then . . . another knock.

Constable Mohan peeked in. 'Dr Thakur,' he said, breathless. 'Vikram Singh Rathore just woke up.'

Anika's eyes snapped up. She looked at Iyer, resolve flashing behind her fatigue.

'Keep digging,' she said. 'Flag everything. And get forensics out to those sites. We need trace material, DNA, anything.'

Then, without another word, she grabbed her coat and bolted from the room.

⁂

The corridors of Jaipur Memorial Hospital were quiet, save for the rhythmic beeping of monitors and the low shuffle of nurses moving between rooms. The scent of antiseptic clung to the air like fog, sterile and unforgiving.

Anika and Singh walked with purpose, their steps measured, heavy with urgency.

'You sure you're okay to do this?' Singh asked, his voice low.

Anika nodded. 'He's the only lead we have right now.'

Singh studied her, as if gauging how much more weight she could carry. She had been unravelling—he could see it—but she hadn't broken. Not yet.

They reached the room. Singh knocked once, then opened the door.

Vikram Singh Rathore sat propped against a stack of pillows, his skin pale and his left arm encased in a cast. Bruises darkened his face and neck. Yet when he saw them, he managed a faint smirk.

'Took you long enough.'

Singh grinned. 'If I'd known you were this charming, I'd have stayed away longer.'

Anika stepped forward. Her voice was sharp. 'We don't have time, Vikram.'

The smirk vanished.

Singh pulled a chair close and sat down. 'What happened to you?'

Vikram shifted, wincing. 'The Wrathbearers. They took me.'

Anika's pulse quickened.

'They wanted information,' Vikram continued.

'About what?'

Vikram looked straight at Anika. 'The Custodians.'

Her fists clenched. 'You knew them?'

He nodded. 'Our family—Rathores—was one of the founding bloodlines. We were sworn to protect the Sacred Chronicle.'

Singh leaned forward. 'So why target you now?'

Vikram's voice dropped. 'Because not everyone in our family agreed with the Custodians' oath.'

Anika narrowed her eyes. 'Who?'

He hesitated, then said, 'Aryan Singh Rathore. My third cousin. He was exiled 12 years ago. But he didn't disappear. He joined the Wrathbearers.'

Singh's jaw clenched. 'You're telling me we've been hunting your cousin this entire time?'

'I found out two nights ago,' Vikram said, his voice brittle. 'That's why they tried to kill me.'

Anika sat down slowly. 'Tell us everything.'

'He was brilliant,' Vikram said. 'Too brilliant. Obsessed with rewriting history, with exposing the lies of the royals. He believed the Rathores were meant to reshape the future, not guard the past.'

Anika felt cold.

'He found the Wrathbearers—or they found him. Either way, he rose through the ranks. Became their master.'

Singh muttered a curse.

Anika leaned in. 'What's he planning?'

Vikram swallowed. 'They called it the Ultimate Sacrifice. I don't know what it is. But Aryan believes it's the final key. The moment everything changes.'

Anika's stomach turned. *Could it be Yuvraj?*

She stood abruptly. 'We need to find Aryan. Now.'

Singh rose beside her. 'And stop whatever the hell he's trying to unleash.'

CHAPTER 16

The converted warehouse that had become Anika's unofficial base of operations hummed with a new, taut urgency. The dusty air now crackled with a focused energy—a collective understanding that the endgame had begun.

They had done it.

The conspiracy was no longer hidden. The secrets of Jaipur's royal families, the buried truths, the manipulation, and the murders—all of them had been exposed. The files had been leaked. Public support had swelled. The shadows were being dragged into the light.

Now, with three days left before the celestial alignment, the team had only one goal.

Aryan Singh Rathore.

The killer. The orchestrator. The man who believed himself chosen to fulfil an ancient prophecy. The so-called master of the Wrathbearers.

The whiteboards, once covered in coded names, symbols, and ancient allegiances, now bore only a single structure—Aryan's movement patterns, his messages, and his mind. His every known location was marked. His words dissected. His rituals interpreted.

Anika stood at the head of the table, surveying her team—Singh, Kumar, Dutta, Dr Kapoor, and Dr Meera Das, the forensic linguist from Delhi who had joined after identifying encrypted texts on the ritual manuscripts. Only Vikram was absent. He was attending diplomatic meetings with other royal families, trying to negotiate restitution for victims.

She nodded to Singh.

He stepped forward. 'Let's start with victimology. What do we know about Aryan's selection process?'

Anika's fingers danced over the map, tracing familiar lines. 'His victims all had ties to Jaipur's royal bloodlines—some distant, some hidden. All targeted for what their ancestors represented, not for who they were.'

Dr Kapoor added, 'And each killing re-enacted a historical execution.'

'Re-enacted?' Anika shook her head. 'He didn't re-enact them. He recreated them. Exactly. The bindings. The settings. Even the time of day.'

She picked up a red marker and connected the sites.

A mandala formed—an elaborate pattern woven into the geography of the city.

Silence fell.

Dutta, who had been scanning the diagram, stepped forward. 'This isn't just ritual. It's geometry. Cosmology. He's not just performing a pattern. He's building one.'

Anika nodded, struck by the clarity of his insight. 'Aryan believes he's constructing a sacred diagram. Something that channels energy. A cosmic key meant to unlock the curse.'

Singh leaned forward. 'So, these aren't symbolic sites. They're active components of a larger design.'

'Yes,' Anika confirmed. 'His choices are both geographical and spiritual. He's obsessed with alignment—not just planetary, but terrestrial.'

She gestured towards the psychological profile beside the whiteboard. 'Aryan is paradoxical. A methodical planner driven by delusional faith. He believes he is enacting prophecy. That his bloodline is chosen. And that only through him can the city's ancient sin be purged.'

Dr Das added quietly, 'The language in the texts—it's not metaphorical. It's instructional. This has been passed down, believed, refined.'

Anika drew a long breath. 'This is a transgenerational delusion. A sacred madness inherited like an heirloom.'

A silence followed—dense and electric.

Then Singh spoke. 'There's something else. Forensics came back on the soil trace found at the last scene.'

Anika's heart skipped. 'Where?'

'Aravalli Hills. Deep layer deposits—minerals consistent with subsurface exposure. That soil came from an underground chamber.'

Kumar's voice was low. 'So that's where Aryan has been hiding.'

Anika turned to the map. The Aravalli ridge stretched across the southern border. Dense. Ancient. Scarred with forgotten trails.

'And it's possibly where they took Yuvraj,' she whispered.

The realisation hit like a thunderclap.

Three days.

That's all they had left.

Anika looked up at the team. 'Public sentiment is with us now. The press knows the truth. There are no more distractions. We move entirely on Aryan.'

She tapped the Aravalli Hills. 'This is our lead.'

Around her, the team mobilised: Kumar reached for maps, Kapoor updated field protocols, and Dr Das cross-referenced soil samples with historical excavation sites.

Singh stayed by her side.

It was he who had discovered the corruption inside the police records.

It had been Dutta, once sceptical, often critical, who cracked the ritual pattern wide open after returning to the case full-time following his exposé for the *Jaipur Chronicle*. After his early coverage of the investigation was dismissed as sensationalist, Dutta had found himself disillusioned with institutional silence. But when the leak broke and the truth spilled into public view, he stepped forward—not as a reporter chasing headlines, but as a committed investigator. His deep archival knowledge, relentless pursuit of truth, and understanding of symbolic patterns made him indispensable. His addition to the inner circle had been unexpected, but earned.

And it had been Meera Das, flown in by Singh when the ritual texts had proven too complex, who had shown them that Aryan's script was not ancient nonsense but deliberate theological engineering.

Anika turned to Singh, the weight of years behind her gaze.

'You did good,' she said softly.

Singh gave a small smile, his usual edge dulled by exhaustion and something else—relief. 'We all did.'

Something passed between them. Not just trust.

Hope.

And for the first time since this nightmare began, Anika allowed herself to feel it.

The air inside Vikram Singh Rathore's private study was thick with the scent of aged teak, ancient parchment, and the faint trace of sandalwood incense that clung to the folds of the past. The room, nestled in one of the haveli's oldest wings, felt like a vault—one built not just to protect relics but to trap memories too dangerous to forget.

Anika stepped in as the double doors clicked shut behind her with a solemn finality. The weight of the moment settled over her like armour—heavy but necessary. This wasn't a conversation. It was a negotiation. Maybe even a plea.

Vikram stood by the tall arched window, back to her, his silhouette sharp against the moonlight filtering through the intricate *jharokha* screen. The light scattered across the stone floor in latticelike shadows. Outside, Jaipur breathed with late-night life. But in here, it was as if time had paused to watch what came next.

Anika didn't speak. Her pulse drummed steadily as she took in the room: old scrolls, ceremonial swords mounted behind glass, and a grandfather clock ticking with imperious rhythm. This was the room where generations had made decisions that shaped the city. Now, she was here to ask Vikram to help unmake one.

'Anika.' His voice, when it came, was low. Weathered. Worn down like stone beneath decades of storm. 'You're asking me to do something dangerous.'

She took one slow step forward. 'I know.' Her voice was calm, almost soft, but it carried the weight of everything she had uncovered, everything she was still carrying.

Vikram turned. The lamplight caught the lines on his face, the bruises still healing. His eyes were no longer just noble or weary. They were haunted. By guilt. By history. By blood.

'You're the only one who can reach him,' Anika said.

He dragged a hand through his hair and looked away, bracing his arms against the window frame. 'Even if I could . . . why would he listen?'

Anika walked farther into the room, stopping just behind him. 'Because Aryan still believes in something. That makes him vulnerable. I just need time to exploit that belief.'

Vikram laughed bitterly. 'Belief? Aryan believes in destiny, not dialogue. He doesn't bend, Anika. He doesn't bargain.'

She met his eyes when he turned. 'I don't need him to bargain. I just need him distracted. Long enough to find my brother.'

The air thickened. Something flickered in Vikram's expression—recognition, maybe. Pain, definitely.

'This isn't just about stopping a killer,' he said quietly. 'This is about Yuvraj.'

Anika nodded, a crack of honesty bleeding through her composure. 'If Aryan still has him . . . he's my only link. And if we take Aryan down without a trace, I may never find out what happened to him.'

Vikram exhaled hard, rubbing the back of his neck. 'You're playing a very dangerous game.'

'I've been playing since the day Yuvraj disappeared,' she said. 'I just didn't realise it until now.'

A silence stretched between them. Then, slowly, reluctantly, Vikram nodded. 'There's an old hunting lodge in the Aravalli Hills. Aryan's been seen there before. If he agrees to a meeting, that's where it will happen.'

Anika's pulse kicked. She stepped back, letting him have space.

'Then ask him,' she said. 'Tell him I want to talk. Alone.'

Vikram hesitated, a war playing out behind his eyes. 'He might say yes. But it won't be for peace.'

'I'm not expecting peace,' Anika replied. 'I'm expecting answers.'

For a long moment, he didn't move. Then he turned to the antique desk and picked up his secure phone.

As Vikram dialled, his fingers tightened around the handset, knuckles pale. Anika stood still, barely breathing.

This was it.

The only thread connecting her to Yuvraj.

And possibly the last chance to bring the nightmare to an end.

She closed her eyes just briefly, bracing herself for what was coming.

Because whatever came next, it would change everything.

The abandoned hunting lodge—once a retreat for royalty, now a husk of forgotten grandeur—stood beneath the pale glow of the moon like a relic mourning its own irrelevance. Its slanted wooden beams groaned under the weight of time, while creeping vines coiled around its cracked lattice windows like fingers too long left unclenched.

The air was dense with jasmine and dust, thick with the scent of wet soil and secrets too old to speak. A faint breeze rustled the dry leaves, whispering stories of bloodlines, betrayals, and curses that had never truly lifted.

Tonight this place would bear witness to a reckoning centuries in the making.

Anika stood near the remains of an intricately carved platform—its wood splintered but its grandeur unmistakable. Her breathing was even, but her pulse ticked faster with each second. She had trained for chaos and mastered control, but standing at the edge of myth and murder, none of that mattered.

A flicker in the shadows.

Then he stepped forward into the moonlight.

Aryan Singh Rathore.

Tall. Poised. As if history had conjured him into flesh. He was dressed in a pristine white kurta embroidered with sacred motifs—half priest, half prince. His face bore the unmistakable symmetry of Jaipur's royal line, yet there was something else in it too—a fire behind his eyes that made him look ancient and dangerous, as if he had walked straight out of a forgotten scripture.

He didn't look mad. That would've been easier.

He looked calm.

And that made him lethal.

'You came alone,' he said, voice low and polished. There was no menace in it—only quiet certainty. As if he'd been expecting her all along.

'I needed to speak to you,' Anika replied, her tone precise, every syllable a deliberate step towards the truth.

Aryan tilted his head, amused. 'You think speaking will stop destiny?'

'I think understanding might.'

He took another step forward, boots whispering against stone. 'You fascinate me, Dr Thakur. A woman of science entangled in prophecy. Logic lured into myth.'

She kept her eyes locked on him. 'I don't believe in fate.'

His smile was slow, like the curl of smoke. 'Then you haven't been paying attention.'

He circled her, not with threat but with ritualistic reverence, as though she were part of the very ceremony he had crafted in his mind. 'You see this as madness. But I—' He stopped in front of her, eyes locked on hers. 'I see completion.'

'You think you're rewriting history,' she said, voice low.

'No.' His smile faltered into something more solemn. 'I'm correcting it.'

The words landed with a force that nearly broke the stillness.

'What's your endgame?' she asked.

Aryan's gaze turned inwards, as if consulting some inner scripture. 'You already know.'

'You believe you're the sacrifice,' she whispered.

'I did,' he replied. 'Until I discovered the illegitimate bloodline . . . Devesh's lineage, buried under royal deceit. Bloodlines must be balanced. The sin must be paid for with blood pure enough to matter.'

Anika's breath hitched.

'And so,' he continued, 'in three nights, beneath the celestial convergence, the final rite will be completed.'

Her voice was iron. 'Who is the sacrifice?'

Aryan's eyes gleamed. 'Yuvraj.'

The name slammed into her like a falling stone.

She didn't show it. Not yet. Her fingers curled inwards. Her face stayed still.

'No,' she said.

Aryan raised an eyebrow. 'No?'

'I'll take his place.'

His expression didn't shift. But something behind his eyes flickered. 'You?'

She stepped forward. Steady. Willing. 'You said the prophecy demands a willing offering. Let him go. Take me.'

For the first time, Aryan faltered. Just a fraction.

'You'd die for him?'

'Yes.'

'You'd leave behind everything?'

'If it stops this, I would.'

A silence pulsed between them, filled with nothing but the night and the weight of ancestral reckoning.

Then Aryan laughed.

It wasn't cruel. It wasn't mocking. It was a surprised, almost sad, laugh.

'You're lying,' he said.

Anika didn't respond.

He stepped closer, the space between them a breath. 'But . . . you would, wouldn't you? For your brother.'

Her throat tightened.

Aryan smiled, slowly and considering. 'I'll think about it,' he said, with the air of a god entertaining a mortal's plea. 'But first, prove your devotion.'

And before she could respond, he stepped back, disappearing into the darkness as if the shadows had reclaimed him.

Anika remained still.

Not because she couldn't move.

But because what he said had shattered her carefully built defences.

Yuvraj was alive.

And Aryan intended to sacrifice him.

She turned sharply, sprinting back towards her car, every nerve in her body ablaze.

There was only one place left that could hold the final truth.

The *Aravalli Hills*, where the curse began.

Where Yuvraj was taken.

And where, one way or another, this would end.

CHAPTER 17

The night hung thick over Jaipur, a breath held in the lungs of a city that now knew too much.

Above, in the moonlit stillness, the streets whispered of royal betrayal, of conspiracies centuries old now laid bare. But here—beneath the palace that had once ruled unchallenged—there was only silence.

The entrance to the underground vaults gaped before them: wide, ancient, and hungry. Time had gnawed at its stone edges, softened its carvings, but could not erase them—symbols of celestial alignments, of sacrifices made in moonlight, and of kings and prophets who believed blood could buy redemption.

Anika stood at the threshold, clad in black tactical gear, her breath steady despite the charge building in her chest. Her gaze was fixed on the darkness ahead, as if she could will it to reveal what lay within.

Behind her, Singh tightened the straps of his holster with economical precision. Kumar keyed his radio, running last-minute diagnostics. Around them, the team waited—ten officers trained for conflict but drawn now into something older, stranger. They didn't speak. They didn't need to.

And yet Anika's thoughts drifted.

To the Aravalli Hills.

To soil samples and ancient journals. To symbols that all pointed west. Her gut told her Yuvraj was out there. But Singh's intel had been ironclad: Aryan had come here. And Aryan never moved without purpose.

Which meant this place—this sealed world beneath the palace—still mattered.

'Everyone clear on the plan?' Singh's voice sliced through the stillness.

'Clear,' Kumar answered, his eyes never leaving the structure. 'We follow the map from Chandravati's scrolls. Locate Aryan. Disrupt the ritual. Nonlethal force unless we have no other choice.'

Anika turned, sweeping her gaze over the group. Their faces were unreadable masks—some stern with resolve, others pale with the weight of what they might face.

'This isn't just a tactical op,' she said, her voice low and unflinching. 'Aryan believes he's here to save Jaipur. That he's fulfilling something ancient and holy. He doesn't see murder. He sees sacrifice.'

The words landed. Heavy. Grounding.

'If there's any chance he can be stopped without violence, we take it.'

Silence answered her.

Then nods. Tight. Reluctant. But real.

Anika turned back to the carved archway. The floor beneath her boots felt colder now. The air drifting up from the chamber was damp, laced with mildew, incense . . . and iron.

'How do you reason with someone who thinks they're a god?' one of the younger officers whispered.

Anika didn't respond.

Because that was the question she'd been wrestling with for weeks.

And now, finally, she was going to get her answer.

The air turned colder as they crossed the threshold, swallowed whole by the passage's narrow mouth. The scent of damp stone, ancient decay, and secrets left too long in the dark clung to them like smoke.

The corridor narrowed as they descended, walls pressing inwards, their surfaces slick with moisture and time. Faded Sanskrit inscriptions spiralled across the stone—hymns, mantras, and curses—and Anika's eyes caught glimpses of familiar verses, fragments she had seen in Chandravati's texts. The words had once seemed academic. Now they felt like a warning.

Her flashlight sliced through the dark, revealing murals worn by centuries—images of cyclical time, rebirth, fallen kings, and crowned martyrs. But as they pressed deeper, the stories turned darker. Bodies arranged on altars. Fire. Blood. Eyes that watched across generations.

A cold shiver traced her spine.

They had only just crossed into the first inner chamber when the ground buckled beneath them with a grinding groan of stone.

'Trap!' Singh barked, his voice sharp.

One of the ops officers stumbled, his boot slicing through a disguised panel. The floor dropped beneath him, revealing a pit of jagged, rust-caked spikes waiting like the teeth of an old beast.

He barely caught the ledge. Fingers white-knuckled around the stone. Singh and Arjun lunged, grabbing him by his arms and hauling him back as debris crumbled into the void below.

Anika swallowed hard, steadying her light. 'He's expecting us,' she said.

Singh nodded, his jaw taut. 'Or leading us.'

And somehow that was worse.

They moved in silence, the narrow corridor twisting tighter around them. Anika kept her gaze sharp, noting the smallest signs—smeared dust, a scuffed footprint on an otherwise untouched surface, and a fresh scratch on a stone edge.

Aryan had been here. Recently.

The air thickened as they moved, vibrating faintly with tension, as though the chamber itself could sense their arrival.

'I hear something,' one of the officers whispered.

So did she.

A low hum. Not electronic. Not mechanical.

A voice. No, many voices.

Chanting.

Ancient. Layered. And growing louder.

The corridor opened with sudden violence into vastness.

The team stumbled into a circular cavern that swallowed the beam of their flashlights. For a breathless moment, Anika could only stare, heart hammering and mind reeling.

The chamber was enormous, its walls rising like the inside of a buried temple. Towering stone pillars stretched to a domed ceiling lost in shadow, each pillar etched with exquisite carvings: celestial alignments, royal executions, and divine punishments. Stories in stone.

The walls pulsed with memory. With madness.

Flickering oil lamps lined the circumference, casting warped shadows that danced like phantoms. Frescoes of rituals stretched above them, their colours faded but their violence unmistakable. Deities watched with painted eyes. Blood spilled in careful spirals. Astronomical charts twisted into symbols of judgment.

But it wasn't just history that greeted them.

It was the present.

Tucked among the bones and relics were machines. Wires. Screens. A table of scientific equipment so modern that it looked like it had been dropped from a different reality. Monitors flickered with cosmic models, projected star charts, and countdown timers—blinking, ticking, and calculating the final convergence.

Anika caught her breath.

This wasn't just a shrine. It was a fusion. A culmination.

A laboratory–temple designed to prove prophecy by force.

At the centre of the chamber stood the altar—slightly raised, its surface smooth and dark, lined with channels and grooves that ran in spirals and symbols: karmic cycles, lunar markers, and sacrifice lines.

It wasn't a slab.

It was a mechanism.

She took a step towards it, her boots echoing in the stillness, the chamber amplifying each sound like a heartbeat.

The team spread out cautiously, weapons lowered but ready, their movements careful, reverent.

This was it.

The beating heart of everything they had been chasing.

And then . . . a shadow moved.

From behind one of the towering rune-covered pillars, a figure stepped forward—measured, deliberate, and utterly without fear.

Anika felt his presence before she saw his face. The air seemed to change—thicker, tighter—pulling her into a silence that vibrated with ancient intent. And when her eyes met his, the cold settled deep into her bones.

Aryan Singh Rathore.

The architect of terror and ritual. The man who had turned prophecy into theatre and murder into scripture. He emerged into the ring of lamplight like a priest ascending to his altar.

He looked just as composed as he had the night before—every inch the heir of Jaipur's royal blood—but tonight something had shifted. The refinement remained, but beneath it was something feral. Something primal. It twisted the elegance of his presence into something darker, magnetic, and dangerous.

His face, chiselled with the same noble precision as Vikram's, held no hesitation. But where Vikram wore his lineage with quiet guilt, Aryan wore his like anointed armour—unrepentant, unyielding, and divine.

His dark eyes locked on to hers—unblinking, unreadable, and filled not with mania but with something far more chilling: certainty.

He stepped fully into the glow, his white ceremonial kurta pristine, untouched by dirt or time. Gold embroidery shimmered along the cuffs and hem, catching the flicker of the lamps with an ethereal gleam, as if he had stepped through time untouched.

And yet behind him, the blood-streaked altar waited.

That contrast—the sacred and the profane—turned Anika's stomach.

'I wondered how long it would take you to find this place, Dr Thakur,' Aryan said, his tone unhurried, as if welcoming her to a long-awaited conclusion. His voice was soft, exacting, the cadence of a man who had rehearsed every word a thousand times.

Anika's pulse thudded, but she kept her gaze steady, her voice level. 'It was inevitable, wasn't it?'

A flicker of something like amusement passed over Aryan's lips. 'Everything is.'

His eyes drifted past her, scanning the armed officers lining the edge of the chamber. Unbothered, he returned his focus to her.

'Put your weapons down,' he said gently. 'You won't need them.'

Anika didn't flinch, didn't turn, and didn't break his gaze. Instead, she raised one hand.

Behind her, Singh hesitated. Then, one by one, the rifles lowered.

A show of trust—or desperation.

'Let's talk,' Anika said.

⁂

The chamber's silence thickened, a dense waiting presence that coiled around them like smoke. Only the soft, rhythmic drip of water somewhere in the distance disturbed the stillness—an echo from deeper within the subterranean dark.

Aryan stood motionless before her, framed by the flickering glow of ancient oil lamps. His pristine white kurta shimmered, as untouched as his belief. His face was a mask of serene determination, carved from the same stone that lined the chamber walls.

Anika's breath was slow and controlled, though her heart thundered in her chest. She had spent her career dissecting minds warped by belief. She had profiled killers who cloaked murder in ideology. But Aryan wasn't lost in delusion. He was not mad. He was clear. Unwavering. Terrifyingly pure in his purpose.

'You think,' Aryan said softly, tilting his head, 'that words will stop what's already begun.'

Anika held his gaze. 'I think you're standing at the edge of your own prophecy. And I know—deep down—you have doubts. If you didn't, we wouldn't be standing here. You'd already have finished it.'

A faint chuckle escaped Aryan's lips, as if her reasoning amused him. 'There she is—the psychologist. Dismantling meaning with logic.' He brushed his hand along the ancient altar's carvings, fingers gliding over grooves worn down by centuries of whispered prayers and silent deaths. 'But you're wrong, Anika. I have no doubts. Only destiny.'

And then . . . he lifted a hand.

From the passageway behind the altar, footfalls echoed. Soft. Slow. Measured.

Anika's spine stiffened. The ops team behind her moved, their hands hovering over weapons and eyes scanning for a threat.

Then they emerged.

Five men in ceremonial white robes, faces obscured beneath low hoods. They moved in eerie synchronicity, solemn and soundless, their arms outstretched—not with weapons, but with weight.

Between them, stumbling, head bowed, and feet dragging across the stone, was a man.

Anika's stomach turned to ice.

The figure was gaunt and frail. His clothes hung in tatters, his hair was long and matted, and his face was hidden.

One of the robed men gripped the prisoner's arm and yanked him upright.

And everything stopped.

The face. The eyes. The familiar tilt of the jaw. The scar on his brow from a childhood fall.

Her brother.

Yuvraj.

The world fell away.

Her breath caught like a punch to the chest. Her knees nearly gave out. 'Yuvraj?' she whispered—fragile and broken, as if speaking the name would wake her from a dream.

For a moment, there were only the two of them. The altar, the chanting, and the men—everything else faded into silence.

Yuvraj's eyes met hers. Hollow and sunken. Recognition dawned slowly, like a memory rising through fog. His lips parted, cracked and dry. He tried to speak.

Anika surged forward, but Aryan's men pulled him back.

'No!' she cried, voice raw. 'Let him go!'

Her voice rang across the chamber, fierce and pleading. Yuvraj struggled weakly in their grasp.

He was thinner. Broken. But alive.

The realisation hit her like a storm. Yuvraj—her brother, lost for years—had been here all along. Held. Hidden. Conditioned.

She turned on Aryan, rage igniting her veins. 'You had him this whole time?' Her voice cracked with fury.

Aryan remained perfectly composed, his expression unreadable. 'He was always meant to be here.'

The chill in those words was deeper than any winter.

Aryan stepped towards the altar again, his fingers resting reverently on the stone. 'It was never about me, Dr Thakur,' he murmured. 'It was always about him.'

Anika's chest tightened. All her years of searching, grieving, and guilt boiled down to this moment. Yuvraj wasn't a casualty of circumstance. He was the key.

And Aryan was seconds from killing him.

No.

Anika stepped forward, her voice a low growl of desperation. 'Take me instead.'

Aryan looked up, mildly surprised. His fingers tapped the stone, considering.

'I'm serious,' Anika said. 'You said the sacrifice must be willing. I'm here. Willing. Let him go.'

Aryan studied her in silence, then smiled—a small eerie thing. 'You'd die for him?'

'Yes.'

'You'd give up everything?'

'If it ends this, yes.'

The chamber held its breath.

Then Aryan chuckled. Not with joy. But disbelief. 'You're lying.'

Anika's fists clenched. 'I'm not.'

He stepped closer. 'Your brother begged for death, Dr Thakur. Thousands of times. That makes him willing.'

Her heart twisted. She forced herself not to imagine it. Not yet.

'But not free,' she said, her voice urgent. 'You know that's not the same.'

She took another step forward, voice dipping into the calm, deliberate cadence she used with hostage takers. 'You've built all this—every murder, every detail, every timing—around one principle: purity of intent. But if you force this . . .' Her voice sharpened. 'Then you're just another tyrant rewriting history through blood.'

Aryan flinched—barely—but she saw it.

'I am willing,' she said. 'And if your prophecy means anything, you'll take me instead.'

Another silence stretched, thick and charged.

Aryan's fingers twitched against the altar.

He looked at her for a long time. And for the first time since she had met him, he hesitated.

'You believe yourself worthy of the sacrifice?' he asked, voice quieter now.

'I believe in saving him,' she answered.

Aryan's jaw tightened. The flicker of uncertainty was there, faint but undeniable.

And then . . . the ground trembled beneath their feet.

Dust fell from the chamber ceiling.

The moment was fracturing.

Time was running out.

A charged silence fell over the chamber—dense and suffocating—as if even the walls were holding their breath. The weight of centuries hung in the air, soaked into every stone and every carving. For a heartbeat, Anika thought the tremor beneath her feet was the earth recoiling in protest. But it was more than that.

A rupture in destiny.

Aryan stood perfectly still. His breath controlled. His hands clenched, as if physically restraining something within himself. The mask of serenity was beginning to crack.

She had rattled him.

'You would take his place?' he asked finally, his voice quieter now, almost disbelieving. There was a tremor in it. Not fear. Conflict.

Anika's pulse thundered, but her words were unwavering. 'Yes.'

He stared at her for a long beat, his dark eyes burning with something she couldn't quite name. Curiosity? Suspicion? Awe?

Then a small weary chuckle escaped his lips. 'You truly are something, Dr Thakur.' He shook his head, pacing slowly in front of the altar. His fingers trailed along the grooves of the etched stone, the weight of ritual thickening around him. Behind him, the machines hummed, calculating and measuring.

His expression changed—sharpened. He turned back to her, his voice cutting through the silence like a blade. 'You think you're clever, don't you? That you can outwit the prophecy? That offering yourself is some final act of defiance that will unravel everything I've built?'

Anika didn't flinch. 'I think belief has always left room for choice.'

Aryan's lips curved—not in amusement this time, but with something colder. Calculated. 'I expected you might try something like this.'

He stepped closer. The light from the altar caught the edges of his gold-threaded kurta, casting shifting shadows across his face. The energy between them changed—darkened.

'That's why I took precautions.'

Anika's muscles tensed. 'What kind of precautions?'

Aryan exhaled slowly, like a teacher disappointed in a student who had missed the obvious.

He turned towards the bank of monitors lining the wall—modern interfaces woven into the sacred geometry of the chamber. With a gesture from him, one of his followers tapped a sequence on the keyboard.

The screens shifted.

Red nodes lit up across a schematic of Jaipur.

Anika felt her stomach plummet. 'What is this?'

Aryan walked to the console, lifted a small silver device from its cradle, and held it up. A detonator.

'The fail-safe,' he said softly. 'In case I didn't make it to the end.'

Anika's voice was barely a whisper. 'No . . .'

His eyes never left hers. 'You see, I accounted for sentiment. For interference. For the possibility that someone, like you, might throw themselves into the gears of my design. So, I created something even you can't stop.'

He nodded towards the screens. More images loaded—grainy surveillance footage of underground corridors, abandoned shrines, and forgotten culverts. Every image showed something similar: crates, wiring, and metal shells.

Explosives.

Anika's world tilted.

'You . . . you planted bombs across the city?'

Aryan smiled, pleased by the horror dawning across her face. 'Markets. Bridges. Historical sites. Hospitals. Places where memory and mortality intersect. If I die—or if this ritual fails—Jaipur will be cleansed by fire.'

'You're insane,' she breathed, the words catching in her throat.

'No,' he said evenly. 'I'm thorough.'

The detonator gleamed in his hand. 'One press. That's all it takes. Every line of blood I've mapped . . . every scar this city has ignored . . . will be written in flame.'

Her mind raced. No threat assessment. No disarm team could neutralize that many targets in time. He had built a martyr's dead man's switch, and now her life was the last fuse left unlit.

Aryan took a step towards her, his expression unreadable. 'Do you understand now, Anika?'

She forced herself to breathe. To think. To respond.

'I do,' she said quietly. 'Which means you need me alive. The ritual must be completed. So, let's finish it.'

Aryan's lips curled into something that resembled a smile. 'Good girl.'

He turned to his followers. 'Take her.'

The words rang in her ears like a sentence.

Two robed figures approached, their movements fluid and silent. She stood perfectly still. Not because she had given up, but because the calculation had shifted. She couldn't win by resistance. Not here. Not yet.

Her gaze locked on to Yuvraj—still restrained and watching. His face, pale with exhaustion and disbelief, was a lighthouse in the rising tide of chaos.

If it meant saving him—saving Jaipur—there was no choice.

She let them take her.

Then . . . pain.

A sharp, blinding crack at the back of her skull.

White exploded behind her eyes. Her knees gave way. The chamber spun violently.

And then . . . only darkness.

꒰❦꒱

A dull, searing pain echoed through Anika's skull, blooming outwards in waves and spreading like fire across her limbs. Every nerve burned, and every breath caught. The world around her felt unreal—distant and warped, as though she were floating just outside her own body.

The air was dense. Smothering. Thick with the acrid tang of burning oil, the wet rot of damp stone, and the sharp metallic sting of blood.

Somewhere beyond the fog clouding her mind, voices murmured—indistinct, echoing, and rising and falling like an incantation she couldn't grasp.

Her fingers twitched against cold stone.

Her mind clawed its way back to consciousness.

Then . . .

'You truly are sentimental fools.'

The voice sliced through the fog like a scalpel. Aryan.

Anika tensed. A jolt of adrenaline surged through her body, snapping her senses back into focus. Her breathing quickened. Her vision sharpened.

She was seated on the floor, propped against the cold, unforgiving wall of the chamber. Her wrists ached—unbound now but raw. Her head throbbed with each beat of her heart.

And then she saw him.

Singh.

Lying on the altar.

Where she was supposed to be.

A noise left her lips—half gasp, half scream—as her world shattered in an instant.

Blood bloomed across his chest, spilling into the ancient grooves carved into the altar's stone and turning ritual markings into runes of death. His uniform—always crisp and always precise—was soaked, ruined, and torn open over the wound.

'NO—NO!'

She lunged, but Kumar caught her, yanking her back just in time.

'LET ME GO!' she screamed, her voice splintering, as she thrashed violently against his hold. But he held fast.

Her entire being fractured. Why him? Why not her?

Singh's head shifted. His eyes fluttered open, glassy but focused. And then . . . that smile. Small. Quiet. The same one he'd always given her before doing something impossibly brave.

'Anika . . .,' he breathed.

Her knees buckled, her nails biting into the stone. 'WHY?' Her voice tore from her throat, shaking and broken.

Singh's breath was shallow, his body trembling. 'Because I couldn't let you die.'

Time slowed. Her pulse roared in her ears. Her vision blurred. She couldn't comprehend it, couldn't accept it. 'No,' she gasped. 'No, Singh, you—'

She tore herself from Kumar's grip and stumbled to the altar, falling to her knees beside him. Her hands trembled as she pressed against the open wound, trying to stop the bleeding, trying to stop the inevitable.

His blood was hot and sticky beneath her palms.

'Why?' she sobbed. 'Why would you do this?'

Singh looked at her through the haze of pain. His hand found hers. Weak. Trembling. But steady in its final purpose.

'Because I knew,' he whispered, 'you would try to take Yuvraj's place.'

Her breath hitched.

He had known.

All along.

The quiet presence behind her. The steady gaze. He'd been watching. Waiting.

Protecting.

'I suspected for a long time,' Singh said, coughing, his voice raw. 'That I might be royal too. Distant blood. An old name we never used. I buried it—until I needed it.'

Her heart shattered.

He'd used it to bring her onto the case. And now . . . to take her place on the altar.

Her stomach twisted. 'You didn't have to do this.'

He smiled again, lips trembling. 'I did, Anika. I had to.' His hand tightened on hers. 'Because I love you.'

The words struck her like a blow.

Her throat clenched. Her vision blurred. 'No. No, you can't—' She shook her head furiously. 'You don't get to say that and leave.'

His breath was shallow. His eyes were heavy. 'You have to live,' he whispered. 'For Yuvraj. For everything that comes next.'

Tears streamed down her face. Her body shook. 'Singh, please . . . stay with me—'

But his grip loosened.

His eyes closed.

And his heartbeat faded into silence.

Her scream cracked the stone.

It echoed across the chamber—raw, unfiltered grief. Rage. Love. Loss.

And somewhere in the shadows, Aryan watched. Silent.

And smiling.

The world stopped moving.

Everything inside the chamber—the flickering oil flames, the metallic tang of blood, and the low, rhythmic chants of Aryan's followers—blurred into insignificance. Nothing mattered. Nothing existed. Nothing but the man who now lay lifeless on the altar.

Singh.

His blood seeped slowly into the carved grooves beneath him, darkening the ancient stone and fulfilling a design that had waited generations to be completed.

Anika didn't move. Didn't blink. Her fingers remained wrapped around his, clinging to the last traces of warmth as it slipped away.

Her mind refused to understand. Her body refused to release him.

This was Singh—the man who had stood beside her through every battle, who had grounded her when she faltered, and who had seen the real her even when she tried to disappear. The man who had carried her unspoken burdens, withstood her walls, and never once let her fall.

And now . . . he was gone.

He had made his choice. But she never got to tell him that she would have made the same one for him.

Her fingers curled into a fist, gripping his hand tighter, her whole body trembling. Her lungs strained to hold in the scream building in her chest.

She looked up—eyes burning and jaw clenched—and spat the only words that could escape.

'You bastard!'

Aryan's eyes were closed, lips moving in the final lines of the ritual. He ignored her cry, his voice calm and sonorous, finishing the words he believed would change the world.

And when the final syllable passed his lips, he opened his eyes and turned to face her.

For the first time, there was something other than smugness in his gaze. Something almost . . . respectful.

'I must admit,' he said, voice low and even, 'I didn't see it coming.' He glanced at Singh's body. 'I expected resistance. Perhaps violence. But not this.'

He looked back at Anika. His expression was unreadable, but his eyes held a flicker of satisfaction.

'The ritual is complete, Dr Thakur. I won. The Wrathbearers won.'

Anika stared at him, unable to comprehend the audacity in his words. Singh's blood was still warm beneath her hands. Her grief rose like bile. Rage burned in her throat.

'You think this is over?' she whispered, voice splintering.

Aryan's smirk returned, infuriating in its calm. 'Of course it is.'

He stepped away from the altar with the casual grace of a man dusting off the last page of a history book. His hands opened at his sides in theatrical conclusion.

'The sacrifice has been made. The city is safe. The curse is lifted. And now . . . we surrender.'

Behind her, Kumar jolted. His voice was hoarse. 'What did you just say?'

Aryan turned slightly, arms still spread in mock absolution. 'Arrest me. Arrest my men. It doesn't matter. Jaipur has been saved.'

The words didn't register.

Anika's vision tunnelled, the sound of her pulse drowning out everything else. Her hearing dulled, except for the echo of Singh's last words. The silence he left behind filled the chamber like a scream too large to be contained.

Tears blurred her vision, her body shaking as grief coiled with fury, twisting into something feral, something she no longer recognised.

'No,' she whispered, her voice a tremor. 'No, you don't get to just walk away from this.'

Aryan tilted his head, the faintest smile curling at his lips.

'I already have.'

Kumar and the team moved forward to secure him, handcuff the Wrathbearers, and guide Yuvraj away from the altar. Footsteps echoed, orders were given, and the chamber slowly began to empty. Yet as the city above unknowingly exhaled in relief, Anika remained on the floor.

Motionless.

Her hands still stained with Singh's blood.

And as she sat there in the cold silence, broken and burning, she stared at Aryan Singh Rathore.

And she realised . . .

She had never hated anyone in her life the way she hated him now.

The chamber throbbed with a heavy, unnatural silence, broken only by the soft crackle of radios sputtering back to life. The air was thick—choking—with the mingled scents of burning oil, sweat, blood, and prophecy fulfilled. It didn't feel like breath could exist here anymore. The space itself felt suspended, held between a past that had just ended and a future not yet born.

Kumar still had Aryan by the wrists, iron tight. His hand went to his radio, pressing the receiver to his lips with a grim steadiness. His voice was calm but frayed at the edges.

'Commissioner Verma, this is Kumar. The target is secure. Aryan Singh Rathore is in custody.'

For the first time, Aryan flinched.

It was barely perceptible—a twitch of the shoulders and a shift in breath—but Anika saw it. Her instincts flared. Something was wrong.

Verma's voice came through the radio, distorted but firm. 'Copy that, Kumar. Jaipur is standing by. Bring them in.'

The words should have ended it.

The city was safe. The prophecy was broken. Singh's sacrifice had meant something.

It should have been over.

But then . . . a sound.

Low. Hissing. Almost imperceptible at first.

Anika froze. Her body responded before her mind did. She knew that sound. She caught her breath, and dread flooded her veins.

A mist slithered into the chamber—white, heavy, and curling low over the floor like smoke from the underworld. It poured in from the seams of the stone, unseen vents, and the shadows themselves.

Aryan's face had changed. No fear. Just knowing.

Anticipation.

'Oh no,' Kumar breathed. His grip on Aryan tightened.

Anika spun, her voice slicing through the rising fog. 'GAS! MASKS ON—NOW!'

Too late.

The smoke thickened in seconds, blanketing the chamber in an impenetrable white. The ancient ritual hall became a void. Sound warped. Shapes twisted.

Chaos erupted.

ॐ

'Hold your positions!' Kumar shouted, his voice booming through the haze, but command had already slipped through his fingers.

The ops team staggered, coughing and stumbling blind. Panic fractured the line. Shadows danced through the fog, disorienting and dismembering cohesion.

Anika fought to orient herself, hands outstretched and boots sliding over blood-slicked stone. She felt hands grab her arm, then vanish. Heard boots scrape. Bodies collide. Screams muffled into static.

And then . . . movement.

Fast. Sharp. Coordinated.

Figures flowed through the mist like spirits loosed from stone. Pale robes. Hidden faces. They weren't panicked. They were executing.

Wrathbearers.

The true believers. The last protectors. The shadows that had been waiting for their moment.

'Protect the master!'

The command cut like a blade through the noise.

Then . . . gunfire. Suppressed shots, dull and deadly. Gas canisters clattered, releasing more choking plumes. And then the sickening unmistakable thuds of bodies hitting stone.

Anika choked, lungs burning. Eyes searing.

'Yuvraj!' she called out, stumbling forward.

A muffled cry answered her.

Somewhere in the fog, struggling. Dragging. A desperate scuffle against the inevitable.

'YUVRAJ!' she screamed, shoving forward with everything left in her body and clawing through the thick air. Her limbs were heavy, her thoughts slipping sideways. But she would not let them take him again.

A shape loomed through the smoke.

Fast. Silent.

A Wrathbearer.

They turned. Masked. Expressionless. But there was purpose in their movement—ritual precision.

Before she could brace, the butt of a rifle cracked into her stomach. The air whooshed from her lungs, her body doubling over.

Then another blow—hard and clean—against her temple.

Pain split her vision. The chamber spun. White turned to red. Red to black.

And then . . .

Darkness.

CHAPTER 18

The world returned in fragments.

First, the steady beep of a heart monitor—slow, mechanical, and too calm. Then the low murmur of distant voices, slipping in and out of her awareness like echoes rising from a well.

The smell hit next: antiseptic. Bleach. Burned fabric. Blood. Beneath it all, the lingering scent of smoke that clung to her skin like a memory.

Anika inhaled sharply.

Pain exploded in her ribs, stopping her breath mid-draw, anchoring her violently back to the present. Consciousness was a brutal tide, dragging her from the dark abyss and slamming her into a reality she wasn't ready to face.

Her first instinct was to sit up. To move. To return to the chamber.

But her body rebelled.

White-hot pain lanced through her side, forcing a gasp from her lips.

'Easy. Easy—'

A firm hand met her shoulder, grounding her before she could do more damage.

As her vision cleared, fluorescent lights bled into focus. A white ceiling. The sterile quiet of a hospital room. And then . . . Kumar. Seated beside her, eyes red-rimmed and shoulders drawn tight with fatigue.

But more than that, he looked defeated.

A weight pressed into her chest, heavier than broken ribs. The chamber. The smoke. The Wrathbearers.

Yuvraj.

Images rushed back—her brother bound, barely able to stand. His voice, muffled in the mist. The feel of Singh's blood on her hands.

Her fingers curled around the hospital sheets, white-knuckled. 'Where is he?' Her voice was rough. Cracked. Barely more than a breath.

Kumar didn't answer immediately. His eyes flickered down. His jaw clenched.

'Kumar.'

He met her gaze. Then looked away again, as if it physically hurt to say the words.

'We got Aryan.'

The words hung like dust in sunlight. Cold. Inert. Hollow.

It should have been a victory.

But Anika felt nothing.

Because if that was what he led with, it meant the real news was worse.

She already knew.

'And Yuvraj?'

Kumar's fists tightened in his lap. 'They took him.'

Her heart stuttered.

The walls tilted. 'No.'

Kumar didn't flinch this time. 'The Wrathbearers got to him before we could extract him.'

A silence stretched between them, deep and choking.

Then it shattered.

'NO!'

She lurched upright, ignoring the pain that clawed through her body like fire. Kumar reached out to steady her, but she shoved at him.

'We have to go after them—right now! We can't just sit here—'

'Anika!' Kumar's voice cut through her panic. Firm. Raw. 'We lost him. But that doesn't mean we won't get him back.'

Her breath heaved in her chest. Her hands clawed at the sheets, her whole body coiled to act, to move, and to fight.

'How long?' she asked, barely able to form the words. 'How long was I out?'

Kumar hesitated.

That pause broke something in her.

'How long, Kumar?'

His voice was quiet. 'Two days.'

The air vanished from the room.

Two days.

She had been lying here—sedated and broken—while they disappeared into the shadows with her brother. Every hour widened the distance. Every second gave Aryan's people more time to vanish, erase, and rebuild.

Her vision blurred. Grief flooded her like poison.

But beneath it . . . something else.

Rage.

'Aryan.' She spat the name like venom.

Kumar's expression darkened. 'He's alive. We have him. Locked in a black site. Maximum security.'

Anika turned to him, eyes blazing. 'Take me to him.'

'Anika—'

'TAKE ME TO HIM.'

The scream ripped from her throat, full of every broken thing inside her.

Kumar flinched . . . but nodded. 'I'll make the call.'

Because this wasn't over.

They had Aryan Singh Rathore.

And now she was going to break him.

Piece by piece.

Until he told her everything.

Because Yuvraj had been stolen again.

And this time, Anika Thakur would burn the Wrathbearers to the ground to bring him home.

No matter the cost.

Jaipur had never been so quiet.

Not even in the deepest hours of night, when the markets lay deserted and the last chai stall extinguished its fire, had the city felt this still. This hollow. The silence that cloaked the streets now wasn't born of sleep. It was the hush of revelation. Of reckoning.

Truth had been pulled from beneath centuries of stone and secrecy. Exposed. Named. And now the city sat with it, unsure whether to mourn or rebuild.

The streets bustled, but not with life as they had known it. Gone were the sing-song haggling of vendors, the clink of teacups in cafés, and the laughter echoing down ancient lanes.

Now Jaipur buzzed with something more fragile. More watchful. A city on the edge of transformation, forced to confront what it had been—so it could decide what it wanted to become.

The grand meeting hall of the City Palace had once been a sanctuary of control—where rulers made history behind silken curtains and stone walls, where alliances were brokered in whispers and betrayals dressed in civility.

Today it was something else.

Today it felt like a reckoning ground.

The air was thick with tension, with the scent of sweat and perfume and fear. The walls, lined with portraits of kings and warriors, bore silent witness as their legacy was questioned at the very table they once ruled from.

At that long polished table, history now stood divided.

On one side, the royal family. Proud faces dulled by sleepless nights and scandal, their silks doing little to mask the cracks in their poise.

On the other, a coalition of government officials, scholars, and public advocates—backs straight, expressions measured, and eyes burning with the righteousness of truth brought to light.

At the head sat Vikram Singh Rathore.

His fingers were laced tightly together, resting against the wood like he was holding the last piece of a crumbling dynasty in his hands. This seat had belonged to his forefathers—men who dictated the city's fate without contest. But today he wasn't dictating. He was listening.

For the first time in the history of this hall, power didn't belong to the crown.

It belonged to the room.

When Vikram finally spoke, his voice was calm, but something raw lingered just beneath. 'Thank you all for coming. We are here to discuss the future of our family's role in Jaipur . . . in light of recent events.'

The words were clinical, careful. But the truth beneath them was a tremor in the bones.

A murmur swept through the royals—tight whispers, barely contained alarm. The walls of legacy, already cracked by the revelations of blood rituals and hidden crimes, were beginning to fracture completely.

Across the table, Aditya Mathur, the senior government representative, leaned forward. His voice was calm. His tone was final.

'Let's not waste time with formalities, Mr Rathore.' The pointed absence of a title hung like a gauntlet on the floor. 'The public is demanding accountability.'

A greying noble to Vikram's left bristled, his voice sharp. 'You can't hold us responsible for what happened centuries ago. We've been patrons, protectors—'

'Patrons of a system built on blood,' a younger woman snapped, her government badge gleaming under the hall's crystal lights. 'The curse may be superstition. But the crimes committed in its name were real.'

Vikram raised a hand.

Silence returned.

'We are not here to debate the past,' he said, his voice steady, though there was something solemn beneath it. 'We are here to decide if the royal family has a place in Jaipur's future.'

The room froze.

Because for the first time, a Rathore had asked that question aloud.

For a moment, no one spoke.

Then Aditya Mathur reached for a file and slid a stack of documents across the table towards Vikram. 'The government recognises your family's cultural significance. But change is necessary.'

His tone was professional. But it had the sharpness of policy carved from anger.

Vikram didn't move. His fingers hovered above the edge of the papers.

Aditya continued, 'We propose a reduction in royal privileges. The transfer of key heritage properties to the state. And the establishment of an independent oversight committee for all future royal activities.'

And just like that, the room erupted.

Voices clashed like swords.

'You can't strip us of everything!'

'We're custodians of Jaipur's legacy!'

'The people won't stand for this!'

'The people are already in the streets,' Mathur's voice sliced through the storm like a blade. 'They're not asking anymore. They're demanding.'

Silence fell again—heavier this time.

Vikram sat unmoving, his expression unreadable. His fingers tapped once—twice—on the edge of the decree.

Then he said, simply, 'Silence.'

The hall obeyed.

And when all that remained was breath and waiting, Vikram spoke again.

'We accept.'

A ripple passed through the room. Shock. Relief. Sorrow.

For the first time in Jaipur's long tangled history, the royal family had surrendered its power. Not to war. Not to rebellion.

But to the truth.

Vikram sat taller, his voice unshaken. 'We accept the need for change.'

Across the table, Aditya Mathur gave a small respectful nod. 'Then it will be arranged. With full oversight.'

And just like that, the last empire fell.

Not with fire.

Not with blood.

But with ink on paper.

And the quiet courage to end what should never have begun.

A new Jaipur would rise.

And for the first time, it would not belong to the kings.

As the sun dipped behind the palaces and ancient walls, Jaipur moved like a city in mourning.

Crowds gathered in hushed clusters outside royal estates and heritage sites, not in celebration or fury, but in stillness. The streets—usually alive with chatter, colour, and rhythm—were subdued, haunted by the ghosts of truth unearthed.

There were protests, yes. Chants, demands, and revolutions of thought. But alongside them were vigils. Rows of candles flickering in the wind. Quiet prayers whispered at street corners. Flowers laid on the courthouse steps. Because in the city's rebirth, there had been blood.

There had been loss.

And one name passed through every mouth—from alleyways to balconies to market stalls.

Singh.

Some called him a fool—a man who had thrown his life away for a dynasty that didn't deserve it.

But most?

They called him something else entirely.

A martyr.

A hero.

The wind moved gently across Anika's balcony, carrying the mingled scents of wet stone, drifting incense, and the aftershock of a city changed.

Jaipur had been saved.

But the price had been everything.

She stood motionless, her hands clenched around the iron railing, staring down at the streets he had died to protect. Street lights cast golden halos on the pavement, and in the distance, temple bells rang as if nothing had changed.

As if a man hadn't bled out on an altar to break a curse woven into the city's bones.

As if her brother hadn't been taken from her again.

As if she hadn't lost the one person who had seen her fully . . . and chosen her anyway.

Her fingers tightened around the railing, her knuckles bone white. Her breath came in shallow bursts.

It had been many hours since Singh's body was taken away. Since the ritual chamber was cleared. Since Aryan was locked behind steel walls.

Since her world had fallen apart.

She had drifted through it all—like a shadow of herself. Attending briefings. Signing reports. Hearing Kumar's voice without listening. The movements of protocol wrapped around her like gauze—functional, numbing.

Because if she had stopped for even a moment, she would have collapsed.

And now . . . now that the silence had returned, now that the wind was the only voice left, there was nothing shielding her from the truth.

He was gone.

Rajesh Singh had chosen to die for her. Had taken the blade meant for her. Had made a decision she never got to contest.

Because he loved her.

The memory of those words—his final breath—pierced her like shrapnel.

'I couldn't let you die . . . because I love you.'

A shuddering breath tore through her. Her body trembled. The pain cracked something open in her chest. The dam broke.

Tears came.

Hot. Blinding. Unrelenting.

She slammed her hands against the railing. Once. Twice. The metal reverberated with the echo of her rage, grief, and helplessness.

'You bastard.'

It came out hoarse, broken. Then louder. 'You stupid, stubborn bastard!'

She didn't know if she was shouting at the sky, the wind, the gods, or herself. She didn't care.

Her fist collided with the iron again. Pain flared up in her arm, sharp and unforgiving. But it didn't stop her.

'How could you?' she screamed. 'How could you just decide for me?'

The words dissolved into sobs as her knees buckled. She collapsed onto the cold tiled floor, her body folding into itself and her forehead pressed to stone. Her hands curled into her hair as the grief ripped from her throat—raw, primal, and unstoppable.

Rajesh Singh had been her compass. Her constant. Her anchor in a world that had tried to unmoor her.

And now . . . he was gone.

She was left in the world he had died to save. Left with the weight of a love unspoken, a goodbye she never got to give.

And she would never get the chance.

The thought was another wound, deeper than the rest.

She didn't know how long she stayed there, sobbing on the balcony floor—minutes, hours, it didn't matter. Because time meant nothing in the wake of that kind of loss.

When the tears finally slowed and her body had no more strength to shake, she sat still, staring at the city beyond the railing. A city that Singh had died for. A city now tasked with being better.

Her fingers slipped into the inside pocket of her jacket and closed around something cold and metallic.

The medal that Commissioner Verma had handed her.

Singh's medal.

Speckled with his blood. The symbol of a legacy he never claimed. A bloodline he never wanted.

And yet the one that killed him.

She held it in her palm, clutching it so tightly her nails dug into her skin. 'It wasn't supposed to be you.' Her voice was barely audible. But the wind carried it anyway.

It was supposed to be her.

And Singh—damn him—had taken that choice from her.

A part of her would never forgive him for that.

But the deeper part of her—the part that knew him, really knew him—understood.

Because Singh had never been the kind of man to let others fight his battles for him.

And in the end, he had fought his last one—for her.

For the city.

For what was right.

Her fingers curled tighter around the medal. Her eyes narrowed. Her spine straightened.

Jaipur had changed. She had changed.

And there was still one war left to finish.

Because Yuvraj was out there.

And the Wrathbearers still lived.

As she rose slowly to her feet, her grief like lead in her bones but her resolve sharper than steel, she whispered one last promise into the night.

'I'll make sure your sacrifice wasn't for nothing, Rajesh.'

And this time, she meant it with every shattered piece of her heart.

The house felt too quiet. The moment Anika stepped through the wooden threshold, she felt a strong wave of exhaustion from all the years lost in this space, making her feel suffocated. The air was thick with the scent of sandalwood and old memories, a mixture of incense from the temple room and the faded perfume her mother always wore.

Everything looked the same. And yet nothing felt the same anymore. Lata sat by the window, her frail hands wrapped around a cup of chai that had long since gone cold. She hadn't turned when Anika entered. She hadn't moved. She just sat there, staring at nothing.

Anika swallowed the lump lodged in her throat, forcing her feet forward. 'Ma . . .'

The sound of her voice, gentle but strained, finally made Lata turn. Her mother's soft brown eyes, once so full of life, now looked at her with something broken, weary.

Anika felt a sharp stab of guilt. She hadn't come home since Aryan's arrest, since the revelation of the curse, and since Singh's cremation the day before. She hadn't had the heart to face her mother since Yuvraj had been taken. She had been afraid. Afraid of facing her mother's grief, hope, and pain. Afraid of saying the words she knew would shatter her all over again.

Lata set down the cup with shaking hands, her expression unreadable. Then, in a voice so soft it almost broke Anika apart, she said, 'You found him, didn't you?'

Anika stilled. Her fingers curled into tight fists at her sides, her breath shuddering in her chest. Her mother had always been too perceptive. She had known from the moment she saw Anika standing at the door.

Anika nodded, slowly, as if saying it out loud would make it more real. 'Yes, Ma.'

Lata inhaled sharply, her lips trembling. 'Yuvraj . . .' Her voice broke.

Anika sank to her knees beside her mother's chair, her hands reaching out, gripping her mother's thin wrists like she was trying to anchor her to the moment. 'Ma . . .' She took a deep breath, steadying herself for what she had to say next. 'He's alive.'

Lata's hands tightened around hers, the breath leaving her in a soft, disbelieving gasp. 'He's alive?'

Anika forced herself to nod again, though the words felt like splinters in her throat. 'Yes. I—' She cleared her throat and started again, 'I saw him.'

A sob racked through her mother's body, silent and shaking, filled with years of unshed grief.

She lifted trembling fingers to touch Anika's face, as if needing to feel her daughter's solidity to believe the words.

'My son . . . is alive . . . ?'

Anika's chest ached. She should have let her mother breathe in that relief, that joy—if only for a moment longer. But she couldn't. Because the truth wasn't that simple. She closed her eyes, steeling herself for the blow she was about to deliver. 'Ma . . . the Wrathbearers, the men who had him, took him again.'

Lata froze. Her breath hitched, her fingers going rigid against Anika's face. Then, in a whisper that held too much pain for such a small sound, she uttered, 'No . . .'

Anika clenched her jaw, her fingernails digging into her palms. 'Yes.' She felt her mother's body start to tremble, her hands slipping from Anika's grip.

'They took him? Again?'

Anika nodded. She had seen many things in her life—murderers at their most depraved, victims in their final moments, and families torn apart by grief. But she had never seen her mother like this. The light that had sparked briefly in Lata's eyes when she heard Yuvraj was alive was now extinguished, replaced with a darkness Anika couldn't bear to look at.

Lata pressed a hand to her chest, her breathing ragged and her body curling in on itself. 'Why?' she whispered, her voice barely holding together. Anika shook her head, blinking past the sting of tears.

'I don't know. But I swear to you, Ma—' She gripped her mother's hands again, her voice fierce, steady, and unwavering. 'I will bring him back.'

Lata's wet, bloodshot eyes locked on to hers, searching her for something—hope, certainty, anything to hold on to. 'You promise me, Anika?' Her mother's hands tightened, as if she could keep her daughter from slipping away just as Yuvraj had.

Anika's own fingers wrapped around her mother's frail ones, the touch an unspoken vow. 'I promise.' The words weren't just for her mother. They were for herself. For Singh, who had died to save this city. For the brother she had lost once and now lost again. For the part of herself that refused to accept that Yuvraj was truly gone.

She pressed her forehead against her mother's hands, letting her grief settle, but not consume her, because she wasn't done yet. Not even close.

CHAPTER 19

Jaipur had once lived in the hush of withheld truths.

Now it pulsed with something else entirely—an energy as raw as it was restless. The streets, still draped in pink sandstone and royal echoes, moved with a different rhythm. A city awakening. A city reckoning. A city becoming.

As dawn unfurled across the City Palace two days after Rajesh Singh's cremation, the sun did not simply cast gold across the sandstone walls. It cast judgment. Illumination. Renewal.

A massive banner draped across the grand façade fluttered in the morning breeze, bold against the fading grandeur of monarchy. It read:

'Truth and Reconciliation: Jaipur's New Chapter.'

Below it, a sea of people had begun to gather—some pulled by curiosity, others by grief, and many by the need to bear witness. What had once been a seat of unquestioned rule was now a stage for collective accountability.

In Chandpole Bazaar, where the sounds of bargaining had once echoed like ritual, another rhythm now filled the air.

Protesters surged through the winding market lanes, their chants rising like thunder between the spice carts and shuttered tea stalls.

'No more secrets! No more lies!'

They carried banners bearing the faces of the forgotten—victims of a fabricated curse, of silence masquerading as tradition. Portraits long buried in dusty family trunks were now held high in the demand for justice.

A shopkeeper, bent with age and time, rested a wrinkled hand atop his stack of saffron-dyed cloth. He shook his head. 'In my day, we respected tradition,' he muttered.

His customer, a woman in her fifties, didn't look at him. Her eyes were fixed on a poster of a young woman whose name had once been whispered and dismissed as myth.

'Maybe,' the woman replied quietly, 'some traditions were built to be broken.'

The shopkeeper fell silent, gaze drifting towards the City Palace—as though seeing it, for the first time, as something both beautiful and terrible.

At Jantar Mantar, the great astronomical observatory once revered for its celestial genius, history was shifting underfoot.

A newly appointed guide, her voice equal parts reverent and resolute, addressed a crowd gathered beneath the shadow of the Samrat Yantra's towering gnomon.

'These were once instruments of knowledge,' she said, running a hand over the cool stone, 'but knowledge was not always used for light.'

She gestured to carvings that scholars now believed had been used to align sacrifices to celestial events.

'The curse,' she continued, 'was never real. But the pain it caused was. The truth we carry now is not a legend. It is legacy.'

A tourist raised his hand. 'So . . . is this place cursed or not?'

She smiled gently. 'No. But it was misused. What we do now is rewrite how we remember.'

The group murmured—some in awe, some in unease—as science and history were rethreaded with uncomfortable truth.

In a modest community hall near Hawa Mahal, tension simmered under ceiling fans that barely stirred the air.

City officials sat shoulder to shoulder with survivors and the children of the disappeared. The air buzzed with grief, demand, and something dangerously close to hope.

A grieving father stood, his voice hoarse with years of silence. 'Will there be compensation for our families? You cannot just apologise.'

Across from him, a councillor—shirt damp and tie loosened—nodded solemnly. 'A justice fund is being established. Some records date back centuries. But we will trace what we can.'

An elderly woman, her knuckles trembling around a faded photograph, rose next. 'My son vanished 30 years ago. He was studying royal archives.'

The room stilled.

The councillor's voice softened. 'We will reopen every case. We owe you that much.'

No one clapped. No one cheered.

But for the first time, no one shouted either.

Because for the first time, someone had said, 'We will try.'

Outside the Albert Hall Museum, history was being unboxed in real time.

A pop-up exhibition titled *Shadows and Light: Jaipur's Hidden History* drew long lines of visitors. Inside, walls bore artefacts once hidden—ledgers of hush money, death records scrubbed clean, forged genealogies, and photographs of the silenced.

One wall featured testimonies of survivors and descendants.

A teenager stared at it in stunned silence. 'How could this happen in our city?'

His friend replied, voice quiet but clear, 'It didn't just happen. It was made to happen. And now we're finally seeing it.'

At Amber Fort, once the crown jewel of royal grandeur, yellow tape now fluttered against the arches.

Sections were cordoned off as forensic teams and archaeologists worked side by side. Hidden chambers were being excavated, secret tunnels mapped.

Among them, volunteers—some students, some retirees—dug with reverence and rage, determined to uncover every secret the walls had tried to keep.

And in the heart of Jaipur's tech district, change was blooming in silicon and circuitry.

Start-ups, coders, and journalists gathered in glass towers, whiteboarding the future.

Apps were being built to trace family histories across caste and class. AI-driven platforms were being coded to match missing person reports with digitised archives. AR tours were in development to show not just the beauty of Jaipur's monuments but their shadows too.

The city wasn't just confronting its past.

It was designing a future that refused to forget it.

As the evening settled over Jaipur, the golden city stirred with conversation—its streets alive not just with footsteps but with reflection.

Restaurants brimmed with the hum of debate. Amid plates of dal-bati-churma, *lassi*, and fresh *rotis*, families, students, and colleagues leaned in close, their voices threading new narratives through old walls.

'It's about time we faced our past,' a young woman said, her tone impassioned, a spoon paused mid-air.

Her older colleague frowned over his glass of *chaach*. 'At what cost? Our tourism industry depends on the romance of royalty. People come for palaces, not political reckoning.'

At the table beside them, a local historian, sipping strong masala chai, leaned in. 'Perhaps it's time for a new kind of tourism—one built not on illusion, but on truth. A city doesn't lose beauty by being honest. It gains depth.'

And beyond these polished spaces—in the heart of Jaipur, where conversation gave way to silence—something quieter unfolded.

A small temple nestled between ancient havelis and stone courtyards became the setting for something sacred. Not ritual. Not pageantry.

A vigil.

They came without banners. Without speeches. Just candles, marigolds, and memories.

They came silently—young and old, royals and commoners, Hindus, Muslims, and Jains. Those who had suffered directly under the so-called curse. And those only just beginning to understand what that legacy meant.

The air was warm, thick with incense and night jasmine. Flames flickered against the darkness, tiny halos of gold illuminating faces etched with grief and resilience.

A father lit a candle for a daughter lost decades ago, whose story had finally been unearthed from dusty records. A college student placed a flower for an ancestor she had learned about only days before. A former palace guard bowed his head, whispering a prayer for the sins he could no longer deny.

Jaipur stood still in that moment—not mourning the fall of a dynasty, but witnessing it.

And from that witnessing came something else.

Purpose.

As the vigil slowly dissolved into the quiet of the night, the participants drifted away, their candles still burning. Some took them home. Others left them on the temple steps, tiny flames standing vigil for truths newly spoken.

And in that warm, flickering light, one thing became clear.

This was not the end of the story.

This was the beginning of a new one.

A Jaipur that didn't turn away from its past.

A Jaipur that wore not only silk and stone but also truth.

A Jaipur that understood that reckoning was not destruction but rebirth.

A city that, for the first time in its long and tangled history, was ready to see itself whole.

The television studio had never felt more claustrophobic.

What was once a space for cultural fluff and polite debate had transformed into an arena of reckoning. The set of *Jaipur Tonight*, usually awash in warm tones and flattering lights, now appeared starker—harsher—under the full force of studio glare. Shadows clung to the panellists' faces, each line and crease exposed under the pressure of truth.

The air felt electric. As if even the walls held their breath, bracing for what was to come.

At the centre of it all sat Priya Mathur, the show's veteran anchor. Her hands rested lightly on the edge of the desk, but her knuckles were white. Her heartbeat thundered in her ears, but she didn't flinch. She met the lens of the camera head-on.

Three. Two. One.

The red light blinked alive.

She leaned forward. Her voice was calm, but beneath it was a current of something sharper—something unflinching.

'Good evening, Jaipur.'

The words fell like a gavel. And in their wake, silence. Thick. Expectant.

'We bring you a special edition tonight. A conversation this city has long avoided—until now. The revelations about Jaipur's secret history have sparked outrage, grief, and soul-searching across the nation. Tonight, we confront it.'

She turned slightly, introducing her guests with careful precision.

'Joining us: Dr Amita Sengupta, historian from Delhi University. Mr Abhimanyu Gupta, political analyst. Dr Harbhajan Kaur, sociologist. And Ms Lakshmi Devi, social activist and direct descendant of a victim family.'

The camera swept across the panel, capturing their expressions— composed but taut.

Priya turned first to Dr Sengupta. The historian sat poised, her eyes sharp with thought.

'Dr Sengupta, how do these revelations alter our understanding of Jaipur's—and India's—historical narrative?'

The historian laced her fingers, her voice steady but brimming with gravitas.

'What we're facing is not merely a footnote. It's a seismic shift. The revelation of a multigenerational conspiracy reframes not only Jaipur's past, but the very tools through which history has been written and sanitised in this country.'

Before the weight of her words could settle, Abhimanyu Gupta leaned back, voice oiled with scepticism. 'Aren't we overreacting?' he asked. 'Every country has shadows. Are we prepared to dismantle our cultural heritage over this?'

The tension cracked across the room.

Dr Kaur, calm but incisive, stepped in. 'This is not about toppling monuments, Mr Gupta. It's about exposing the systems that used culture to commit and conceal systemic abuse. This wasn't incidental. It was deliberate.'

He offered a polite scoff. 'Still, we risk a cultural unravelling. Is that wise?'

Then Lakshmi Devi spoke.

Her voice was quieter, but it sliced through the noise. 'My grandmother was taken in the name of that "culture". My father lived his life with that silence wrapped around his throat. This isn't theoretical. This is trauma. And we have been told to bear it for generations—for the sake of your comfort.'

The studio stilled.

Priya turned to her gently. 'Ms Devi . . . what does healing look like?'

Lakshmi's hands trembled in her lap. But her voice didn't. 'It starts with accountability. It continues with reparations. But more than anything, it requires that we no longer be told that our pain is inconvenient.'

Before anyone could respond, Gupta cut in, 'So what now? Do we tear down centuries of history?'

Dr Sengupta's eyes flashed. 'No one's tearing down anything. We're contextualising. Reconciling. We can honour Jaipur's artistry and architecture—and still call out the crimes committed in their shadow.'

The discussion spiralled, voices overlapping—

'Will the royals be prosecuted?'

'Are we rewriting history?'

'What about national unity?'

Priya raised a hand. Her voice carried.

'Dr Kaur, how does a city—and a nation—recover from this?'

He paused, choosing each word with care. 'This is a moment of profound societal reckoning. Jaipur was a symbol of royal romance. Now it has the potential to become something greater: a symbol of truth, of self-correction. If we face this honestly, we model for the nation how to address caste, class, and inherited violence.'

Lakshmi nodded. 'This doesn't end with Jaipur.'

And everyone knew she was right.

The temperature in the room rose—not from heat, but from the weight of legacy rubbing up against the friction of transformation.

Finally, Priya sat back, her tone shifting.

'As we near the close of tonight's programme, I'll ask one final question to each of you: What is the most crucial next step?'

Dr Sengupta: 'Truth. However uncomfortable it may be.'

Mr Abhimanyu: 'Balancing justice with institutional stability.'

Dr Kaur: 'Crafting new narratives that don't erase the past—but don't glorify it either.'

Lakshmi Devi: 'Healing. That's the revolution now.'

The cameras blinked off. The debate did not.

As the panellists gathered their notes and the lights cooled, the echo of their words lingered in the room.

Jaipur had begun to speak. And now the country was listening.

Weeks after Aryan Singh Rathore's arrest, dawn broke gently over Jaipur—its light subdued, as if the sky itself were treading softly.

The city remained fragile in its rebirth. It no longer whispered lies, but it hadn't yet learned how to speak truth without trembling.

Tucked away in a quiet quarter—far from the opulence of palaces and the din of bazaars—stood the newly inaugurated Memorial Garden, a sanctuary carved not for kings but for the silenced.

No statues. No marble. Just a single monolith of unpolished grey stone, framed by marigolds and jasmine. On its face, chiselled deep and without ornament, were the words:

'In Memory of Those Lost to Shadows. May Truth Bring Light.'

It was not built to glorify.

It was built to remember.

And this morning, for the first time, Jaipur would gather—not to worship, but to reckon.

Anika arrived before the crowds.

Her steps were slow, deliberate, her heels tapping softly on the winding path of smooth stone that threaded through beds of white flowers. Above, old peepal trees swayed in the morning breeze, their leaves whispering like the voices of the lost.

She hadn't slept since Singh's cremation. Nor since her mother's strangled sobs filled the house the night she confessed that Yuvraj was alive, only to be taken again.

She had come today not as the woman who cracked open Jaipur's secrets, not as the forensic psychologist who exposed a royal conspiracy. She came as a sister who had lost her brother—twice. As a woman who had knelt in blood, watching the man she cared for give everything to a city that would never speak his name with the reverence it deserved.

She came because she owed it to Singh, to Yuvraj, and to every name carved in stone before her.

As the morning sun rose higher, the city came too.

Families trickled in. Some walked like they carried centuries on their backs. Others moved lightly, but with eyes that had seen too much. They brought flowers, black-and-white photos, prayer beads, and folded letters never mailed. Their grief was private—but shared. Each story wrapped itself into the next.

An elderly woman bent to place a photo at the foot of the monument. The man in it was young and joyful. Forgotten by history. Swallowed by silence. But today, remembered.

A couple stood quietly near an engraving—parents of one of Aryan's final victims. They did not speak. Their clasped hands did all the mourning.

Anika stood apart, watching. The wind tugged gently at her sleeves.

This was the real legacy of power: not palaces or lineages, but lives extinguished and voices erased.

Eventually the officials came.

No garlands. No fanfare. Just tired suits and heavier eyes.

Among them, Mayor Agarwal, whose voice, when he reached her, was quiet. 'Dr Thakur . . . thank you. For forcing the truth into the light.'

Anika gave a slight nod. Her voice was barely above a whisper. 'It's a beginning.'

He understood. This garden, this gathering—it wasn't closure. It was a first step.

The ceremony began.

The garden swelled with hundreds, the pathways and shaded benches blooming with silence, sobs, and stories.

Mayor Agarwal stood before the crowd, his voice raw but resonant. 'We gather not to bury the past, but to confront it. To remember the lost. And to build a city where silence no longer protects violence.'

There were no political speeches. Just words that tried to hold centuries of pain.

A priest read a Sanskrit prayer, a maulvi whispered a dua, a Sikh granthi recited from the Guru Granth Sahib, and a Christian pastor offered a benediction.

In that moment, there were no divisions.

Only loss. And the fragile, desperate hope that memory could be a kind of healing.

One by one, survivors and families shared their stories.

Of brothers taken without warning.

Of women branded as cursed.

Of children buried not in earth but in silence.

Each voice carved something new into the air: a promise that history would not be erased again.

Then came Anika's turn.

She stepped forward, the silence wrapping around her like a shawl.

Her voice did not waver. 'I stand before you not just as a professional, but as a daughter of Jaipur. As a sister. As someone who has known the cost of secrets too intimately to ever forget them.'

She let the words settle before continuing.

'This garden is not an end point. It is a threshold. A promise to remember. To seek justice. And to end the cycles of silence and suffering with us.'

The words sank into the soil like seeds.

As the ceremony ended, the crowd remained. They lit candles. Touched the stone. Left behind petals, letters, and names.

Anika stayed long after the others had gone.

She knelt before the monument, her fingers tracing the carved inscription. Her shadow stretched long across the stone path as the afternoon sun dipped low.

Jaipur had taken its first honest step.

The path ahead would be jagged.

But today the dead were no longer forgotten.

And that, at least, was something.

A promise written in stone.

And carried in the blood of those still fighting.

The conference room at the Rajasthan Police Headquarters had never felt like this.

Usually a space burdened by the bureaucratic lull of file-heavy meetings and procedural debates, today it thrummed with something entirely different—a sense of purpose.

The long table was filled. Senior officers, junior investigators, and members of the special task force sat shoulder to shoulder, not out of obligation, but from an unspoken understanding: They were part of something historic.

At the far end, Anika sat in silence, her hands folded before her. Her eyes were steady, but her mind replayed the events that had led them here—the unmasking of the Wrathbearers, the shattered veil of royal legacy, Singh's sacrifice, and Yuvraj's disappearance.

This moment was not just a coda. It was the crossroads between memory and mandate.

Then the door opened.

Commissioner Verma entered, his uniform crisp but his face drawn by sleepless nights. Tucked beneath his arm was a thick folder—the kind that usually promised procedural tedium. But today it felt like a blueprint for change.

He took his place at the head of the table. The room stilled.

'Thank you all for being here,' he began, his voice steady, tinged with something weightier than usual. 'Recent events have made it clear—we must re-examine not only how we investigate, but why we've failed to see what needed to be seen.'

He scanned the room, his gaze lingering on Anika, Kumar, and those who had stood in the storm and refused to yield.

Then he set the folder down, opened it, and said the words that would redefine Jaipur's relationship with justice.

'Effective immediately, we are establishing a Historical Crimes Unit.'

Silence followed. Not stunned—reverent.

Then a shift rippled through the room. Heads nodded. Eyes sharpened. A quiet understanding bloomed.

This wasn't just about crime. This was about history's reckoning.

Verma continued, his voice gaining strength, 'This unit will investigate unresolved cases tied to historical patterns of abuse, disappearances, and cover-ups—including those we uncovered in the Wrathbearer investigation. It will have full authority to revisit archives, reopen cold cases, and work across departments. We owe this to the people of Jaipur. And to those we failed.'

He turned to Anika. 'Dr Thakur, I want you to lead it.'

For a moment, the world tilted, not from shock, but from the weight of earned trust.

Anika sat up straighter. 'Thank you, sir. I accept.'

Verma nodded. 'You'll have full autonomy to build your team. I suggest a mix—veteran detectives, fresh thinkers. People who understand both history and trauma. We're not just solving crimes. We're restoring truths.'

Her mind was already assembling names—those who believed in the work, who had seen the rot beneath the surface and still chosen to stay.

Verma's tone turned sharper. 'Alongside this, we're implementing reforms—mandatory ethics training, new whistle-blower protocols, transparency measures when dealing with prominent families and sacred sites, and official collaborations with historians and forensic experts.'

Anika could feel the shift. This wasn't lip service. This was systemic change.

The room, once sceptical, was now electric with resolve.

Ideas flowed. Strategies were shared. Barriers were acknowledged and dismantled.

Anika spoke, drawing from her experience. 'We'll need trauma-informed interview practices. Survivors of historic abuse respond differently. The truth lives in silence and scars. We'll have to learn how to listen—differently.'

Nods followed. Respect bloomed where doubt once lingered.

When Verma finally stood, ready to close the session, he didn't posture. He promised.

'The road ahead won't be easy. But if we walk it with integrity, it will lead us somewhere better. Not just for the victims. But for Jaipur.'

The meeting adjourned, but no one rushed to leave. Conversations crackled across the room. Files were passed hand to hand. Officers leaned in, not just to talk, but to build.

Beside her, Kumar leaned back, his expression lighter than it had been in weeks. He nudged her with a smirk.

'Looks like you've got your work cut out for you, boss.'

Anika let out a breath, one that didn't ache this time.

'We've got our work cut out for us.' The correction wasn't just about humility. It was about unity.

They stepped out together, towards a small side wing where a new brass plate had just been affixed:

HISTORICAL CRIMES UNIT—JAIPUR METRO

And as Anika pushed open the door to her new office, she knew the work ahead would be exhausting, messy, and relentless.

But finally—finally—it would be just.

She looked out across the city as the sun lifted over the horizon.

Jaipur had chosen truth.

Now it was her turn to deliver justice.

One name.

One story.

One shadow at a time.

EPILOGUE

Eight weeks after Aryan Singh Rathore was sentenced to life in prison, the early morning sun cast long fractured shadows over the decaying façade of an old haveli nestled on the outskirts of Jaipur. Once a monument to aristocratic grandeur, it now stood under scaffolding, its jharokhas draped in netting and its carvings weathered by monsoon and time. Yet even in ruin, the haveli seemed to resist silence—as though it had more to say.

The air vibrated with the low hum of machinery and the sharp barks of workmen, the restoration team moving methodically, balancing preservation with the risk of disturbing something long buried.

Dhiraj, the site foreman, leaned over a makeshift worktable, squinting at blueprints with a furrowed brow. He had overseen dozens of such heritage restorations, but something about this one had gnawed at him for days—a spatial anomaly in the layout that made no architectural sense.

'Raju,' he called, not looking up. 'Bring the sonar scanner over here. I need to check something.'

Just as Raju wheeled the equipment over, Dr Meera Kapoor, a historian from the Historical Crimes Unit, joined them. She had been supervising the excavation for any artefacts or hidden clues that might be tied to Anika Thakur's ongoing investigations. She noticed Dhiraj's tension immediately.

'What's wrong?'

He tapped a section of the blueprint and pointed to the haveli's oldest wing. 'There's a three-foot discrepancy between the map and the actual measurements. It's either a mistake, or something's been sealed off.'

Kapoor's eyebrows lifted. 'A hidden chamber?'

He nodded. 'Looks that way.'

The sonar whirred to life, its frequency slicing through layers of stone. Raju squinted at the screen. 'There's definitely a void. A room. It's not on any blueprint.'

A current of anticipation passed through the crew. Jaipur's havelis held their share of secrets—false walls, passageways, and family vaults—but the stillness in the air now felt different. Like the building itself was holding its breath.

'Proceed carefully,' Dhiraj ordered. 'No drilling. Manual removal only.'

With slow chiselled precision, workers began peeling away the ancient masonry. Dust poured out in thick clouds. And then came the smell—old earth, desiccated wood, and something older still. Something metallic. Decay and memory.

'Flashlight,' Dhiraj murmured.

A beam cut through the dark. The chamber opened before them like a wound in the haveli's heart—shelves lining the walls, filled with ancient manuscripts, rusted lockboxes, ceremonial instruments, and objects no one could immediately name. The air went taut with awe and unease.

Kapoor caught her breath. 'This . . . this could be centuries old.' Her fingers brushed over the filigree of an ornate box. 'Predates even the earliest royal archives.'

Dhiraj moved towards the back wall and froze. 'Dr Kapoor, over here.'

She stepped carefully through the scattered debris and then saw it—an inscription carved into stone. Faint, hidden behind cobwebs, but unmistakably deliberate.

She leaned in. 'This is an older dialect. Not Sanskrit. Possibly a proto-Rajasthani script.' Her voice trembled slightly. 'It speaks of a guardian . . . and a choice.'

Dhiraj stiffened. 'What kind of choice?'

Kapoor hesitated. 'If I'm translating this correctly . . . the curse we thought was broken?' She looked up, her face pale. 'It was just a fragment. There's another one. A deeper one.'

Silence fell like a veil.

Before anyone could speak, Dhiraj's radio crackled. 'Sir, someone's here from the Historical Crimes Unit. Says it's urgent.'

Moments later, Dr Anika Thakur stepped through the threshold, her silhouette framed by swirling dust. She scanned the room and clocked the uncovered chamber, the artefacts, and the look on Kapoor's face.

'What have you found?' Her voice was low, already bracing for the answer.

Kapoor stepped aside, revealing the inscription.

Anika moved closer. She didn't need a translation. The weight in the air told her everything. The past had spoken again, and it hadn't finished its tale.

'We need to document everything,' Anika said, eyes still fixed on the wall. 'Catalogue, photograph, bag the evidence. I'll go over the findings tonight.'

She gave the chamber one last look and left.

The afternoon light slanted through the blinds of her new office, casting gold and shadow across the cluttered desk of the Historical Crimes Unit. State-of-the-art forensics sat beside cracked manuscripts. A whiteboard sprawled across one wall—an expanding nexus of threads and timelines, murder scenes, and dynastic maps.

Anika sat motionless, eyes closed, rubbing the bridge of her nose. The revelation at the haveli refused to leave her mind. Just as the city had begun to heal, the past had cracked open again.

A knock at the door.

'Come in,' she said without looking up.

Constable Mohan stepped in, holding a plain manila envelope. No return address. Just her name.

'It was dropped by courier,' he said. 'No sender. No cameras.'

Anika took it, instantly alert. 'Trace the origin. Get me everything.'

He nodded and left.

She opened the envelope with care. Inside—one page, filled with precise symbols and numbers. No letter. No signature.

She snapped a photo and sent it to Meera Kapoor. 'Does this match anything?'

Kapoor called seconds later. 'Some of these symbols, yes. They match the Chandravati archive and today's chamber. Especially the last line.'

Anika crossed to the whiteboard, marker in hand, transcribing the strange glyphs.

'These numbers . . .,' she murmured. 'They don't belong to any historical date.'

'Could be coordinates?' Meera offered. 'Or a key?'

Anika caught her breath. 'Or . . . astrological data.'

She dropped into her chair, pulled up a celestial alignment tracker, and punched in the sequence.

A beat, and her screen lit up.

'Oh my God,' she whispered. 'Meera . . . these alignments—they're not from the past.'

'What are they?'

Anika stared at the date. 'They haven't happened yet.'

Silence. Cold and immediate.

A warning. Not from history, but from the future.

And just like that, she knew.

The Wrathbearers weren't finished.

Not yet.

Far from Jaipur, in the snow-shadowed stillness of a Himalayan monastery long thought abandoned, a single candle burned in the heart of a subterranean sanctum. Hooded figures stood in a circle, their faces hidden and their silence absolute—until one of them stepped forward and placed a slip of parchment onto the altar. Upon it was drawn a familiar symbol. The same that now haunted Anika Thakur's whiteboard.

A low chant began, soft at first, then swelling—a single phrase echoing through the frozen stone walls:

'The Seal has fractured. The guardian must awaken.'

And somewhere, deep within the earth . . . a second chamber began to stir.

ABOUT THE AUTHOR

Dr. Ramesh Pattni OBE brings a rare fusion of forensic psychology, Indian history, and philosophical depth to the world of crime fiction. With doctorates from both Oxford University (DPhil) and the New School of Psychotherapy & Counselling (DCPsych), and decades of research in Indian psychology and cultural trauma, Dr. Pattni crafts psychological thrillers rooted in historical truth and emotional authenticity. Echoes of Time: A Jaipur Mystery draws on his unparalleled expertise in ancient Indian texts, intergenerational trauma, and the legacy of colonial power, delivering a mystery that is both intellectually rich and emotionally compelling.

As a professor of psychology and former Oxford tutor, Pattni's storytelling weaves intricate symbolism, archival secrets, and psychological nuance into a gripping narrative. His background as a psychotherapist and interfaith leader infuses his work with layered character development and moral complexity. Readers will be drawn to his unique voice—grounded in rigorous scholarship yet driven by personal resonance and deep empathy. This is more than a murder mystery; it's a journey into memory, myth, and the unresolved past. Dr. Pattni doesn't just write about justice—he reveals how truth, when buried, always leaves echoes behind.

Printed in Dunstable, United Kingdom

69209184R00188